Lestrade and the Dead Man's Hand

Lestrade and the Dead Man's Hand

Volume XI in the
Lestrade Mystery Series

M.J. Trow

A Gateway Mystery

REGNERY
PUBLISHING, INC.
Since 1947 • An Eagle Publishing Company

Library of Congress Cataloging-in-Publication Data
    Trow, M.J.
            Lestrade and the dead man's hand / M.J. Trow.
                p. cm. — (A Gateway mystery) (Lestrade mystery series v. 11)
                ISBN 0-89526-288-6
                1. Lestrade, Inspector (Fictitious character)—Fiction. 2.
                Police—England—London—Fiction. 3. London (England)—
                Fiction. I. Title. II. Series.

    PR6070.R598 L466 2000
    823'.914—dc21   99-059916

Published in the United States by
Regnery Publishing, Inc.
An Eagle Publishing Company
One Massachusetts Avenue, NW
Washington, DC 20001
www.regnery.com

Originally published in Great Britain

Distributed to the trade by
National Book Network
4720-A Boston Way
Lanham, MD 20706

Printed on acid-free paper
Manufactured in the United States of America

10 9 8 7 6 5 4 3 2 1

Books are available in quantity for promotional or premium use. Write to Director of Special Sales, Regnery Publishing, Inc., One Massachusetts Avenue, NW, Washington, DC 20001, for information on discounts and terms or call (202) 216-0600.

The character of Inspector Lestrade was created by the late Sir Arthur Conan Doyle and appears in the Sherlock Holmes stories and novels by him, as do some other characters in this book.

1

The snows lingered long that year. And the iron hand of winter lay like a vice over the mountains of the Hindu Kush. By day, only the tiny khaki column moved, like a foraging party of soldier ants, over the great white wilderness. By night, only the wind held sway below the shrouded peaks of Tirach Mir. Until the dawn came again. And the bugle shattered the stillness and the pack animals strained and the rifle butts thumped into buckets. And the little column moved on.

Lieutenant John Sleigh commanded the skirmishers of the 32nd who fanned out on the rocky outcrops, their fur-mittened fists tight on their Lee-Enfields. They moved like ghosts, grey against white, their copper faces tinged with blue and icicles hanging in their ringlets.

They'd seen it long before the Lieutenant's hand shot skyward. A single horseman winding uphill towards them. Their senior officer, a Havildar of particularly fawning disposition, scuttled through the snow to Sleigh's side.

'What do you make of it, Havildar?' The Lieutenant's breath snaked out on the morning air.

'O illustrious one, your eyes burn brighter than the temple heights of Kashmir; your vision is as far-seeing as the kite . . .'

'Yes, yes, Sanji,' Sleigh muttered. 'Stop buggering about and answer the bloody question, will you?'

'It is a horseman, omnipotent one.' The Havildar squinted through the snow.

Sleigh sighed. 'That much I'd managed,' he said, fiddling with his field-glasses. 'Remind me never to buy Zeiss again. It's like looking into a fog.'

'I will remind you, O great and wise purchaser.'

Sleigh abandoned the binoculars and took off his Wolseley helmet to use as an eye shield. It didn't help either. So much for the fatherly chat the old man had given him at Meerut when he'd first arrived in India. So far none of it had been any use at all, especially that bit about carnal relations with the sacred baboons. The animals inflamed his manly passions scarcely at all.

But by now the horseman had ridden within rifle range.

'Havildar.' Sleigh thought it best to dismount. Alone among his infantry men, he presented too easy a target in the saddle. 'Get Gupta over here, will you?'

The Havildar barked an order in his native Hindustani and the Sepoy the Lieutenant had singled out dropped his pack and Pioneer's pick, and saluted briskly at the white man's side.

Sleigh returned it. 'Stout fellow,' he said. 'Havildar, tell Gupta to fire a warning shot over the rider's head. He is not to hit him. Merely let him know we've seen him. All right?'

The Havildar turned to his private and jabbered in the lilting, wheedling tone common to the Frontier tribes. 'The son of a harlot wants you to shoot at that poor bastard coming up the ridge.'

'Why doesn't he do his own dirty work?' the Sepoy asked in the same tongue.

'Because you, Gupta my son, are the best shot in the Thirty-second and because that dromedary's prepuce couldn't shoot his own foot with any degree of certainty.'

'Flattery will get you a reasonable way, Havildar,' the Sepoy said. 'Couldn't I just take an ear off?'

'What's the fuss, Havildar?' Sleigh broke in, agitated in the freezing morning by all this jabber.

'Gupta is extolling your virtues, illustrious one,' the Havildar said. 'He draws blessings on your house for allowing him to show his humble skill and thanks Allah for the opportunity of serving you . . . oh, Jesus Christ Almighty!' The Havildar reeled sideways as Gupta's rifle crashed by his ear. He screamed at the man, 'You know what this bloody Afghan cold does to my eardrums, you jackal's nipple!'

'Oh, good shot, Gupta.' Sleigh focused again with the field-glasses. 'Yes, Havildar. You did right to praise him. Wait a minute. What's he doing now?'

Several pairs of eyes squinted at the solitary figure on the slopes below. Gupta's shot had stopped him short and now he had swung from the saddle and was shouting out, waving something frantically.

'It is a flag of truce, powerful one,' the Havildar said. 'Either that or the worst bit of semaphoring I've ever seen.'

'Is he a Pathan?' Sleigh steadied his binoculars on the Havildar's shoulders.

'If he was,' muttered Gupta in his native tongue, 'you'd have a jezail bullet where your forehead used to be.'

'What's he say, Havildar?'

'He asks whether he will have the pleasure of kneeling beside your excellency's horse so that he will feel the exquisite pressure of your boot on his neck as you mount, unparalleled one.'

'I say, steady on, old man.' Sleigh's blue face turned a shade of magenta rarely seen this far north of the Chitral ranges. 'One thing they taught us at Sandhurst was "Never step on a chap's neck." I believe it's in the Articles of War. What's that fellow shouting down there, Havildar? Can you make it out?'

'You have the ears of a flitter-mouse, all-hearing one. There is no one in the Thirty-second Pioneers with your lobes.'

'Oh, come off it, Havildar.' Sleigh scuffed the snow with his boot. 'I bet you say that to all the Subs.'

'Bloody hell!' Gupta trilled in Hindustani. 'That poor sod down there is speaking English.'

'English?' the Havildar said in English.

'What?' Sleigh turned to him.

'He is speaking that most superlative of tongues, O elocuted one. The Mother Tongue of all the Empire. The language of diplomacy and of the law. The Pax Britannica . . .'

'That's Latin, Havildar.' Sleigh was still trying to focus his glasses. 'The language of the Romans.'

'Ah yes.' The Havildar placed his hands together. 'And were not the Romans taught their Latin by you English! You still teach it in your public schools, I know. *Amo, amas, amat.* What a thrill! What a culture! This is why you are the rulers of a quarter of the world, sophisticated one – because you have mastered Latin gerundives.'

'Shut up, Havildar, and get down there with a squad of the

7

chaps. If that fellow speaks English, he could be useful to us. And *juldi, juldi.'*

The Havildar saluted and pointed to Gupta and four of the others. 'Come on, lads. The chinless wonder's trying out his only word of Hindustani again. Let's get down there before he tries Hither Lao. That Kipling bloke's got a lot to answer for, you know.'

'Hay-Winthrop, Thirty-seventh Dogras.' The officer held out his gloved hand.

'Good Lord, you're English!' Sleigh caught it.

'Well I was the last time I looked. I'm bally glad I found you chaps. Didn't fancy gasping my last on a bally mountainside in the Chitral. Lieutenant . . . er . . . ?'

'Oh, sorry. Forgetting my manners. The cold does that to a chap, doesn't it? Sleigh, Thirty-second Pioneers. You're not from the column?'

'Lord, no. Out from Peshawar week last Thursday. Had a touch of frostbite and couldn't march with my unit. But as soon as the swelling went down, orff I set. And here I am.'

'Alone?' Sleigh fumbled for a cigar.

'Oh, thanks.' Hay-Winthrop accepted it. 'Alone save for a native bearer, a cholera belt and a packet of Janos Hunyadi's laxative powders, yes. I seem to have lost him somewhere, the bearer that is, not Janos Hunyadi. I expect he'll turn up around tiffin. Good chaps, your Punjabis?'

'The best,' said Sleigh. 'What's that?' He pointed to the flag of truce that Hay-Winthrop had waved at them from the lower slopes.

'Oh,' the officer of the 37th snorted. It was what passed in the Dragoons for a laugh. 'It's *The Times*! I always knew the bally thing had a purpose. Think I'll take out a patent when I get home.'

'Can I have a look?' Sleigh took the tattered thing between freezing fingers. 'I haven't seen a white newspaper since I left Meerut.'

'Be my guest,' Hay-Winthrop told him, struggling to put some feeling into the blackened toes of his left foot. 'It's rather old, I'm afraid.'

Sleigh could just make out the date, 16 February.

'I've a tin of Mrs Gittings' Bread and Butter Pudding in my saddlebags. If one of your chaps wouldn't mind . . .'

'No. Of course not. Havildar.'

The NCO snapped to attention. 'I am the servant of your merest whim, O unblemished one.'

'Yes, yes. Send Gupta to bring up Mr Hay-Winthrop's horse, will you? Rather stupid of him to leave it down there, actually.'

'Indeed it was, great judge of men. I shall personally remove his kneecaps.' He turned to Hay-Winthrop. 'May I ask the Dogra Sahib if he speaks the lowly language of Hindoostani?'

'Lord, no,' Hay-Winthrop said. 'No need in the Thirty-seventh. All my people speak English like natives. Except Major McPherson of course, but he went to Haileybury.'

'Ah,' Sleigh nodded. That said it all.

The Havildar smiled. 'Right, Gupta. I bet you never thought you'd find a wonder as chinless as this one, did you? But lo, Allah has directed another idiot to cross our paths.'

'What is this tinned stuff of which the other idiot speaks, Havildar?' the Sepoy asked, shouldering his rifle ready for the run.

'Bread and Butter Pudding? Allah knows! Some repulsive spiceless sap, I shouldn't wonder.'

'Oh, my God!' Sleigh stood as though transfixed by a Pathan *tulwar*, staring at *The Times*.

'Oh, yes, it's true, I'm afraid.' Hay-Winthrop sensed the trouble at once. 'Rosebery *is* Prime Minister. I thought of returning my Suakin medal in protest.'

'Rosebery be buggered!' Sleigh said. 'Hay-Winthrop, you've come from Peshawar. Is the road clear to Gilgit? And the telegraph intact there?'

'It was when I took it, yes. My dear fellow, are you all right? You look as though you'd seen a ghost.'

Sleigh looked at his man, the cool public school eyes, the frozen moustache like a dead hedgehog lying across his lips. 'Perhaps I have, Hay-Winthrop,' he said, 'perhaps I have.'

The old man's telegram to Lord Roberts was curt enough.

'Lieutenant Sleigh gone. Stop. Berserk. Stop. Probably gone berserk. Stop. Command of his company of the 32nd Pioneers temporarily taken by Lieutenant Hay-Winthrop, 37th Dogras. Stop. Sleigh's Havildar says he'd been expecting it. Stop. Weather getting better. Stop. Hope this finds you as it leaves same. Stop. On campaign. Stop. Chitral. Stop.'

Sleigh himself, his uniform hanging on the back of an old, one-eyed bazaar dealer in Gilgit, the copy of Hay-Winthrop's *Times* stuffed into the Afghan coat he'd swapped it for, sent a telegram too. To Australia.

You could have heard a jumbuck drop that morning in the Dandenong. And the air so thick in the outback it could choke a man. The next train wasn't due until Thursday and in the purple clouds of dawn a tiny spiral of dust was all that told of the horseman's approach.

William Sleigh sat his saddle patiently, the hunting rifle cradled in the crook of his arm. He tilted his bush hat, the one with the corks dangling from it, and scanned the flock one more time. Three thousand head of the bleating bastards. But all of them struck dumb as the February heat already climbed in the heavens and the scent of fire raked their ovine nostrils. A kookaburra jarred the moment, hopping among the jacarandas.

The second stockman turned his pony into the wind and walked it through the yellowed scrub to Sleigh's side.

'Dingo in the wind, boss,' he said, the flies buzzing around his broad, black nostrils and tightly frizzed grey hair.

'I don't see anything, Croajingolong,' Sleigh said.

'That easy for you to say, boss. But he about, boss,' the herdsman grinned. 'They smell 'im. I smell 'im.'

Sleigh looked uncomfortable. Marlborough. Trinity. The Classics Tripos. And here he was outsmelt by an aborigine of dubious parentage and 3,000 sheep. What a country!

'Who's that?' Sleigh gestured with his rifle to the growing dust.

'Doknow, boss,' Croajingolong squinted. 'I got the family nose. Don't got the family eyes too.'

A third stockman, lean, dusty, white, trotted over the rise to Sleigh's right. 'Who's that bloody gallah? He'll scare the dingo.'

'Croajingolong can't make him out, Tom.'

'Course he can't. Too much jungle juice at the bloody Korroboree. You watch I don't point a bone at you, boy. Well, that bloody dingo won't turn up now.'

'He's had thirty-six of my sheep, Tom. I'm not giving up.'

'I'm not saying you should, Mr Sleigh. I'm just sayin' no rogue dingo is goin' to show up obligingly and play dead when there's all this bloody activity. I dunnow, you don't see another white bloke from one Christmas to the next and suddenly, it's like bloody Bendigo Junction around here.'

Sleigh steadied his horse as the rider took the slope below them. The peaked cap and the blue tunic caked with dust told the story. In the name of the Empress, this was the Overland Mail. He reined in his flagging mare, and the ewes, alarmed by the thudding, trotted away with the smaller lambs springing at their heels.

'Mr Sleigh?' the postman said, fighting for breath.

'Yes,' said Sleigh.

'Mr William Sleigh?'

'Yes.'

'G'day, Mr Sleigh. Telegram for you.'

'Thanks. How did you find me?'

'Passed your camp down by the billabong. Up came three squatters and told me where you was.' He suddenly sniffed the wind. ''Ere, I smell dingo.'

'Really?' Sleigh was impressed. 'Do you have any aborigine blood in you?'

'Christ, no. Do you mind? Na, my old dad used to have a sheep farm over at Yarra Yarra. That's 'ow I earned my pocket money as a kid, keeping watch on the flocks. Didn't see no bloody Angel of the Lord, neither. Hey, you're a pom, aren't you?'

'I'm British, yes.' Sleigh was slightly affronted. 'But then, aren't we all?'

The postman winked at Tom. 'You speak for your bloody self, mate. I knew you was by your whinge. That and the corks around your hat.'

'Oh, my God!' Sleigh had ripped open the buff envelope.

'Not bad news, Mr Sleigh?' Tom leaned in the saddle to read the news. He couldn't what with the angle of the sun and Sleigh's trembling hand – and the fact that he couldn't read.

'When was this sent?' the Englishman asked.

'From Melbourne three days ago. I've ridden bloody day and night, you know.'

'Yes. Yes, thank you, Mr . . . er . . . ?'

'Dundee.'

'Mr Dundee. You'll find some tucker in Croajingolong's saddlebags.'

'No, thanks,' the postman grimaced. 'I've gone right off locusts.'

'Watch the stock, Tom.' Sleigh rammed the rifle into the leather bucket. 'I'll be back.'

'What? Where are you going, Mr Sleigh?'

'Home,' he shouted. 'Don't wait up.'

'Eh? When will you be back.'

'Octoberish, all being well.' And he was gone, lashing his pony with his reins, thudding away in a cloud of red dust.

'That's all right,' muttered Dundee. 'Never mind my tip. I *was* right, then. Another bloody whingeing pom.'

'Well,' Tom steadied his animal. 'Maybe he left the iron on.'

And when William Sleigh's exhausted pony finally carried him into the dingy suburbs of Melbourne, the whingeing bloody pom found a post office and sent his own telegram. To South Africa.

The flickering torchlight lit the bearded faces that crossed the kraal. Arthur Sleigh stood half in shadow and watched them assemble. Some he knew. Farmers like himself. One or two of the men from the mine. He heard them muttering in guarded tones, the hum of conspiracy through the ages. Then he heard a rifle-bolt snick behind him.

'Come along now, Mr Sleigh,' a gruff voice called. 'You shouldn't be lurking in the bushes. You'll have us thinking you're a damned Boer.'

Sleigh crossed the open space with his hands in his pockets, chewing the veld grass with the stubbornness of a Durban cow. The rifleman crossed with him and tapped with his butt on the ramshackle door. Three thuds and a tickle. The accepted sign.

'Yes?' a low voice called from within.

The rifleman lifted the latch and ushered Sleigh in. The knot of men he had seen outside had now formed a circle and some of them held knitting in their hands.

'Arthur.' A balding gent with a clipped moustache and the distinct look of an ambassador to Matabeleland stood up and shook his hand.

'What a splendid cardie,' Sleigh said.

The ambassador chuckled. 'You're right. Not altogether a sensible cover, is it? Whose idea was it by the way, the knitting circle?'

'I don't believe you've met Christian de Wet of the Johannesburg Uitlanders?'

'I thought we agreed, Dr Jim,' the South African said in the tortured tongue of that country. 'No real names.'

'It's all right, de Wet, Arthur Sleigh is one of us. Most of the chaps here I think you know. Except perhaps Mr Whitecross of *The Times* and Mr Tait, direct from Rhodesia.'

'How is dear old Cecil?' Sleigh asked. 'Still asthmatic?'

'Getting better,' Tait assured him.

'Well, then. To business,' the ambassador said. 'The Chartered Company means business, gentlemen. That's why I've asked you all here tonight. I've got nearly five hundred men ready to ride at a moment's notice and with de Wet's Uitlanders in tow, I estimate that we can take the Transvaal in one or two weeks. Arthur, how many blacks can you muster?'

'Thirty-three,' Sleigh said. 'But I'm not sure it's their fight, Jameson.'

'Of course it is,' the ambassador assured him. 'Who treats the blacks worse than anybody? Cronje and his damned Boers, that's who. Lobengula has promised me a thousand of his warriors.'

De Wet spat copiously on to his knitting. 'Black levies!' he snarled. 'You can't trust 'em, man. I remember the levies we had in the Zulu war. Ran away at the first whisper of *Usuthu*.'

'*Usuthu*?' the *Times* man repeated.

'It's a Zulu word,' Jameson explained. 'It means kill.'

'Oh, I say,' Whitecross put down his knitting and Tait dropped a stitch entirely, 'I'm not sure we're talking about violence . . . are we?'

There was a silence. Jameson broke it. 'I thought we agreed,' he said, looking wildly around at them, 'the Transvaal must be secured for Britain. These damned Boers have a lesson coming. We can't teach them that with gentle reminders – or letters to *The Times*. I think, Tait, if Cecil heard you talking such nonsense as Whitecross here, he'd have you shot!'

'Oh dear,' gulped Whitecross, not exactly a leader of Empire at the best of times.

There was a thud at the door, followed by two more and a tickle. Everyone but Sleigh snatched up their knitting again in the candlelight.

'Yes?' Jameson called.

The rifleman popped his head round the door. 'I'm sorry Dr Jameson,' he said, 'but there's a fellow here with a telegram for Mr Sleigh.'

'Who?' Jameson tried the cool approach.

'Mr Sleigh.' The delivery boy emerged from the gloom, only the whites of his eyes and his pearly teeth flashing.

'Get out of here, Kaffir!' de Wet snarled.

'No, no,' Jameson interrupted. 'This fellow is simply doing his job. Deliver away, Johnny.'

'Thank you, Dr Jim,' the Bantu said.

'Er . . .' Jameson did his best not to be surprised. Then he remembered that the Kaffir had heard the stupid guard use his name, so he calmed down.

'Dis came all de way up de Limpopo, bwana,' the Bantu beamed. 'I rowed all de way myself.'

Sleigh slapped him on the shoulder. 'Just like a Trinity chap, I shouldn't wonder,' he said.

'Ah, Mr Tait,' the Bantu grinned. 'How is Sir Cecil? Got over his asthma, I trust?' He turned to *The Times* man, standing open-mouthed with the others. 'Mr Whitecross, how marvellous to see you, bwana. Did you get my solution to de *Times* crossword number three four one? I particularly liked de cheeky vulgarity of eighteen down.'

'Who the bloody hell are you, Kaffir?' de Wet growled, rounding on the little black man.

14

'Good God!' Sleigh had read the telegram and visibly paled in the candlelight.

'Bad news on the wool supplies, er . . . George?' Jameson attempted to keep the façade going.

'Wool supplies be buggered,' Sleigh snapped. 'You'll have to postpone the Jameson Raid, gentlemen. I have urgent business in London.'

And he saw himself out.

All eyes turned to the Bantu who held up his hands in submission. 'Can I wind de wool for anybody, bwanas?'

2

Chief Inspector Abberline's favourite colour was flesh. Especially somebody else's. Especially if that somebody else was the right side of thirty with a figure like the Venus de Milo; before her arms dropped off of course.

Such a one, alas, was not Mrs Ermintrude Abberline, née Pargeter, of the Neasden Pargeters. She was decidedly the wrong side of thirty, but then it could be argued that Mrs Abberline was the wrong side of everything, especially Chief Inspector Abberline. And flesh was certainly not her colour. Indeed, the last time she had been pestered by the Chief Inspector he was a detective sergeant and Mr Disraeli was Prime Minister. That had been in 1874.

She faced him that early April morning over the marmalade and the toast, wondering what on earth she had seen in the whiskered stranger moronically dunking his rookies in his soft-boiled egg. Once, perhaps, he had been a dashing, and undoubtedly white, sergeant, at a time when Dundrearies were still the height of fashion. Now he, and they, looked a trifle passé.

'That Chinaman called yesterday with your shirts, Frederick,' she said.

'Hmm,' he responded wittily, checking the obituaries in the *Police Gazette*.

'Yes, he was very apologetic.'

15

'Hmm,' said Abberline, ever one for the dry quip and the variety of response.

'He said he and his family had been in the laundry business ever since the First Opium War and he had never known lipstick stains so stubborn.'

'Lipstick?' Abberline's composure cracked at last. He would rather face the Yard's rubber-truncheon room any day than Mrs Abberline at her most persistent. She made the Spanish Inquisition look like a casual inquiry.

'Yes, Frederick.' She had the pursed lips of the habitual lemon sucker. 'You know, it's the pink stuff that young girls paint on their faces nowadays. In my day . . .'

'In your day, Ermintrude . . .'

'How dare you interrupt me when I'm making a moral and historical observation, Frederick!' she thundered and the windows shook. 'In my day, those females who wore lipstick were harlots. No better than they should be, Frederick. Creatures of the night.'

'Come, come, dearest.' The Chief Inspector folded the *Gazette*. 'This *is* 1895.'

'I am aware of the date, Frederick,' she assured him, 'but it does not give you licence to debauch yourself.'

'Debauch?' Abberline gulped the last of his coffee. 'Ermintrude, I don't know what you mean.'

'Indeed?' She narrowed her eyes at him. 'So you've no idea how lipstick came to be on the collar of your number three shirt?'

'None whatever.' He'd decided to brazen it out. 'If indeed it *was* lipstick.'

"If indeed it was"? I have just given you Mr Wu's pedigree in the ancient Oriental Art of Cleansing and Starching. I imagine the man is thoroughly immersed in the whole sordid spectrum of stains, many of them of unmentionable origin.'

'Some damn chink?' Abberline grumbled. 'Needs his own collar feeling, that bloke, I shouldn't wonder. Think I'll send a few of the boys round to cut his pigtail off.'

'It was number three shirt,' she reminded him. 'The one you wore last Wednesday.'

'Really?' The Chief Inspector knew exactly when to look blank.

'Last Wednesday.' Ermintrude Abberline was clearly descended from a long line of terriers. 'Surveillance at Penge, wasn't it?'

'Was it?'

'That's precisely the question I would like you to answer, Frederick,' she said.

He looked at her under his shifty lids, taking in the lariats of fake pearls around her throat, the throat he longed to squeeze. He focused briefly on the pile of hair, grey as barbed wire and twice as tangled, balanced high on the cranium he longed to split with the axe he kept carefully honed in the garden shed.

'Wednesday!' He clicked his fingers. 'Of course. I remember now.' The frozen grin was a mark of his desperation. 'Detective Constable La Rue.'

Her eyes widened. 'La Rue wears lipstick?'

'Oh, only in the course of duty, my dear,' he smiled. 'Nothing funny about La Rue, I assure you. I can't tell you too much, of course . . .'

'Of course not, Frederick,' she had the grin of a basilisk, 'lest you incriminate yourself. Why was La Rue wearing lipstick?'

'We're on to the Penge flasher,' he told her.

She shuddered. 'Revolting!'

'Quite, my dearest, quite. This is why I don't tell you these things. It is not for the fair sex,' and it had positively hurt him to force his lips to form the words, 'nor for the faint-hearted.'

'You haven't explained how La Rue's lipstick ended up on your collar.'

'Ah, well, yes, now, let me see . . . May I trouble you for a little more of your delicious coffee, heart?'

Her lips almost disappeared into her huge, grey face, like a prune that's been too long in the sun. With the speed of a salamander in full rut she poured it all over his hand.

He screamed and leapt upright, bandaging the raw fingers in his handkerchief.

'Tsk, tsk,' she smiled. 'How very careless of me. And just as you were about to invent a rather unconvincing explanation about the lipstick.'

'It happens to be true, Ermintrude,' he assured her. 'I was just giving La Rue his final instructions, checking the half brick in his handbag, that sort of thing, when the damned bus lurched forward; horse startled by a velocipede, I shouldn't wonder. La Rue and I collided. Fair damaged my gardenia, I can tell you.'

'Bunkum,' snorted Mrs Abberline. 'Sit down, Frederick, and tell me the truth.'

The cavalry arrived just then for Frederick Abberline and it came in the form of a sharp rap at the door. 'Ah,' the Chief Inspector was already fighting his way through the aspidistras that choked the conservatory, 'that'll be the postman. He always knocks twice.'

'More of a rap, I'd say,' she told him. 'I've told that idiot about that. He's definitely rapping again. And remember.' Her circular-saw-like tones held him rigid in the hallway. '*I* open the post in this house.'

'Of course you do, my pet,' he hissed and closed the conservatory door.

'Oh, it's you, Mr Abberline,' the postman clipped his peak.

'Who did you expect?' Abberline snapped. 'Spring-Heeled Jack?'

'All right, all right,' the postman said, 'keep your 'air on.' But he realized that advice came far too late. 'Uh-huh.' He withheld the letters as Abberline snatched at them. 'Mrs Abberline and I have a little arrangement.'

The Chief Inspector's heart missed a beat as he saw the pale turquoise envelope with the Penge postmark. 'All right,' he whispered. 'Two bob?'

The postman grinned and pocketed the silver. 'Sorry as 'ow you 'ad no post today, Mr Abberline. My mistake.' And he stuffed the letters into the Chief Inspector's hand and vanished.

'Well?' Ermintrude's reminder rattled the elephant's foot umbrella stand. The Chief Inspector steadied it and snatched his hat. 'No, it wasn't the postman, dear,' he called, briefly inhaling the heady perfume of the Penge letter. 'It's the Yard. Urgent business. God knows when I'll be back. Don't wait up.'

And he didn't stay to hear Ermintrude scream after him. He was only sure she had because at the end of the road a gas lamp had shattered.

The home life of Detective Constable Walter Dew was altogether different. The inside of his little wooden locker in the back basement of Scotland Yard was testimony to that. A lovingly photographed sepia portrait of Mrs Dew and the two little Dews, right next to the tripe sandwiches she made him every morning with her own fair hand.

The Constable still had brown hair in those days and the immortality he was to acquire on the case of Dr Crippen lay murderous years ahead. Even so, he had been a detective of sorts now for some little time. Time enough certainly for him to give the once over to the two rookies who now stood before him in the latrine-turned-office on the first floor. It was only five years since the Metropolitan Police had obtained this building, designed as an Opera House, and Constable Dew still winced to read the sign ARTISTES THIS WAY in the corridor. Whenever he passed it he strode with a particularly manly bearing; lest someone should equate him with an artiste, he thought it best to walk *that* way.

'Russell?' He twitched his regulation moustache at the new man.

'Yessir.' The lad was all of twenty.

'This can't be right.' Dew peered closer at the pro forma. 'Lordjohn? Is that your name, Russell? Lordjohn?'

'Yessir. My grandad was a staunch Whig, sir.'

'Don't call me sir, lad,' Dew said, though he only predated the man by seven or eight years. 'If we take a shine to you here, we'll be colleagues in an odd sort of way. Experience?'

'Two years on the beat, s . . . Constable.'

'C Division?' Dew looked at his man through narrow eyes.

'Yessir . . . er . . . Vine Street.'

'Precisely,' growled Dew. 'Never known an honest copper out of Vine Street.'

'But I . . .'

'All right, son.' Dew raised an already avuncular hand. 'No cause to get hot and bothered. You're on probation, so to speak. And we speak as we find. Next.'

Next was another man, but altogether older and greyer than the boyish Russell.

'Bromley,' he said. 'Ex-Essex Constabulary.'

'Essex, eh?' Dew stroked his chin. 'That's that place north of here, isn't it?'

'That's right, Constable.'

'Just call me Mr Dew, lad.' Mr Dew ignored the fact that Bromley could have been his father. 'Well, twenty years in Chipping Ongar Nick doesn't exactly fit you for a career living on the razor's edge, does it? Why did you leave it until now to transfer to the Met? And why so long before you transferred to the Criminal Investigation Department?'

'Well, I may be slow,' Bromley mused, 'but I'm thorough. There isn't a horse trough or public urinal in Ongar which I am unfamiliar with.'

'Oh good,' sighed Dew. 'Credentials enough for any man, I'm sure. All right. Perhaps for the first and last time in your careers, Russell and Bromley, you may sit down in the presence of a senior officer of Scotland Yard, vit and to wiz, me. There are a few little rules you need to know.'

The new boys did as they were told, wedged between the piles of shoe boxes as they were, rapt in their first-day attention, sticky in their regulation suits.

'The guv'nor,' said Dew, leaning back with his boots on the scarred leather of the desk; he always took them off on hot mornings when the guv'nor wasn't in, 'he isn't in. So now is a good time to talk about him. His name is Lestrade. His second name, that is. His first name needn't concern you at all. For the record, it is Inspector. You call him "Mr Lestrade" or "sir". He's got the mind of a razor, the memory of an elephant and the pugnacity of a pug. You cross him at your peril, I'm telling you. Oh, by the way,' he leaned forward, 'he likes his tea from a little emporium in the Strand and is partial to a quick dunk of the Bath Olivers. Your first important jobs will be to provide huge quantities of both. And if ever you go out on a recce with the Inspector, be sure to carry plenty of spare change 'cos he's never got any. Any questions?'

Bromley shrugged and shook his head. He had enough years on a Force to know you never asked questions of superiors. Russell was altogether greener. 'Is he married, Mr Dew, the guv'nor?'

Dew's bovine face darkened. 'Was, laddie, was. His wife was a Mrs Manchester; before she became Mrs Lestrade, that is. She passed away now, ooh, two years last January. He still wears a black bowler in her memory. So don't you go mentioning his wife, God rest her, or the name of Manchester. Got it?'

'Yes, Mr Dew,' Russell promised. 'The name shall not pass my lips.'

The man in the black bowler made his way to the second floor. He padded down the worn corridor carpet past cluttered offices from which the keys of Remingtons rattled in the morning. The hat of which Dew had spoken was in fact in the crook of his arm and the heat of that spring meant that it was soon to be replaced by an altogether more suitable boater. And since, at least in the 1890s, they didn't make boaters in black, there went another of Constable Dew's theories out of the window.

He knocked on the frosted glass marked ASSISTANT COMMISSIONER and waited. Nothing. He knocked again. A tiny, grey-haired woman in grey opened it, greyly.

'Ah, Miss Featherstonehaugh, radiant as ever this bright spring morning.'

'Inspector Lestrade.' She peered at him through her pince-nez. She'd know that missing nose-tip anywhere. 'I'm afraid the Assistant Commissioner is . . . out.'

'Out? But I got a memoranda.' He shook a piece of paper at her. 'It *is* Wednesday, isn't it?'

She consulted the calendar thing on the Assistant Commissioner's desk. 'Indeed,' she concurred.

'Well,' Lestrade slapped his leg with his bowler, 'I'll be downstairs. If His Nims returns, perhaps you can trot down with that curious way of going of yours, can you? I'm up to my dickie in cases.'

'No, no.' She held his arm, a curiously passionate gesture for one who was of her generation and had been hacked from a block of pure granite. 'I don't mean Mr Frost is out, exactly. He's in.'

'In? Out? Come on, woman, is he shaking it all about?'

There was a tell-tale gurgle as the Yard's plumbing was put through its paces. A grocer's son from Grantham with a girth the length of the Embankment emerged from a side door, buttoning up his flies. 'Ah, Lestrade,' he said. 'Just popped out for a pee. Oh, sorry, Miss F. Tea, Lestrade?'

'I wouldn't say no, sir.' Lestrade noticed that the old woman had turned even greyer, clutching various parts of her frock. She took a deep breath, summoned up the blood and swept from the room, her chatelaine rattling in disgust.

'The trouble with that woman,' Frost said, 'is that she doesn't believe people should have private parts, let alone use them.' He sat heavily, and at nineteen stone he had no choice, in the great leather Chesterfield he'd inherited from his predecessor, McNaughten. Then it had been a magnificent piece of furniture. Now it hung like an old sack, horsehair trailing on the floor. Lestrade perched on the only other chair in the room, so hard that it made his eyes water and so narrow that his buttocks draped over each side.

'Tell me about that railway murder.' Frost fixed him with his old Grantham grocer's stare.

'Er . . .'

'The one back in February.'

'Er . . .'

'L Division had it. Inspector Julius Greatorex.'

'Oh, Julie. Yes, I remember now. What can I tell you about it?'

Frost frowned at him. 'Well, nothing apparently. I thought it was referred to you.'

'No, sir. Chief Inspector Abberline.'

'Abberline?'

'Yes, sir. Frederick Abberline. Chief Inspector. You must know him. Thinning hair. Dundreary whiskers. Lovely wife.'

Frost was slowly turning purple. 'Don't be flippant with me, Lestrade. A man hoping for a pension one day should be careful how lippy he is. Am I getting through?'

'Loud and clear, sir,' Lestrade beamed.

'All right, then.'

There was a rustle of grey clothing beyond the partition and Miss Featherstonehaugh emerged like a ghost, rattling her teacups.

'Three sugars, Mr Lestrade?' she asked.

Lestrade looked aghast. 'Will there be room for any tea?' he asked.

'Mr Frost always has three,' she told him.

Lestrade groaned inwardly. Another giant leap for idiotkind.

'No éclairs, Miss F?' the Assistant Commissioner asked.

'The éclair man hasn't been this morning,' she said. 'Would you settle for a muffin?'

'No,' scowled Frost, 'but I could hide my acute disappointment by eating three.'

'Mr Lestrade?' she asked.

'Nothing, thank you, Miss Featherstonehaugh. Your tea, as always, is sheer nectar.'

She simpered at him and scuttled away in search of muffins.

'Don't butter her up, Lestrade,' Frost said. 'I've got to pay her two-thirds of a man's wage as it is. Where was I?'

'Three sugars?'

'No, the railway murder. I was going to tell you.'

Lestrade unglued one numb buttock from the chair. 'I'm sitting comfortably,' he lied.

'Then I'll begin,' said Frost. 'Fourteenth of February, wasn't it? St Valentine's Day. The gentlemen of the Press called it the St Valentine's Day massacre. Erroneously, as always. I don't think one victim can be called a massacre, do you?'

'I wouldn't have thought so, sir.' Though it had to be said that Lestrade had missed the lecture on Semantics for Policemen. But it didn't matter; he'd had plenty of experience of the Chosen People anyway.

'Her name was Sarah Culdrose. She was twenty-eight years of age; married; childless.'

'That's right,' Lestrade remembered. 'The husband did it.'

'Or did he?'

'Pardon?'

'I'll get round to Mr Culdrose in a minute. Her body was found in the early hours of the morning at Liverpool Street in a carriage from Aldgate. Her purse was still in her handbag and she'd been strangled.'

'And Abberline got his man within three days. It's all coming back to me now.'

'That's right. Except he didn't.'

'Ah.' Lestrade was not surprised. Abberline's track record was not what it might have been.

'Ask yourself – why would a husband who wants to terminate the relationship he has with his wife go to the extraordinary lengths of taking her on the Inner Circle of the Metropolitan line's Underground, where he would have been seen by scores of people, strangling his wife, having carefully disarranged her clothing first, and leaving her corpse for anyone to find?'

'Fair question, sir,' Lestrade ruminated. He'd had no breakfast. 'But if this doubt has crept into your mind, may I ask why Mr Culdrose is still in custody? If I remember rightly, he's in the Scrubs on remand.'

'He is. And that's where you're going this morning, Lestrade. To ask him a few more questions – this time from a totally different angle.'

'And that angle is?'

'As though he were innocent.'

Lestrade frowned. 'I thought all men were until proven guilty.'

It was Frost's turn to frown. 'I'm seriously worried about you, Lestrade,' he tutted, shaking his bulldog head. 'You are not as other policemen. Still, we'll have to hope for an improvement.'

'May I ask two questions, sir?' Lestrade said.

'You may ask, certainly,' Frost told him.

'First, why aren't you giving this back to Chief Inspector Abberline, whose case it actually is?'

'That's simple. He's on extended surveillance on the omnibuses of Penge, looking for the pervert who haunts the public transport in that district. So far the cunning swine has eluded the police, thwarting Abberline's efforts at every turn. Your next question?'

'Second, why are you sending me to interrogate a murder suspect, when you have no less evidence against him now than when Abberline arrested him?'

'No less evidence? Well, not quite. You see, the Railway Police found another one this morning.'

Lestrade blinked. 'Another one?'

Frost nodded grimly. 'Her body is at the Old Montague Street Morgue. When you've seen Culdrose, get along there.'

'I'd prefer to go there first, sir.'

'Why, Lestrade? She isn't going anywhere for the moment.'

'But there may be vital . . .'

'I'm sure there will be, Lestrade. And you're wasting time nattering about it. You know how serious a matter it is to waste the police's time. Cut along. Oh, when you've finished your tea, of course.'

Lestrade gulped down the cup's dregs and made for the door. He paused. 'I don't suppose you've considered,' he said, 'why the Penge pervert has so far eluded us, sir?'

Frost scowled at him. 'I smell a theory in the wind, Lestrade,' he said. 'Go on. Out with it.'

'Well, sir,' the Inspector said, 'it's unprofessional of me to say it, I know, but have you considered the possibility that Chief Inspector Abberline *is* the Penge Flasher?'

'Get out, Lestrade,' Frost told him, levelly. 'And wipe that smile off your face. Culdrose's barrister is a shifty bastard called Marshall Hall. God help you if he's got wind of this morning's little discovery.'

The Victorian pile of Her Majesty's Prison Wormwood Scrubs lies in the borough of Hammersmith on the twenty-two acres beside the recreation ground. Once a lung of London, it now stood dumb in the unseasonal heat of that spring, the sun beating mercilessly on its slated roofs and the grilles of its little windows through which the hopeless stared in vain.

Inspector Sholto Lestrade and Constable Walter Dew took the tram to Shepherd's Bush and walked the rest of the way through the great lunchtime throng to the great studded gates. Beyond these, the sun never shone. They followed a rattling warder down endless bleak corridors, in regulation chipped green and cream, past the treadmill that counted 930 steps to nowhere and the crank that broke the back and the spirit. On up to the first floor overlooking the grey exercise yard where years of hobnailed boots had worn a tight and ghastly circle. In the centre was the flagpole where they ran up the black flag on execution days and they passed the execution shed where men died crying or cursing their God or asking for forgiveness. Calcraft, Berry, the Billingtons, public executioners past and present were deaf and blind to such entreaties. The white hood. The pinions on the legs. The noose. The trap. Scientific death in nine seconds.

The cell door crashed back as the prison clock struck eleven. A hollow-faced man, his skin parchment yellow above the rough arrow-grey, sat curled on the plain iron bedstead in the corner. The remains of an indescribable meal lay on the wooden plate on the table. There was no knife, no fork, only an ancient spoon. And there were no laces in the man's boots.

But it was someone else who held Lestrade's attention. A man of nearly his own age, but boyish, clean-shaven and in an immaculately cut suit. The Apollo of the Bar.

'I am Marshall Hall,' he said, hands on hips. 'Who are you?'

It was what Frost had feared. The Persians had sneaked around the pass at Thermopylae, the Scots were late at Glencoe, General Custer had forgotten his sabres at the Little Bighorn. It all added up to one thing – defeat.

'I am Inspector Lestrade,' said Lestrade. 'This is Detective Constable Dew.'

Marshall Hall nodded. 'You have the papers for my client's release?'

'I have no instructions as to that,' Lestrade told him.

Marshall Hall crossed to his man, the grey eyes cold and lethal. Lestrade had seen him in action before, at the Bailey. He delighted in destroying policemen when it suited his book and it was unfortunate that the two policemen on the case of Sarah Culdrose were Julius Greatorex and Frederick Abberline. It was as though Marshall Hall read Lestrade's mind.

'Let me see,' he said. 'Inspector Greatorex. L Division. Made sergeant at thirty-eight after nearly nineteen years on the Force. Number of arrests – two hundred and sixty-eight. Number of convictions – sixteen. Promoted to inspector one month after marrying the least eligible daughter of Sir Charles Warren, late Commissioner of the Metropolitan Police – a lady whose face has been known to frighten horses. Chief Inspector Abberline. Consistently promoted to the level of his own incompetence. Signally failed to catch the Whitechapel murderer seven years ago. Consistently succeeds in catching his own tail, but then he's had a great deal of practice. Has faced a string of paternity suits since the spring of 1874 since which point he has become increasingly estranged from the increasingly strange Mrs Abberline, she who almost took the title "London's Most Homely Woman" from the aforementioned Mrs Greatorex.'

'To what conclusion is this going?' asked Lestrade, perfectly able to use court-room jargon when the devil drove.

Marshall Hall looked at him oddly. 'To establish the incompetence of the police officers in charge of my client's alleged case,' he said.

Lestrade breathed a silent sigh of relief.

'Unless of course I choose to believe the literary ramblings of Doctors John Watson and Arthur Conan Doyle in the *Strand Magazine.*'

'Which you don't,' Lestrade checked.

'I'd be a solicitor's clerk if I did,' the barrister said. 'But if ever you're tempted to sue, I'd be delighted to act for you. No one can accuse me of partisanship. Now come, Lestrade, I'm a busy man. Time is money and my client has been wasting away in custody here for three months.'

'I have come to ask your client some questions.'

'Come off it, Lestrade,' Marshall Hall chuckled. 'The sole reason you are here is to eat humble pie on the part of your superiors. The case against my client is circumstantial at best. And the little discovery this morning of a woman's body at Blackfriars Station has left you with an entire omelette on your face. Admit it.'

'Some have cases thrust upon them,' Lestrade said. 'That is my position this afternoon. I know nothing about the woman at Blackfriars, nor will I until this afternoon. But if your client intends to get out of here, I suggest that he cooperates.'

Marshall Hall perched himself on the corner of the table. 'George,' he said, 'you aren't obliged to say anything to these . . . gentlemen.'

Culdrose nodded slowly. 'I know, Marshall,' he said. 'But as I have said repeatedly since February, I have nothing to hide.'

'Very well, Lestrade,' said Marshall Hall, 'but rest assured I shall interfere if I find your questions improper.'

Lestrade nodded. 'Constable Dew will take notes,' he said.

'And I will see his notebook,' Marshall Hall said.

'You will not,' said Lestrade.

'Then you will receive no answers,' said the lawyer.

'Please,' Culdrose interrupted, 'I have been in this stinking cell for three months. Can we get on with it? Ask me your questions, Inspector.'

The seconds were out. It was Round One. And the first blood had gone to Lestrade.

'How long had you and your wife been married, Mr Culdrose?'

'A little less than five years,' the grey man said.

'Children?'

'None.'

'What is your occupation?'

'I am . . . was a speculator.'

'I see,' mused Lestrade. 'And in what do you speculate?'

'You needn't be too precise here, George,' Marshall Hall was quick to point out.

'I don't mind,' Culdrose said. 'I began in railways. I now dabble chiefly in South African mining. And I'm heavily involved in rubber, Inspector.'

Lestrade flashed a knowing glance at Constable Dew, but the man was still struggling with the spelling of speculator and the moment passed him by.

'How's business?' Lestrade asked.

'For the last three months, non-existent,' Marshall Hall reminded him.

'Quite.' Lestrade had, not for the first time, shot himself in the foot. 'Tell me, Mr Culdrose, did you love your wife?'

'Objection,' said Marshall Hall.

'This is not the Old Bailey, Mr Marshall Hall,' Lestrade reminded him.

'Neither is my client in the dock,' said the lawyer. 'Not yet.'

'I am giving him the chance to do something he cannot do in court,' said Lestrade, 'and that is to speak in his own defence.'

'Please, Marshall,' Culdrose struggled on the edge of his seat, 'I want to get this over with.'

Marshall Hall's cold grey eyes flashed at his client, at Lestrade, at Dew. He threw his arms into the air in one of those histrionic gestures the Bailey clientele knew so well and admired so much.

'No, Mr Lestrade,' Culdrose almost whispered. 'I did not love my wife. Sarah was the daughter of a business partner. It was a marriage of convenience that became an inconvenience; a pact made in hell. And all in the name of consoles.'

'And did anything console you, sir?' Lestrade raised an inquisitorial eyebrow.

'If you mean did I take a mistress, no. I was brought up

in the Methodist faith, Inspector. A tot of medicinal brandy would have me up before the minister; but a mistress . . .' He positively shuddered. 'I'd be excommunicated.'

'When did you last see your wife?' Lestrade asked, trying not to look like that man in the painting.

'We had a row on that Tuesday morning . . .'

'George . . .'

But Marshall Hall's growled warning went unheeded as Culdrose stormed on. 'I can't actually remember what it was about now. I left to go to the City and that was that.'

'Did she say anything before you left, about going out?'

'No. Sarah was a hypochondriac, Mr Lestrade. She never left the house in the winter unless she had to.'

'Er . . . excuse me, sir.' Dew's wrist was flagging at his notebook. 'Is that a branch of the Methodist movement?'

'What?' Culdrose was confused.

'The Hypochondriacs.'

'Never mind, Walter.' Lestrade patted the man's arm. 'I'll explain it later.' The Constable had been the first policeman on the scene to find the battered body of the last of the Ripper's victims in the slaughterhouse of Miller's Court. You had to make allowances.

'Do you have servants?' Lestrade asked.

'One maid of all work. The bottom had fallen out of rubber late last year and I had to let old Gonad go.'

'Best thing for it,' Lestrade nodded. 'When was the first time you were aware anything was amiss?'

'When I came home that night. Amelia – that's the maid – said that Sarah had gone out shortly before dark.'

'Did she say where she was going?'

'No. Except that she couldn't bear to be in the house on my return.'

'Had she done this sort of thing before?'

'Once. About a year ago. She went to her mother's.'

'Which is where?'

'Uxbridge.'

'Make a note of that, Dew.' Lestrade peered over his man's shoulder and tapped the notebook. 'The Underground train from Aldgate to Liverpool Street does not go to Uxbridge. I assume that your mother-in-law had not seen your wife?'

'No. I called her on the telephone.'

'You have a telephone?' Lestrade asked.

'Oh, a hideous expense, I know. And for long I racked my conscience as to which should go – the telephone or old Gonad. But in the modern world of lofty technology, Mr Lestrade, the telephone was indispensable.'

'To your mother-in-law too, it would seem.'

'Sarah insisted upon it. The old crone is over eighty and deaf as a doornail. I had to shout. There was no need for the telephone at all, come to think of it.'

'What did you do when you realized that your wife had gone?'

'I called my mother-in-law as I said. Then I went to the police.'

'Straight away?'

'As I told you, Inspector, my wife never left home voluntarily in the winter months. She was not at her mother's. We have few friends to speak of, merely business acquaintances, and she had been very upset when I'd left her in the morning.'

'This would have been . . . which police station?'

'Wimbledon. I caught a train.'

'And what was next?'

'I was visited the next morning by an Inspector Greatorex.' Marshall Hall snorted.

'He proceeded to drop cigar ash all over Sarah's mother's Wilton and was generally unpleasant.'

'About par for the course,' Lestrade and Marshall Hall choroused.

'He began questioning me in the most belligerent manner, asking personal things about . . . personal things. He insisted on seeing our bedroom.'

'Outrageous!' hissed Marshall Hall. 'The man hasn't the remotest idea of procedure.'

'In the end I showed him the door.'

Lestrade nodded. He knew 'Julie' Greatorex of old. All people ever showed him was the door. Ever since his first adolescent fumblings with the vicar's daughter, behind the rhododendron bushes.

'I thought they were the worst days of my life,' Culdrose

went on. 'Then Chief Inspector Abberline called and I knew they weren't. He began pleasantly enough . . .'

'Cunning bastard,' chorused Marshall Hall and Lestrade.

'Then he came right out with it.' Culdrose had turned a whiter shade of pale. 'He said they'd found Sarah in a carriage of a train in a siding at Liverpool Street. An Underground train. She'd been dead, apparently, for nearly three days. The train had not been in service. She'd been . . . strangled. He cautioned me that I need not say anything and then I was arrested for Sarah's murder.' Culdrose buried his face in his hands and hung there, like a man tired of London and tired of life.

'And what brought you thundering to the rescue?' Lestrade turned to the lawyer.

'Bowker, my clerk,' Marshall Hall said. 'He has a nose for a good brief. Until this morning, I think you'd have found us more than ready, Lestrade, to devastate the puerile case for the prosecution. Pity, really. I was particularly relishing the prospect of cross-examining Abberline. Bit like swatting a fly in a way.' He yawned ostentatiously.

Lestrade sighed in sympathy. 'Until this morning?' he said.

'Come on, Lestrade,' the lawyer chuckled. 'Are you telling me there are *two* stranglers working the Underground at the moment?'

The Inspector looked at him, then at Culdrose. 'I don't know if this morning's victim *was* strangled,' he said.

'That's because you don't read the lunchtime edition of the *Standard*.' Marshall Hall threw it at him. 'Headline news. The gentlemen of the Press are so subtle, aren't they? I remember, as I'm sure you do, the field day they had with the Ripper Case. The only occupation they didn't point a finger at was, surprise, surprise, journalists. Odd that. Show me an innocent journalist and I'll show you an intelligent policeman.'

'Or an honest lawyer,' Lestrade said levelly. 'Doubtless with your vast experience, Mr Marshall Hall, you will be aware of copycat killing. Mr Culdrose kills his wife on the Underground . . .'

'*Allegedly*,' bridled Marshall Hall.

'And someone else does the same thing "just for jolly, wouldn't you"?'

'Why?' Marshall Hall challenged him. 'Tell me why?'

Lestrade summoned Walter Dew to his feet. 'Because it's

there, Mr Marshall Hall. The Underground. Dark and deadly and half-way to hell. We'll see ourselves out.'

The mortuary attendant, the one with the stoop, slopped his bucket along the marble slab in the silent basement of Old Montague Street. He sniffed. Why did all mortuary attendants sniff, Lestrade wondered. Was it an essential part of the job, which they automatically included in their curriculum vitals?

'Cup of tea, Mr Lestrade?' he asked.

'No thanks, Igor. It's a little early for me.'

The attendant looked at the morgue clock. On the stroke of four. He'd always thought this was precisely the time the English took their tea, but it had to be said he lived in the Marie Walewska Home for Polish Immigrants off the Commercial Road and he didn't meet many Englishmen. Not live ones anyway.

'Tram accident in Holborn,' he explained as he gathered up the fingers.

'That's a long way from here,' Lestrade commented, fanning the flies away with his bowler.

'Some of dem are in Charing Cross Hospital; some in St Bartholomew's. One of dem is in Wards Four, Six and Seven. Vell, you can't get the staff dese days.'

Lestrade looked at the increasingly green face of Walter Dew at his elbow. 'Indeed not. Get up, Walter, and have a little walk around. I can manage here.'

'Very good, guv'nor.' And the grateful Constable was gone, his hobnails clattering on the stone steps that led to the air and the sun.

'Now, Igor. This morning's little find.'

'Ah, yes. The strangulation.'

'Was it?'

'Oh yes. Ven I vas at home in Cracov, I vas, vat vould you call dem? A surgeon's gofor. I attended many courts of de coroner. I hef seen dese tings before.'

He hauled the green blanket off a body that lay in the far corner, noting Lestrade's expression. It didn't change. Here was a cool one.

'Inspector Lestrade,' Igor said, 'say hello to Mrs Hollander.'

'You know her?'

'I don't,' the Pole said, 'but she has been identified.'

'By whom?'

'De paperwork is upstairs. Shall I get it for you?'

Lestrade nodded and the attendant hobbled away, sniffing. Mrs Hollander lay naked with her eyes closed and her arms crossed over her breasts. Lestrade took the cold hand and prised open the fingers now that the tension of rigor was leaving them. He noted mechanically the blue nails, the pale line where the wedding band had been. He looked at the face. A comely woman once; the strangler's grip had changed all that. Her lips were bluer than her nails and there was a dark trickle of blood around her nostrils, running down in a brown streak across her right cheek and into her auburn hair. Her tongue protruded as though in a permanent gesture of contempt to those who had come to gaze on her now. Lestrade's eyes focused on the throat. Finger-marks, nearly black, had discoloured the area below the jaw and there was a ragged line of cuts where the murderer's finger-nails had torn the flesh. The jawline and the breasts were mottled where the blood vessels had burst in her death agony. He knew that the hyoid bone had snapped and the windpipe collapsed beyond that once-pretty neck. He let his eyes wander down over the ribcage, the flat belly, the pubic mound. Nothing appeared untoward down . . . there, but he would reserve judgement for now.

'Comte de la Warre,' Igor said from the steps.

The voice shook Lestrade out of his silence. 'What?' he asked.

'Dat is de man who came to identify her. De Comte de la Warre.'

'A Frenchman?' Lestrade was nothing if not cosmopolitan.

Igor shrugged. 'It seems like. I vas not here but I tink he said he vas her husband.'

'Her husband?' Lestrade was confused. 'You mean he was Mr Hollander?'

'I do not know how you say it in England,' Igor said, rummaging in his pockets. 'Mrs Hollander lived wid him.'

'Ah.' Realization dawned. 'She was his common-law wife. Did the Comte leave an address?'

'No.' Igor perused the ledger he was carrying.

'Marvellous!' sighed Lestrade. 'What's all this?'

'Dese are de things Mrs Hollander had on her perzon ven she vas brought in.'

Lestrade checked the items that Igor had splayed on the corpse. A wedding ring, of brass. Three coins. A small comb. A ticket for the Metropolitan line dated yesterday. A yellow season ticket to the Earls Court Exhibition. And a bracelet in the form of brightly coloured beads with a curious design that Lestrade had never seen before.

'Vait a minute.' Igor was resting the ledger on Mrs Hollander's breasts. 'Dis is peculiar.'

'What?' Lestrade asked.

'Three udder people came to identify her.'

Lestrade remembered the Ripper Case, when there had been queues to view the corpses. 'Why is that peculiar?'

'One of dem says dat she is Frau Hauptmann.'

'Frau . . . ?'

'Dat's German,' Igor helped him.

'I know.' Lestrade *had* been to the lecture on German for Detectives. 'What is his name?'

Igor squinted and shook his head. 'I can't read dat.' He gave it to Lestrade, sniffing. 'Can you read dat?'

Lestrade sniffed in reply. No, he couldn't.

'And dere's somebody else,' the attendant tutted, clearly amazed. 'If only I hadn't been off zick vid dis cold dis morning. Bitches, aren't dey?'

'Who?' Lestrade asked.

'Zpring colds,' Igor explained. 'Dat's who.'

'Who did the somebody else claim she was?' Lestrade couldn't read the ledger from that angle.

Igor stared at it in something akin to disbelief. 'Mrs Sun Dat Warms De Mountains.'

'Of course,' muttered Lestrade. 'A name well known in the Home Counties.'

Lestrade and Dew reached the giant complex that was Earls Court a little before dusk. The place was closed now and the spring crowds had gone home. The Great Wheel stood huge and silent dominating the approaches from Brompton Road Station.

A tall man with a broad white hat and long hair cascading over his shoulders sat in a brightly painted caravan near the central stadium. He appeared to be lassoing his right foot with unerring accuracy. Lestrade showed him Mrs Hollander's yellow season ticket.

'Yeah, we're closed, buddy,' he said. 'Come back tomorrow.'

'What is this?' Lestrade asked.

The long-haired man looked at the pair before him. Both in regulation serge. Both in bowler hats. He checked their ankles for the tell-tale signs of the manacles which would have proclaimed that they had escaped from somewhere.

'It's a ticket,' he said.

'To the Wild West Show?' Lestrade asked.

'Not really a show right now,' the American said. 'Justa sorta retainer. But it's nearly seven o'clock, Great Britain Time, mister. You and your pal come back tomorrow, y'hear.'

'I am Inspector Sholto Lestrade of Scotland Yard,' said Lestrade. 'This is Constable Dew. We are here on official police business.'

The long-haired man took the cigar from his mouth for the first time. 'No shit?' he said. 'I'm John Burke, but you can call me Arizona John. What'll I call you? Scotland Yard Sholto?'

'You can call me Inspector,' Lestrade told him.

'Sure,' Burke shrugged. 'Well, what can I do for you guys? Police Benefit, some'n like that?'

'In this country, Mr Burke,' Lestrade said, 'nobody gives policemen the benefit. We're here in connection with the murder of the late Mrs Hollander.'

'Mrs . . . Holy shit.' He took off his hat. 'So it's true, then?'

'What is?' Lestrade gave nothing away, least of all to foreigners with silly hats and long hair.

'That Jane Hollander's dead. Holy shit.'

'Did you know the lady?'

'Sure,' Burke said, pouring himself a stiff shot of Redeye from a decanter on the table. 'Well, not in the biblical sense. I'm about the only fella round here who didn't. Oh, apart from Old Birdie, that is. And I ain't so sure about him.'

'Old Birdie?' Lestrade was giving Dew time to cope with the longhand.

'Her paw.'

'Her paw?' Lestrade and Dew had clearly both misheard.

'Father,' Burke said.

'Is there a Mr Hollander?'

'Yeah. And that's where the going gets a little rough, Inspector. I guess there *was* a Mr Hollander once, but now there's four of 'em with claims on her.'

'Indeed?'

'Well, there's the Comte, the beauest of beaux sabreurs around here. Then there's Michail, a monosyllabic moron from Minsk. Not forgetting Bruno, one of the sourest Krauts it's been my misfortune to tangle with. And then of course there's Sun That Warms The Mountains.'

'Sun That Warms The Mountains?' Lestrade was afraid he'd heard right.

'He's a full-blooded Oglala Sioux. I sure hope you ain't packin'.'

'We're not going anywhere,' Lestrade assured him.

'What? Oh, no, I mean I sure hope you ain't packin' a gun. Sunny's fine with blanks. Whoops it up like all get out, attackin' the Deadwood Stage an' all. But you go within thirty paces of him with a loaded thumb-breaker and he'll part your hair.'

'The friendly type then?' Lestrade smiled.

'Like a crate of rattlers,' Burke nodded.

'Are they all here?'

'Sure. They all stayed on after Bill's last show. I've just come over to take 'em home.'

'Bill?' Dew asked.

'Buffalo Bill.' Burke frowned, appalled at the ineptitude of the British police. 'Prince of Plainsmen. He tamed the West single-handed.'

'Yes,' said Lestrade. 'Constable Dew here did much the same thing to Shepherd's Bush a few years ago. I'd like to talk to Old Birdie first. Can you point us in his direction?'

The direction in which Old Birdie lay took the policemen and the showman through a labyrinth of alleyways and cattle pens where great shaggy buffalo stood stamping and steaming in the evening. Long before they had reached their destination, a dingy little shed marked with a single star and the legend

Lestrade had put both feet right in it and Dew was careful to sit upwind of him.

One by one John Burke sent the men to them, beginning with the father of the dead woman. Old Birdie still carried himself erect, for all his years. Only the eyes betrayed his age and a certain stagger in his step. He stood in that little shed at Earls Court, before Lestrade and Dew, in the yellow-braided jacket and forage cap of the Light Cavalry.

'State your name,' said Dew, today playing the role of the nasty policeman.

'Sergeant 1209 Bird, William, late Eight Royal Irish Hussars, sir.'

'At ease, Sergeant,' Lestrade said. He had worked with old soldiers before, on the Brigade Case. He knew they had their pride and they still responded, after all these years, to the old commands. Bird's shaky old nether limbs slid apart and he locked his hands behind his back. 'It's about your daughter, Mr Bird,' the Inspector said.

'She's dead, y'know,' the old soldier said, staring straight ahead.

'That's why we're here,' said Lestrade. 'We're from Scotland Yard. How did you find out about your daughter?'

'Wolfgang told me, sir.'

'Wolfgang?'

'Captain Bruno. Proper gen'leman he is. Unlike some of 'em around 'ere,' and the old man spat into a pile of sawdust in the corner. "E went to see 'er in the morgue this morning. I couldn't bear it. Seein' her . . . like that. It's not decent.'

'We have to find out who murdered her, Mr Bird,' Lestrade said. He had a daughter himself. Little Emma. Not quite two. He wouldn't want to see her . . . like that either.

'I know who murdered her,' the old Hussar said.

'Really?' Lestrade and Dew exchanged glances. 'Would you care to tell us who?'

'That damned Rusky, that's who.'

'Er . . . you'll have to forgive us, Sergeant,' Lestrade humoured him. 'Which damned Rusky?'

'That bloody Cossack; that Bogdanovitch. Son of a bitch, more like. I haven't forgotten the Charge, y'know.'

Who had?

'Damned Cossacks. Killed my horse, they did, old Daisy. Or was it Buttercup? Ah, the old memory isn't what it was.'

'How old are you, Mr Bird?' Lestrade asked.

'Sixty-three . . . I shouldn't wonder,' the old soldier said. 'Took me prisoner, y'know.'

'Who did?'

'The Ruskies. That bloody general of theirs. That Liprandi. Know what he arsked me?'

'No.'

'How much bloody rum I'd had that morning – the morning of the Charge. And me a lifelong teetotaller. If I'd 'ad me health and strength I'd have put one on him, I tell you.'

'You didn't have either?'

'Either what?'

'Your health and strength?'

'Lord love you, no. I'd 'ad cholera something dreadful. What with that and the lance in me buttock.'

The policemen glanced at the man's buttock.

'Still rolls to the left when I canter.' He slapped his haunch.

'So you think Bogdanovitch killed your daughter?' Lestrade thought it best to keep the old boy to the matter in hand.

'Stands to reason. 'Ate us, they do.'

'The Ruskies?'

Bird nodded. 'Sneaky bastards wear grey, y'know. I tell you, sir, never trust a man in a grey uniform. Look at that Robert Bloody E. Lee.'

'Is he another Russian, sir?' Dew whispered to Lestrade out of the corner of his mouth.

'Let it go, Walter.' The Inspector patted his shoulder. 'Would you like to sit down, Mr Bird?'

'No thank you, sir.' The old Hussar straightened. 'Hi'll stand hif it's all the same to you.'

It was. 'Tell us about your daughter,' Lestrade said.

He smiled and a single tear rolled the length of his battered cheek. 'She were a good girl. Or so they said. I never believed 'em, mind. Pure and innocent she were. That's why 'e killed her.'

'Oh?'

Bird nodded. 'I saw it in Turkey,' he said. 'Blokes queuing up for the 'arlots. If they saw a girl who wouldn't let 'em, they'd

38

call 'er heveryfink under the sun. She wouldn't let that bastard Cossack 'ave his end away with her so 'e killed 'er.'

'I see. When did you see your daughter last, Mr Bird?'

'Jane? Ooh, must 'ave been larst week some time. She come 'ere regular – just to see 'er old man.' He smiled affectionately. "Ad a Hannie Hoakley.'

'A Hannie Hoakley?'

'It's what we in the show call a season ticket. Yellow thing looks like it's been shot full of 'oles.'

'Where is Mr Hollander?' Lestrade asked.

'Kensal Green.'

'The cemetery?'

Bird nodded.

'When did he die?'

'Who said 'e was dead?' Bird asked. "E cuts the grass up there, that's all. They're hestranged.'

Lestrade could see that. They didn't come any hestranger than this lot. 'Where did she live?'

'Thirty-one Quex Road.'

'Kilburn,' said Dew, whose knowledge of such things was encyclopaedic.

'How well did she know the others here – in the show?'

'Scarcely at all,' said Bird. 'Major Burke, 'e's a proper gen'leman 'e is, for all 'e's a bloody Yank. 'E looked after 'er.'

'Indeed?' Lestrade glanced at Dew. 'Tell me, Mr Bird. Did your daughter have any enemies? Anybody who would wish her ill?'

'Nah.' The old man didn't have to think. 'Little Janey was always very popular. Just like 'er mother, Gawd rest 'er. Specially with the lads. Hever since she used to go into the bushes with them at home in Kilburn.'

'How old was she then?'

'Eight. 'Ad a passion for nature, she did. Used to take the older boys into the bushes to show 'em birds' nests and that. Knew all about the birds, did my little Janey.'

'And the bees?' asked Dew, although perhaps it was not his place to do so.

'Good Methodist stock we are, us Birds,' the old soldier said. 'She was a saint, that girl. A bloody saint. Now, if that's all, gentlemen, I've got things I've got to be a-doing.'

'Yes, of course, Mr Bird,' said Lestrade. 'What is it you do here, exactly?'

'I parades with the Union Jack, sir,' the ex-Sergeant told him. 'For all it's a Yankee show, can't 'ave them bloody Stars and Stripes all over the bloody shop. Back in '87 I used to re-enact the Charge, but there was six of us then. The other five have cocked their toes up since and my buttock ain't what it was. I just walks round with the flag now.'

'I can't think of a finer calling, Mr Bird,' said Lestrade. 'Thank you for your help.' And the old man saluted and saw himself out.

Dew had barely had time to lick his pencil when a dapper little beau sabreur bounded in. He was easily twenty years younger than the old Hussar, with a cheeky upturned moustache and the sky-blue jacket and kepi of the Chasseurs d'Afrique.

'Messieurs,' he bowed, 'the Comte de la Warre, at your service. 'Ow may I 'elp?'

'You called at the Old Montague Street mortuary earlier today?' Lestrade asked him.

'*Oui.*'

'To identify a woman called Jane Hollander, née Bird.'

'*Oui.*' The Frenchman threw his scabbard and sabre over the arm of a chair in the corner and threw his buttocks in seconds later. Clearly they were made of sterner stuff than Sergeant Bird's for he scarcely winced at all.

'What was she to you?' Lestrade inquired.

''Ow you say, she was my common-law wife.'

'For how long had this been the case?'

'Nearly three years.'

'Your common-law father-in-law seems blissfully unaware of the fact,' Lestrade pointed out.

'Pah!' the Frenchman laughed. ''E is, 'ow you say, a few troopers short of a squadron, *n'est-ce pas?*'

'So you've been with the Wild West Show for three years?'

'*Oui,*' said de la Warre, 'I 'ave said so. Do you doubt my word? Ze word of an officer in the glorious Cavalerie de la France?'

'No, no,' Lestrade assured him, not at all pleased with the gleam in the man's eye or the man's sabre. Cutlass drill was all a long time ago and Walter Dew was a slouch. 'How often did you and Mrs Hollander . . . I mean . . .'

'Monsieur,' the Frenchman stood up, his spurs jingling with umbrage, 'a Frenchman takes 'is pleasure where 'e will. I was a young man at Mars-la-Tour. Having scattered that damned Bosch cuirassier regiment, I took a girl behind a 'edge.'

'Really?' asked Lestrade. What with the young Miss Bird's proclivities, there was an awful lot of hedging going on, one way or another. 'Where was the regiment, all this time?'

'Looking on. Applauding.'

'Hmm,' Lestrade mused. 'Weren't you people beaten at Mars-la-Tour?'

The Frenchman turned an unusual shade of cerise, not at all at odds with his sky-blue. 'A gross slur,' he said. 'German propaganda. I thought you wanted to ask me about Madame 'Ollander.'

'Indeed,' said Lestrade. 'Constable Dew and I are looking into her murder.'

'You need look no further,' the Comte said.

'Oh?'

'Hauptmann Wolfgang Bruno is your man.'

'He is?'

Dew added another suspect to his already bulging pad.

'*Mais certainement*. The Bosch bastard is my inferior in every-thing. 'Orsemanship, swordsmanship, panache. 'E envied me my little Janey. I 'ave of course sworn to kill 'im.'

'Of course.' Lestrade's eyebrow rose just a little. It would take some doing to remind these foreigners that Earls Court was actually on British soil and that British law did not look kindly on affairs of honour.

'Consumed with jealousy, 'e chose 'is moment to choke the life out of 'er. But fear not. 'E will be impaled on my blade by sunset. So, if you will excuse me . . .'

'One more thing, Comte,' Lestrade said. 'When did you see Mrs Hollander last, apart from this morning at the mortuary, I mean?'

'Ooh, you 'ave me there.' The Frenchman screwed up his little face. 'It would 'ave been last Tuesday, I think. I 'ad the night off from restaging the rout of the Prussians at Jena by Marshal Murat of blessed memory and I visited 'er in Kilburn.'

'Quex Road?'

'Ze same.'

'Why did you refer to her as Mrs Hollander rather than the Comtesse de la Warre?' Lestrade asked.

The Frenchman chuckled. 'Please, monsieur. I am a member of an old aristocratic family. It would be improper. A *bientôt*, messieurs.' And he clicked his heels and left.

Talking of heel clicking, no sooner had the door closed on the policemen than a large, square-looking horseman with a razor-cropped haircut and wearing the attila of the seventh Rhenish Hussars stood before them, doing just that.

'Er . . . Hauptmann Bruno?' Lestrade guessed.

The German bowed fiercely as though his neck had snapped.

'Won't you sit down?'

'In a chair vere a Frenchman has sat?' The Captain raised a sabre-scarred eyebrow. 'I vas a young man at Mars-la-Tour. I don't sit down with Frenchmen or in chairs zey hef vacated.'

'I see,' said Lestrade, rapidly wondering what sort of show Buffalo Bill and John Burke were running here. 'I understand that you had . . . er . . . a relationship with Mrs Jane Hollander.'

'Yah. Zis is correct. She vas my wife.'

'You were married?'

'Zere vas no religious ceremony. But ve shared ze conventions of ze marriage bed.'

'We are making inquiries into her murder.'

'Goot. You hef saved me ze trouble of coming to Zcotland Yard.'

'We have?' Lestrade smelled confession.

'Your murderer is zat damned frog who just left.'

'It is?'

Dew sighed and turned over another page in his notebook.

'Of course. He knew zat Frau Hollander and I were betrothed. He could not bear to be beaten. Rather ironic, zat, isn't it, in an army zat von its last battle forty years ago?'

'You . . . er . . . haven't any plans to fight him, then?' Lestrade ventured.

The Captain looked askance. 'Of course not,' he said. 'I did not come down with ze last shower of rain. I know zat duelling has been illegal in zis century since the thirteenth of Elizabeth. Besides, ze Frenchman is a mere lieutenant. I cannot fight someone of a lower rank. It zimply is not done.'

'But he *is* a nobleman,' Lestrade pointed out.

'If 'e is a nobleman, I am a Dutchman, as ve zay in Alsace-Lorraine.'

'And when did you see Mrs Hollander last?'

'Ach, zere you hef me. I believe it was last Zursday.'

'You went to Kilburn?'

'*Nein*. She came to see me here at Earls Court.'

'I see. Well, thank you, Captain,' and Lestrade made a point of taking the man's hand.

Lestrade had never seen a Cossack before. Dew had never even seen a man from Lancashire, but then he was a particularly parochial policeman.

The Russian appeared eight feet tall in the long, cartridge case-embroidered khurtka of those regions pleasantly watered by the merry Don. His beard reached to his waist and he seemed to be bristling with weapons at every orifice.

'Do you speak English?' said Lestrade slowly and steadily.

'Of course,' the Cossack said. 'At school in Minsk I learned three languages.'

Lestrade shrugged. So much for Burke's assessment of this monosyllabic moron. 'We are investigating the murder of Jane Hollander in the early hours of this morning at or near Blackfriars Station.'

'Tragic.' The man nodded slowly.

'What was she to you?'

'A pleasant diversion, tovarishch, nothing more.'

'She was not your common-law wife, then?'

'Good God, *nyet*. If Mrs Bogdanovitch found out, there'd be hell to pay.'

'So how did you know the dead woman?'

'Intimately,' the Russian said. 'In my country a mistress is dandy if the wife is not handy. But another wife, albeit common-law, would be defying the laws of nature and of God.'

'I see.' Lestrade tilted his bowler to the back of his head. 'And who do you think killed her?'

The Russian shrugged this time. 'Obviously, that senile degenerate, her father.'

'Ah.' All par for the course so far. 'And why do you assume that?'

'Inspector,' said the Russian, 'we Russians are a deeply moral people. In the snows of the Urals if a father discovers that his daughter is promiscuous he takes her into the forest and leaves her to the wolves.'

'Really?'

'Of course. East European folklore is full of such stories. Take the Grimms.'

Lestrade would rather not. 'So, to you, this is perfectly natural.'

'Perfectly. Justifiable filicide.'

'But the Metropolitan line is hardly the forests of the Urals,' Lestrade commented.

'This is true, tovarishch, but then you have no forests to speak of in this little country, do you? Old Birdie obviously spoke as he found.'

'I see,' Lestrade cleared his throat, 'well, thank you . . . er . . .'

'Colonel,' beamed the Cossack, 'I outrank all these expatriate reprobates, but I'm not one to boast of these things.'

'You'll be here if we need you?' Lestrade checked.

'Of course. I have to do the pursuit over the Beresina again tomorrow. How we'll keep the water frozen in this weather I've no idea.' He looked at the darkening sky through the small window. 'Ah, to be in Petersburg now that April's there.'

It had to be said they missed the clatter of booted spurs on the hard ground beyond the door. Had Burke gone home? Forgotten to remind the last witness? Or had he lost patience waiting? Dew flexed his throbbing fingers and soothed the writer's ridge of hard skin that had formed along them. He fumbled with his lucifers to light the oil lamp on the table.

Lestrade peered silently through the window at the last of the sun's rays gilding the Great Wheel. He was in a world of his own watching Old Birdie at a treadle whetstone, sharpening his old sabre. Across the stadium from him, Lieutenant Comte de la Warre had hung his braided jacket on a pole and was advancing on it sword in hand, posturing before it as if warming up for a duel, moving in slow motion, as though in a dream.

Dew's scream therefore brought the Inspector jarring back to reality. The Constable dropped the match and the lamp and kicked over the table.

'For God's sake, Dew!' Lestrade snapped. 'You've seen a mouse before, surely?'

But it was not a mouse that moved soundlessly into the fading daylight. It was a figure the height of a man with a dark face shrouded in fur and horns and feathers trailing to the ground. Two parallel white lines were painted across the bridge of his aquiline nose and down his gaunt copper cheeks. A necklace of bears' teeth rattled on the bone breastplate as he folded his arms across his chest.

'Ah,' said Lestrade slowly, stooping to pick up Dew's lamp and what was left of the Constable's dignity, 'you wouldn't be Sun That Warms The Mountains, would you?'

'If you asked me nicely, He Whose Feet Smell Of The Droppings Of The Buffalo. You are a policeman. At the Reservation, the policemen kill my people. You will empty your pockets.'

'Guv'nor?' Dew whispered.

'Do as he says, Walter,' Lestrade told him. 'Carefully, now.'

'He Who Is Afraid Of His Shadow would be wise to do as his white chief says.'

Dew would have contended that remark but something in the glint of the Indian's eyes and the glint of the Bowie knife in the Indian's hand made him think again.

Sun's sharp eyes fell on the brass knuckles that Lestrade placed on the table. He snatched them up, cradling them in his massive painted fist. 'Good,' he said without smiling. 'My cousins the Cheyenne could have done with a few of these at Wounded Knee.' He clicked the tiny button and the deadly four-inch blade licked out in the darkness. 'Well, well, *hokai-hey*,' he chuckled. 'Isn't eastern technology wonderful? I must send for one of these the next time I get a replacement for my bears' teeth necklace.'

'You get these from the white man's city in the east?' Lestrade said, waving his hands in all directions. He'd had a sneaky read of a few of Ned Buntline's Dreadfuls. 'Chicago?'

'Birmingham,' the Indian told him, 'and not the one in

Alabama.' He snatched up the bead bracelet that Lestrade had tugged from his pocket. 'Ah. Where did you get this?' The Oglala closed to his man.

'From the body of Jane . . . Sun That Warms The Mountains,' Lestrade said.

The Oglala sheathed his knife and held the bracelet briefly to his cheek. 'Manitou, Wakan Tanka will punish the wrongdoer.'

'And who is the wrongdoer, Sun?' Lestrade asked.

'Wakan Tanka knows,' shrugged the Indian. 'That's what you fellas are paid huge amounts of wampum to find out, isn't it?'

'Indeed,' said Lestrade. 'When did you see your wife last – apart from this morning?'

'Three suns ago,' the Indian said, 'at her tepee in the Quex Road. She was on her way to see me today. The brothers and I were re-enacting the Little Big Horn. Major Burke, One Who Looks Like Bill Cody But Hasn't Got His Essential Je Ne Sais Quoi, he say a woman wearing a Sioux bracelet found dead. It was written in your papers. Smoke signals would have been quicker, of course.'

'Of course,' Lestrade was forced to agree.

'Er . . . sir . . .'

'Not now, Walter,' Lestrade said. 'Tell me, Sun . . .'

'Guv'nor, you know that French bloke . . .'

'Dew! I said not now.'

'It's just that he seems to be trying to kill the Kraut, sir.'

'What?'

Lestrade joined his subordinate at the window. Across the stadium, in the darkening O, two men were knocking seven bells out of each other with sabres. Feet from them, a doddery old man was using both hands to slash the fur cap off an unsuspecting Cossack. Lestrade heard him say that the next one would be his head.

He didn't wait to hear any more.

3

Frost's grandmother had the most annoying tic in the world. But she lived in Lincolnshire and it was the Assistant Commissioner's clock that got right up the nostrils of Inspector Lestrade the next morning.

He stood with his legs planted firmly apart, hands locked behind him, staring defiantly ahead. To his left and slightly behind him, Constable Dew looked appallingly sheepish, partly because he was holding two bowlers, Lestrade's and his own.

Facing them across the well-worn mahogany sat 'His Nims' himself, he of the bulldog breed, and a smug Chief Inspector Abberline, never happier than when a subordinate was on the carpet. Especially if that subordinate was Sholto Lestrade.

'I'm looking at a bill,' Frost said softly, 'to the tune of four hundred and six pounds three and eightpence from the Earls Court Exhibition Committee. Is your constable there capable of the mental arithmetic to work out how old you two will be by the time you've paid that little lot off?'

Only the clock broke the silence.

Then Dew shifted his weight from one foot to the other. 'I've got the eightpence, sir,' he said.

'Shut up, Dew!' the other three chorused and in the face of such a unanimous order, the Constable fell silent.

'Then of course,' Frost went on alone, 'there are the charges. One,' he held up the relevant digit, 'breaking the nose of a lieutenant of the Chasseurs d'Afrique. Do you have any comment on that, Lestrade?'

'I'm not sure if you saw that, did you, Walter? The Comte de la Warre walking into that flagpole?'

Frost cleared his throat. 'A frozen shoulder suffered by a Cossack of His Imperial Majesty's Bodyguard named Michail Bogdanovitch.' He waved another sheet.

'Hum,' Lestrade mused thoughtfully, 'that'll be the cold in Siberia,' he said. Had not Mr Poulson himself, all those years ago at the Blackheath Academy for Nearly Respectable Gentlefolk, taught the future Yard man all there was to know about the lack of global warming?

Frost twisted his already incredulous lip. 'I'm not sure the heart attack suffered by ex-Sergeant William Bird, late Eighth Hussars, is down to you or not,' he said. 'But just thank your stars it was a mild one.'

'We were merely following a line of inquiry, sir,' Lestrade said.

'A line of inquiry, Lestrade?' Frost's jowls trembled. 'A line of inquiry? Three men are in hospital, half a stadium is wrecked, tonight's show at Earls Court has had to be cancelled and sixteen policemen had to be taken off other duties to assist you and this idiot in your line of inquiry. I don't have the men, Lestrade. I don't have the money. Above all, I don't have the time to bail you and Dew out every time you ask people a few questions. And I don't even want to know what a war bonnet is and how you came to bend it. You realize of course that you've created an international incident? Any minute now there'll be a telegram from the French Embassy, a memorandum from St Petersburg, smoke signals or whatever from the Standing Rock Indian Agency. And,' Frost had quivered to his feet, his knuckles white on the desktop, 'you know of course that this overdressed marjorie Buffalo Bill is a close friend of the Prince of Wales, don't you? Now I'm not one for personal aggrandizement, God knows, but I would like to keep my job for a while!'

He subsided, purple in the face. The ever-solicitous Miss Featherstonehaugh stuck her wizened little head round the door, constantly on the defensive as Protector of Her Master's Arteries as she was. One look at the Assistant Commissioner, however, and she beat a hasty retreat.

'It was a fraught situation, sir,' Lestrade explained calmly. 'If it had not been for Constable Dew and myself, someone would have been killed.'

Frost's look might have accomplished much the same, but he broke away to the window where the April sun was already spreading spring along the Embankment. 'It's the Railway Police for you, Lestrade,' he said through clenched teeth.

The Inspector positively blanched. He saw Abberline's poisoned grin and checked himself. 'Oh, goodie,' he said, quietly.

'Two women murdered on the Underground in three months,'

Frost went on without turning, 'and you're having punch-ups with a maniac bunch of foreigners at Earls Court. Inspector Tomelty's your man. You'll find him at Finchley. Now get out.'

Lestrade spun on his heel.

'And Lestrade . . .' The Inspector stopped.

'Keep your bloody nose clean. Or it's the horse troughs. Understood?'

'Perfectly, sir,' Lestrade said and left, Dew at his elbow.

No sooner had the door closed than Frost snarled out of the corner of his mouth at Abberline, 'Follow him.'

'I beg your pardon, sir?'

'I said "follow him", Abberline. Follow him.'

'Why?'

'Why?' Frost's flabby face was turning spectrum-hued again. 'I am not given to explaining myself to subordinates, Abberline, but I cannot allow Lestrade to plant his elephantine feet all over internatonal sensibilities. I know that man. He's what the Americans call a maverick.'

'Isn't that a cow?' Abberline had once read a Buntline Special.

'No. Well, yes. It is. But it's a cow that goes its own way. Doesn't like the herd. Well, I'm all for a certain unconventionality. My father was a grocer for God's sake. But Lestrade, well, he's beyond the pale.'

'I am fully aware of Lestrade's method, sir.' Abberline folded his arms smugly, careful to avoid the gardenia. 'You should have seen his performance on the Attaché Case. But the point is that I am a Chief Inspector.'

'You're a half-wit, Abberline,' Frost corrected him, crashing back into his chair, 'which at least gives you the edge over Lestrade.'

Abberline tried a different tack. 'But I'm on extended surveillance at Penge, sir. The flasher . . .'

'Ah, yes. Leave that to whatsisface.'

'Inspector Cottingley, sir?' Abberline was aghast.

'Yes. "Fairy" Cottingley. Good man. Good man. Besides,' Frost winked at the Chief Inspector, 'following Lestrade around the Inner Circle, you'll be home that much earlier. Now wouldn't Ermintrude like that?'

*   *   *

Quex Road, Kilburn, was like any other Victorian suburb. Row upon row of villas, each identical with the rest, all built by Norwood builders as the metropolis grew outward and the well-to-do moved further to escape it and allowed the middle classes to live as a buffer between them and the People of the Abyss who walked the mean streets of the East End.

Jane Hollander had occupied a tiny set of rooms in the upper storey of Number 31. It was neat but not gaudy, and the two policemen who trampled all over it now had the task of piecing together the broken jigsaw of her belongings.

'Well, Walter?' Lestrade stretched his feet out on the *chaise-longue*. 'What of Mrs Hollander?'

'A kept woman, sir,' the Constable said.

'Why do you say that?'

'No visible means of support. She's got . . . what . . . three changes of clothes in the wardrobe. That's too many to be walking the streets. And yet . . .'

'And yet?'

'No job. At least none we've come across. Her old man didn't mention one. The landlady downstairs . . .'

'Mrs Dunnose.'

'Mrs Dunnose, she said Mrs Hollander went out irregularly, so there's no daily job. Unless . . .'

'Unless?'

'Unless she's a woman of the streets.'

'But?'

'But if she is, she's doing well on it. What do you reckon the old bag charges for rent?'

Lestrade took in the damp walls, the shabby furniture. 'Enough, I expect. So, a kept woman, then?'

'Right.'

'But by whom, Walter – that is the question.'

'Well . . .'

'Come on, man, out with it. You've been at my knee now for what – seven years? You've served your apprenticeship. You know my methods, Dew. You're a detective, man. Detect.'

'Well, I'd prefer to deduce at this stage, sir.'

'Perhaps we should be called deductives, then?' Lestrade mused. Kilburn did that to some men. It made them pensive, philosophical. 'All right, Walter. That kettle should have boiled by now, shouldn't it? I'm sure Jane Hollander wouldn't begrudge us a cup of tea. After all, we are in the process of catching her murderer. Start with Mr Hollander. I'll hear you.'

'Well.' Dew busied himself in the kitchen, out of sight of Lestrade. The quality of his tea was legendary the length and breadth of the first floor at Scotland Yard. 'Mrs Dunnose was very forthcoming on that point. Apparently, the Hollanders occupied half the house until the summer of ninety-one.'

'And then?' Lestrade lit a cigar.

'They fell on hard times.'

'What was he again?'

'He was then in ladies' underwear. Do you think we should follow that up, by the way?'

'Live and let live,' Lestrade shrugged. 'This is the Naughty Nineties.'

'Oh, right. Anyway,' Dew brought in a tray with two steaming cups, 'financial penury caused a rift in the family superstructure.'

Lestrade raised an eyebrow. Dew had clearly been at the dictionary again. 'Handles, Walter!' he said, taking the cup. 'What an unaccustomed luxury. You didn't find any Bath Olivers, I suppose?'

'Sorry, sir. Only half a packet of Garibaldis, but there seem to be flies squashed on them.'

'Yes, it's the heat,' Lestrade commented. 'So what happened to Hollander?'

'I'll have to confirm this with the shoe boxes, guv'nor, but Mrs Dunnose says they parted and he's still in ladies' underwear somewhere in Beckenham. Old Birdie says he cuts the grass in Kensal Green. It's a separation, not a divorce, and she doesn't think he contributes anything.'

'No children,' Lestrade observed.

Dew shook his head.

'So as far as we know, there's been no contact between the deceased and her husband for four years?'

'As far as we know,' Dew said.

'Go on.'

'Sir?'

'Well, if Hollander isn't paying the rent, who is?'

'Er . . .'

'The old man,' Lestrade prompted him. 'First-class bevy, Walter.'

'Thank you, guv'nor,' Dew smiled. 'Tripe sandwich?'

'Er . . . no thanks. Bit early for me. The old man.'

'Yes. William Bird. Ex-hussar. Crimean hero. Cantankerous old bastard. Homicidal in a geriatric sort of way.'

Lestrade would really have to confiscate that dictionary. 'Is he our man, then?'

'Well, he's earning peanuts carrying a flag around a ring,' Dew said. 'Unless he's an eccentric with a bit stashed away for a rainy day, he couldn't afford to pay his daughter's rent.'

'Could he have killed her?'

Dew looked blank. 'What would be his motive, sir?' he asked.

'We must accept, Walter,' the Inspector said, 'that the late Mrs Hollander put it about a bit. What if he found out about the Frenchman, the German, the Russian and the Indian? Had it out with her? They quarrelled and he killed her.'

'Of course!' Dew clicked his fingers. 'Brilliant, sir. I'll get the warrant.'

'Now, hold on, Dew. We're still in the realms of suppository here. The problem with strangulation is what?'

'Er . . . ?'

'How long does it take?' Lestrade prompted again.

'Well, that depends.'

'On what?'

'Age and strength of the victim. Age and strength of the killer. Actual method used.'

'Make a guess then with Jane Hollander.'

'Well, she was young and strong. Two, perhaps three minutes.'

'There goes your theory,' Lestrade said.

'It does? Why?'

'Look at me, Walter.'

Dew did.

'You've annoyed me.'

'Oh, I'm sorry, guv.' The Constable shifted in his chair.

'No, no. Just for the sake of argument. You've annoyed me and I lash out. What do I lash out with?'

'Er . . . your spoon?'

'My fist,' Lestrade told him. 'That first punch takes away the bulk of my anger. If I'm really miffed, I might hit you again. Perhaps a third time. Then what?'

'Well, by that time I'm on the floor, sir, and you kick the shit out of me.'

'Yes, that's the police manual way, Walter, but we're not talking about that. After three or four punches, I've worked it out of my system. Anything else is planned, calculated, premeditated.'

'I see. So the murder method . . .'

'Implies a deliberate will to end life, yes. This is no chance blow in the heat of the moment.'

'What if, once started, the killer wanted to silence his victim? What if she went to the authorities and charged him with assault and battery? Perhaps he had to shut her up?'

'Perhaps,' Lestrade agreed, 'but it takes a special kind of maniac to watch the daughter he gave rise to turn blue and choke under his hands. Do you think Old Birdie is that man?'

'No, sir. I don't.'

'Neither do I. What about the others?'

'Ah, more than likely,' Dew said gleefully. 'They're all foreign.'

'Your British sense of fair play does you credit, Walter,' Lestrade smiled. 'But unfortunately we've got to play the white man about all this.'

'Well, it's not the Indian,' Dew said.

'Oh, why?'

'Well, stands to reason. We've had no sightings, have we? No one was seen with the dead woman. On the Tube, I mean?'

'The papers say not. But we'll need to check that with the Railway Police.'

'Well even if he left off all that warpaint and stuff, he'd be noticed, wouldn't he? There can't be many Ogl . . . Oga . . . Sioux Indians riding around the Inner Circle.'

'Especially not on Thursdays,' Lestrade agreed. 'Which leaves us with?'

'The Frenchman, the German, the Russian.'

'And the American,' Lestrade sighed.

'Major Burke? But I thought he hadn't been intimate with the dead woman.'

'You'd have thought he comes from Arizona, too, but a little chat with Captain Bruno as we were carrying the others into hospital elicited the information that he's never been near the place.'

'That's it!' Dew clicked his eurekan fingers again. 'Burke did it precisely *because* he had not been intimate with the dead woman.'

'Go on.'

'Well, he knew she was putting it about with all the others in the show, except him. He made advances to her. She didn't want to know. So he killed her.'

'On a train.'

'Yes, on a train. Is that a problem?'

Lestrade nodded. 'It is, Walter. You see it *could* have been any one of them. The motive is jealousy if it's de la Warre, Bruno, Mountains or Burke. It could even have been the old man after all if he disapproved of his daughter's lifestyle that strongly. But if it was any of them, they'd kill her here, wouldn't they? They all knew about this place, I'd stake my reputation on it. The last place they'd kill her is at Earls Court – too many fingers would point too soon in their direction. But Kilburn is perfect. It even sounds a suitable place for a murder. But a train. Why a train?'

'Well . . .' and Constable Dew had run the gamut of his deductive powers.

'Well, Walter,' Lestrade sighed, 'there's nothing for it. We've got to bite the bullet and visit Superintendent Tomelty of the Railway Police. Get a cab, will you? Oh dear,' he flicked out a pocket lining, 'I appear to have no change.'

'Why a train?' Superintendent Tomelty of the Railway Police repeated. It wasn't a question that had ever been put to him before. Which was odd for a man in his position. That position was four storeys up in the Railway Police Headquarters at Finchley Central, perched on a narrow window sill, watering his geraniums.

'Let me answer that by asking you a question, Lestrade. Know anything about gerania?'

'I fear not, sir,' the Inspector said, then, on reflection, 'Oh, they're those little red things aren't they? You find them in gardens and so on.'

Tomelty's face was a picture, 'I'm very much afraid you're a philistine, Lestrade,' he said.

'Please sir,' the Inspector bridled, 'not the f word if you please. I was sent by Assistant Commissioner Frost to lia . . . leea . . . work closely with your department.'

'Were you?' Tomelty clambered back to his desk and produced a magnifying glass of the type purported to have been used by the late Mr Sherlock Holmes of 221B Baker Street. 'Aphids,' grunted Tomelty. 'Those little green bastards are the worst foes known to man.'

'Really, sir?' Lestrade sighed. So much for departmental co-operation.

'Did you know that if an aphid were the size of a man it could munch its way through Hyde Park in a fortnight? I find that sinister, Lestrade, sinister.'

'I find murder sinister, sir,' the Inspector said.

'Eh? Oh lor, yes. Rather. Well, how can I help?'

'Two women have been murdered by the same method of dispatch on the Underground in the last three months. I have a feeling that the answer lies on the train in this case and not in the soil. I have, in effect, been sent to solve the murders for you.'

'Ah yes. Righto. Well, look,' Tomelty vanished below his desk and re-emerged with a lethal-looking spray gun, 'I don't know much about the Underground myself. Not much about railways, really. It's mostly lost property anyway. Do you know how many lawnmowers were left on the Underground system in the financial year just gone?'

'No,' said Lestrade.

'Oh, really,' Tomelty was disappointed, 'I was hoping you'd seen the figures. I can't seem to get hold of them. Anyway, in 1887 it was sixty-three. I ask you, Lestrade! Why should sixty-three people be carrying lawnmowers on the Underground, let alone forgetting they'd got them? Unless it's some vast underground conspiracy of course.'

'I will need to talk to the officers who dealt with the bodies.'

'Ah yes. My man at the desk will give you their names,' and he blasted the foliage at point-blank range.

'And I will need detailed times of all the trains.'

'Ah yes. Bradshaw's. My man on the desk will have a copy. But actually, you can't do better than to ask Melville Lavender.'

'Who?'

'Melville Lavender. He runs a little museum off Covent Garden somewhere. Apparently he always wanted to be an engine driver when he grew up but he was allergic.'

'To steam?'

'Work. My man at the desk will have his address. Good morning. Oh . . . and if I can be of even more assistance, don't hesitate to ask.'

'I wouldn't dream of it, sir,' Lestrade assured him. 'Helpful isn't the word for what you've been.'

Melville Lavender lived four floors up an increasingly rickety stairway in Maiden Lane. The walls of his rather shabby drawing-room were hung with railway timetables and paintings, in his own fair hand, of locomotives past and present. He was a wizened little man with a pencil moustache Lestrade suspected he'd pencilled in himself. He wore a scarf which appeared to be two or three stitched together and moved as though on castors over the threadbare carpet.

'Welcome to my little museum,' he said with the rattle of a simple railman.

'Fascinating,' said Lestrade looking in vain for somewhere to sit. The climb had taken it out of him. After all, he would never see forty again.

'Oh, I'm sorry.' Lavender sensed his predicament and removed a cat. The ginger beast showed the most amazing fortitude by maintaining perfect rigidity as its master lifted it. Even when he rested it upside-down on a sand-filled bucket, the creature neither demurred nor purred. Only slowly did the observant Inspector realize that the animal was stuffed and it stared at him from its curious angle with sightless glass eyes.

'The old station cat,' beamed Lavender. 'Unfortunately it mistimed its daily crossing of the line at Crewe some years ago and caught the eight-thirty-five to Runcorn. It didn't stop bouncing until Congleton. Tea?'

'Thank you.' Lestrade eased his buttocks on the excruciatingly wooden slats of a Great Western Railway station seat. Luckily they were not broad gauge so he didn't fall through them.

'It's only LNER, I'm afraid,' Lavender apologized.

'So you're a railway enthusiast?' Lestrade checked, staring at the life-size locomotive front that appeared to be coming through the wall facing him.

'Now, how did you know?' Lavender stuck his head round a beaded curtain. 'This is from Marrakesh Central, by the way,' he explained.

'Ah,' Lestrade looked relieved. He thought he hadn't seen its like on the South-Eastern recently, 'Superintendent Tomelty sent me.'

'Ah, how is Prufrock?'

'A little narrow in his interests, I thought.' Lestrade placed his bowler on the seat. It landed on a small piece of green cloth, heavily stained.

'Yes, I know,' Lavender said. 'About the width of a window-box, am I right?'

The Inspector nodded.

'How some people can let their hobbies dominate their lives, I really don't know. Oh, just a minute.' And he abandoned the tea making in mid-brew and leapt to the window, flicking a half-hunter out of his waistcoat pocket. 'Listen,' he said. 'That's the six-five special coming down the line.'

'Really?' Lestrade could only hear the usual early-evening shouts of the vegetable vendors, calling the prices of caulis and carrots.

'The six-five special's right on time,' beamed Lavender with evident satisfaction. 'Now, where was I?'

'Expressing amazement that people allowed their hobbies to dominate their lives.'

'Quite. Quite. Oh, mind that, won't you?' He gingerly removed the cloth from below Lestrade's bowler.

'This bit of rag?'

'Rag?' He was barely audible. 'It may be a piece of rag to you, Inspector.' He rubbed it lovingly against his chin. 'It is in fact the coat tail of Mr William Huskisson, late President of the Board of Trade and the first man to be killed by a train.'

'Really?' Lestrade hoped his face wasn't betraying his indifference.

'The poor man was attending the opening of the Liverpool to Manchester line in 1830 when the Rocket jolted forward without warning, catching Mr Huskisson's coat tail in its moving parts. Look, here is the very oil that smeared the garment.' And he pointed lovingly to the dark stains that tracked it.

'Oh, yes,' noted Lestrade, less than fascinated.

'The Duke of Wellington was there of course. And for the second time in his life the man observed that a colleague had lost his leg inches from him.'

'Ah well, luck of the Irish, these aristocracy,' Lestrade observed.

'Your tea.' Lavender poured for them both. The china was crested GWR and the liquid was the colour of engine oil. 'What do you think of this?' He held up a rusted bolt, sheared at one end.

Now Lestrade had been a detective, man and man for nearly twenty years. Trained to observe, not to miss one single clue, however small. 'It's a rusted bolt,' he said, 'sheared at one end.'

'Good, good,' gloated Lavender, 'but not just any old bolt, Mr Lestrade. I have reason to believe it is *the* bolt which snapped and caused the terrible accident at the Tay Bridge during the night of 28 December 1879, when thirteen of the seventy-four spans fell ninety feet while a train was passing over them.'

'Ah yes,' Lestrade remembered. 'I believe I've read the poem.'

'There were ninety deaths,' Lavender said grimly, 'but that's nothing in comparison with this.' And he held up a glass case beneath which was a shrivelled mess of greyish-green.

'Er . . . ?' Lestrade had never seen anything quite like it.

'It's a sandwich, Mr Lestrade,' Lavender whispered. 'The first of its kind to be sold in station buffets at Swindon. Man, in the wrong hands, it could cause an epidemic.'

Lestrade didn't doubt it.

'Still, you didn't come here to listen to my nonsense. How can I help?'

'Superintendent Tomelty said that you knew more about the Underground than any man living or words to that effect.'

Lavender turned puce. 'Oh, he's too kind, Mr Lestrade. Too kind. To be precise, the Underground is not my forte. It's true that Tubes help you breathe more easily. But there's too much wheeling and dealing for me. I've no head for business.'

'It's the business of murder I'm interested in.'

'Murder?' Lavender narrowed his eyes. 'Ah, that poor unfortunate who died at Liverpool Street the other day.'

'Why do you say that?'

'What?'

'Unfortunate.'

'Well, I assume anyone who meets his or her end by foul means to be singularly unfortunate, Mr Lestrade. I was only saying to my good friend Dr Watson the other day . . .'

'Dr Watson?' Lestrade interrupted. 'Dr John Watson?'

'Yes. Do you know him?'

'Hardly at all. Go on.'

'Well, there's no more to say. I merely felt sorry for the lady.'

'And Sarah Culdrose?'

'Er . . . ?'

'Sarah Culdrose was found dead on an Underground train at Blackfriars in February last.'

'Oh good Lord, yes. But didn't her husband do it? I seem to remember the *Standard* said . . .'

'Yes, well, the *Standard* wouldn't know the truth if it got up and bit it. Both women died on Tube trains. They both died by strangulation. If Mr Culdrose did it, then he has some extraordinary powers. He was in a remand cell at Wormwood Scrubs when Jane Hollander died.'

'I see.' Lavender swirled the dregs of his cup. 'But I don't see how I can help.'

'Mr Lavender,' Lestrade edged forward on the station seat, 'what I am about to ask you is highly irregular.'

'Oh goodie,' Lavender beamed.

'But from time to time Scotland Yard is forced to ask for expert help outside the realms of conventional police work. I'd like you to come with me to Liverpool Street. And to Blackfriars. I want you to tell me how it is possible for a man to strangle two women and walk away from it.'

'Oh, Mr Lestrade,' Lavender chuckled, 'on the Underground, anything is possible.'

* * *

'So, Dew,' Lestrade crossed his ankles on the paper-bestrewn surface of his desk, Standard III, Inspectors, for the use of, 'let me have it again.'

The Detective Constable's collar was awry. It was an extraordinarily hot night for April, and the Yard was its usual stifling self.

'Righto, guv,' he said. 'The body of Jane Hollander was found by a guard on the ten-twenty up line at Blackfriars. He blew his whistle and two railway policemen turned up.'

'What time was that?'

'Er . . . half past eleven.'

'An hour and ten minutes later?' Lestrade raised an eyebrow to the level he reserved for the reproach of incompetence. 'What do you deduce from that, Russell?'

The young rookie sat to attention. 'Er . . .'

'Good,' nodded Lestrade. 'Loyalty to brother officers. I like that. Go on, Dew.'

'PCs Dogberry and Verges of the Railway Police reported as follows . . .'

Lestrade held up his hand. 'Wait a minute,' he said. 'We've heard these names before, haven't we? Bromley?'

The old rookie frowned. Years on the Essex Force had taught him caution, circumspection even. 'Er . . .'

'Think, man, think. You're supposed to be a detective.'

Inspiration came to him. 'Shakespeare, sir,' he beamed. *Twelfth Night* or *As You Like It* or one of those.'

Lestrade's look would have withered a civilian. 'Don't be ridiculous, Bromley. You're not tramping the Essex marshes now, you know. Look to your laurels. Assuming, that is, you have any laurels to look to. Go on, Dew.'

'They reported that the deceased was lying slumped on her back with . . .' he peered to read his notes by the gaslight, 'her nether limbs spread and her skirts raised.'

Russell tugged at his collar.

'If this gets too much for you, lad,' the Inspector said, 'you know where the door is. There are any number of bobbies' helmets to vomit into.' He nodded at Dew.

'She was fully clothed. No actual sign of outrage.'

'From which you deduce, Bromley?' Lestrade was giving the old rookie a second chance.

'Our man is impotent,' the new detective ventured.

'That's about the eighth possibility I had in mind,' Lestrade said, stirring his tea with his pen. 'What else could explain it . . . Russell?'

'Er . . .'

'Exactly, lad. Well done. Our man dithered, just as you're doing now. He intended assault on Mrs Hollander. She wasn't having any – which meant that he wasn't either. She struggled. He killed her – and then panicked.'

'Could he just walk away though, sir?' Bromley asked.

'Certainly he could,' Lestrade said. 'Assuming he wouldn't be daft enough to attack the woman in a crowded carriage. With luck, in three or four minutes the job would be done and he'd get off at the next station.'

'Temple,' said Dew.

'Fact, Walter?' Lestrade raised the ever-censorious eyebrow.

'Suppository, guv'nor,' Dew confessed.

'I'd put my money on Charing Cross,' Lestrade proffered. 'Our man could lose himself more easily there. And if no one got on until Blackfriars, that gave him time to vanish.'

'He took a chance, though,' Bromley said.

'Murder is a chancy business, Constable,' the Inspector said. 'But as long as he stopped Mrs Hollander from reaching the communication cord and as long as no one got into the carriage as he got out, it was a chance worth taking. From Charing Cross, he could have caught a train on the down line of the Circle, travelling west. Or . . . Dew?'

'He could have got off the train and cut back down Villiers Street to the Arches; thence across the bridge.'

'Or . . . Bromley?'

'Er . . . west along the Strand into Trafalgar Square, then any point of the compass, really.'

'Vague but reprehensible,' Lestrade nodded. 'Or . . . Russell?'

'Er . . . east.'

'East,' Lestrade agreed after a pause. 'You've summed it up well there, son. Along the Strand, you mean? Down Fleet Street? And into the City. Well, we've no hope of catching him there, thanks to our colleagues in the City Force. Any pieces of evidence at the scene of the crime, Dew?'

'Dogberry and Verges didn't report anything, sir. The floor

of the carriage was full of rubbish, of course, it being the last train.'

'Of course,' Lestrade nodded. 'Theatregoers. Pub crawlers. And only three million to choose from. Right, gentlemen. It's time we went to work . . .'

There was a rattle at the door. The unmistakable knuckles of a uniformed man.

'Sergeant Dixon,' Lestrade greeted the avuncular face, 'what brings you out from behind your desk this sultry evening?'

'Evening all,' the Sergeant saluted. 'Beggin' your pardon, Mr Lestrade, sir. There's been another one. On the City and South London. Down the Elephant.'

The growler dropped them at the domed entrance to the station at the Elephant and Castle. It was young Russell's first murder; old Bromley's third. As for Lestrade and Dew, they'd long ago lost count. At the turnstile, there was a delay while the buck was passed down the chain of command. Dew would have coughed up willingly enough, but the Yard Maria fleet was undergoing its annual refit, and the growler had just cleaned the Detective Constable out. There was nothing for it, then. Russell was paying.

They wedged into the wooden-panelled Otis Elevator and a bewhiskered attendant kicked the contraption into motion. It whirred and clanked to the bottom. The bewhiskered attendant tugged the peak of his cap. 'Every trip,' he managed through ill-fitting dentures. 'Clunk. Click.'

The four policemen ignored him, especially the hand held out for the tip, and paced the dim, green platform to where the No. 6 Mather and Platt locomotive sat hunched like a little yellow bee over the electric line that gave it life. The place was full of policemen and there were mysterious light shafts darting to and fro in the distant, dusty tunnel like deranged fireflies. Mass salutings followed and Lestrade entered the metal-gated tail platform alone. Inside the dim, brown interior of the padded cell, four lights barely illumined a bizarre scene. Two women sat there, one with her head in her large, workmanlike hands; the other, oddly upright, some seats away in the central carriage, her eyes staring sightlessly ahead, her lips blue, her tongue forced

62

obscenely between her teeth. Her bodice had been ripped away and there were the tell-tale purple marks of a maniac forming a necklace of bruises around her throat.

Lestrade blinked, trying to take in the scene. Time enough to cope with the dead. She wasn't going anywhere. Perhaps the live one was a witness. He took off his bowler as a mark of respect. 'Please don't be alarmed, madam,' he said. 'I am a police officer.'

The woman looked anything but alarmed and slowly pulled the tousled hair from her head. 'So am I, Lestrade,' she said.

'Good God,' Lestrade sat down heavily, 'Johnnie "Upright". What are you doing here?'

'Trying to stop this, would you believe?' He jerked his head in the direction of his travelling companion.

'What?'

'I've gone underground on the Underground, Lestrade. Didn't they tell you?'

'Not a dickie bird.' Lestrade clicked his teeth. 'Abberline?'

Johnnie "Upright" nodded. 'Do you know, I've been under-cover now in various guises since 18 bloody 88. The Ripper Case – that was my first one.'

'That's right.' Lestrade ignored the NO SMOKING sign and lit up a cigar. With a generosity rarely paralleled, he passed it to the posing policeman. 'I remember it well. You haunted the Ten Bells in Whitechapel.'

'Damn near took my liver, that little job. D'you know, I was downing ten, eleven pints a night.'

Lestrade tilted back the bowler he'd put back on. 'Get away,' he said. No wonder the Whitechapel murderer had never been caught. 'So how long have you been on this one, then?'

'Two days.' He eased a lump of wadding out of the left breast of his bodice. 'Ooh, that's better. How these women carry these things around with them, I'll never know.'

A young constable put his head round the door. 'Mr Lestrade, the line Inspector wants to know ... Oh, my God ...' and Russell lolled over the metal tail gate, depositing his supper on to the City and South London line.

'What's the matter with him?' Johnnie "Upright" asked.

'It gets some men that way, Johnnie,' Lestrade explained, 'especially the young green ones. Seeing a bloke like you in a frock; well, it's their natural bigotry, I suppose. Gives rise to a certain revulsion, don't you think?'

'If you think I'm enjoying this . . .' Upright moaned.

'Oh, I know, I know. Constable Russell,' he called to the still-heaving detective, 'if I can drag you away from all the fun for a minute. This is Detective Inspector Thicke; he's one of us.'

Russell didn't need to turn round to be apprised of that.

'If I read the sentence you so gamely started aright, the line Inspector wants to know when he can have his train back. The answer to that is when I'm good and ready. Tell him he can play with his armatures until then. Now, John, let's have the details. And take your time with that cigar. There aren't any more where that came from.'

The policemen turned their attention to the only real lady in the carriage.

'I was in the next cell, would you believe?' Thicke said. 'If only I'd chosen to ride in this one.'

'If you had, Johnnie, he'd only have waited until later and killed somewhere else. What made you take the City and South London in the first place?'

'A hunch.'

'A what?'

'A spinal curvature I've had since childhood. The seats on the Metropolitan line stock are bloody agony, I can tell you. I thought a padded cell of the C and SL would be comfier.'

'And was it?'

'No. Rather worse, in fact.'

'Of course,' Lestrade observed, 'the corsets don't help. Tell me what happened.'

'Well, I was just going off duty actually.' Thicke took Lestrade's proffered bowler as a matter of course as the more senior of the inspectors peered into the bodice of the dead woman. 'I'd been to Stockwell and back three times today already.'

'Any luck?'

Thicke shook his head. 'Not unless you count the old boy on the eleven-seventeen up line.' He gave Lestrade an old-fashioned look and the more senior inspector thought it best not to press the matter.

'The lights went very dim as we took the Elephant gradient. There was a family of four in my carriage. It was like bloody

Bedlam, I can tell you. I blame the government of course. It's stopping those school fees that's done it. Kids these days have no respect. They were climbing all over the seats, pulling faces at the guard, God knows what. Bloody railway children! When one of 'em told his mother he was going to be sick, I got out.'

'Where was this?'

'Right here, at the Elephant. I changed carriages and here she was.'

Lestrade felt the dead woman's hand. 'Still warm,' he murmured.

'I must have walked right past the bloke,' Thicke ruminated.

'You don't remember anything?'

Thicke shook his head. 'Nothing,' he admitted. 'Whoever our man is, he's a cool bugger. I don't think I could strangle a woman feet away from a potential eyewitness and get off a train as if I was . . . getting off a train.'

Lestrade patted Thicke's fol-de-rols. 'That's why you chose to become a policeman, Johnnie,' he said, 'and not a homicidal maniac. Have you . . . er . . .' he nodded to the corpse's lower limbs, 'has she been . . . er . . . ?'

'Come off it, Lestrade,' Thicke said. 'I'm a married man. Oh . . . sorry, Sholto. I heard about your wife. Bad luck, eh?'

'Damn bad luck,' Lestrade nodded and carefully lifted the lady's skirts. 'Nothing untoward here,' he said.

'Still, there wouldn't be time, would there? The platform was pretty busy at Kennington.'

'You didn't notice anybody getting on or off this carriage there?'

'That's the trouble with these padded cells – no windows to speak of. Our man would have had an easier time of it here – no windows to overlook him. No communication cord to pull for emergencies.'

'But two guards,' Lestrade observed.

'Ah, that's why he struck in the middle of the three coaches,' Thicke realized. 'With the doors closed at both ends, you can't see through, at least not all the time.'

'So how do you know where you are?' Lestrade asked. 'I usually take a cab.'

'The guard flicks up a next-station sign at that little window at the end. Without that, you'd be going round for ever. You can't see the station name on the platform for the bloody advertisements. Some American bloke asked me yesterday where Fry's Cocoa was. I said "Eh?" And he said, "Fry's Cocoa." He couldn't find it on the map of the Underground, but he'd definitely passed through it at least three times.'

'That's why I take a cab,' said Lestrade. 'Do we know who she was, John?'

'I found these in her handbag.' Thicke held up a wad of paper.

'Money?'

'Three pounds eighteen and sixpence three farthings.'

'She wasn't robbed, then?' Lestrade left no stone unturned.

'I wouldn't say so. Quite well-heeled to look at her shoes.'

Lestrade had. Everything about the body smacked of opulence and good taste. The senior Inspector riffled through the contents of the dead woman's bag. 'Emily,' he said. 'Her name was Emily.'

'My deductions entirely,' nodded Thicke. 'But who's the William who's writing to her?'

Lestrade took in the address. 'Albany,' he said. 'A bachelor's address if ever there was one. Dew!'

The constable of that name had been swapping suicide stories with the railway police on the platform and popped his macassared head inside the 'cell'. 'Sir?'

'Get over to Albany. You're looking for someone called William.'

'William who?'

'Just William, Dew,' said Lestrade.

'Isn't the Albany a pub, sir?' Dew said.

'No, it's a rather nobby tenement building, Constable. No doubt you'll need some help, so take those rookies with you. And be circumscribed. Upset any of the inmates there and you'll be on the horse troughs for the rest of your natural. Got it?'

'Yessir.'

'And make sure you do the talking. Your unparalleled eloquence will take you far.'

'Yessir. Er . . . it's nearly midnight, sir.'

'So?'

'The lads and I went off duty nearly an hour ago, guv'nor.'

Lestrade got up and crossed to his man. 'There's a woman dead, Dew,' he said solemnly. 'And we never sleep, do we?'

'No, sir,' said Dew, a little shamefaced, 'we never do.'

'Get along, then,' said Lestrade.

'What do you make of the letter, then, Lestrade?' Thicke asked.

The senior Inspector perused it again, 'Not a love-letter,' he said, sniffing it. 'Too cordial – "Your ever-loving" – what is that? Father? No. He'd sign it "Papa" or "Dad". Brother perhaps? What's all this about a match? Grace? Who's Grace?'

'Some friend of hers, I shouldn't wonder,' Thicke surmised.

'"I'm playing with Grace on Saturday",' Lestrade read. 'Hallo, hallo, hallo.'

'That's what I thought,' said Thicke. 'Bit forward if you ask me. Doesn't that count as an obscene publication?'

'My God.' Lestrade read further.

'What?'

'Huish Episcopi,' Lestrade said.

If this was an ejaculation, it was a new one on Thicke. 'What?' he repeated.

'He's invited her to Huish Episcopi for Saturday.'

'Where?'

'It's a village, Johnnie, in Somerset.'

'Bloody hell.' Thicke was impressed. 'I can see why you Yard blokes get on,' he said. 'Minds like gazetteers, you've got.'

'Not really,' Lestrade smiled. 'I have every reason to know this particular village very well indeed.'

It was the wee small hours when Lestrade's knuckles barked painfully on the door of Melville Lavender's rooms in Maiden Lane.

A rather dishevelled figure in a nightcap peered round it at him. 'Mr Lestrade,' he said, 'have you any idea of the time?'

The Inspector flicked out a half-hunter. 'It's nearly two-thirty, sir,' he said.

'Good,' said Lavender. 'The milk train will just be limbering up at Budleigh Salterton now. Cocoa?'

'That's extraordinarily kind, Mr Lavender,' Lestrade said, 'bearing in mind my intrusion.'

'Ah, I couldn't sleep anyway. There's been another, hasn't there?'

Lestrade paused in the passage. 'How did you know?' He collided briefly with a GREEN FOR GO signal arm that jutted out from the wall. The miracle was that he had missed it on his first visit.

'Oh, I've been half expecting it,' he said. 'And I don't suppose you'd knock me up at this hour to inquire into the braking capacity of a Beyer Peacock 4-4-OT.'

'How right you are.' Lestrade patted the blood from his forehead where the signal had drawn it.

'Where?'

'Elephant and Castle,' Lestrade said.

'Oh, the City and South London.' Lavender looked perplexed.

'You look perplexed,' Lestrade observed with the eagle eye of a born detective. The other one was already beginning to close where the signal arm had caught it.

'Well, it's just that . . . oh, never mind.'

'No, no.' Lestrade removed a scale model of Mr Greathead's tunnelling shield from the sofa before he landed on it. 'Please go on. I could use all the help I can get at this stage.'

'Well, I did have a little theory,' Lavender said, 'about the Jane Hollander murder. And that of Sarah Culdrose. This one's rather blown it, though.'

'Yes?' Lestrade was not too proud to pinch someone else's theories. He'd done it all his working life.

'If I remember rightly,' Lavender caught the rising, bubbling milk in the pan on the embers of the fire in the nick of time, 'you told me Mrs Culdrose was found at Liverpool Street?'

'That's right.'

'And Mrs Hollander at Blackfriars?'

'Yes.'

'Lovely Moorish façade at Blackfriars,' Lavender mused.

'Indeed. Your theory?' Lestrade harried his man.

'Theory? Oh yes. Well, that means that both ladies died on the Metropolitan and District line.'

'So?' It was half past two in the morning and for Lestrade it had been a long day.

'So I did have a little surmise that perhaps someone was out to discredit that company.'

'What? By committing murders on them?'

'Exactly. But this new one has spoilt it. Sugar?'

'Two please. Why?'

'Because,' Lavender explained as though to an idiot, 'the latest was committed on the City and South London. If someone from the City and South London wanted to discredit a rival, he'd hardly commit a murder on his own line.'

'Ah,' Lestrade was ahead of him, 'but shitting on one's own doorstep *could* be a clever ploy,' he said, 'to divert suspicion. Thank you, Mr Lavender, you've been very helpful.' He rose to go, his cocoa untouched.

'Have I?' Lavender asked. 'I hardly think so.'

'One more thing,' Lestrade said. 'The guards.'

'Guards?'

'Unlike the Metropolitan and District, there are guards on the City and South London, aren't there?'

'Well,' Lavender sipped the froth off his cocoa, so that it settled like foam along the iron-grey line of his moustache, 'as you know, I'm no expert on the Underground, but yes; I believe there are two, one at the end of each carriage.'

'Well, they must have been short-staffed tonight, because there were only two per train as I understand it.'

'Ah, there you are,' Lavender said, 'but they're quite meticulous about the calibre of chap they employ, of course. No one who has failed to reach Grade III in the National Schools has any chance at all – and those with the rudiments of calculus are preferred.'

Lestrade shrugged. That was clearly why he had become a policeman all those years ago. The City Force was not that choosy. Still less the Metropolitan. 'You've intrigued me, Mr Lavender, with your theory of the City and South London. Thanks for the cocoa – perhaps some other time? Don't worry,' he swung under the signal arm, only grazing himself this time, 'I'll see myself out.' He opened his blacking eye gingerly. 'Just about.'

4

Lestrade caught the 4.50 from Paddington. Billycock-hatted men in workers' overalls carrying tin flasks of tea trudged grumbling along the platform towards him, longing for the Independent Labour Party to come of age and for Mr Keir Hardie to *do* something in the House of Commons. These were a new race – the commuters of the metropolis – for whom special cheap trains were run which arrived with the milk from Budleigh Salterton.

By the time the locomotive had whistled and hissed its way out of Praed Street, Lestrade was asleep. Through his dreams a phantom floated, with hideous grin, howling 'Mind the doors' at him. It turned through the endless chill tunnels of the Underground where rats played leapfrog with the live rail of the City and South London screaming 'Mind the gap,' and he was trying to lift his feet to do just that when a bemused ticket inspector woke him, demanding to see his ticket.

By now the sun was up and threatening another hot day, ridiculously hot for April, turning as it was into May. Lestrade had cast a clout or two already despite the adage advising against it, and his suit was now a natty lightweight serge and his bowler was left at the Yard. Tilted on the back of his head was a regulation straw boater, Inspectors, for the use of, 1 May to 30 September. The ghosts of the Great Western's broad gauge still lay by the trackside where three years ago, on a frenzied Sunday, the 7-foot 1/4-inch sleepers had been hacked and sawn to the regulation Stephenson length. Everyone knew it had to come, but even so Isambard Kingdom Brunel must have been revolving slowly in his grave.

At the Georgian city of Bath that the Romans had called Aquae Sulis for reasons best known to themselves, the Yard man changed trains and travelled south–west through the mid-morning, blowing billows of cigar smoke at the prominent NO SMOKING signs and ignoring the looks of contempt from a clergyman and his wife. He alighted at Street on the Fosse Way and found a cabman dozing in the sun on his perch. For a trifling amount at which Lestrade felt faint and for which he demanded a receipt, the growler rattled over the tortuous, rutted roads of Somerset, across the King's Sedge Moor, through the Hams (and Lestrade felt every jolt of this), over the battlefield of Langport where Roundhead buggers and Cavalier buggers had clashed long ago (or so the cabman told him) and over the Parrett into the charming little village of Huish Episcopi.

He found the Bandicoot and Piglet without difficulty as the only hostelry in the village and took a jar of his host's excellent West Country cider while deciding on his plan of attack.

'Here for the match, sir?' his host had the temerity to inquire.

'Er . . . yes,' Lestrade lied.

'Ar. Mr Bandicoot's eleven, I'll be bound.'

Now this was something of a facer for Lestrade. He had known Harry Bandicoot, the local squire, man and boy for four years. Ever since he turned up where Russell and Bromley stood now, as rookies at the Yard. There had been a misunderstanding while young Bandicoot was at Eton. He had joined the cadet force there and the chaps had told him that it was a sure way into the police force later. Chump that he was, he had believed them. But although Harry Bandicoot's deductive powers were limited, he was a crack shot, had boxed for his school, had saved Lestrade's life and was now bringing up the Inspector's motherless daughter. Wouldn't it therefore be a *little* uncharitable to agree with the landlord's estimation of Harry's mental age?

'Twenty-five, surely,' Lestrade said.

The host's face fell a little. 'Twenty-two, sir,' he corrected the visitor, counting both teams. Perhaps the man was a foreigner. The parchment face, the dark circles round the eyes, the tipless nose. Perhaps they played by different rules in different parts of the Empire.

'Is there a telegram for me?' Lestrade asked.

'Who might you be, sir?'

Lestrade might have been the Akond of Swat for all the landlord knew.

'Lestrade,' said Lestrade.

'Lord love you, I believe there is,' and he wiped his hands on his greasy apron before scurrying away for it. Lestrade leant back in the inglenook by the empty fireplace. Three smocked yokels sat opposite him, sipping the froth from their ale and watching him intently. There were a lot of foreigners in their parts this particular weekend, but they all bore watching.

Lestrade read the telegram his host had brought. 'Only William at The Albany is William Bellamy. Stop. Not here. Stop. Cricketer. Stop. Inhabitants of The Albany took umbrage at police intrusion. Stop. Seeing my superior. Stop. Is that you? Stop. Dew.'

Lestrade clicked his tongue in admiration. Typical of his hardy Lieutenant to pull out all the stops.

'Has Mr Bellamy arrived?' Lestrade asked.

'He have, sir,' his host told him. 'Come last night. They're all up at the Hall now, having luncheon. You'd better put your skates on if you're playing.'

Lestrade of course had no intention of playing. Especially on skates. He had no idea the game he had played with an old stick and an onion in the backstreets of Pimlico all those years ago differed so much from the real thing.

'Do you know the way, sir? Or shall I get old Tadger to show ye?'

'No, no,' Lestrade wobbled a little uncertainly for the low door and the sunlight beyond, 'I know the way.' Old Tadger could rest undisturbed.

He took the little road over the bridge and wound his way through the May blossom to the great wrought-iron gates. The stone wildebeeste sat sejantly, looking down their quivering nostrils at him. Not eighteen months before he had walked this way, on a night of rain, carrying a little motherless babe in arms to the only safe house he knew. To Bandicoot Hall.

Today was very different. There were servants, white-aproned and capped, hurrying this way and that, and the lower lawns had been marked out for a match. Gentlemen and players strolled in the sunshine, coloured ties around their waists and tasselled caps on their heads. A huge bearded man was prodding the ground and talking to Harry Bandicoot.

'Well, you'll just have to play with ten men, Harry. There's no help for it.'

The squire turned to see a sallow, rat-faced fellow in dark serge standing on his own and carrying a battered Gladstone.

'Oh no, we won't', he grinned. 'Sholto!' He ran across to grip the Inspector's hand and shake it warmly. 'Sholto Lestrade, a keen batsman if ever I saw one; meet the famous W. G. Grace.'

'Grace,' Lestrade repeated dumbly, remembering the letter on the dead woman. 'Of course.'

'Delighted.' The huge bearded man shook Lestrade's hand. 'Who do you play for, Lestrade?'

'Er . . . the SYC,' Lestrade bluffed.

'South Yorkshire?' Grace guessed.

'No.'

'Salop Yeomanry?' Though the good doctor had never heard of such a team, he assumed they must have one.

'Scotland Yard,' he said.

'By Jove,' Grace chuckled so that his whole body wobbled, 'I had no idea. Well, sir, your timing's perfect. See you on the field. Better make a start, Harry,' and he jogged off to join his team.

'Harry . . .'

'I know, Sholto. You've never played first-class cricket before . . .'

'Harry, I haven't played *any* class of cricket before. I don't know the rules!'

'The point is,' Bandicoot explained earnestly, 'that "Leg-breaker" Lawson's been laid up with a recurrence of his old trouble. Didn't let us know until this morning. This match has been arranged for ages. Look at the crowds coming in. We can't let them down. I'll put you in as eleventh man. You probably won't have to bat.'

'Good,' Lestrade groaned. The crowd in fact was becoming sizeable. In London there'd have been a bobby on a white horse to control that lot. As it was, they took their places on the temporary benches, muttering Mummerset, while several top-hatted dignitaries and the odd bishop (Bath and Wells being the odd bishop in question) sauntered from the marquee adjusting the strings on his headgear as white-shirted fielders began limbering up.

'It's good to see you, Sholto.' Bandicoot led his old guv'nor across to the robing pavilion. 'Let's see, I think we've got a pair of ducks somewhere.'

'Well, that's what I'll score if you put me out there,' Lestrade warned. 'Which one is William Bellamy?'

'Oh, Sholto,' Bandicoot stopped in mid-selection of a coloured tie for Lestrade's waist, 'so this isn't a social visit?'

The Inspector shook his head.

'And I thought you'd come to see little Emma.'

'How is she?' her father asked.

'See for yourself,' Bandicoot beamed, pointing to a little thing no higher than a cricket stump, all lace and golden curls, who staggered between Letitia Bandicoot and a frosty old nanny with a barbed-wire bun. 'She took to Nanny Balsam like a duck to water,' the squire said.

Lestrade found himself nodding, grinning inanely. Was that the baby he'd left all those months ago? The helpless pink little thing with the neck that smelt like nothing he would know? The one now bashing seven bells out of two little boys until Nanny and Letitia broke in as the good seconds they were? It didn't seem possible.

'No, Harry,' Lestrade said, 'it's not a social call. Which one is Bellamy?'

Bandicoot scanned the players passing a ball from one to another. 'There,' he said. 'The chap with the little goatee. Next to the Black Prince.'

'Who?'

'Ranjitsinhji. The Black Prince of cricket. This is quite a coup for Huish Episcopi, Sholto. The two greatest cricketers in the world on my turf. All the gate money goes to one of Letitia's charities of course.'

'Gate money?' Lestrade was incredulous. 'You mean people are actually paying to see me make a complete idiot of myself?'

'No, no,' Bandicoot laughed. 'That's an added bonus, Sholto,' and the Old Etonian winked audibly. Then he was serious. 'Whatever it is,' he said, 'can you wait until the game is over? These people have come a long way.'

Lestrade nodded. It wasn't likely that William Bellamy would be leaving.

'He's in sixth man,' Bandicoot said, reading the Inspector's mind better than he read his own. 'He's in our team and you can watch him all afternoon if you like.'

Lestrade nodded.

'But, Sholto,' Bandicoot placed a warning hand on the older

74

man's shoulder, 'that's a bumping pitch and a blinding light. While you're keeping an eye on Mr Bellamy, keep an eye on the ball as well, there's a good chap.'

Lestrade was led out on to the sacred turf. Somebody threw a ball at him and it hit him in the ribs. The damn thing was like a red cannonball, but twice as hard.

'Oh, bad show,' called the thrower and Bandicoot picked it up and threw it to somebody else.

'You're supposed to catch it, Sholto,' he murmured out of the corner of his mouth.

'Right.'

Then there was a flurry in the centre and two men wearing long white coats and swathed in other people's jumpers were tossing a coin in the air. Grace and Bandicoot faced each other. 'Mr Bandicoot's eleven will open the batting.'

Grace and Bandicoot shook hands and the squire and his men trotted back to the pavilion.

'Sholto!' a female voice called above the hum of spectators. 'Sholto Lestrade!'

He turned and saw Letitia, Harry's wife, running towards him, little Emma bouncing in her arms. He paused before they reached him. 'I didn't know you'd be here,' she said. 'Why didn't Harry tell me?'

Lestrade glanced across to where the captain was giving last-minute instructions to his team. 'He didn't know,' he said. 'Letitia, how are you?'

'I'm well,' she said breathlessly. 'Sholto, say hallo to your . . .'

He held up a hand. 'We agreed,' he said.

'Of course,' she checked herself. 'Say hallo to little Emma. Emma, darling, this is Uncle Sholto.'

Little Emma screwed up her face. Then, with Letitia's encouragement, she reached out and ran her stubby little fingers across his tipless nose, the scarred cheeks, the walrus moustache. Without warning, she clouted him hard on the bridge of the nose.

'Emma!' Letitia scolded, but the reeling Inspector quickly forgave and squeezed her fingers very gently.

'Hold her,' Letitia said.

As though handling the most precious Sèvres, Lestrade reached out and took the girl. Her neck still smelt the same, though she weighed more than when he'd held her last. He held her to him, closer, tighter. She gurgled and wriggled, then frowned into his face and said with great solemnity, 'Ga.'

'What's that?' Lestrade asked.

'That's what she calls the cat, Sholto,' Letitia giggled. 'We're strange cattle, us women.'

'No, I mean that.' He held up a damp left hand from where it had supported little Emma.

'Ah, you're very lucky,' Letitia laughed. 'She doesn't do that on just anybody, you know. Nanny Balsam!' And she took the little girl away, to do whatever it is surrogate mothers and nannies do at times like that.

There was a ripple of applause as Harry Bandicoot strode out in his Eton cap, waving a bat at the crowd, and took his place at the crease.

Huish Episcopi's famous – and indeed only – sports commentator, John Arslightly, took up the running over a loud hailer. 'And it's Mr Bandicoot in to bat first, ladies and gentlemen. What a lovely action. Such grace – oh, beggin' your pardon, doctor. What a perfect afternoon we have, ladies and gentlemen, for the sound of leather on willow . . .'

'Uncannily hot.' Lestrade eased himself down beside William Bellamy, sitting on one of Harry's wicker chairs before the pavilion where generations of Bandicoots had stretched before him.

'Deuced,' said Bellamy. 'What are you in?'

Something of a spot, Lestrade thought, but he was man enough not to show it. 'The police,' he admitted.

'No,' Bellamy smiled. 'What number are you batting?'

'Er . . . eleven,' Lestrade told him. 'That's somewhere near the end, isn't it?'

Bellamy gave him an odd look.

'Sholto Lestrade.' The Inspector introduced himself.

'William Bellamy.' He caught the outstretched hand. 'Kent.'

'Is this your first visit to Bandicoot Hall, Mr Bellamy?'

'It is. Charming fellow, Mr Bandicoot.'

'He is,' Lestrade grinned.

'His wife is rather a looker, isn't she?'

'Letitia?'

'Bless you,' said Bellamy. 'Oh, well played.'

Lestrade had heard Arslightly's crack of leather on willow and guessed something must have happened. Harry and another man were running backwards and forwards to the polite clapping of the spectators.

'Not exactly Headingley,' Bellamy said, 'but Bandicoot has style.'

'Yes,' Arslightly was droning, 'it's a soft shot down the field. Quite a hard pitch this and there's plenty of bounce . . .'

Lestrade had noticed his man scanning the crowd across the field from him. 'Looking for someone?' he asked.

'My sister was supposed to be here,' he said. 'At least I wrote to invite her. Perhaps her train has been delayed.'

'Where was she coming from?' Lestrade asked.

'London. She lives in the Walworth Road.'

'Good address,' Lestrade commented. 'Isn't that a little unusual?'

'To live in the Walworth Road? People do.'

'No, no. A woman interested in cricket.'

Nanny Balsam passed at that moment with the Bandicoot boys in tow. 'Well, hit the bally thing, man!' she screamed stentoriously at Bandicoot's partner. Then she glanced at Lestrade. 'What *do* they teach them at school these days?'

Lestrade was about to search for an answer but the play had carried on and Bandicoot's partner, chipping for dear life against the deadly momentum of Grace's bowling, had snuck an easy one into the slips, where Prince Ranjitsinhji was waiting to claim his first victim of the day. The luckless batsman returned under a broiling sun to the patter of appreciative hands.

'Well, there goes batsman number two. Just not his day . . .' Arslightly's Mummerset came and went on the breeze.

'Bad luck, Hooch,' Bellamy called. 'No, Lestrade. Cricket was a woman's game in the last century as much as it was a man's. Emily and I were brought up in the shadow of the Oval. Cricket is in our blood, I suppose. Father and Grandfather both played for Kent in their time.'

The third batsman took his place at the crease. He'd barely asked for middle and leg when a whistling ball from Grace demolished him and a few of the less genteel members of the crowd began a slow handclap.

'Oh dear, oh dear,' chuckled Arslightly's loud hailer. 'Well, he'll be cussing himself for not covering himself on that one . . .'

'Bad show, Gotham!' Bellamy called. 'This isn't going too well,

Lestrade. Scratting's in now and we've scored three. It'll be the wooden spoon for us at this rate. What's your average?'

'Well, I . . .'

'Ah, that's better.' Bandicoot had sent one of Grace's balls out of sight into his own grounds. The deafening shatter of glass told everyone that it had found a greenhouse.

'I hope we have no more of those.' Nanny Balsam was perambulating back the other way. 'People with glasshouses shouldn't hit sixes.'

For the next hour, Lestrade watched in horrified fascination as Scratting, Cower, Bellamy and all the others fell either to Grace's bowling or Ranjitsinhji's fielding. He'd have fallen fast asleep to Arslightly's commentary if it hadn't been for the incipient rising terror inside him. At last there was a tap on his shoulder. 'You're in, old man. Good luck.'

Someone had already strapped Lestrade into his pads, noting with a certain apprehension that the Inspector had them on upside-down.

'You might need this,' Bellamy told him, handing him a saucer-shaped device with a padded edge. 'W. G. isn't fast, but he's devilish accurate.'

Lestrade took the bat, hopefully at the right end, and crossed to the spot where he assumed he'd have to stand. But Harry Bandicoot was standing there already.

'Other end, Sholto,' the squire whispered. 'I'm sorry about this. W. G. is back on form with a vengeance. I'll do what I can.'

Lestrade hurried down the pitch to the other end. He took his place as he'd seen the others do.

'Er . . . Mr Lestrade?' the good doctor called. 'Could you stand a little to the side, please? You're rather in my line of fire.'

'Sorry.' Lestrade stood back. A huge, bearded meteor hurtled past him and the next thing Lestrade knew was Harry Bandicoot yelling 'One!' at him. The squire was dashing towards the Inspector and the Inspector dashed in return. He jabbed at the ground with his bat as he had watched the others do and was half-way back when Bandicoot yelled, 'No, no. That'll do.'

Lestrade lunged back for the crease. Now there was an ominous silence. The umpire was peering down the wicket, apparently somewhat annoyed by Lestrade's stance. W. G.

stood, mouth open. Never in thirty years of professional cricket had he seen such a posture. If he weren't a doctor he'd have thought it anatomically impossible.

'Would you care to put that on, sir?' the umpire called to him.

Lestrade realized the man was referring to the strange padded box that Bellamy had given him. 'Er . . .'

'I'm sure the ladies will turn their backs.'

There was an embarrassed cough over Arslightly's loud hailer, as though the Great Commentator had been goosed.

Lestrade had no clue where the thing was supposed to go, so in desperation he shoved it down the front of his trousers. The umpire's outstretched hand came down. Lestrade saw Bandicoot poised like a hawk on a lure (an analogy he'd learned in the case of the Pekinese Falcon) and the good doctor lumbering towards him, rubbing the ball for some reason against his groin. And that in effect was the last thing the Inspector remembered for some time. There was a burst of stars, a scream of 'Owzat?!', a fuzzy 'Oh dear' over the loud hailer. And silence.

'Well, there you are,' a frosty, corrective voice was saying, 'if you will play silly mid-on.'

'Thank you, Nanny,' Lestrade heard Harry Bandicoot say. The tall Etonian seemed to have shrunk. It was only minutes later that Lestrade realized that was because he was sitting down.

'Harry?'

'Sholto? Sholto, are you all right?'

'Um . . . I'll let you know, shall I?'

'Look, I'm deucedly sorry, old man.' A huge bearded doctor was patting the Inspector's head with something cold and wet. 'Pop into the surgery in Bristol tomorrow, will you? There might be a slight concussion. There's this chap Röntgen somewhere in Germany . . .'

'What happened?' Lestrade asked.

'Damned if I know,' Grace told him. 'Fluke, I suppose.'

'Ah,' Lestrade let his tortured head fall back, 'I remember now. The ball hit me on the head.'

'Er . . . well, not exactly,' Grace said. 'You missed the ball entirely. In fact, it took out your middle stump. For some reason you just hit yourself on the head with your bat.'

'Shame,' sneered Nanny Balsam.

'Yes, it was,' Bandicoot agreed.

'No,' she corrected him, 'I mean that's why he did it. Very common in small children. They're so ashamed of the dog's breakfast they've just made of something that they mutilate themselves with sheer embarrassment.'

'Oh, come off it, Nanny.' Bandicoot defended his old guv'nor. 'It wasn't *that* bad a shot.'

'Anyway,' insisted the dour domestic, 'You were *out*, Mr Lestrade, in all senses of the word.'

'Oh, I'm sorry, Harry. What was the final score?'

'Three hundred and six, all out.'

'Three hundred and . . .' Lestrade cradled his head. 'I'm sorry, it must be the bump. I thought you said "three hundred and six".'

'I did.'

'But . . .'

'Yes, I know. When you stepped in we had forty-one, all but seven scored by me; but in view of your injury, W. G. was kind enough to let me play a twelfth man.'

'Who was that?' Lestrade asked.

'Nanny Balsam,' Bandicoot said a little sheepishly.

'We kept them at bay,' she of the barbed-wire hair said, knowingly. 'You're coming on, Harry. A year or two and you'll be a useful sort of batsman. Ah,' she raised a finger as the clock struck something or other, 'it's the children's bathtime.' She looked severely at Lestrade. 'I suggest you have one of those,' she recommended. 'A bath that is, rather than a child. Although both would, I suspect, be a salutary experience for people like you.' And she swept from the room.

'Harry?' Lestrade propped himself on his pillow. 'William Bellamy?'

'Is still here, Sholto,' the squire said. 'He knows you want to see him. W. G.? Dinner shouldn't be long. I wanted to see that action of Ranjitsinhji's you talked about.' And he led the good doctor away.

William Bellamy joined Lestrade shortly afterwards. Gone were the flannels and the tasselled cap. Now the man stood before him in a lightweight Kashmir, whose embroidered pocket bore the arms of the Kent Cricket Club. 'How are you feeling?' he asked, pulling up a chair.

'A little blurred,' Lestrade confessed.

'Could have happened to anyone,' Bellamy said kindly, though he didn't believe it. 'Demon bowler, W. G., isn't he?'

Until today, Lestrade had thought that phrase referred to something he habitually wore on his head. 'Mr Bellamy, there is no way to soften what I have to say to you,' he said.

The smile faded from the man's face. 'It's Emily, isn't it?' he said. 'It's my sister.'

'What makes you say that?'

'Please, Mr Lestrade, don't play games with me. I left all that out there on the pitch. If you know anything, I have a right to know.'

Lestrade nodded. 'I am afraid, sir, that Miss Emily Bellamy is dead. She was found murdered on an Underground train belonging to the City and South London Railway at the Elephant and Castle Station in the early hours of this morning.'

'Oh, my God!'

'It's been a shock, clearly. I'm sorry that I couldn't tell you earlier.'

'That explains why she didn't arrive. It makes sense now. She never missed a match – even a charity local – if she could avoid it. Oh, my God! Emily. Emily.' Her brother hung his head.

'Did she live alone in the Walworth Road?' Lestrade asked. He was less than at ease. His vision still doggypaddled rather than swam, and he was sitting in somebody else's bed, wearing somebody else's pyjamas, his head wrapped in a bandage. Hardly the most commanding way to conduct an inquiry.

'Yes. It was our parents' house. After they died, she naturally lived on there.'

'No maid?'

'Yes, two. Faithful old biddies. They'll be devastated.'

'Forgive me, Mr Bellamy, but there are painful questions I must ask.'

'Of course, Mr Lestrade. I understand. Bowl away.'

'Did your sister have any . . . gentlemen friends?'

'No. She lived for her cricket.'

'I see. That was her only interest?'

81

'That and her house. She loved beautiful things. Had a penchant for *objets d'art*. Finest collection of fire-irons in eight counties. That sort of thing.'

'So her interests were cricket and the hearth, you might say?'

'*You* might, Mr Lestrade. Tell me, how ... how did she die?'

'She was strangled, Mr Bellamy. I cannot pretend that her death was either quick or painless. But one thing I assure you. As soon as I am out of this bed, I shall set about nailing the bastard responsible.'

Dr Grace insisted that Lestrade attend his surgery in Bristol. Prince Ranjitsinhji insisted he try an old Indian remedy handed down by the Moguls which seemed to consist of the yak droppings so plentiful in the West Country; Letitia was adamant that the Inspector spend at least the next day in bed and some time with his daughter. Nanny Balsam couldn't see what all the fuss was about, and aided and abetted the Inspector by driving him to the station in her donkey cart.

'Thank you, Nanny,' he said, the boater sitting uneasily atop his bandage, 'for looking after little Emma.'

'It's nothing that a trained saint and martyr such as myself wouldn't do for anyone,' she told him, gathering up her reins. 'And I couldn't see the little waif starve, which is what she would surely do if left to your devices. She was an orphan of the storm, Mr Lestrade, but she is safe now. Now I'm a very busy woman. I've verrucas to lance and the Lord knows what else. You, I assume, have some murky business to unravel; some depths which you must plumb.'

'Indeed I have,' he sighed. It was the story of his life.

When Lestrade reached the Yard that Sunday morning, all hell had broken loose. What Fleet Street referred to in more jocund moments as its newspapers smelt linked murders and incompetent policing. Fine, upstanding guardians that they were, they bayed for blood and when they saw an exposed jugular, they went for it.

They caught Lestrade in an unguarded moment as he crossed Whitehall.

'T. A. Liesinsdad,' a bald man snarled at him, '*Daily Graphic*. Three women butchered on the Underground. Is the Ripper still at large, Inspector Lestrade? Is Jack back?'

'No, Mr Liesinsdad.' Lestrade had met the reporter from the Principality before and the Welshman never failed to climb up his nostrils. 'The ladies in question were strangled. There were no mutilations.'

'David Newman, *Catholic Herald*.' Another one blocked his way, pad poised. 'Is sex involved?'

'Does the *Catholic Herald* really want to know that?' Lestrade threw it back.

'Ezekiel Ledbetter, the *War Cry*. Is there a Methodist connection, Inspector?'

'Not that I am aware. Gentlemen, please!' He held up his hand to still the noise. 'At the moment, we are pursuing every inquiry. No stone will be unturned.'

'Barry Bucknell, the *Woodworker*. Is a man helping you with your inquiries?'

'Some are, some aren't,' said Lestrade, 'and at the moment, you're not. Now, please can I get on with the job in hand?'

'Albert Wedgewood, the *Sun*. If we came out with a headline like "Daily Murders. Lestrade Has No Clue", would you sue us for libel, Inspector?'

'No,' sighed Lestrade, 'I'd have you shot. Good morning, gentlemen.'

'Mr Lestrade,' and the Inspector turned in time to have his face blackened by the sulphur flash of a photographer from the *Monthly Exposure*.

He vaguely acknowledged Sergeant Dixon on the front desk. He slammed angrily into the lift that jarred and rattled its way to the first floor. He marched off down sunlit corridors until he found his office where the sun never shone. But here, as his boater unerringly missed the hat rack, was a brilliance of its own – a radiant smile on the face of Detective Constable Walter Dew.

'Well, well,' Lestrade snapped. Journalists always left him frayed, tetchy, past his best. 'Got lucky crossing the Common last night, Dew?'

The Constable looked a little hurt. 'I am a happily married man, sir,' he said.

Lestrade collapsed into the rickety chair, the one with the peeling leather. 'Of course you are, Walter,' he said. 'The world is full, is it not, of married men? So, why are you so happy?'

'We've got him, sir.' Dew's beam returned.

'Who?' Lestrade toyed with reaching for the teapot, but the strain was too great and he let Dew do it.

'Our man. Our Underground murderer.'

Lestrade sat bolt upright. 'We have?' he said slowly.

Dew nodded. 'He's downstairs now. Constable Corkindale is keeping an eye on him.'

'Corkindale?' Lestrade roared. 'Dew, the man is an animal!'

'Don't worry, guv,' Dew grinned. 'I left the door open.'

But Lestrade wasn't listening. He'd gone, in a flurry of pro formas and liniment, his bandage streaming out in his wake, like the wrappings of some unusually healthy mummy. Down the corridors they ran, the Inspector and the Constable, leaping over saddles on the stairways, brushing the dust off aspidistras in their haste, hurtling past the ancient graffito in honour of a former Assistant Commissioner which read 'McNaughten Rules'. They aimed for the lift, but Assistant Commissioner Frost was filling that all by himself, so they took the back doubles and reached the cells in double-quick time. A man the height of a Clydesdale, with shoulders to match, stood at the door of a cell. Lestrade thrust a practised eye to the little grille in the centre thereof and rounded on the vast Constable.

'Corkindale, have you touched this man?'

'No, sir,' the man droned, but some seconds after the question was asked.

'Are you sure?'

'Yes, sir,' after the same time had elapsed.

'Open up, then.'

They waited while the order permeated to whatever levels of consciousness Corkindale possessed and they swept into the room.

'I am Inspector Lestrade,' said Lestrade to the man sitting at the small wooden table. 'Who are you?'

'Edward Bayreuth,' he said, but Lestrade ignored him.

'Dew,' he snapped, indicating the door, 'a word in your ear.'

The confused Constable led the way and Lestrade slammed the door behind them. He looked at the constables before him.

Dew, ever-loyal, ever-eager. He might make sergeant if hell froze over. He looked at Corkindale. And he shook his head. In the same length of time he might become a human being. But all in all, it wasn't likely.

'Tell me, Dew,' said Lestrade softly, 'did that man have only one arm before he was in Constable Corkindale's company? Or do we have a rather tricky police brutality case on our hands?'

Dew breathed a sigh of relief. 'No, sir,' he said. 'Mr Bayreuth lost his arm in a printing accident many years ago.'

Lestrade nodded. The same printing accident had led, or so he believed, to some of Miss Corelli's outpourings. He turned to the vast Constable. 'Tell me, Corkindale, what do you weigh?'

'Er . . .'

'How heavy are you?'

'I'm seventeen stone, sir, give or take.'

'Right. Are you right-handed?'

'Oh yes, sir. Mrs Minniver up at the school taught me to be, sir.'

'Excellent. Did she teach you to think as well?'

'Sir?'

'Never mind. Put your left arm behind your back, will you?' The confused Constable did.

'Good. Now. I want you to strangle Constable Dew here. But only with that one hand. Got it?'

'Er . . .' The chorus came from both constables, both of them, for different reasons, unsure about the experiment that was about to take place.

'Well, go on, man,' Lestrade insisted.

Corkindale's giant palm slid forward and locked around Dew's throat. The man began to turn a rather attractive shade of purple. Then he gurgled a bit.

'Well, do something, Dew!' Lestrade thought it best to command.

The smaller man's right knee came up, catching Corkindale a nasty one in the groin. As his strangling hand gave way, Dew swung both fists into the man's face, then hobbled away, clutching his knuckles under his armpits.

'Sorry, Walter,' Corkindale mumbled, 'I hope I didn't hurt you.'

'No, no, Herminius,' Dew bit his lip to prevent the scream, 'not in the slightest.'

'Thank you, gentlemen,' said Lestrade. 'A useful little test, I think. Now, Dew, let's see this murderer of yours.'

Edward Bayreuth was a wizened little man with the mien of an idiot. In fact, as idiots go, they probably didn't come any meaner. His doleful eyes took in the re-entry of the detectives and he watched carefully as Lestrade took out a cigar, lit it and blew the smoke into his face.

'Now, then,' he said, 'I believe you've met my assistant here before.'

'I have, sir,' Bayreuth said.

'When?'

'Within the last hour.'

'And what did you tell him?'

'That I'm the one that you want. I'm the murderer.'

'Of whom?'

'Whom would you like me to be the murderer of?'

Lestrade leaned forward so that his cigar smouldered dangerously near to the nose of the man. 'Do you imagine this is some sort of game, Mr Bayruth?'

'Bayreuth.' He corrected the Yard man's pronunciation. 'Not at all, sir. I am guilty and I deserve to be punished. Horribly. Painfully.'

'All right.' Lestrade leaned back. 'Tell us about it.'

'Well, I saw this woman on the Underground. She got on at the Oval. I at Stockwell. She showed a clean pair of ankles. It was her ankles that inflamed me.'

'Go on.'

'No, it's true. I've always had this thing about ankles. Ever since I can remember, I've been an ankle man.'

'What happened?'

'Well, I started . . . you know . . . talking to her. She seemed upset. Moved away. So I sat by her.'

'Which compartment was this in?'

'The end one,' said Bayreuth.

'Was it just the two of you in the carriage?'

'Yes.'

'What happened next?'

'She tried to get away. Well, I couldn't feel her ankles from a distance, could I? So I strangled her.'

'How?'

'Eh?'

'I said,' Lestrade was a model of patience, 'how did you strangle her?'

Bayreuth's eyes bulged anew and he swallowed convulsively. 'With my bare hands,' he explained.

Lestrade looked at Dew. 'Shouldn't that be hand?' he asked.

'What?' Bayreuth had obviously lost the gist of the interrogation.

'Mr Bayreuth,' sighed Lestrade, 'I don't know whether it has escaped your notice, but you have a deformity.'

'How dare you?' Bayreuth turned an even more malevolent shade of grey. 'I find that remark highly offensive, that's what I do.'

'Perhaps you do.' Lestrade lolled back in his chair. 'But we are in the business of facts here at Scotland Yard. And it is a fact that you have only one arm.'

Bayreuth shot a lightning glance at his empty sleeve as if to confirm the fact. 'Well, that doesn't mean I'm not a murderer!' he snapped.

'If the lady in question was shot, stabbed or even bludgeoned, I might agree with you,' Lestrade said, 'but the lady in question appeared to have been a healthy lass until somebody snuffed out the candle of her life. How did you hold her down while you strangled her?'

'Ah,' Bayreuth's eyes rolled wildly in his head, 'it was surprise, you see. The effluent of surprise. I come up on her blind side.'

'Her blind side?' Lestrade repeated. 'Ah, I see. You're referring to her one eye.'

'That's right.' Bayreuth clicked his limited choice of fingers.

'Was that her right or her left?'

'What?'

'Her missing eye. The one with the patch. You must remember. One-eyed women can't be all that common on the Underground. She'd have stood out like a sore thumb – oh, I beg your pardon.'

'Left,' Bayreuth guessed. Then, when he saw Lestrade's expression, blurted, 'Right. It was her right. Of course. I remember now.'

Lestrade scraped back the chair. 'I'm afraid, Mr Bayreuth, you've given my Constable here hours of paperwork for nothing. Turn the light off on your way out, will you?'

'But I done it!' Bayreuth was on his feet, shouting. 'I killed her.'

'With your bare hand. Yes, I know. You told me. Now, what is it you want, Mr Bayreuth? The limelight of an Old Bailey trial? The kiss of the rope? Or just a month or two in custody? Because the first two I'm afraid I can't provide. But the last one is easy. All I have to do is to charge you with wasting police time. Good morning.'

'Your trouble is, you're not grateful,' Bayreuth screamed as Lestrade saw himself out. 'Here I am giving you the collar of your career and you're throwing it all away. Bloody philistine, that's what you are. That bandaged head don't fool me.'

At the bottom of the stairs, Lestrade paused. 'The f word again,' he sighed. 'Constable Corkindale, see Mr Bayreuth out, would you? I'll leave his condition largely up to you.'

The Horse and Collar had closed an hour ago. But to them, the landlord reckoned, it was still open. The little back room that is, furthest from the river. It was here that Lestrade sat, in his waistcoat and shirtsleeves, across a gnarled old table from Walter Dew.

'Right, Walter, now that we've disposed of Mr Bayreuth; any other little surprises I should know about?'

'No, sir,' Dew said confidently. 'Mr Bellamy came to identify his wife.'

Lestrade's feet fell off the table to crash on to the uneven brick floor, thick with sawdust. 'Who?' he managed.

'The dead woman's husband, guv.' Clearly the bandage round the Inspector's head covered a more serious wound than Dew imagined.

'She didn't have a husband, Walter,' Lestrade said.

'Ah, that's what we assumed, yes. But in point of fact, she

did. I've got it here.' He flicked open his notebook. 'Name of William.'

'But William's the brother,' Lestrade said. 'I played cricket with him yesterday – after a fashion.'

'Well, he definitely said husband, guv'nor.'

'Why wasn't I told about this, Dew?'

The young Constable was clearly a little flustered. 'I'm sorry, sir. What with Mr Bayreuth's confession and all, I sort of forgot about it. All he did was identify her.'

'As Emily Bellamy?'

Dew nodded.

'What did he say – precisely?'

'Er . . . he said he'd come to look at the body and I said, "Who might you be?" And he said, "The husband of the deceased." And I said, "She didn't have a husband," and he said, "Oh yes she did," and I said, "Oh no she didn't" . . .'

'All right, Walter,' Lestrade cut in, 'perhaps "precisely" was a trifle strong. Just give me the gist.'

'Well, he gave his name as William Bellamy. Said he didn't have the marriage lines exactly on him, but he'd read in the papers about the woman on the City and South London line and it fitted his wife's description. He hadn't seen her since Tuesday last.'

'So you showed him the body?'

'Yes, sir.'

'What was his reaction?'

'Seemed fascinated by the throat marks,' Dew remembered. 'I thought that was a bit peculiar, but you know how it takes them in different ways. Remember that woman who brought a change of underwear for her old man? The one who'd been run over by that tram? Not a lot of point, really. She said she'd brought it in in case he was involved in an accident.'

'Yes, yes. What time was this?'

'What, the tram accident?'

'No, no. Bellamy's visit to view the remains. Do try to stay with it, Dew.'

'Oh, yes. This would be about three o'clockish yesterday afternoon, sir. Sergeant Dixon will have logged the exact time.'

Lestrade grunted. He could see it now in old Dixon's immaculate copperplate: 'William Bellamy. About three o'clockish.'

Well, you couldn't get the staff. 'At more or less the same time he was going down to a particularly clever yorkie from W. G. Grace,' the Inspector said. 'What did this man look like, Dew?'

'Er . . . about my height, sir. Blond. Clean-shaven. Had a slight accent.'

'Really? What?'

'Well, I don't know . . .'

'Well, think, man. This is important. What was it? Close your eyes. Right. You're in the morgue in C basement, West Wing. What do you smell?'

'Formaldehyde.'

'And?'

Dew screwed up his nose. 'The river.'

'Good. Now. Bellamy's talking to you. He's saying . . . what's he saying?'

'"Yes, my God, yes. It's her. It's my wife." Something like that.'

'Fine. Now, how's he saying it?'

'Eh?'

'Well, is he shouting? Crying? Whispering?'

Dew's face relaxed and his moustache slumped. 'He's just . . . saying it.'

'Right. No emotion. Odd for a man who's staring at the light of his life stretched out on a marble slab. Now what's the accent? Bermondsey? West Ham?'

Dew shook his head, the mental effort too great.

'All right.' Lestrade held the man's arm. 'Class. Did he have a plum in his mouth? A silver spoon? Was he gentry? A nob?'

'Sort of . . .'

'Right. Public school, then. Did he sound like Harry Bandicoot?'

'No, it wasn't Harry Bandicoot, sir.' Dew opened his eyes. 'I'd know Harry Bandicoot.'

'I *know* it wasn't Harry Bandicoot, Dew, you nincompoop! I mean, could he have gone to Eton, this Mr Bellamy?'

'Possibly. Wait a minute.'

'What?'

'His address. He'd have left an address with Sergeant Dixon.'

'Yes. And it would have been a false one. That's the trouble with the bloody newspapers in this country. They printed the dead woman's name. Any maniac can crawl out of the woodwork and claim all sorts of connections. Look at Bayreuth. And I haven't forgotten the Ripper Case . . .'

Neither had Dew. He shuddered.

'Two hundred letters all signed "Jack". I'd give Bayreuth's right arm to know who leaked her name to the Press.'

Dew hoped his blush wouldn't show in the darkened confines of the snug of the Horse and Collar. Lestrade blew a hearty sigh. He was rather as he had been the day before, totally stumped.

'I know this sounds ridiculous, sir . . .' Dew began.

'It does, Walter, but I'm getting used to it. Go on.'

'Well, if anything, the accent sounded . . . Australian.'

'Australian?' Lestrade repeated.

'Does that make any sense?' Dew asked hopefully.

'No, Walter,' Lestrade said, 'no sense at all. But I know one thing.'

'What's that, sir?'

Lestrade lifted his empty glass. 'It's your shout.'

5

She lay where the murderer had left her, on the ridged floor of the padded cell, her bonnet beside her. She'd turned her head, as though to watch out for the guard's posting of the next station. Her left hand had clawed the leather of the seat in her death throes, and in the lashings of her agony she'd kicked off both her shoes as she died.

Lestrade knelt before her, wedged between the seats. Around him, on the platform at Stockwell, policemen stood in knots, muttering darkly.

'This is number three, isn't it?' The voice made him turn.

'Who's there?' In the flickering gas lights, all the Inspector saw was a shape.

'Melville Lavender. You sent for me?'

'Ah, yes. Thanks for coming so promptly.' Lestrade shook his hand. 'We must stop meeting like this.'

Lavender stared at the corpse at Lestrade's feet. He was shaking imperceptibly and had turned a whiter shade of pale.

'Are you all right?' the Inspector asked.

'I think so,' the Railway Police's expert said. 'Perhaps we could sit in the adjacent car?'

'Yes, of course. Bromley.'

The constable of that name popped his head round the double door. 'Sir?'

'Get Litchfield at the double.'

'Who, sir? Where, sir?'

'Police photographer at the Yard. Tell him I want this car covered. All angles, with the body in position.'

'Won't he be in bed, sir?'

'We were all in bed an hour ago, Constable,' Lestrade snapped. 'This isn't sleepy Essex, lad – and I use the word advisedly. It's Scotland Yard. We never sleep. And tell Litchfield I can do without the studio backdrop and the aspidistras. No frills. Got it?'

'Very good, sir.'

'Who was she?' Lavender plodded past caped policemen to the car nearest the locomotive.

'Verity True,' said Lestrade, 'or so her pelisse label says. What sort of person writes their name in their clothing, I wonder?'

Lavender leaned heavily on the metal balustrade that enclosed the entrance to the car. 'Soldiers, sailors, domestic servants, anyone who's attended boarding school or doesn't have a very trusting nature.'

For a rhetorical question, Lestrade hadn't done badly in terms of an answer. 'And it's number four, by the way,' he said.

'What?' Lavender gulped something sedative from a hip flask.

'Miss True. She's the fourth victim of the Underground.'

Lavender shook his head. 'This is awful,' he muttered. 'It's not safe to use these lines any more. It's funny, a few weeks ago, I'd have said there was no safer form of travel in the world.'

'I've heard rickshaws have a very low accident rate,' Lestrade said.

'Ah, that's because there are so many Chinese,' Lavender informed him. 'The very magnitude of their population means that it's impossible to fall over in China. The throng keeps you upright.'

'I've heard that the whole of the world's population could stand upright on the Isle of Dogs,' Lestrade said.

'That's the Isle of Wight, surely,' Lavender said.

'Nobody stands on the Isle of Wight, do they?' asked Lestrade. 'At least not after closing time.'

'Thank you, Mr Lestrade,' Lavender smiled.

'Hmm?'

'The very banality of your conversation has a marvellous soothing effect. I feel better now.'

'Oh, good,' Lestrade grinned through gritted teeth. He'd never been accused of banality before and anyway, the law against it had been repealed in the 24th of George III if he had remembered that lecture on Hansard for Policemen correctly.

'I'm not used to seeing murder victims, that's all,' Lavender explained.

'Of course not,' Lestrade said. 'I'm afraid it's something we get manured to in our business. Feel up to a spot of sleuthing?'

'I'll do my best.'

'Miss True's body was found here a little over an hour ago. I estimate she died a little before eleven.'

'The last train,' Lavender nodded.

'On the down line from King William Street?'

'Correct. How long would . . . that . . . have taken?'

'The killing? It depends,' Lestrade said, 'on the strength of the attacker, the strength of the victim, the element of surprise. Probably between two and four minutes.'

'A bit dicey from the Oval, then?' Lavender observed.

'Really?'

The railway expert pointed to the locomotive. 'Number eleven,' he said, 'a four-wheeled frame, fourteen feet wide over the central buffers. Driven by two series-wound engines with Gramme armatures. Fifty horsepower at three hundred and ten revolutions per minute.'

That sounded rather like the Balkans to Lestrade, ever the man of current affairs thanks to the editorial excellence of the *Sun*.

'Both motors are connected in series and controlled by a plain rheostat switch and a reversing switch.' Lavender was in full flight. 'The starting current is one hundred and fifty amperes and the drawbar pull two thousand and fifty pounds. On the Kennington level it would be managing twenty-five miles an hour.'

'God, that's frightening,' Lestrade observed.

'On average, of course, it would slow to eleven and a half miles an hour.'

'Why the difference?'

Lavender's flask contents had given him the *joie de vivre* to chuckle. 'Human nature, Mr Lestrade,' he said. 'It's knocking-off time. Ever seen a fire engine late at night, and no fire?'

'Well . . . yes.'

'An ambulance and no accident?'

'Well . . .'

'What better way to get home fast through the streets? Just lash the horses and ring the bloody bell. People leap aside and thank God it isn't happening to them. No need of a bell down here. Just open the throttle full up and hang on to the dead man's hand.'

'The . . . er?'

'The brake. That lever over there.' Lavender pointed to it. 'There's no air pump for it, but two reservoirs under the sides of the cab. They're recharged every night on the down run from the Stockwell reservoir. But in case they fail, or in case the driver collapses with apoplexy or anything, he has to keep his hand on that lever at all times. As he falls, his weight will slide it forward and the train will stop.'

'I see.'

'Of course,' Lavender looked into the nearest car, 'it would have been dark.'

'It would?'

'Of course. The Stockwell gradient drains the power considerably. About where Spurgeon's orphanage stands in the Clapham Road, the City and South London had to use cables to haul the cars up the gradient until last year. Well, it is one in three and a half. They've got over it now by more juice.'

'Juice?' Lestrade was confused.

'Electric current. But it still knocks out the lights, if only for a few seconds.'

'Time enough for our man to strike?'

'If he waited until after the Oval, yes. But that's only a journey of three minutes. Would that give him time?'

'It would if he struck north of the Oval, say after Kennington.'

'After Kennington,' Lavender obliged thoughtfully. 'But what if someone got on at the Oval? Wasn't that taking a hell of a chance?'

'What if they didn't?' Lestrade asked. 'You said yourself it was the last train. All murder is chance, Mr Lavender. You show me the perfect murder and I'll show you a good time. What if he's seen? What if he's left a clue at the murder scene? What if the victim fights back? What does he do with the body? It's all chance. All luck. We've just got to weigh our luck with his and hope for the best.'

'Is that it?' Lavender asked, horrified. 'Is that all modern detection is all about?'

'Modern detection?' Lestrade repeated. 'That's a rather silly phrase invented by Dr Conan Doyle, isn't it? Some of us live in the real world, you know.'

Camberwell Library stood in Camberwell Church Street. Within it, that bright May morning, a ferret-faced little man in regulation serge stood at the Romantic Fiction counter, his features dappled by the shafts of sunlight that threw red and amber rays on to the shelves through the stained glass.

'Can I help you?' a frosty-faced woman the wrong side of the counter asked.

'Do you have periodicals?' the ferret-faced man asked.

The frosty-faced woman's eyes filled with loathing and she shrieked and fled through Gardening and Taxidermy in search of a male superior. The ferret-faced man was aware that the avid readers had looked up sharply at the intrusion, had indrawn their respective breaths and had read on.

'Do you have a ticket?' a much less severe woman asked him.

'No,' he said, 'I have not come to borrow a book.'

She glanced at his suiting. He seemed respectable enough.

At least he wasn't wearing a long raincoat with his trousers tied at the knee with string. All seemed in order. What *could* have so frightened her colleague?

'Is there a particular book you wish to borrow?' she asked.

'I am here on another matter,' he told her. 'I am Inspector Lestrade of Scotland Yard. I am looking for Miss Agnes True.'

'You've found her,' the librarian said.

'Trottie!' A male voice shattered the quiet.

A dozen fingers shot to a dozen lips and the common cry of 'Ssshh!' rent the air.

'Get away from that man,' the male voice went on. 'He just asked Miss Dalrymple an improper question.'

Miss True took a step backwards.

'Who's that?' Lestrade asked her.

'Mr Hathersuch, the Chief Librarian,' she whispered. 'He means well.'

'And I assume Miss Dalrymple is the one with the moustache General Kitchener would be proud of?'

Miss True giggled.

A large, balding man squeezed himself between Horticulture and the slim section marked Humour of the Medes and Persians, and made boldly for the Inspector. The frosty-faced woman with the moustache bustled at his elbow. 'We get undesirables like you, fellow, from time to time. If they are not publishers' representatives, they are ruffians from the Elephant and Castle. Well, let me tell you, this is a respectable neighbourhood. John Ruskin used to live up the road.'

'Ah, I must pop in on my way home.'

'I would like you to leave.' The librarian stood at the height of his dignity. 'Indulge your animal instincts elsewhere. This is England, sir. More – it is Camberwell. Is librariankind safe nowhere?'

'Certainly not in Romantic Fiction.' Lestrade winked at Miss Dalrymple who shuddered and clutched her date-stamper convulsively. 'I think Miss Dalrymple may have misheard me. I am Inspector Lestrade of Scotland Yard and I have business with Miss True here.'

'Trottie?' Hathersuch rounded on her. 'Is this true?'

'Well.' The girl was a little nonplussed. 'He showed me his card.'

'I'm sure he did!' Miss Dalrymple shrilled.

'Look, do you mind?' a crotchety voice called. 'I've read the last line three times already.'

'What are you reading?' Hathersuch instinctively asked.

'*Who Killed Lady Agatha?*' the reader told him.

'It was Samson the gardener,' said the Chief Librarian. 'Bashed in her head with a hoe after forcing her to change her will. I'd got it by page eight.'

'Well, really!' The reader slammed shut the book and stormed out.

'I think he'd find *All About Chartered Accountancy* marginally more gripping. Mr Lestrade – if that is your name – I am afraid Miss True is still on duty until five of the clock. I cannot . . .'

'Is there a back room?' Lestrade asked her.

There was a further inrush of breath from Miss Dalrymple.

'Follow me,' Miss True said.

She led him down a spiral staircase where his hobnailed boots rang and scraped on the treads to a basement wall-to-wall with remaindered copies that no one read any more. There were an awful lot of Marie Corellis, Lestrade couldn't help noticing.

'Trottie?' Lestrade said. 'Is that what they call you?'

'Well,' she smiled at him, 'Agnes is rather awful, isn't it? I don't mind being called after a pigeon.'

Lestrade saw, in the dim light as she put a match to an oil lamp, how like her dead sister the girl was. But this one was bright, vivacious. A smile played around her mouth. Her eyes danced. She was alive.

'I don't think I've met a real Scotland Yard detective before.' She offered him a chair.

'I'm not sure you've missed much, miss,' he said.

'Call me Trottie,' she said. 'Everybody does.'

'Are you all right down there?' a stentorian voice called from above.

'Fine thank you, Mr Hathersuch,' she called back. 'Tell me,' she said, 'are you any relation to the Inspector Lestrade who crops up from time to time in the *Strand Magazine*? In those Sherlock Holmes adventures?'

'No,' said Lestrade, 'none whatever. Now, you tell me, Trottie. Who is Verity True?'

'Verity? She's my sister . . .' The girl's face darkened. The bright eyes lost their shine for a moment. 'What's happened?'

'You must prepare yourself for a shock,' Lestrade told her.

The girl swallowed hard. 'Go on,' she said.

'I have reason to believe that your sister is dead, Trottie,' he said softly. 'She was murdered on the Underground near Stockwell Station late last night.'

For a moment she looked at him, her head to one side, wistfully, as though browsing her shelves for a good book. She tried to speak, but the words would not come. She wanted to scream, but she couldn't. A thousand thoughts hurtled through her brain. She saw a laughing girl with a bucket and spade on a sandy beach; the rush of water through childish fingers; heard the tinkle of sisterly laughter. Then blackness.

The periodicals, mention of which had so outraged Miss Dalrymple, came in extremely handy later when Lestrade remembered his First Aid for Policemen and fanned Trottie True back to consciousness. Admittedly, he had had to compromise her honour by loosening a stay or two and despite the fact that part 2, page 316 of that journal had specifically recommended such action, it was clear that neither Miss Dalrymple nor Mr Hathersuch had read it. Instead they kept peering round the door at the pair until Lestrade used his ultimate authority and threw all eight volumes of *With Rod and Line Up the Titikaka* in their general direction. After that, the nosiness stopped.

'I . . . I'm sorry,' she said. 'I don't know what happened.'

'You fainted, Trottie.' He stopped rubbing her hand. 'It's only natural after the shock you've had.'

She looked at him, her eyes full of tears, but determined not to cry. 'What happened to her?' she asked, afraid to hear his answer.

'She was strangled,' he said.

She closed her eyes.

'Trottie.' He leaned back against a remaindered stack. 'There are questions I must ask you. This is of the essence. I cannot wait.'

He fancied he heard a sharp intake of breath from the staircase overhead, but it was probably the swish of Miss Dalrymple's stamp and he passed it off. 'Did your sister know a lady called Emily Bellamy?'

'No,' Trottie said, 'I don't believe she did.'

'What about Jane Hollander?'

The librarian shook her head.

'Sarah Culdrose?'

'These names mean nothing to me, Inspector. Who are they?'

'Let's just say fellow travellers,' he said grimly, 'on life's Underground.'

'Wait a minute. They're the others, aren't they? The other women who've died. I remember reading about them now. Who can it be? What sort of madman is responsible?'

He looked into the desperate, pleading eyes, at the outreaching hand in the shadows of the basement room. And he could not tell her. He could not tell her anything.

'Was your sister . . . did she have any gentlemen friends?'

'Yes. Two.'

'Two?'

Trottie's glance fell to the ground. 'She was to have made her choice last night. She went for a walk, she said. To be alone. To think things through.'

'What time did she leave?'

'About six, I think.'

'Weren't you alarmed when she didn't return?'

'I went out too. By the time I got back, it was gone midnight. I didn't want to disturb Very, so I went straight to bed.'

'And this morning?'

'I overslept. Very wasn't in her bed and I assumed she'd gone off as usual.'

'Gone where?'

'My sister does . . . did . . . good works, Inspector, as I do. I'm only here one day in sixteen. I believe she was due at Dr Barnardo's today.'

'You didn't find it odd,' he asked, narrowing his eyes, 'that her bed had not been slept in?'

'My sister was fastidious, Inspector. She always made her bed as soon as she rose.'

'You have no maid?'

'No. We are not well off, Mr Lestrade. Librarian's wages are woefully inadequate. And good works pay not at all.'

'How do you live?'

'Carefully,' she told him. 'We have a modest endowment from our father. We eke.'

'Pardon?' Lestrade looked round for the mouse.

'We eke out an existence. But Very had been about to change all that.'

'Ah, yes,' Lestrade ran a finger over the thick dust that carpeted *One Hundred and One Things to Do With a Piece of Knotted String*. 'Her choice of lovers.'

He thought he saw a librarianly blush flush her cheek, but it was probably a trick of the light. 'Lovers is too strong a word, Mr Lestrade. We Trues have been brought up with propriety.'

'I shall need their names,' he said.

'Clarence Holdsworth and George Cross,' she told him, 'of the Sylvester Theatre Company.'

'Actors?'

'Dancers,' she said.

'Dancers?' he repeated.

'Yes,' she told him. 'Formerly of the Ballet Rambo.'

This was a new one on Lestrade. He'd never heard of men dancing professionally before. He changed tack accordingly. 'You said your sister went out for a walk. Can you tell me how she came to be riding the Underground?'

The girl thought for a moment, a quizzical expression crossing her lovely face. 'I don't know,' she said. 'I wish I did.'

He helped her to her feet. 'Thank you, Trottie,' he said. 'You've been very helpful.'

'No, I haven't,' she told him. 'I feel so . . . so useless. So empty. Do you know what it's like?' She looked up at him. 'To lose someone you love. Do you know what it's like?'

He thought of his dear, dead Sarah, alone in the cold of Abney Park. He leaned forward and kissed the girl's forehead. 'Yes,' he said, 'I know.'

An orchestra was tuning up, for want of a better phrase, in the aptly named pits the next morning. Lots of bow and not much rosin, the sounds screamed through Lestrade's ears as he fumbled forward in the darkness of the theatre. To be fair to him, he was not to know that there was a mop resting in a

100

pail a little to his left. He walked straight into it and it caught his right as well, doubling him up for an instant and bringing tears to his eyes. The clatter of the pail brought an instantaneous reproof in the form of a sharp 'Sshh!' from a tall, elegant man with locks that flew all over his shoulders.

He clapped his hands. 'Now, gentlemen, if you please.'

The orchestra struck up and a row of men in ludicrous tights hurtled across from stage left and disappeared stage right.

'Is that it?' the tall man wailed after a stunned pause.

One of the chorus line stuck his head round the door. 'No good, George?'

'Like a row of beans,' George mumbled into the carefully manicured hand that covered his face in horror. 'Not that I know what that looks like. Some of you . . .' he shouted stentorianly, and he waited for them all to appear on stage like a gaggle of naughty schoolboys caught behind the temporary buildings with their first cigarette, 'some of you clearly do not know a *jetée* from a harbour wall. May I remind you, gentlemen, that you are supposed to be Lords of the Spirit World, come from the Realms Beneath to rescue Fair Eleanor . . . By the way, has anyone seen Morag?'

'Who?' one of the chorus line asked.

'Morag Finisterre . . . Fair Eleanor. The prima ballerina. Oh, this is hopeless.'

'Of course it is, George,' another arch voice called from the darkness. '*You're* directing.'

The silence could have peeled wallpaper.

'Not now, Clarence. My head really couldn't take it. It's going to be one of those days, I just know it is . . .'

His voice tailed away as a gormless fellow in a nasty brown suit stumbled on to the stage, walking as though his arabesque was decidedly penché.

'Ah,' George managed, when his artistic temperament had mentally stripped away the modern impedimenta, 'at last. We've been waiting for over an hour. Don't bother to change now. What do you do?'

'Er . . . solve crimes,' Lestrade said.

'Oh, very droll,' George snapped. 'Clarence, is he one of yours?'

'Never seen him before,' Clarence said, peering at Lestrade

through a pair of ivory opera-glasses. 'Doesn't appear to have the calves for it.'

'Well, just give us some attitudes. We'll build to the *fouettée en tournant* when I'm feeling stronger.'

'I beg your pardon?'

'Oh, Lord, that's all we need. A deaf primo ballerino. I said . . .' he shouted.

'I know what you said.' Lestrade moved forward so that his face was a ghastly green above the sulphur of the footlights. 'What I didn't do was understand it. I am Inspector Lestrade of Scotland Yard. I am looking for Clarence Holdsworth. Would you be him?'

The tall man's nostrils quivered with emotion in the half light. 'Not if you ripped out my quadriceps femoris.'

Lestrade wouldn't know where to look for that, let alone rip it out.

'*I* am Clarence Holdsworth.' The disembodied voice emerged into the light, half a head shorter than the other, but with the same aesthetic hair. All he lacked was a lily. And he was probably carrying that somewhere where the sun never shone.

'And George Cross,' Lestrade continued.

'I have that pleasure,' George said.

'Though not often,' sneered Holdsworth.

'May I see you gentlemen in private?'

'Oh, really!' Cross threw up his hands with the exasperation of the encumbered impresario and bellowed to the yellow-tighted oafs on stage, 'Take five minutes, gentlemen. And while you're taking them, you might learn to dance.'

He led the way through a maze of corridors, scraping past painted flats and flapping paint. At last they entered a dressing room with a single star. 'Well?' Cross snapped. 'As you see, we are very busy men – at least, I am.'

'Gentlemen,' Lestrade said when the door was closed, 'it is not normally my custom to interview two murder suspects simultaneously . . .' and he waited for the strangled cries to reach fever pitch until a raised hand quieted them. Such was the long arm of the law.

'Murder?' Cross challenged him.

Lestrade nodded. 'Of Miss Verity True,' he said.

They looked at each other. Suddenly, Holdsworth lashed out

with a powerful right leg and Cross pranced away out of reach, up on the points of his toes. Lestrade, not quite ready for the *alongée*, was still standing there when a shin caught him in the place earmarked by the mop minutes earlier.

'You swine!' Cross hissed at his partner in mime.

'Beast!' Holdsworth countered.

'Do I assume,' Lestrade squeaked, stepping a little less than manfully between them, 'that you believe each other guilty of her murder?'

'Of course.' Holdsworth tossed his lion's mane and reached in his long coat for a cigarette holder, then a cigarette. 'You see, Constable, Very was about to accept my hand in marriage.'

'Yes,' Cross hissed, 'it was the rest of you she couldn't stand.'

'That's what made George so unnaturally jealous.' Holdsworth ignored him. 'Not only has my talent as a dancer and choreographer eclipsed his, but I had also won Very's heart.'

'I expect you cut it out, you degenerate,' Cross countered. 'You'll be charging him, of course, Sergeant?'

'All in good time,' said Lestrade, finding odd comfort in the stock police phrase now and again. 'Perhaps we could all sit down, gentlemen. I'm not the man I was when I came in here,' and he breathed a sigh of relief when the lethal legs on both sides of him crossed over their respective knees and came to a stop. 'Now,' he said, 'Mr Cross, when did you see Miss True last?'

'Wednesday,' Cross said. 'We both did.'

'That's right,' Holdsworth said. 'Except of course that George saw her at least once more.'

'Oh?' Cross and Lestrade chorused.

'Of course.' Holdsworth blew elegant smoke rings from his cigarette. 'When he killed her.'

'That's an outrageous slur,' Cross sneered.

'You're the outrageous slur,' Holdsworth told him. 'A blot on the scutcheon of ballet.'

'How long have you gentlemen known Miss True?' Lestrade broke in lest the pair resort again to footicuffs.

'I met her last year,' Cross said, 'April. Over a year ago. She came backstage to congratulate me on my *pas de deux*.'

'Why is one of the unanswered questions of our time,'

Holdsworth bridled. 'It was actually *my* arabesque she admired – it was the talk of the town.'

Cross snorted. 'Let's face it, Clarence, that little lad we saw in Russia last year has more poise than you, that lad Nijinski.'

'Ah, yes,' Holdsworth remembered. 'He had the legs of a racehorse.'

'Well, there you are, Inspector.' Cross snapped his fingers. 'I knew it. Little boys and their legs are about the summit of Clarence's sexual experience. He is secretly a misogynist.'

Lestrade had not expected the Masonic connection. But then no one ever did.

'Rubbish!' Holdsworth sneered.

'Fact!' snarled Cross. 'The only reason you feigned interest in Very at all was so that people wouldn't talk about you . . . though who would wish to talk about *you* I can't imagine.'

'You'll take that back!' Holdsworth was on his feet.

'Come any nearer and I'll scratch your eyes out!' Cross assured him.

'Gentlemen, please, please!' Lestrade was the only one still sitting. 'A woman is dead. Could we have a little decor, please?' But his reasoned words were drowned by the flutter of dancers' feet leaving the floor, and two flying drop kicks aimed by Cross at Holdsworth and Holdsworth at Cross fell a little short. And they felled Lestrade.

'Playing cricket?' An incredulous Assistant Commissioner Frost recovered the use of his lower jaw.

Chief Inspector Abberline nodded with evident satisfaction. 'He then managed to get himself knocked out – that must be unique in the anals of the game, I would have thought.'

'Hardly unique to Lestrade, though,' Frost grumbled. 'About par for the course for him I'd say – or is that a different game?'

Abberline consulted his notepad. 'We then have the complaints from Camberwell Branch Library.'

Frost hid his chubby face with his chubby hands. 'I don't think I want to hear this. How overdue was he?'

'For suspension you mean, sir?'

'Let's get one thing straight, Abberline. *I'll* decide on matters regarding suspension. Clear?'

'As a bell, sir,' the Chief Inspector said. 'No, it was a little more serious than that. First, he made an improper suggestion to an unmarried librarian lady, a Miss Dalrymple. Then he took another one from her place of work into a back room and was seen to catch her as she fell into his arms and he loosened her clothing.'

Frost grimaced. 'This complaint came from the young lady herself?'

'No, from the Chief Librarian, a man called Hathersuch or Hoversuch – Sergeant Dixon wasn't sure.'

'He never is,' muttered Frost. 'It sounds to me as if this Hoversuch was a little miffed that the lady didn't collapse into his arms. And until we appoint policewomen to accompany detectives on forays like this, such bodily contacts are inevitable.'

'Policewomen?' Abberline's sidewhiskers twitched in horror.

'All right, I know, I know,' Frost said. 'Such things are beyond your ken. But believe me, the time will come. Don't you dare breathe a word of it to Miss Featherstonehaugh, though, or she'll be first in line to volunteer. Where is he now?'

'Lestrade? In hospital.'

'Hospital?'

'What I hadn't got to, sir, on page forty-three of my Lestrade Surveillance Report, is that we have complaints from two Maryannes who run some sort of dancing school. They both accuse him of accusing them of murder.'

'So why is Lestrade in hospital?'

'They both kicked him in the head. Unfortunately, Charing Cross say he'll recover.'

'Hmm.' Frost considered his options. 'This could be the answer to an Assistant Commissioner's prayer,' he said. 'Compassionate leave. Thank you, Chief Inspector.'

'Sir,' Abberline folded away the notepad, 'may I come off this surveillance now? Events in Penge are hotting up.'

'Oh, very well. But I'm not giving you much longer on that bus business, Abberline. Your flasher hasn't struck for a while, has he?'

'I believe not, sir, but flashers are like buses themselves – there'll always be another one along in a minute.'

*   *   *

For the second time on this case, Lestrade gave an audience from a bed. True, he got some funny looks from a man with a hacking cough to his left and some wheezes from another to his right, but all was relatively discreet after Constable Russell had the presence of mind to draw a screen over the proceedings.

'Well done, lad,' Lestrade said, the new bandage swathed in place of the old one. 'I wondered when somebody would think of that. Well, Walter, touched though I am by your concern for my well-being, I can't help inclining that you have something to tell me.'

'Right, guv.' Dew finished the last of the grapes he'd brought the Inspector. 'It's this.'

He handed Lestrade a letter. The Inspector read it. 'Where did this come from?' he asked.

'Postmarked Bermondsey, guv,' Dew told him.

'Three o'clock yesterday.' Lestrade could read envelopes too. 'Addressed to the Yard.'

'To Whom It May Concern,' Dew quoted.

'To whom indeed. All right, Bromley, let's see what eighty-odd years on the Essex Force have taught you. Give me your views on the character of this anonymous letter – and don't let me see your lips moving as you read.'

Bromley did his best. But, in fact, the expert on Essex horse troughs was out of his depth. 'Er . . .'

'Well, thank you, Bromley. Russell?'

The younger rookie took over. He was as incisive on these matters as his older colleague.

'Disappointing,' Lestrade told him. 'Still, graphology is not an easy art. Dew, tell them.'

'Well, sir,' the old hand shifted uncomfortably, 'written by a . . . pen?'

Lestrade closed his eyes. For seven years this man had served his apprenticeship with the World's Second Greatest Detective, in the most famous police station in the Northern Hemisphere. 'Very good, Walter,' he said. 'It's this sort of blistering brilliance which allows the editors of *Punch*, not to mention Drs Conan Doyle and Watson, to poke fun at us. Listen, children, while a grown-up is speaking . . .' He checked the letter again and cleared his throat. 'First, notice the arches of the arcade letters

– the "m" and the "n" – they tell us the writer was a woman. Next, the loops on the "g" – she's about fifty years old. This at the bottom – 'Guess Who' in loo of a signature; the hallmark of the exhibitionist.'

'Why?' Bromley had the temerity to ask.

'Because I say so, Constable,' Lestrade told him. 'The cross on the "t" is a give-away – middle class, definitely. Almost certainly Church of England. Probably born near Uttoxeter.'

'Where's that?' Bromley asked.

Lestrade turned to the man as far as his hopelessly ricked neck would allow. 'When I find her, I'll ask her,' he snarled. 'Now, as subtly as you can, gentlemen, pick up these screens around me and we'll sidle to the door. Dew, you brought the change of clothing?'

'Yes, guv. In the station wagon outside.'

'Good man. Last one back at the Yard buys the Bath Olivers.'

George Dixon had been the Desk man at the Yard for as long as he – or Lestrade – could remember. He was the acceptable face of the police: gnarled, wrinkled and grey, like an old oak. But he was solid and honest and patient and kind, like policemen were in the old days, before they asked them to think. Like Walter Dew's tea, Sergeant Dixon's cocoa was legendary. And he'd made some now, hot day though it was in the middle of May.

'Just think of it, miss,' he was saying. 'Dr Grace is forty-seven and he scored two hundred and eighty-eight against Somerset yesterday. Makes your googies wither, don't it?'

'How long have you been on the Force, Sergeant?' she asked him.

'Ooh, now you've asked me, miss,' the old man twinkled. 'Let's just say, when I joined first we still wore stovepipe hats and carried rattles. I forget who was on the throne – prob'ly 'Er Majesty, same as now. She's a wonder an' all, ain't she? Must be over a 'undred. Well over a 'undred.'

'Sergeant!'

Lestrade's dulcet tones had the Desk man standing to attention, staring straight ahead. 'Morning sir.'

'Nothing better to do?'

'I was waiting for you, Inspector,' the lady said. 'The Sergeant was kind enough to keep me company.'

'Miss True.' Lestrade couldn't help smiling. For all his dour exterior, he was secretly pleased to see her. 'What can I do for you?'

'I've come to help,' she said.

'Help?' he repeated.

Bromley and Russell exchanged glances. Dew flashed a knowing wink at Dixon.

'I behaved disgracefully the other day,' she said, 'fainting like that. But I'm over it now and I'm here to offer my services.'

'You're not one of these New Women, are you, Trottie?' he chuckled.

'Ah,' she laughed, 'one of those who dress like men, talk like men, live like men and don't like men? No, no, Sholto. I promise I won't get in your way.'

'Indeed you won't,' he led her to the door, 'because you won't get the chance.'

She pirouetted around him. 'I'm not going,' she said, 'so you may as well get used to me being around.'

Lestrade looked at her. In the background he caught the expectant faces of Dew, Dixon and the rookies. Detectives going off or coming on duty also gave him funny looks. He closed to his woman. 'Murder is not a pleasant business, Trottie. It's not a woman's place.'

'It wasn't my sister's place, either,' she said, 'to die at the hands of a madman, but she did. Now I don't know much about murder, Sholto, but I know a lot about her. I think you need me on this case. I think you need me desperately.'

He stood dithering in the hallway, for a moment uncertain, unglued. Then he acted. 'All right,' he said. 'Come with me. Dew, you and Russell and Bromley will get me addresses on the owners of the Metropolitan and District and City and South London Railways. You will visit them and get their views on all this. Assure them the usual; no stone unturned, full manpower, arrest imminent, etcetera, etcetera.'

'Where will you be, sir?' Dew asked.

Lestrade paused at the entrance to the lift. 'The usual, Dew – in the thick of it.'

*   *   *

It was on the fourth floor that Lestrade and Trottie True found him – in an annexe that ran transwise towards Whitehall. He was of an indeterminate age but probably the wrong side of sixty, and his spectacles appeared to have been made from the bottoms of porter bottles.

'Good God, is that a woman?' he said.

'Indeed it is, Stanley. I was just telling Miss True, Stanley, how erudite and sharp you are. You've just confirmed that admirably.'

'Well, come in, come in.'

Trottie True had never seen such a laboratory in her life. The regulation green tiles were all but hidden by shelves which bowed in the middle like a one-string fiddle and contained jars of things she'd rather not inquire too closely about.

'This is the Police Museum,' Lestrade told her. 'People nowadays seem to be calling it the Black Museum, though I don't believe you have any negroes here, Stanley, am I right?'

'Not unless you count Wesley Levine, the Chocolate-Coloured Coon,' the boffin said. 'That's his death mask over there – the one with the funny lip.'

'Corkindale?' Lestrade cocked an apprehensive eyebrow.

'Accident of birth. That's what hanged him of course. Even under that make-up, a witness recognized his lip. Is this a social visit, miss? We don't get many women – visitors that is. There are a few residents, as it were. That's Mrs Pearcey's perambulator in the corner, the one she wheeled the dismembered Mrs Hogg and her equally dismembered baby round in. And this,' he handled it lovingly, 'is the rope used on Mary Ann Cotton the poisoner.'

Trottie True turned to Sholto Lestrade. 'If this is designed to frighten me,' she said, 'it's failed.'

Lestrade held up his hands. 'Nothing of the kind entered my head,' he smiled. 'Welcome to the world of homicide. No, Stanley,' Lestrade pulled up a chair, 'this is not a social visit – but let's have a few niceties anyway – how is Mrs Stanley?'

'Comatose at breakfast, but then what do you expect from a social worker? How's that little boy of yours, the one young Harry Bandicoot adopted?'

'Girl – and she's fine, thanks. Leaks a bit.'

'Ah, they all do.'

'Right.' Lestrade fished in his pocket. 'That's all that over with. What do you make of this?'

The boffin lifted his glasses on to the top of his head and read the letter. 'Friedrich Schiess is the one you want. I seen him on the Tube the other night near where that woman was killed. He done it or my name's not . . . Guess Who?'

'Well?' Lestrade said.

'Well . . .' Stanley held the paper to the light of a table lamp. 'Common enough paper. Writing slopes to the right, which indicates honesty, but there's a reluctance here. Whoever wrote this didn't really want to, yet felt it his duty.'

'His?' Lestrade was nonplussed.

'Oh yes,' said the boffin. 'The writer is definitely a man – the arcade letters of the "m" and "n" tell us that. He's fortyish.'

'Er . . . are you sure?'

'I said "ish", Lestrade,' Stanley reminded him.

'Can you tell us anything else?'

'Our man has a damaged right arm. He wrote this with his left.'

'Really? He's from Uttoxeter, though?'

'Edmonton,' Stanley corrected him. He sniffed the letter. 'And he works with horses. His wife's called Emma, he's five feet nine inches with brown hair and brown eyes. No, wait a minute. I tell a lie – hazel eyes.'

Trottie True and Sholto Lestrade sat open-mouthed.

'You can tell all that from those few words?' she asked.

'Come off it, Stanley,' Lestrade sneered. 'You know something we don't.'

'An awful lot, Lestrade,' the boffin smiled. 'But in this particular case, yes, you're right. I must come clean. One of my little hobbies is collecting signatures of famous people.'

'Would you like mine?' Lestrade asked.

Stanley ignored him. 'I've got Napoleon's here somewhere and Frederick the Great's. King John's from Magna Carta should be somewhere too . . .'

'I thought King John *sealed* Magna Carta, Mr Stanley,' Trottie True said.

'Ah, my dear,' and he patted her hand, 'how nice to find an astute person on the distaff side. You're absolutely right, of course. It's actually a rather clumsy forgery of Lord Macaulay's. Ah, here we are.' He handed a piece of paper to Lestrade.

'A clumsy forgery of Lord Macaulay's?'

'No,' Stanley tutted, in the wrong job of course to escape the suffering of fools gladly. 'The actual signature of one Frederick Hitch, VC, late twenty-fourth Foot, now the South Wales Borderers. Notice the capital H – as in "Guess Who".'

'Yes, you're right.' Lestrade compared them. 'A dashed odd way to spell "Who". Stanley, you've got a mind like a knife blade.'

The boffin bowed. 'Photographic memory, that's all,' he said. 'But it keeps me off the streets.'

'What do you know about this Schiess?' Lestrade asked.

Stanley shrugged. 'Not famous enough for me, I'm afraid. I suggest you ask Private Hitch.'

'I will.' Lestrade ushered Miss True to the door. 'I don't suppose you have an address?' he asked and moved nimbly aside as the boffin threw a book at him.

'You're supposed to be the bloody policeman!' they heard him call as they bustled away down the corridor and into the sunshine of Whitehall.

'This could be dangerous, Trottie,' Lestrade said, checking the brass knuckles in his pocket just in case. 'I've no idea what this man is about.'

'He's about an inch taller than you, Sholto. And you've had police training.'

'Yes, but he's faced four thousand Zulus on a bad day.'

'Has he?'

He looked at her oddly. 'It's obviously before your time,' he said. 'The defence of Rorke's Drift, Natal. That's Africa.'

'I know,' she said. 'I *am* a librarian, albeit part-time.'

'Sorry.' He peered again round the corner.

'Eleven Victoria Crosses awarded in one day to the garrison of the mission hospital for valour against a Zulu Army led by King Cetawayo whose impis had destroyed their regiment at Isandlwana the day before.'

'Er . . . quite,' he said. 'Fred Hitch was one of the eleven.'

'What do you see?'

He poked out the remnant of his nose beyond the brick wall. Before him lay a deserted Edmonton Street, dumb in the afternoon heat. Flies droned lazily around the hansom horse, which occasionally responded with a deft flick of its tail. But these were the first flies of the season, brought out by the unseasonable heat and they were too fast for it, darting from its back to its ears and then to investigate the feed sack roped over his nose.

'Leave this to me,' he told her, but as he glanced back, she had gone, marching past him defiantly, out into the street.

'Trottie!' he hissed, but whether she heard or not made no difference, because she didn't look back.

'Why have you been writing anonymous letters to Scotland Yard?' he heard her ask of the cabman lolling against the lamppost.

'Who says I have?' He stood up to his full five feet nine.

'A very clever man at the Yard named Stanley.'

'Well, he's a liar,' the cabman said.

By this time, Lestrade had caught up with the pair, dashing along the street for all he was worth. 'Frederick Hitch?' he asked.

'Who wants to know?' the cabman rejoined.

'My name is Inspector Lestrade, Scotland Yard.'

'Oh.'

'In pursuance of my . . . colleague's question: why *have* you been writing letters to Scotland Yard – or at least, the one?'

'What makes you think it was me?' the cabman asked.

Lestrade stood nose to nose with the man. 'Are you or are you not Frederick Hitch?' he said.

'What if I am?'

'Why is it,' Lestrade said levelly, 'that the working classes always answer a question with a question?'

'All right, I'm Hitch,' the cabman said. 'What of it?'

'You tell us, Mr Hitch,' Lestrade said. 'I assume you didn't write this for laughs?' He held up the letter.

'Look, it's Schiess you want, not me. I didn't want to write in the first place. I knew I shouldn't of. But my Emma – that's my trouble and strife – she made me, see.'

Lestrade moved aside lest Hitch's horse took it into its head to empty its bowels. As a young constable he'd ridden, for want of a better word, with the Horse Patrol. It was not an experience he cared to repeat. 'All right,' he said. 'Tell us what you know.'

''Ere,' Hitch frowned under his billycock. ''Ow long 'ave you 'ad donnas on the beat, then?'

'It's an experiment,' Lestrade lied. 'And this is Policewoman Jenkins, not a donna.'

'Oh, pardon me for livin'.' Hitch tugged at the rim of his hat. 'Look, guv, I ain't no squealer, 'onest. Only I was on the Tube the night o' that last murder.'

'Of Miss Verity True?' Trottie asked.

'Yeah, that was 'er name. You could 'ave bowled me over wiv a cabwheel, so you could. There was Schiess, large as life.'

'Why did that strike you as peculiar?'

'Well, for one thing, 'e was a City and Sarf London guards-man.'

'Was he now?'

''E was, right down to 'is buttons. The second fing is . . . what a bloody coincidence – oh, beggin' your pardon, Policewoman.'

'Why coincidence?' Lestrade asked.

'Well the last time I seen 'im, it was at Rorke's Drift an' 'e was killin' them Zulus like it was goin' out of fashion.'

'You didn't know he'd settled in London?'

'Nah. A lot of blokes fought 'e was Dutch. In fact it turns out 'e was a Swiss.'

'I see. Where and when did you see him?'

'Comin' off of locomotive Number Eleven at Stockwell. This would of been near midnight.'

'What were you doing at Stockwell? You live here in Edmonton.'

'Visitin',' Hitch told the real and imaginary policepersons. 'A few of us old sojers meet up on Fursday nights for a 'and of gin. We rotates it. It was old Dobbie's turn this week.'

'And old Dobbie lives in Stockwell?'

'Right enough,' Hitch confirmed.

'What did Schiess say when you hailed him?'

'Well, that's just it,' Hitch said. ''E looked right frough me. Like I was a ghost or sunfink. Mind you, 'e'd aged a bit.'

'He had?'

'Well, yeh. 'Im and me, we was of an age, see. Bofe of us born in 1856. That makes us bofe thirty-nine. 'E looked sixty.'

'How do you explain that?'

'Dunno,' Hitch shrugged. 'Course, Schiess 'ad been brought up in an orphanage – that couldn't of helped. 'E was a sojer at fifteen. I 'eard 'e'd fell on hard times.'

'How?'

'Oh, you know, on the old grapevine.'

'When did you discover there'd been a murder?' Lestrade asked.

'It was in the *Stannit* the next day. My trouble Emma puts two and two together and she says, "Fred, that was when you saw Corporal Schiess. 'E must of done it."'

'Why must he of . . . have?'

'Stands to reason, don't it? 'E come off the very carriage in what they found her in. It's too much of a coincidence. I didn't want to shop an ol' messmate, especially one wot's stood by yer elbow against farsands o' darkies. But you don't know my trouble. So I sent the letter anonymous, like. 'Ow did you blokes – beggin' yer pardon, Policewoman – find it was me?'

'We have our ways,' Lestrade said cryptically. 'You will talk to no one else about this, Mr Hitch. If we need to talk to you again, can we find you here?'

"Ere or out on the road,' he said.

'Thank you,' and Lestrade held out his hand.

The cabman offered his left and Lestrade had to change hands accordingly. To a casual passer-by, it looked as though it were a meeting of Masons from the Edmonton Lodge.

'Arm still giving you trouble?' the Inspector asked.

'Yeah,' Hitch winced. 'Those Zulu buggers got some Lee-Enfields orff our blokes at Sandawhana. I copped a bullet. Some days it's bloody murder, I can tell you.'

'Yes,' said Lestrade, leading Trottie True away. 'I know exactly what you mean.'

6

That was the night that Goron arrived. He caught a packet at Le Havre and the Pullman out of Portsmouth. Like another famous Frenchman (who wasn't quite) he found his Waterloo and crossed the bridge to the Yard.

A rather wary Sergeant Dixon let him up, but as soon as he was in the lift, lifted the speaking tube down from the wall to inform the guv'nor.

'There's a Frog on 'is way up, sir. Thought I ought to warn you. Forearmed is forewarned, isn't it?'

'Probably, Dixon,' the tube crackled back at him after much blowing and scraping.

'Right, sir. Mind 'ow 'e goes, won't you? Only I 'aven't forgiven 'em for the Peninsular War yet. My ol' grandad lost his right leg in Badajaoz's breeches, you know.'

'Fascinating,' said the tube and hung up.

Goron was Head of the Sûreté. He had the mind of a thesaurus or some other ancient lizard, the memory of an elephant and the little pocket pistol which was the one he claimed killed Abraham Lincoln. In his headquarters in the Rue des Saussaies he had a little suite of rooms known affectionately by all as his cookshop. There were no windows in the cookshop and the walls were very thick. It was rumoured that they were painted crimson so that the blood did not show and many was the silent scream that failed to puncture the Parisian night when M. Goron was asking the questions.

'Le Strade.' The Frenchman held out his arms and hugged the Inspector violently.

'I thought for a moment you were going to kiss my cheeks, Goron,' Lestrade said.

The Frenchman frowned. 'What do you zink I am – une Marie-Anne?' he said. "Ow long 'as it bin?'

'Since the poisoned breakfast at the Grand? Four years.'

'Ah.' The Frenchman turfed Dew out of the only other comfortable chair and threw himself into it. 'I am still, 'ow you say, a little *comme ci, comme ça* about ze full English breakfast since zat day. Ze other man who collapsed choking wiz me – Monsieur Bain de Coute – 'e is well?'

'Very,' said Lestrade. 'Married now with two boys.'

'*Bien,*' nodded Goron. He leaned forward suddenly, earnest, humble. 'I was sorry to 'ear about Madame Le Strade, Le Strade.'

'Thank you, Goron,' the Inspector said. 'Walter, a cup of your best Darjeeling for the Head of the Sûreté.'

'Sûreté.' Goron felt compelled to correct the man's lamentable pronunciation.

'Now,' Lestrade leant back in his chair, 'what brings the great Goron to the Yard at this hour? In a few minutes you'll have the pleasure of watching Constable Bromley turn into a pumpkin.'

Goron fumbled in his waistcoat pocket. "Ave you seen zis man?' he asked. Lestrade took the artist's impression.

'This man has orange hair?' Lestrade thought it best to double-check.

'Damn Toulouse-Lautrec!' snapped Goron. 'I said to 'im, "Henri," I said, "just ze basics, never mind all zat *merde* zat wows zem in Montmartre."'

'Well,' Lestrade tilted the likeness to the light, 'he is a *little* familiar. It's not the Prince of Wales, is it?'

Goron shook his head.

'Sarah Bernhardt?'

Clearly Lestrade was getting colder.

"E goes by several aliases or *noms d'autres*,' Goron said, 'Pierre La Touche, Henri Chauvon, the Abbé Fiennes, the Comte de la Warre. I of course know 'im as the Monster of Montparnasse.'

'The Comte de la Warre?' Lestrade repeated.

'Ah,' Goron beamed, 'ze ringing of ze little grey bells. You know zis man?'

Lestrade looked at the picture again. Clearly Mr Toulouse Lautrec had been given too much licence. 'I did interview a man calling himself that,' the Inspector said. 'The likeness is not great.'

'Pah,' Goron dismissed the artist's work. 'What do you expect from a man who does not often reach women's navels. 'E is always selling 'imself short. I am all *oreilles*.'

Lestrade had never doubted it. Dew arrived with the finest bevy in the world and waited with pride while the World's Greatest French Detective partook of the same. He wasn't quite prepared for the grimace from Goron, but he'd faced worse disappointment in his life.

'Why is it', Goron asked through gritted teeth, 'zat over zere,' and he pointed vaguely in the direction of Paris, 'all is *la belle époque* and over 'ere . . . zis? Ze pee of ze gnat. Never mind, M. Dieu, a brave effort, *n'est-ce pas*? As we say at the Sûreté, back to ze drawing-board. Now, Le Strade, de la Warre?'

And Lestrade told him the tale of the skeleton crew at Earls Court and the curiously rough riders of Colonel Cody's circus.

'What has he done, this Monster of Montparnasse?' the Inspector asked when he had finished.

'What 'as 'e not done, *mon vieux*,' Goron said unwrapping an expensive foreign cigar.

'Walter!' Lestrade snapped his fingers. 'Monsieur Goron's cigar. Look sharp, man!'

Dew looked as sharp as he could, but in the event it was young Russell who struck a light.

''E is a rapist,' Goron said. For a split second, Lestrade flashed an unbelieving glance at Russell, but then realized that the Frenchman was talking about de la Warre. It had been a long night. And the chimes of midnight had yet to strike.

'I want to talk to 'im in connection wiz eight unsolved rapes in and around ze Montparnasse district of Paris within ze last year. I nearly 'ad 'im zere, but 'e got away from one of my lads and took a ship from Dieppe. We lost 'im zere, but I 'ave reason to believe 'e was seen in ze London area.'

'This is very interesting, Goron,' Lestrade said. 'You see, the lady of whom I spoke, Jane Hollander, is one of four such women who have died on the Underground since February. You don't have an Underground in Paris, do you?'

'*Non*,' said Goron, 'because ze boulevards of Paris are so wide, we do not need zem. But it is only a matter of time, I fear. 'Aussmann 'as a lot to answer for.'

'Let me pick your brains, Goron,' Lestrade said, helping himself to the Frenchman's tea having finished his own. 'Like our own Metropolitan trains, we're going round in circles on this one.'

'If ze astonishing intellect of Goron can be of service, Le Strade,' said the unassuming Head of the Sûreté, 'it is at your disposal. Fire away.'

'Tell him, Russell,' Lestrade commanded. 'Murder One.'

'Sarah Culdrose,' Russell said, wandering, if that was the right term in an office converted from a lavatory, before the wall chart of the Underground killings, 'wife of George Culdrose, still on remand at Wormwood Scrubs Prison.'

'Yes, we'd better get him out,' Lestrade said, 'before Mr

Marshall Hall brings an action for wrongful arrest. That's your job first thing next week, Dew. Get the necessary paperwork from Abberline, will you? He's finished following me around now I think. Unless my memory serves me awry, you'll find him at Number Forty-eight Fitzloosely Street, Penge, the home of one Mrs Cadogan, a divorcée of unusual accomplishments picked up by her when she was a bareback rider at Charlie Hengler's Circus. Well, go on, Russell; we're waiting.'

'Er . . . right, sir. Mrs Culdrose was found strangled in a railway carriage at Liverpool Street station in the early hours of 14 February.'

'Ah,' smiled Goron, ever the romantic, 'the Day of St Valentin, n'est-ce pas?'

'The motive was not robbery, because her purse was untouched. Her clothing was in disarray but there was no sign of forced entry.'

'Does that fit the modish operandus of your man, Goron?' Lestrade asked.

'Non,' the Frenchman said, 'the Monster effects entry but 'e does not kill. At least 'e didn't in Montparnasse. Still, doing it on a moving train demands timing and precision. I am not sure zat even ze great Goron could do it . . .' He thought for a moment. "Ow long between stations?'

'Four, five minutes,' Lestrade said.

'It is a possibilité,' Goron said. 'In ze 'eady days of my youth, I made love three times between Survilliers and ze Gare du Nord.'

'How far is that?' Lestrade was astonished.

'Seven, perhaps eight kilometres,' Goron said.

Lestrade was even more astonished. Dew, the upright family man, was appalled. Somehow he knew that the object of his affections was not Madame Goron.

'Go on, Russell,' Lestrade said.

'L Division passed the case over to the Yard and Chief Inspector Abberline arrested the husband.'

'Ah,' Goron shook his head, 'la Cour Ecosse is not what it was.'

'Abberline never has been,' Lestrade told him, unprofessionally. 'Russell?'

'Well, that's about it, sir.'

118

'Excellent, lad. You'll go far. All right, Bromley,' the Inspector turned his attention to the other rookie, 'as someone who won't; we'll pass on Mrs Hollander. I've just told Monsieur Goron about her. Now you can give us your words of wisdom on Emily Bellamy.'

'Murder Three,' said Bromley, flashing out his middle finger in the tired old Essex tradition. 'Miss Emily Bellamy, a spinster lady of twenty-five. Found strangled in a carriage on the City and South London at Elephant and Castle on Thursday last. Again, robbery doesn't seem to have been the motive and there was no actual evidence of how's your father.'

'*Comment*?' Goron broke in. "Ow is your father?'

'It's an expression, Goron,' Lestrade said, 'rather a meaningless one in fact.' He flashed a withering glance at Bromley. 'Note the change of track, Monsieur – the first two women died on the Metropolitan line, the third on the City and South London.'

'What is ze significance of zis?' Goron asked.

'Er . . . quite,' said Lestrade. 'We'll get to theories later. Get on with it, Bromley. Monsieur Goron is waiting.'

'She lived in the Walworth Road and our inquiries there have turned up nothing. She seems to have been a very ordinary young woman who loved cricket and collected fire-irons.'

'Such a woman is ordinary?' Goron asked.

'This side of the Channel, yes,' Lestrade assured him. 'Is that it, Bromley?'

'At the moment sir, yes.'

'Right. Walter. Verity True.'

'About Miss Agnes True, sir . . .' Dew's Puritan instincts obliged him to bring up the subject.

'What about her?' Lestrade asked quickly.

'Well, she's sleeping on the couch in what was Public Carriages, sir.'

'Yes, Walter, now tell me something I don't know.'

'But . . . well, it's not for me to say, sir.' Dew clammed up.

'Correct,' Lestrade told him, but he sensed that the eyes of four policemen looked to him for some sort of explanation. 'Miss True is the sister of the dead woman, Murder Four, Goron,' he said. 'She is of a highly nervous disposition and is determined to track down her sister's murderer herself. Rather than have that, I decided to keep an eye on her.'

'Ah,' smiled Goron, 'she is a cracker, zis Miss True?'

'I've no idea,' Lestrade lied.

'Monsieur Russell?' Goron fixed the young man with his cold, grey eyes.

'Rather, sir,' he admitted.

'Well, I'd never noticed,' Lestrade insisted.

'It is a commonplace at the Sûreté.' Goron finished his cigar. 'I often 'ave several young ladies 'elping me wiz my inquiries. Especially after a 'eavy day. Of course, if Madame Goron ever found out . . . *Merde*! It does not bear thinking about.'

'The deceased had no enemies that we know of,' Dew said, attempting to keep the Rabelaisian detective on the straight and narrow. 'She was prone to good works.'

'Ah,' Goron said, 'you mean she 'elped ze working classes?'

'Yes sir,' said Dew.

'Zere you are – it is one of zem.'

'Zem?' repeated Lestrade. He ever valued the Frenchman's expertise.

'What we used to call in my country ze *sans-culottes*, ze *va-nu-pieds*, ze Fronde. Zey are ze great unwashed, Le Strade – ze shirking classes. Anarchists, Socialists, Bohemians, Jews, members of ze Académie Française – I trust zem as far as I could throw zem. Zey are an ungrateful lot. Didn't your Mr Disraeli give zem ze right to picket recently?'

Disraeli had been dead for fourteen years, but Lestrade could not fail to be impressed by Goron's grasp of once-current affairs.

'What zat Jewboy did not know was zat it never gets better if you picket. Take my word for it, Le Strade. Your man is an ingrate of ze working classes.'

'You mean – the real target was Verity True and all the others merely a blind.'

'But of course.' Goron produced a second cigar. 'Delve deeper into zis Verity True,' he advised. 'Someone close to her is your man. Or woman . . .'

'Woman?' the English policemen chorused.

'What do you know about zis Agnes True?' Goron asked.

All eyes turned to Lestrade.

'Er . . . nothing much,' he said. 'She works part time as a librarian in Camberwell. She's a very determined lady. Er . . . that's about it.'

'Zere you have it,' Goron said.

'What?' Lestrade asked, not unreasonably in the circumstances.

'Did I never tell you about Chantal LeClerc, the demon librarian of St Germain-en-Laye?'

'Never,' yawned Lestrade as Big Ben told the otherwise sleeping city that it was Tuesday already.

'I was a very young coppaire,' Goron said, 'green as ze Bois de Boulogne. Chantal LeClerc killed thirteen people in ze St Germain district before we brought ze librarian to book – zat is a French policeman's joke, by ze way.'

Nobody had laughed at it in France either.

'How did she kill them?' Lestrade asked.

'Prussic acid,' said Goron. 'Not only a murderer, but an unpatriotic one. You know 'ow we French feel about ze Bosch?'

'Poison,' said Lestrade.

'*Mais oui*,' said Goron.

'Not strangulation?'

'*Non.*' Goron was patience itself. 'I 'ave said, Prussic acid.'

'My point,' said Lestrade, 'is that poison is the traditional murderess's weapon. It is relatively easy to administer and the time factor means that the murderess herself can be miles away from the death scene, thereby not only giving herself a perfect alibi but avoiding anything messy.'

'Zo?'

'So strangulation is altogether more brutish, nasty and short,' Lestrade explained.

'*Non, non, non,* ze method is of secondary importance, *mon vieux*,' the Frenchman said. 'Consider ze life of a librarian. Hours wiz nothing to do but *read*. To pick up all kinds of dangerous and unhealthy ideas – Voltaire, Rousseau, Descartes – perverts all – and have nothing to do wiz zose ideas but to plot. Zen zere is ze strain.'

'The strain?'

'Zis is ze age of ze strain, Le Strade,' Goron told him. 'Can you imagine going through your professional life allowed only to whisper? You long to scream, but you may not. You are, as a great Frenchman once said, "Cabin'd, cribb'd, confined." Zat was ze motive of Mademoiselle LeClerc – 'er carefully concocted cocoa was her scream of revenge. 'Er *cri de coeur*.'

'What happened to her?' asked Lestrade.

'She 'ad a rendezvous wiz death,' Goron said. 'A meeting wiz Madame Guillotine. Now, I suppose, she is in zat great library in ze sky.'

'A moment ago you said it was one of the working classes,' Lestrade observed. 'Now you appear to be fingering Miss Agnes True.'

'We 'ave a saying at the Sûreté,' Goron said. 'Leave no stone unturned. Keep your options – and your bowels – open. I am merely offering zuggestions, Le Strade. After all, I am not in full possession of the facts.'

'Are any of us?' sighed Lestrade. 'All right, Dew – Theory One.'

Dew cleared his throat of Darjeeling. 'Theory One,' he said, 'is as Monsieur Goron has indicated – one murder cloaked by four.'

'Problems with that, gentlemen?' Lestrade asked.

'Er . . . the risk, sir.'

'Excellent, Russell. Go on.'

'Four times the murders; four times the risk.'

'That's right,' said Lestrade. 'The mad mathematician's equation.'

'If your man is mad,' said Goron, 'ze risk will not bother 'im. Ze impulse to kill knows no boundaries. Crime knows no frontiers – which is why I am 'ere.'

'Theory Two,' Lestrade said. 'Bromley.'

'Er . . . there's a maniac loose. A random killer of women.'

'What do we know about him?' Lestrade asked, then flashed a glance Goron's way and added, for the sake of making the *entente* a little more *cordiale*, 'Or her?'

'Strong,' said Russell.

'Good boy,' said Lestrade.

'Crafty,' said Bromley.

'Obviously,' said Lestrade.

'Knows the Underground,' said Dew.

'Does he?' Lestrade asked. 'Or she?'

'Enough to kill at the end of the line, on the last train, when he knows he's not likely to get caught.'

'That will stop now that we're wise to that one,' Lestrade said. 'Both the Metropolitan and the City and South London have increased their guards and Superintendent Tomelty has drafted every available man on to that shift.'

'Even the Graffiti Squad?' Dew asked.

'Even the Graffiti Squad,' Lestrade said. 'A Constable McMurdo, the Railway Police's answer to vandalism. What that man can do with a bucket and mop would bring tears to your eyes, Goron.'

The Frenchman didn't doubt it.

'Theory Three,' said Lestrade. 'Dew?'

'Well, guv. It *was* Corporal Schiess.'

'Who?' Goron asked.

'Tell him, Walter.'

'Well, sir, we had an anonymous letter to the effect that a man had been seen getting off the very train aboard which Miss True died. The anonymous informant's name, it expires, was one Frederick Hitch – a war hero . . .'

'Thank you, Walter,' Lestrade interrupted.

'Hitch had won the VC for the defence of Rorke's Drift.'

'Yes, thank you, Walter.'

'In the Zulu War.'

'Oh my God,' muttered Lestrade, briefly burying his face in his hands.

Goron rose slowly to his feet. 'You mean you gave men ze VC for zat débâcle?'

'No, sir.' Dew stood his ground. 'For the defence of Rorke's Drift.'

'You are aware,' Goron stood level with the Constable's tie-knot, 'zat our great and glorious Prince Impérial was killed by ze cowardly and incompetent behaviour of a British officer whose name I will not soil my lips wiz?'

'Er . . .' Clearly this had come as a surprise to Dew.

'He is not aware, Goron,' Lestrade cut in. 'Diminished responsibility – that's what I'll do – diminish his responsibility. It's the water troughs for you, Dew,' the Inspector shouted, winking surreptitiously at his man. 'Now, get on with it. Monsieur Goron,' Lestrade whipped out a cigar, 'have one of mine.'

'Havana?' Goron wavered.

'Prince Willem's,' he answered.

Goron shook his head. 'Too Dutch,' he said. 'I'll stick to zese,' and he sat down and lit up another.

'Well,' Dew cleared his throat again, vaguely grateful that Goron had left it where it was, 'this Hitch fingered an old mate of his – Corporal Schiess.'

'And?' Goron blew smoke into the Constable's face.

'And we tracked him down.'

'Wiz what success?'

'None,' Dew admitted. 'He was dead.'

'Ah,' Goron nodded, 'zuicide.'

'Not quite that simple. All right, Walter. I'll take it from here. Don't look so glum. It turns out that Friedrich Schiess, known – sorry, Goron – as "Dutchie" to his friends – is actually Ferdinand Christian Schiess and was Swiss.'

Goron spat into the upturned boater lying beside the Remington.

'Er . . . quite,' smiled Lestrade.

'I'll just go and wipe your hat, sir,' Russell said.

'Thank you, my boy,' the Inspector said. 'He was born at Bergedorf on 7 April 1856 and fought for you chaps in the late war against Prussia.'

'Which we lost by a whisker because of treachery and double-dealing,' Goron explained.

Lestrade had always believed it was a combination of ruthless Hunnish efficiency, a massive superiority in railway lines, the firepower of the Dreyse needle-gun and the brilliance of Helmuth von Moltke, but he could have been wrong.

'Corporal Schiess served with Lonsdale's Horse and won the VC against the . . . enemy in the war to which Constable Dew so appallingly referred. He was a shy bloke by all accounts and worked in the telegraph office in Durban, South Africa. By 1884, however, he'd fallen on hard times and, unable to get the prison job on which he'd set his heart, emigrated. He took sick on board the *Serapis*, however, and died on 14 December of that year off that place . . . where was it, Walter? They make woollens there . . . you remember.'

'Angola, sir.'

'Yes, that's right.'

'Zo is zis man a *hareng rouge* – a red herring?'

'Yes and no.' Lestrade could be cryptic when the moment was right. 'We contacted the Twenty-fourth Foot as was, the South Wales Borderers as they are now, stationed at Brecon.'

'And?'

'And,' Lestrade drew a telegram from a bundle of papers at his elbow, 'this is from Captain Penn-Symons of that regiment – "I saw Corporal Schiess in November 1891 in Allahabad, India. He had been working in a jeweller's shop and was just going to Australia. Being afraid to lose his Victoria Cross, he has sent it on ahead by registered post to his destination."'

'From which you conclude?' Goron asked.

'Either,' Lestrade matched the Frenchman smoke ring for smoke ring, 'Captain Penn-Symons is an idiot who wouldn't know Corporal Schiess from his elbow *or* Corporal Schiess did not die aboard the *Serapis*, and could therefore be alive and well and living somewhere in London.'

'What would be his motive?'

Lestrade shrugged. 'Perhaps he's as mad as a snake. Perhaps he doesn't approve of unaccompanied women riding the Underground. Who knows? I'll tell you that when we've found him. I'd be happier if we knew what Corporal Schiess looks like.'

'Well,' chuckled Goron, 'don't ask Toulouse-Lautrec!'

'Because I have a feeling that one of us in this room knows what he looks like.'

'Oh?' They all looked at each other.

'Apparently,' Lestrade said, tapping Penn-Symons's telegram, 'Schiess spoke perfect English.'

'Zo?'

'So – where was he going from Allahabad?'

'Er . . . Australia.' Goron had been listening all the time.

'And where do you believe, Walter, did that man come from – the one claiming to be the fictitious Mr Bellamy?'

'Australia!' Dew clicked his fingers.

Lestrade stubbed out his cigar butt. 'The rest, Goron, is mystery. Tomorrow, Constables Russell and Bromley here will escort you with full powers of arrest to Earls Court. If we can find the Monster of Montparnasse, you can have him for breakfast.'

The Comte de la Warre, alias Pierre La Touche, Henri Chauvon and the Abbé Fiennes, had done, as the French say, a bunk. Goron was disappointed of course but consoled himself by jabbing Hauptmann Bruno in his vitals during the course of his inquiries. It happened so fast that neither Russell nor Bromley saw it, and when asked (by an examining magistrate) why he had done it, Goron explained that the man was German. Enough that may have been in the boulevards and under the bridges of Paris, but Englishmen with their eminent sense of fair play couldn't accept it. Goron was quite prepared to settle the matter on Hounslow Heath or Regent's Park or anywhere. Pistols, swords, medieval maces, he didn't have a preference. But the magistrate saw things differently and caused an international incident by arresting and imprisoning the Head of the Sûreté which only the Fashoda affair of three years later and the Eurovision Song Contest of another century would eclipse in terms of Anglo-French hostility.

It had been none of Lestrade's doing of course, but he, it transpired, had other problems.

She took the stairs for safety, keeping a tight grip on the handrail that spiralled to the right. All the way down, posters told her to use Pear's Soap and Nestlé's Milk and Senna's Laxative. The old advertisements gave her comfort as her heels clicked hollow on the metal treads until she reached the ground.

There was no one on the platform, but the clock told her it was 11.38. If she stood quite still she could see the huge metal hand move upwards, in uneven jerks, towards the Roman eight. Overhead the covered walkway along which she had just trudged boasted the fact that a Remington typewriter had a longer life than certain other typewriters, and another display asked her, rather rudely she thought, whether she had tried Allsopp's Pale Ale.

The gas lamps flickered green on the white letters of Charing Cross. The last train. Why had she left it this long? Why hadn't she taken up his gallant offer of a lift home? A cab would have been far more sensible. Still, the newspapers were just scaremongering, weren't they? It was obviously a ploy by Sabbatarians or somebody to keep women off the Underground. Well, it wouldn't work. This was 1895. Women could vote in municipal elections. Some of them followed their menfolk all over the Empire, climbed mountains, made their own cream teas. She wasn't going to be frightened by a lunatic who pounced on women travelling alone. But just in case, as the last locomotive slowed on the curve before the platform and she saw its yellow lights like eyes glowing in the dark, she remembered her mother's advice and jammed the blunt end of her hatpin between her lips. Let anybody come near her now and they'd be in for a surprise.

She tried to find a crowded compartment, a carriage with women, children. Perhaps a clergyman? Or even a policeman? But they were empty. The whole train was empty. Still, the carriages had a communication cord. The driver could stop on a sixpence, she'd heard. She'd be all right. She chose the end carriage. She opened the door and hauled up her skirts and climbed inside. Yes, the end carriage was the safest – the one with the guard.

They found her at four the next morning. As dawn crept over the Moorish façade of Blackfriars and the cleaner shuffled down the platform with his bucket and broom, she half fell out of the end carriage – the safe one with the guard. Her hair was unpinned and her bonnet had gone. Her blouse had been ripped open and her breasts were bare. Still clamped between the blue, bloated lips was a steel hatpin of fearsome dimensions. Her skirt was hitched up to her waist and her unmentionables had been ripped aside. Her hands were clawed, the nails embedded in the leather of the seats. But it was her eyes the cleaner would never forget. Before they retired him weeks later with the shakes and an inability to sleep, he had seen those eyes watching him every waking hour of his life. Eyes that spoke in silence of the terror they had seen. Of a nameless dread that stalked the Underground. Of a ghost that came in the night.

'Mr Wells?' The policeman stood silhouetted against the sun. 'Mr Herbert George Wells?'

'Yes.' The younger man sat up from his dozing alongside the picnic cloth and the relics of a *déjeuner sur l'herbe*. Lestrade knew that if this had been the redoubtable Goron picnicking, the woman with him would have been naked.

'Would this be Mrs Wells?' Lestrade asked.

The straw-boatered young lady in the frothy summer blouse blushed a softer shade of crimson. 'Not for a few months yet,' she said.

'This is Jane Robbins, Mr . . . er?'

'Lestrade,' said Lestrade.

'My wife is at home,' Wells explained. 'Who are you?'

'Let's just say we have a mutual acquaintance.' Lestrade squatted by the pair, tilting the boater back on his head.

'Oh? Who?'

Lestrade sucked his teeth. He never enjoyed embarrassing people, although he was excellent at it. 'Are you the author of a book called *The Time Machine*, Mr Wells?' he asked.

'I am.' Wells was clearly proud of the fact and produced a pen from his waistcoat pocket. 'You know, old chap, you don't have to claim a mutual acquaintanceship just to get my signature. I'd be delighted to sign your copy.'

'Good,' said Lestrade, hoicking the man upright by his writing arm. 'There's a boat over there. Let's talk about your book, shall we?'

'But . . . that's *my* punt,' said Wells.

'We shan't be long, Miss Robbins,' Lestrade called. 'Why don't you rinse the dishes in the river, or something?'

'Look here . . .' But Wells's uncomprehending protests were to no avail as Lestrade bundled him into the working end of the punt and lowered himself down as nonchalantly as he dared.

It had to be said that this was not the ideal position. A suspect in a murder inquiry was looming over the prone policeman and he was armed with a murderous ten-foot pole. Neither was this a stretch of the Thames with which Lestrade was totally familiar. Give him the murky swirling depths of Shadwell Stair, the impenetrable stagnant gloom of Blackwall Reach. Here were fields and trees and bulrushes standing sentinel along the bank. Mallards flapped skywards from the reeds and moorhens patted on their floating nests, poking their white noses into some other river dweller's business.

'I'm not going anywhere,' Wells stood defiantly on the platform, 'until you tell me what this is all about.'

'I didn't want to compromise you in front of a lady, Mr Wells,' said Lestrade, 'but I have reason to believe that you are acquainted with a Miss Henrietta Fordingbridge of Lower Streatham.'

'Henrietta? Yes, I am. Is anything wrong?'

Miss Robbins was kneeling up now, shielding her eyes from the sun and listening intently to snatches of the men's conversation.

'Can you use that thing?' Lestrade pointed to the pole.

'After a fashion,' said Wells. 'That is, I got us here.'

'Then row,' Lestrade advised. 'I have some grave news for you, Mr Wells. I am a policeman.'

The author of *The Time Machine* slid the pole into the river mud and the punt glided effortlessly away from the bank. Ducks were a-dabbling up-tails all, but neither man noticed.

'That's not very grave. Go on,' said Wells.

'I'm afraid she's dead.' Lestrade watched his man for signs of reaction. The pole slipped slightly in the strong zoologist's hands. The handsome face darkened and the luxuriant mustachios, blonded by the brilliance of the spring sun, visibly drooped.

'I knew it,' he said.

'Did you now?' Lestrade sat up, balancing himself in the shallow skiff as best he could. 'Would you care to elaborate, sir?'

'It's my fault,' said Wells.

'Ah.' Lestrade sensed his prey slowing, wavering before headlong panic set in to escape the long arm of the law. He'd settle for a confession on Henrietta Fordingbridge. The rest could come later. Then he could clear himself with Frost, cock yet another snook at Abberline and perhaps put in for some long-overdue leave.

'I should never have let her go home alone. How did it happen?'

'You tell me, sir.' Lestrade had been to the Spanish Inquisition school of police interrogations; not quite vicious enough for Her Majesty's Tax Inspectors.

'What?'

'When did you see her last?'

'The night before last.' Wells applied his pole again. 'She'd been to the theatre with me.'

'What did you see?'

'That little-known piece by Chekhov – *Ward Number Six*. Do you know it?'

'No,' said Lestrade. The last time he'd gone to the theatre it was to see a translation of Corneille's *Le Cid*. He'd asked for his money back. There wasn't a single mention of the Criminal Investigation Department, just a load of tosh about some Spanish bloke. Very disappointing. 'What time did you leave her?'

'Let me see.' Wells thought. 'It'd be about ten-thirty, I suppose.'

'Where?'

'Outside the Prince's, Haymarket.'

'How was she to get home?'

'Well, I offered to call her a cab, but she wouldn't hear of it. She was an independent spirit, Mr Lestrade. Insisted on paying for her own theatre seat and so on. I should have insisted!' He jabbed the butt of the pole down on to the boat's end and it wobbled violently.

'So,' Lestrade's mind was racing over the map of London he knew so well, 'from the Haymarket, her nearest Underground station was Charing Cross?'

'Er . . . yes, I suppose so.' Wells was less familiar.

'So where was she between ten-thirty and eleven-thirty?'

'I don't follow,' said Wells, scanning the river ahead for other craft. 'Hello, Jerome!' he called to the three men in the passing boat.

'Afternoon, H.G.!' the clean-shaven member of the trio shouted back. 'Loved *The Time Machine*, by the way.'

'Thanks. What do you mean?' He'd returned mentally to Lestrade.

'We know from a platform guard that she caught the eleven-thirty-eight at Charing Cross Station. At that time of night it takes . . . what, five minutes to reach Charing Cross – and that's with a headwind. So where was she for the other fifty-five minutes or so?'

Wells shrugged.

'Where did you go?'

'Home,' he said, 'by cab. Oh God, Lestrade, this is terrible.'

'Can you tell me, sir,' the Inspector leaned forward, 'what was Miss Fordingbridge to you?'

'A dalliance, that's all.'

'Whereas Miss Robbins . . . ?'

'Is my fiancée, Mr Lestrade. I appreciate your circumspection, by the way, but it wasn't strictly necessary.'

Lestrade closed his legs. He didn't know it showed. 'And Mrs Wells?'

'Isabel and I are divorced,' the writer told him. 'I may as well come clean, Lestrade. I am a believer in free love.'

'You mean you don't approve of prostitution?'

'No. I mean that I don't believe that a man and a woman should be shackled by the conventions of a Christian marriage where sex is concerned.'

Lestrade raised an eyebrow. No wonder the nineties were naughty. And thank God Walter Dew wasn't there. 'You mean you expect *any* woman to have sex with you?'

'Only if she wants to,' Wells explained. 'Never without her consent – and never on the Underground. Was Henrietta raped, Mr Lestrade?'

'The police surgeon thinks not,' Lestrade said. 'Tell me, Mr Wells,' he peered closely at his man, 'how did you come to scratch your cheek?'

'My . . . ?' Wells felt the red claw marks as though for the first time. 'Oh, my cat, Mr Polly. A vicious old Tom with homicidal tendencies. I was moving him off some notes I'd written for the *Graphic* yesterday and he didn't appreciate the gesture. Why do you ask?'

'Did anyone witness this murderous attack on you by your pet?'

'No, I don't think so. What is its significance?'

'The police surgeon is a good man. Chap called Quincey; he'll go far. He noticed, under Miss Fordingbridge's finger-nails, a quantity of human skin.'

'You mean . . . ?'

'I mean, Mr Wells, that as she was being strangled to death by a powerful pair of hands,' and he glared meaningfully at those handling the pole with such expertise, 'she clawed the face of her attacker.'

'I see,' said Wells, 'and you think . . . ?'

'I'm not paid to think,' Lestrade confessed. 'Merely to ask questions and to act upon information received.'

'It's a tragic world, Mr Lestrade,' Wells said. 'You clearly haven't read my *Time Machine* and that's a pity. You see, I'm something of a prophet. Oh, I'm not Elijah or Elisha and I don't have a crystal ball, but I know there are terrible things coming. One day – and not too long in the future – there'll be war from the air; great bombs that will destroy whole civilizations; men and women created like some ghastly Frankenstein experiment; and worst of all, people will pay good money to eat pieces of minced beef thrust with onions between two pieces of bread. I tell you, that's not a future I want to see.'

It was Lestrade's turn not to follow.

'Don't you see?' Wells took in the puzzled face, the hangdog moustache. It spoke of incomprehension beyond comprehension. 'It's started already. The End Of Civilization As We Know It. Some lunatic is going round slaughtering women haphazardly on the Underground. This isn't an England I want; an England I can believe in; an England in which my children will grow up. There's only one solution, Lestrade.'

'There is?' The Inspector longed to hear it; was ever open to suggestion.

'A one-class society. Oh, not this nonsense the Fabians are jabbering about. Some Marxist dogma of a proletarian uprising, be it by bloody revolution or be it by ballot. No, the creation of a Utopia in which Jack's as good as his master because Jack has no master. And master has no Jack.'

Lestrade's expression became ever more fixed as the philosopher began to tremble, then cough. He ferreted in his pocket for a handkerchief, failed to find it, then spewed blood all over his shirt and waistcoat. He dropped to both knees, the pole sliding into the water as he went down. Lestrade leapt forward, cradling the convulsing man in his arms.

'Look out!' he heard someone shout over an increasingly loud rush of water. 'The weir. Watch out for the weir.'

Weird was right, Lestrade observed. The erstwhile hearty Mr Wells, punter extraordinary, draper's assistant, zoologist, teacher, novelist, free lover and Utopian prophet, lay bleeding in Lestrade's arms, the bits that weren't red a deathly white. It was only gradually, as the punt began to speed up and rock with a life of its own, that Lestrade realized the danger they were both in. Some yards away, the river appeared to vanish over a sliding, hurtling, silver drop. A ledge had developed unaccountably in the river bed and he saw at a glance what had happened. Wells's seizure had sent the boat off course, past those large red signs that said DANGER. WEIR.

Lestrade fumbled about in the boat's bottom and came up with a single paddle. Like a man with one arm he dipped it into the frothy turbulence of the Thames. If only, like Harry Bandicoot, he had rowed for Eton. If only, like Jane Robbins, he had stayed on terra firma. And his terror now was complete. The roar of the river was deafening and Lestrade's unskilled sculling made no headway against the foam. Wells looked up through the fog of his fit, half realized their predicament and murmured, helpfully, 'Here we go, here we go, here we go,' before passing out completely.

Lestrade did what all Englishmen do when faced with the intransigence of machines. He blamed the boat. As he and Wells disappeared over the edge of forever, he was heard to cry, 'You stupid punt!'

7

They let Lestrade and Wells out of Surbiton General the next day. Both men, the doctor said, were lucky to be alive. They'd pumped enough water out of them to refloat the *Revenge* and if they'd gone in any lower down the Thames Reaches it would have been a case of poisoning, not drowning.

Jane Robbins had sat at Wells's bedside, clutching his hand, smoothing his delirious brow and feeding him nourishing broth. Walter Dew had sat by Lestrade's, continuing to make inroads into the grapes he'd brought (like last time) and whittling his initials on the bed frame. He was always careful in these situations to carve a broad arrow between the W of Walter and the D of Dew so that the whole thing had an aura of officialdom and the War Department got the blame.

'What of Herbert George Wells then, guv'nor?' the Constable asked as the growler took them through sleepy Surbiton and on into bustling Barnes.

'An odd cove, certainly,' Lestrade said. 'Confessed to an amorous dalliance with the late Miss Fordingbridge.'

'Ah, so who was the lady I saw him with just now?'

'That was no lady,' said Lestrade 'That was his fiancée.'

'But . . .'

'Don't ask, Walter,' Lestrade rested his head gratefully against the leather seat of the growler. 'We are not, you and I, of the Thinking Classes. We're one-woman men, at least at a time. Mr Wells believes in getting it where he can as often as he can.'

'So he killed Miss Fordingbridge because she had become an encumbrance?'

'Possible,' said Lestrade, 'but I'd have emptied her pockets first.'

'Eh, sir?'

'I wouldn't risk killing a woman and leaving my calling card in her fol-de-rols, would you? Without that, we might never have linked her with Wells at all.'

'No, I suppose not. But what if he didn't know it was there?'

'Well done, Dew. I'd hoped you'd spot that one. The fact is that Mr Wells has such a philosophy of life that he really doesn't care that much who knows about his dalliances. He certainly wouldn't kill to keep them quiet. No, I think our Mr Wells is in the clear, but we'll just put him in the shoe boxes for now, shall we? Put him on ice, so to speak. We may have need of him again. Now, any news in my absence?'

'Not a lot, sir. Formal identification of the body in question.'

'Not a fictitious husband this time?' Lestrade asked.

'Oh, no, guv,' Dew chuckled. 'Bromley was meticulous.'

'Bromley?' Lestrade's face fell an octave.

'He double-checked with me, sir.' Dew sat on his dignity a little. After all, he had been a detective man and boy now for seven years. A bloody apprenticeship, it had to be said. And if he could just lay his hands on one arch-criminal, it would be the making of him.

'Did he, now?' Lestrade was unimpressed 'Who was this person, then?'

'Father, sir.'

'Father? How old did Bromley say he was?'

'Er . . . on the youngish side, he said.'

'I bet he did!'

'Why, guv?' Dew sensed that all was not well.

'During my conversations with Mr Wells over the last four hours in our adjacent hospital beds, he told me, apart from his plans for world Socialism, and the plot of a fairly ludicrous novel about blokes from Mars invading earth, he told me that Henrietta Fordingbridge had no dependants. She was orphaned in the Great Diphtheria Outbreak in eighty-nine. Come to think of it, I didn't feel so good myself that year.'

'Oh, God.'

'A little late for that Great Commissioner in the Sky, Dew, if you'll permit me that observation. You know, I've had this conversation with you before – and recently. I assume we're talking about our Australian friend?'

'No, sir. Or at least, Bromley didn't mention an accent. In fact, the bloke kept talking to him in Indian.'

'Indian?'

'"Hither lao" and "juldee juldee". Hindoostani, isn't it?'

'Might as well be,' Lestrade corroborated. 'What did he look like?'

'Well set-up chap, Bromley said. Auburn 'tache. Military bearing.'

'Not a turban and a loincloth?'

'Oh, no, sir. He was a white man all right. Not a fakir or anything like that.'

'Ah, but he was, Walter. He faked his identity and Bromley fell for it like the Essex constable he is. You just can't get the staff. Look, when we get to the Yard, I want you to trot along to N Corridor and get hold of Constable Hockney.'

'The police artist?'

'Yes. I've got a feeling that when he draws your Mr Bellamy and Bromley's Mr Fordingbridge from the careful and meticulous descriptions you're both going to give him, they're going to look horribly alike.'

'But why didn't you take me with you?' she asked, trying to catch his gaze.

'I couldn't, Trottie,' he explained, untwining his fingers from beneath hers. 'I shouldn't even be doing this.'

'You're only winding my wool for me,' she said. 'Is that a crime in Rosebery's England?'

'Now, now,' he warned her, 'let's not get political.'

'But you might have been killed.'

'Who told you that?'

'Walter Dew.'

'I'll kill him.'

'No, you won't. Hold still. I've nearly finished. He's very fond of you, Sholto Lestrade. Lieutenants like him aren't easy to come by.'

He looked at her. The evening sun was sinking behind the solid, respectable villas of the Walworth Road, gilding her hair where it lay in tresses across her shoulders. 'If you say so,' he said.

'Tell me about her,' she said.

'Who?'

'Your wife.'

His eyes hardened. She felt the wool tense as she continued to wind around his hands. 'Walter Dew?' he asked.

'It's not his fault, Sholto,' she said. 'I'm a very persuasive woman when I want to be. When he was kind enough to bring me breakfast at the Yard yesterday, I pinned him down.'

'He must have thought his luck had changed!' Lestrade scowled.

'Tell me about her,' she said again.

'There's not much to tell,' he said. 'Her name was Sarah. Sarah Manchester. She was a widow. Her husband died when his gig overturned at Hyde Park Corner five years ago. She was . . . and he smiled at the remembrance of it, 'she was actually my landlady, but there was a joke between us that she was my housekeeper. I needed somewhere to lay my hat. She needed the rent. It worked well.'

'And then?'

'Then we . . . fell in love. That worked well too.'

She lowered his arms. 'Poor Sholto,' she said. 'Walter told me. She died, didn't she?'

He nodded. 'One of those things,' he said. 'There was no reason for it. Oh, I expect the doctors had some scientific explanation. It was beyond me.'

She lifted his chin, gazing into the sad, dark eyes and placed

136

a finger on her lips. Then she passed it across the space between them, a space grown small in that moment, and touched it against his lips. For an instant they looked into each other's eyes, his face closing imperceptibly to hers.

Then there was the ring of her doorbell and the moment was broken for ever.

She swirled away to the window that overlooked the little courtyard below. A carriage and pair stood beyond the myrtle hedge, a coachman in the livery of the old Prince of Wales Theatre perched on the box.

'Damn!' she muttered, biting her lip.

'I'd better go,' he said. 'That was mighty fine gooseberry pie, Trottie.'

'But you haven't had your coffee,' she frowned. 'Look. Wait in there,' and she shoved him into an ante-room.

'Who is it?' he asked, remembering to snatch up his boater.

'That old duffer Squire Bancroft,' she said. 'Impresario Extra-ordinary – and that's his phrase, not mine. He wants me for Ophelia.'

Jesus wanted Lestrade for a sunbeam or so he'd always believed but this wasn't the time to say so. He wedged himself against the flock of the wallpaper and waited.

He heard the booming of the voice in the hall, then the crash of the drawing-room door as the Great Thespian made his entrance. He put his eye to the keyhole and saw a sight for sore eyes. Squire Bancroft was easily the wrong side of his half-century with wild grey hair under a shiny topper and a superb pair of Piccadilly weepers that threatened to entangle themselves with the rope of his monocle that flashed like a firefly in the sunset.

'Trottie, my jewel,' and he chewed his consonants with relish, 'I'm not compromising you, am I?' And Lestrade saw the Actor's Actor close a rather sweaty arm around the slim waist of Miss True.

'No, you're not,' she assured him and took his arm just as purposefully away.

'Well, well,' he glanced at the grandfather in the corner, glad that it was made of wood and metal rather than flesh and blood, 'the night is young. Just wanted to say, the most deuc'd thing has happened. You'd never believe it.'

'Nellie Melba's hit the right note?'

'Haw, haw,' he guffawed and his monocle fell off. 'My, but you're a waspish little filly,' he observed, showing a curious ignorance of the animal world. 'No, no. It's my gel for Ophelia. You'll *have* to take the part now.'

'Squire,' she turned to face him, 'I've told you. I'm not very good. What's happened to the girl you had?'

'Well, that's the devil of it. It was in *Greasepaint* this morning – she's dead. Been strangled by this bally maniac on the Tube. I don't know what the bally police think they're at. This is London, for Jove's sake, 1895. Not Chicago in the Middle Ages.'

'Yes,' she said levelly, 'it's tragic. I didn't know you knew Miss Fordingbridge?'

'Oh Lord, yes. Er ... not in the biblical sense of course. But I saw her Lady Teazle last year at the Hippodrome. Don't tell Mrs Bancroft, but it beat hers into a cocked hat, I can tell you. Now, tomorrow, lotus flower, we're having to rethink the whole thing. Well, you know what a perfectionist Forbes-Robertson is.'

'Can't you cancel?'

'Cancel?' Lestrade saw the Great Pretender turn ashen. 'My dear girl, Irving himself is coming to the opening night. And it's three weeks away. Fair makes your footlights dim, I can tell you. Shall we say ten-thirty then, at the POW? Give Mrs Bancroft time to put her face on. Not to mention the other parts of her anatomy.'

'Squire . . .'

'My dear,' and he leapt to her side with a theatrical sweep, snatching up one hand and wiping his mustachios all over it, 'who needs Sarah Bernhardt when I can have you?'

'You can't have me,' she told him defiantly, ungluing his lips from her fingers. 'Oh all right, I'll be there. But I can't promise anything much.'

'"Divine perfection of woman",' he said, leering in the sunset, 'you've made a nearly middle-aged man very happy. *A bientôt*,' and he swirled his cape and exited, stage left.

Lestrade oozed out of the cupboard where Trottie True had placed him in lieu of the ante-room in her haste. 'Who was that?' he asked.

'Didn't I tell you?'

'Let me put it another way.' He shivered the nets aside to watch the Great Entertainer spring lightly into his waiting trap. '*What* was that?'

'Oh, he means well enough.' She joined him at the window. 'He actually retired ten years ago, but you'd never think so. He was manager of the Prince of Wales and the Haymarket. He's raised twenty thousand pounds for hospitals you know, by giving recitals throughout the country.'

'They pay him to stop, do they?'

'Sholto,' she flicked him with a curtain, 'that's unkind. His Little Nell is legendary.'

'Yes, of course. I could see that. Almost. Tell me, Trottie, didn't he know about Verity?'

She shook her head and busied herself with a lamp. 'It's getting dark,' she said. 'So much for June's long-lighted days. No, I don't suppose he does. I haven't seen him for three months or more. Ever since I initially turned Ophelia down. Notice he only read about poor Miss Fordingbridge in *Greasepaint*. I expect it's the only reading he does apart from plays.'

'Rather a coincidence, that,' Lestrade said.

'What?'

'That he should know one murder victim and the sister of another.'

A chill flicked over her heart and she caught her breath, standing with the glass chimney in her hand, the oil glow lighting her face. 'Sholto,' she said, 'you don't think . . . that Squire Bancroft . . . ?'

'This play he's doing – the one with Ophelia in it. What is it, exactly?'

'*Hamlet*,' she said, looking oddly at him.

'Any blokes in that?' It had obviously slipped his mind for a moment.

'Several,' she said.

'Good. I'll come with you tomorrow. Introduce me as an actor – from the provinces.'

'Do you do accents?' she asked.

'Somerset,' he demonstrated, lapsing into fluent Lancashire.

'Is this a good idea?' she asked.

'Links like these are important,' he told her, making for

the door, 'when one name can join two victims. Who knows, perhaps Squire Bancroft is the missing link.'

'I wouldn't be at all surprised,' she nodded.

'Good night, Trottie. I'll be back at ten tomorrow morning with a growler. Sleep well.'

She didn't. Through her tortured turnings under the coverlet, Squire Bancroft loomed over her, moaning, 'Murder,' and grinning like some hideous death's head. In the wings of her dreams her sister lay garotted, a gaping hole where her throat used to be and her face a deathly white, like a pierrot whose cheeks ran with glycerine tears.

The solid, comfortable, lived-in face of Sholto Lestrade came as an errant in shining armour to her dragons of the night. The growler took them to Coventry Street, to the side door of the Prince of Wales Theatre. Here, amid dusty flats and the smell of sulphur, an old crone took bookings on the telephone machine.

'Gerard 7483,' she croaked. 'Yes. Yes. Upper circle? You must be joking, sonny. No. Out of the question. Only the pit. One and eightpence. Well, take it or leave it. I don't have to do this job, you know. I could have been a contender.' And she slammed the phone down.

'Get a lot of bookings, do you?' Lestrade asked Trottie as they climbed a set of rickety stairs to the stage. Once again, the darkened auditorium. Once again, the floodlit stage. A tall man of Lestrade's own vintage, but with hair swept back and wearing a faintly outrageous codpiece, stood in the centre and an enormous woman in a nightie with a crown on her head knelt with obvious discomfort at his feet.

'Johnston,' Lestrade recognized Squire Bancroft's voice bellowing from the blackness, 'you'll have to help her up, I'm afraid. It's her knees.'

The fairy queen on the floor wrenched off her crown and scowled into the darkness. 'Will you stop mentioning parts of my body, Squire?' she bellowed back.

'You're supposed to be a queen for God's sake, Effie. At least manage *some* of the dignity that the Bard in his brilliance bestowed on Gertrude. Ah, Trottie. Marvellous! Marvellous! I was just congratulating Mrs Bancroft on her lofty portrayal of Denmark's queen. Who's that with you? Your driver?'

'Er . . . no, Squire,' she called over the footlights. 'This is Anthony Lister, the actor.'

'*The* actor?' Bancroft repeated. 'Take five minutes, everybody. Johnston, darling, see to Effie, will you?'

And the leading man nearly ruptured himself trying to lift her.

'Here goes,' Trottie whispered, crossing everything she had, and waited while the Great Actor-Manager ascended the stage. There was deafening applause from a solitary inhabitant of the balcony above and Squire Bancroft turned to bow.

'A shilling a day he pays that chap to do that,' Trottie said to Lestrade from the corner of her mouth.

'Well, well,' the impresario held out a theatrical hand, 'Squire Bancroft Bancroft.'

'Er . . . Anthony Lister Lister,' said Lestrade, following what was obviously a theatrical convention.

'What have you done?'

'Nothing,' Lestrade admitted quickly.

'Nothing?' Bancroft was a little confused. 'Trottie, darling . . .'

'Mostly pantomime, Squire.' Trottie came to Lestrade's rescue as he had to hers not an hour before.

'Ah, the nursery of the theatre.' Queen Gertrude thrust her way into the gathering. 'You can't beat a good burlesque, that's what I always say. Isn't that what I always say, Squire?' She nudged him disarmingly in the ribs and his monocle fell off.

'Oh, er . . . quite. Mr Lister, this is my wife . . . um . . . Mrs Bancroft Bancroft.'

'Charmed.' Lestrade took the proffered hand, but thought better of the kiss the Great Actress clearly expected.

'Likewise,' she bobbed. 'You may call me Effie . . . Anthony,' and she proceeded to paw his arm.

'Known Trottie long?' Bancroft asked.

'Not really,' Lestrade said.

'We thought perhaps the gravedigger,' Trottie suggested.

'But I've got a gravedigger, dear,' Bancroft explained. 'George Arliss will be very disappointed . . .'

'Nonsense, Squire,' Effie Bancroft retorted. 'You can never have too many gravediggers, that's what I always say. I'm sure if Gilbert and Sullivan ever get their hands on the Bard, they'll have a whole chorus of gravediggers.'

'Oh, very well.' Bancroft threw up his arms. 'We'll try you out, Anthony, darling, but I can't promise,' and he turned to his wife. 'He hasn't even got George's stupendous lip, you stupid old trout. And remember, if I hire him, you are not to wander into the men's dressing-rooms; understand?'

'That was a mistake,' she hissed. 'You know perfectly well I got lost.'

'Not fourteen times you didn't.' He rounded on her. This *sotto-voce* tête-à-tête had nearly reached the street and the loving couple both turned to the waiting company and tittered before gliding apart.

'Johnston, darling. Sorry about this. We'll have to work on the bedroom scene later. You're marvellous, of course. It's just a pity about the queen, that's all . . .' and he ignored the venomous scowl Mrs Bancroft flashed at him. 'Right, every-body!' And he clapped his hands. 'I want to give Anthony a try-out. Gravedigger scene. I'll have to be George Arliss; he's having his monocle reground today. Somebody give Anthony a script.'

A sheaf of tatty papers appeared from nowhere and Lestrade tried to read it. The lights dazzled and the sweat began to trickle down his temples. True, his Sarah Bernhardt in the Police Revue was legendary, but perhaps a gravedigger in drag might raise an eyebrow or two.

'Perhaps if you took off the boater,' Bancroft suggested. Mrs Bancroft had marched off to a corner where Lestrade was horrified to observe that she was lighting a pipe.

'We'll go from page forty-one. Johnston – "think it be thine indeed" – Anthony, you can read George's part for now.'

Like a book, thought Lestrade, though it had to be said he read better upside-down.

Johnston adopted a peculiar stance as though his codpiece were playing him up and placed a hand over his breast. 'I think it be thine indeed,' he said, 'for thou liest in't.'

Silence.

'That's you, Anthony darling!' Bancroft roared and Lestrade heard the Great Director slap his thigh, or probably someone else's, with exasperation.

'I'm sorry,' said Lestrade. 'I thought I was reading the gravedigger's part.'

'So you are, dear boy,' Bancroft replied.

'It's just that it says "1 Clo". I was a bit confused, that's all.'

'Aren't we all?' sighed Bancroft. 'First Clown, Anthony. First Clown. "You lie out on't sir". Can we get on, Anthony? We open, heart, in three weeks. I don't want anyone to panic or go to pieces or anything, but I've got to break in a new Ophelia, Gertrude needs work – and how – and the deuc'd ghost machine is playing up. Other than that, we're laughing, aren't we, dears?' And he was screaming his head off by now. 'Now, once again, Anthony, from the top.'

Lestrade decided that Bancroft was more over the top than from it and went into his part with a will. 'You lie out on't sir, and therefore it is not yours: for my part, I do not lie in't, and yet it is mine.' He peered at the page. Yes, he'd got the words right, but they made no sense to him whatsoever. Clearly Johnston understood, however, because he came back with, 'Thou dost lie in't to be in't, and say it is thine: 'tis for the dead, not for the quick; therefore thou liest.'

'Er . . . "'Tis a quick lie, sir: 'twill . . ."' Lestrade thought twill was a sort of material the cavalry wore. He couldn't get into this play at all. "'twill away again from me to you.'

'What man dost thou dig for?' Johnston asked, dropping to one knee.

'For no man, sir,' Lestrade answered.

'Go with him, Anthony,' Bancroft bawled. 'Go with him.'

Lestrade dropped to one knee as well and there was an audible crack as patella hit board.

'What woman, then?' Johnston asked.

'For none neither,' Lestrade hissed through the pain.

'Who is to be buried in't?'

'One that was a woman, sir; but, rest her soul, she's dead.'

'Oh, God!' Johnston broke away from the imaginary graveside and Lestrade thought how good that was. He couldn't find the line in his script, however, and erred for a while while Mrs Bancroft blew a cloud of smoke from her lips and rushed to the leading man who stood, head in hands, in the wings.

'What's the matter now?' Bancroft roared from the darkness.

'Don't be such an insensitive bastard, Squire!' his wife commanded. Obviously all this queen-playing had gone to her head. 'Can't you see Johnston's upset?'

'Oh, give me strength!' Bancroft wailed. 'I never had this trouble with Mrs Patrick Campbell. We'll break for elevenses. Where's that chap who makes the tea? Aubrey Smith? If you're off playing cricket somewhere, I'll flay you alive!'

Lestrade followed the pale-faced Hamlet through the bowels of the building. Trottie True was at his elbow, but he raised a finger to his lips and asked her, in sign language, to return to the stage. At the dressing-room door, the one with the single star that said in large letters painted by Squire Bancroft himself 'MEN ONLY', Lestrade collared his man.

'My performance wasn't that bad, was it?' he said.

The leading man pulled himself together and sat before a mirror dazzling with light bulbs. 'I'm sorry . . . er . . . Lister. I don't know what came over me. I'm Johnston Forbes-Robertson, by the way,' and he extended a hand before deftly whipping off his codpiece. Lestrade noted with some satisfaction that he was nothing without it.

'I've suffered a bereavement recently,' he said, blowing his elegant actor's nose into a Leichner tissue. 'Your lines up there brought it all flooding back – "One that was a woman, sir" . . .' and he shook his head. 'You know we actors, Lister,' he sniffed. 'Emotional types, eh?'

'Was it your wife?' Lestrade fished.

'No. Closer than that.'

'Sister?'

'My leading lady. My Ophelia. Oh, Trottie's all right, but Squire Bancroft tends to pick 'em for the length they measure on the casting couch rather than their talent.'

Lestrade *had* heard they were all the same length lying down, but that was obviously an ugly rumour.

'Henrietta was just starting out. She'd been third spear bearer for a year or two and then got the Aladdin at the Hippodrome, Weston-Super-Mare. This would have made her. She'd have been up there alongside Mrs Patrick Campbell, Sarah Bernhardt . . .'

'Lily Langtry?' Lestrade extended the list.

'No, I meant she was an actress, Lister,' Forbes-Robertson sneered.

'What happened to her?'

'Lily Langtry? I haven't the faintest idea.'

'No, I mean Henrietta . . . er . . . I didn't catch her last name.'

'Fordingbridge. She met her death three days ago at the hands of a madman.'

'Ah, of course,' Lestrade said, putting on his finest performance. 'On the Underground, wasn't it? I seem to remember reading about it in *Greasepaint*. Shocking. Shocking. You've . . . er . . . no theories, I suppose?'

'None. Except . . . oh no, that's ridiculous.'

'What?' The gravedigger was all ears.

'Well, didn't Trottie True's sister meet a similar end?'

'Good Lord! Did she?'

'Well, surely you know that?'

'Squire Bancroft didn't.'

'What?'

'I have a confession to make to you, Mr Forbes-Robertson. I am not an actor.'

'Oh no!' Forbes-Robertson clapped a theatrical hand to his theatrical forehead. 'Shock! Horror! Tell me it isn't so.'

'Ah,' said Lestrade, 'you'd guessed.'

'Let's just say I had an inkling,' Forbes-Robertson said. 'Just a teensy one, of course. You're a policeman, aren't you?'

'You'd guessed that too?'

'Well, not at first. But your face was a little familiar. Didn't I see you in a Metropolitan Police Revue at the Alhambra a year or two back? You were Widow Twankey.'

'Sarah Bernhardt,' Lestrade corrected him, a little hurt.

'Well, I was close.'

'Inspector Lestrade.' The actor *manqué* came out of the closet at last.

'Are you on his trail?' Forbes-Robertson asked. 'The madman who stalks the Tubes?'

'On his trail, certainly, but as to how close, that's anybody's guess. Tell me all you know about Henrietta Fordingbridge.'

*   *   *

Forbes-Robertson had known Henrietta Fordingbridge in the biblical sense, but he was far too much of a gentleman to go very far into that. After all, he had been educated at Charterhouse and Rouen and his first part was as Chasteland in *Mary Queen of Scots*. As to the rest, he had loved her in the way that actors do, passionately and strong. Yes, he had proposed. No, she had not said yes. There was someone else, she had told Forbes-Robertson – a writer and visionary. Forbes-Robertson had offered to kill him, but Henrietta had just laughed. When he'd threatened to kill himself, that had elicited the same response.

'So he killed her instead,' was the conclusion to which Walter Dew had immediately leapt. Alas, it was the wrong one and Lestrade continued to dunk his Bath Oliver without moving his lips.

Friday morning found him padding up the shady side of Garrick Street, in search of the club of the same name. Dray horses snorted and champed their bits under a burning sun and flies droned about those bits they tried desperately to champ. A top-hatted gentleman in brown livery hailed Lestrade at the door.

'Are we a member, sir?' he inquired.

Lestrade assessed the situation at a glance. 'You may be,' he said. 'I am not.'

'Then may I ask your business, sir?'

'Certainly. Now let me pass.'

The flunkey was of the determined variety, however. This was a club unlike any other, composed of lawyers, literary men and thespians – men who made enemies like other people made excuses. To the flunkey, Lestrade could have been a client, dissatisfied with a barrister's defence; an author whose latest opus had been cruelly mangled by an editor's whim; a theatregoer who objected to an actor's performance. He could take no chances.

'I cannot let you in, sir,' he said.

'Official police business.' Lestrade flashed his documentation.

'That's what they all say,' the flunkey said.

'Do let him in, Kennedy,' a rich, mellifluous voice said, as it swept past them both.

'Very good, sir, Mr Marshall Hall, sir. This way, sir, if you please,' and he led Lestrade into a cloakroom to the left where the Inspector solemnly deposited his boater before ascending the marble and brass staircase. Great actors stood before him, adoring the spotlight on their gilded faces. Advocates in wigs and gowns bore down on him in cross-examination. He was shown into a drawing-room where anonymous gentlemen snored the morning away under copies of *The Times* and flunkeys ran to and fro with amber nectar decanters on silver trays.

'Thank you, Mr Marshall Hall.' Lestrade bowed to his man, already perusing his paper.

'What for, Lestrade? The entrée? I'd offer to buy you luncheon, but I know the food would be too rich for someone used to Scotland Yard fare. Looking for someone else to hound?'

'I was hoping to find Squire Bancroft.'

'Well, you must be virtually unique in that. I believe I heard him shattering glass in the next room. Thank you, by the by, for dropping charges against George Culdrose. The man was patently innocent and alas, not rich enough to interest me for long.'

'As you say, Mr Marshall Hall, patently innocent.'

'Yes, and it *just* saved you from charges of wrongful arrest, didn't it? I'll swear you chappies have a sixth sense when it comes to that sort of thing. Pity you haven't the same sense – or indeed any sense at all – when it comes to stopping this sort of thing.' He tapped *The Times* with his index finger. '"Terror of the Tubes",' he quoted, '"Whose Line Is It Anyway?" Tsk, tsk. This rag gets more like a penny dreadful every day. *Any* ideas, Lestrade?'

'Ah, Squire Bancroft.' The Inspector felt the furniture wobble as the Great Actor-Manager's dulcet tones preceded him into the room.

'Good God, er . . . ?'

'Inspector Lestrade, Scotland Yard,' said Lestrade.

'Really?' Bancroft sat down beside the advocate unasked. 'Haven't a brother or cousin or something in the theatre, have you?'

'Would that be the operating theatre?' Lestrade asked solemnly. 'Or the theatre of war?'

'Er . . .'

'Never mind. I would like to ask you some questions.' Lestrade looked in the direction of Marshall Hall, who showed no sign of leaving.

'Morning, Bancroft. I believe you need a lawyer. I am that man. Shall we say fifteen guineas?'

'Oh, morning, Marshall Hall.' Bancroft screwed in his monocle. 'I didn't see you there . . . eh? Fifteen guineas? Are you mad? Anyway, I have a lawyer.'

'Oh, yes, for contracts and slander and so on. But I'm talking about a criminal lawyer. I have a feeling that Lestrade here is about to arrest you for murder. Of course, if he doesn't get his words quite right, the cautioning and so on, the judge will throw it out. And even if he does, I'm sure I can get you bail. It might mean putting up the Prince of Wales of course as surety, but I'm sure you're good for it.'

'Arrest me for murder? What is this all about? I haven't understood a bally word for the last five minutes. Lestrade? What's going on?'

'I fear Mr Marshall Hall is a little premature, Mr Bancroft,' he said. 'I merely want to ask you some questions.'

'Well, I'm not sure it's convenient; not at all sure.'

'We can do it at the Yard.' Lestrade stood up.

'Er . . . no, no. All right,' the Great Actor fluffed. 'Er . . . is that fifteen guineas an hour, Marshall Hall?'

'Good Lord, no. I'm a generous man,' the lawyer said. 'It's only fifteen pounds an hour. From my vast experience of police procedure, this will take an hour and ten minutes. Lestrade?'

'Wait a minute,' Bancroft said, flicking his fingers at a flunkey. 'I need a drink.'

'Three brandies,' said Marshall Hall, 'on Squire Bancroft's slate. Well, Lestrade?'

'Better than I was,' the Inspector said. 'Mr Bancroft, how well did you know Miss Henrietta Fordingbridge?'

'I barely touched her, for Jove's sake,' the Actor-Manager flustered. 'Is that a proper question, Marshall Hall?'

'Perfectly proper,' chuckled the lawyer. 'It's the answer that bothers me. For example, as I'm sure Mr Lestrade is about to follow with – *where* precisely did you touch her? *When* was the last time you touched her? And so on. Am I right, Lestrade?'

'In a manner of speaking, Mr Marshall Hall, but unless you let me conduct my own inquiries, I shall have to ask you to leave.'

The lawyer sat back. 'Feel free,' he said. It was a rare moment of generosity from a lawyer.

'Well?' Lestrade looked at Bancroft.

'Well, she was a sweet girl, certainly,' the Actor-Manager remembered. 'Not without a pinch of talent.'

'Pinch?'

'Well, perhaps that's the wrong word. Modicum.'

'Go on.'

'I first met her last year. I was giving advice in my capacity as chairman of the Extremely Dramatic Theatre Association and there she was, the most charming Principal Boy I had ever seen. I signed her upon the spot. Well, one thing led to another and . . .'

'Oh?'

'Look, Lestrade, I won't have this innuendo. I did nothing improper with Miss Fordingbridge. I'm expecting a knighthood in a year or so. It's more than my career's worth. The only reason I'm baring my soul here is that I happen to know that all my fellow club members are deaf, senile or both – oh, present company excepted of course, Marshall Hall.'

'Eh?' The advocate was clearly miles away.

'Did you ever visit Miss Fordingbridge's home?' Lestrade asked.

'Never. It could have been on the Greek island of Mossbros for all I know. We only ever met at the theatre – either the Prince of Wales or the Haymarket.'

'Yet you called at Miss True's home,' Lestrade challenged him.

'How the devil do you know that?' Marshall Hall asked.

'I'll ask the questions,' Lestrade said.

'Trottie and I go back a long way,' the Actor-Manager explained. 'I knew the family.'

'Yet you didn't know about her sister?'

'Who?'

'Verity True.'

'Of course. What of her?'

'She too died at the hands of the Underground murderer,' Lestrade said.

'The deuce she did!' Bancroft's monocle fell off. 'Well, fan my flies. Now I see why you're asking me all these questions.'

'It *is* a coincidence, is it not, Mr Bancroft? Your old leading lady and the sister of your new leading lady both strangled to death in the same month.'

'By Jove, yes,' Bancroft pondered while the flunkey served the brandies. 'Yes, I see.'

'What's that?' Lestrade asked.

'It's a brandy,' Marshall Hall told him. 'Rich people like us drink it regularly.'

'No, I mean *that*.' Lestrade pointed more precisely.

'That's my thumb, Lestrade,' the Actor-Manager confessed.

'*That*.' Lestrade poked a purple ridge running transwise across it.

'It's an old scar,' said Bancroft. 'I'd like to say it was the result of an old flesh wound from *Macbeth*, but actually I fell off my rocking horse when I was a boy.'

'Well, Mr Bancroft,' Lestrade downed his brandy, 'offer up a prayer to that wooden charger tonight. That fall may just have saved you from the drop. Good morning, gentlemen.' And he exited, stage right.

'Well, you were useful, Marshall Hall!' Bancroft thundered.

The advocate smiled. 'That's the price you pay, Squire,' he said. 'I'll send my man Bowker around tomorrow morning, shall I? Give you a chance to embezzle a bit of ticket money.'

'I'm sorry, guv. I know your views on the matter, but Mr Abberline insisted.'

'Did he now?' Lestrade pushed his way down the basement stairs at the Yard, where, on a clear day, you could hear the lap of the water and the swishing of the tails of the rats.

He didn't stop until his hand was resting on the cell door that Constable Corkindale had banged open with his shoulder. The only damage was a slight dent in the metal.

'Mr Bayruth,' the Inspector said.

'That's Bayreuth,' the suspect corrected him again.

'Is it?' said Lestrade, throwing his boater on to the bed and squatting on Bayreuth's latrine. 'Do you know what they call you in the sergeants' mess next door?'

'If it's anything unpleasant, I shall sue,' Bayreuth said, shaking his stump with some defiance.

'Your first name is Edward, isn't it?' Lestrade asked.

'It is.'

'They're calling you Edward the Confessor. Now you see the position that puts me in, don't you?'

'Up for promotion, I would have thought. Here I am, on a plate.'

'Yes, and I'm tempted to let Constable Corkindale over there eat you. How about it, Corkindale?'

'Ooh, no, sir,' the Constable grimaced. 'That would be cannibalism and contrary to the laws of nature.'

Lestrade looked at the man. 'Did Mrs Minniver up at the school teach you that?' he asked.

'No, sir. It's in the *Police Manual*.'

'Is it?'

'Yessir. Sergeant Dixon read all that to me when I joined, sir.'

'Of course. I remember. You followed the lines with your finger, didn't you?'

'Yessir,' Corkindale beamed.

'Right. Now to weightier matters.' Though it was difficult to find much that was weightier than Corkindale. 'Who have you killed this time, Mr Bayreuth?'

'The latest one,' the prisoner answered. 'Henrietta Fordingbridge.'

'Why?' Lestrade lit a cigar.

'Give me the come-on, she did. Well, what do you expect? She was an actress, wasn't she?'

'I fully believe that you are guilty of reading the papers, Mr Bayreuth. What I want is one cast-iron reason why I should charge you for the murder.'

'Chief Inspector Abberline was convinced,' Bayreuth said petulantly.

'Yes, of course he was,' Lestrade said. 'That's because Chief Inspector Abberline makes Constable Corkindale look like a college professor. Now I thought I made it clear last time that a man with your ... infirmity ... cannot possibly kill a full-grown, healthy woman, come-on or not.'

Bayreuth stood up, his jaw flexing. 'I may be manually disadvantaged,' he said, 'but my bosom harbours thoughts the like of which the world cannot encompass.'

'Really? You know, Bayreuth,' Lestrade rose to go, 'you're the sort of bloke who ought to report to a police station every Thursday for a damned good smacking . . . Except that you'd probably enjoy it too much. See this . . . gentleman out, Corkindale. Take him the pretty way via the river. I don't want Joseph Public thinking he's helping us with our inquiries.'

At the bottom of the stairs, Lestrade turned to the faithful Dew. 'Are they ready?'

'In your office, sir,' the Constable told him.

And they were. Three ladies of the night, each encased in whalebone and plastered with make-up.

'Well, bounce a bit, Bromley,' Lestrade snapped. 'Good God, man, you're about as enticing as a cardboard box.'

The detective of that name swayed his hips but only looked as if he was limbering up for the Metropolitan Tug-o'-War Team.

'Show him, Johnnie,' Lestrade sighed.

Inspector John Thicke obliged. After all, he had been doing it for years. 'Like this,' he said. 'More flair. More grind. Remember, you're not coppers now; not for tonight, anyway. You're part of the oldest profession in the world. And look as if you're enjoying it.'

'What's your view on our man, Johnnie?' Lestrade asked.

'Well,' the Inspector rolled down his bodice to pull a cigar from his cleavage, 'I've been trailing madmen now for seven years, man and woman. The Ripper, the Penge Flasher and now the Underground Strangler. Oh, and in between, the Toilet Torch of Teddington.'

'Who?'

'Dunno. Never caught him.' Thicke lit up so that the lucifer flame lit up his strangely convincing features. 'Never caught the Ripper neither, come to think of it. And now La Rue's in charge of dressing up, I don't hold out much hope for the Flasher. However, I digress.'

'Indeed you do,' Lestrade agreed.

'Let's get to cases, then,' said Thicke. 'Our man is a sexual pervert. He doesn't have time to carry out the appalling interference he plans and dreams of because he has to wait for his moment. A crowded train is no good. So he waits until the last one or maybe the one before. But he can't risk striking when somebody might get on at a station, so he has to kill on the last stretch. That doesn't give him time to do more than lift the lady's skirts; which makes him more exasperated and frustrated than ever. The blood lust in him must be rising, which for us is good.'

'Not so good for some unsuspecting woman, though,' Russell observed.

'I'll do the morality, lad,' Thicke told him. 'You just stick out your bum at any bloke on that last or pen ... pelu ... last-but-one train. *Any* bloke, understand? Be he bishop or woman. I know our friend's sexual proclivities, but I'm buggered if I know what he looks like. These women are still out there riding the Underground, despite the warnings Mr Lestrade has issued and the field day the Press have had. That points to one thing. Well, two things. Well, three, I suppose.'

'And they are, Johnnie?' Lestrade tried to pin his man down. It would soon be time for the last trains.

'One,' and he held up a thumb with a long red nail, 'the women in question can't read. Two,' a finger joined it, 'they like a laugh. Three,' and he'd stopped the use of the digits by now, 'they think that they can trust the bloke. Which means he could be a vicar or a woman.'

'Or a guard,' Bromley said.

'Don't be bloody ridiculous, Bromley,' Lestrade and Thicke chorused.

'Right,' said Lestrade. 'Now, no heroics. You're all armed, gentlemen?'

Thicke hauled up his frock to reveal the ebony life-preserver tucked alluringly in his garter. Russell flicked a catch in his handbag to flash a set of gleaming steel knuckles. Bromley pulled out a powder puff.

'What in God's name will that do to him?' Lestrade asked. 'Make him smell nice as he chokes the life out of you?'

'It's pepper, sir. It'll blind him. My boots'll do the rest.'

'I hope you're right, son,' the Inspector said. 'Who's on where, Johnnie?'

'Russell's on the Circle moving east from Earls Court. Bromley's doing the reverse, heading west. I'm going up and down the City and South London like a yo-yo in drag. And I calculate our chances of catching him are about three hundred and eighteen thousand to one.'

'I know,' sighed Lestrade, 'but we've got to try something. He's making fools of us all – well, Abberline, anyway. Good luck, ladies – and don't talk to any strange men.'

'I've been propositioned by Sergeant Challoner already,' Russell moaned.

'What did he do?' quipped Thicke. 'Pull rank?'

Russell fluttered his false eyelashes. 'A lady doesn't answer that kind of question, Inspector,' and he held open the door while the others flounced out.

A tight-lipped man of indeterminate age sat open-mouthed as the three traipsed through the outer office to the whistles and applause of passing detectives. Lestrade caught his eye. 'Well, we don't get many perks on this floor, Mr . . . er . . . ?'

'Galton,' the man said, 'Francis Galton. Are you Inspector Lestrade?'

'I am. What can I do for you?' Lestrade offered a chair. It was Walter Dew's.

'Ask rather what I can do for you,' he beamed.

'Ah, it's riddle night,' said Lestrade. 'You'll forgive me if I'm a little frayed, Mr Galton, but it's late and I've forgotten where I live. Could you get to the point?'

'Clearly,' Galton bridled, 'you don't realize who I am.'

'Clearly,' agreed Lestrade.

'I am Francis Galton the anthropologist.'

'Oh, we never discuss politics here,' Lestrade assured him.

'The meteorologist.'

'Or religion.'

'I am the originator of the theory of eugenics . . .'

'Well, I'm happy for you,' said Lestrade. 'Allow me to be the first to congratulate you.'

'A few years ago.'

'Ah, then I'm too late.'

'Give me your hand, Mr Lestrade.'

'What?'

'Your hand.'

With some trepidation, the Inspector did so. He sensed Walter Dew peering over a pile of papers at him.

'Ah,' Galton said, squinting in the bad light at Lestrade's thumb, 'the bifurcated ridge. Don't ever commit a crime, Mr Lestrade. That thumb would hang you.'

Lestrade had said something curiously similar to Squire Bancroft that very morning. 'Why so?' he asked.

'The lines,' said Galton triumphantly. 'Five years ago I proved conclusively that each of us has a unique pattern of lines on the tips of our fingers – and thumbs. Your loops and whorls will be the same now as on the day you were born – and will not change until the day of your death. Moreover, yours are quite unlike mine or anyone else's.'

'So?'

'So, all you have to do is to check the throats of your Underground victims and you've got him.'

'Who?'

'The murderer.'

'I see.' Lestrade looked at his fingertips. 'It's that simple?'

'It is. The Chinese were using thumb prints as signatures as long ago as two hundred years before Christ. Purkenje at Breslau suggested a classification system in 1823 and William Herschel in Bengal . . .'

'Doesn't this depend on one thing?' Lestrade asked.

'What?'

'On knowing what our man's whoops are like?'

'Ah, yes. But all you need to do is take fingerprint samples from all the passengers . . .'

'All the passengers?' Lestrade roared. 'Well, that's a mere fifteen thousand a day on the City and South London line alone, Mr Galton. That's assuming they'd actually let us do it, of course. You'll be telling me next that you can divide people up by the kind of blood they've got or tell a man's physical characteristics by his bodily secretions! Now, I'm a very busy man, Mr Galton. Have you ever thought of writing sketches for the music hall?'

8

All that was left of Fanny Chattox lay in a smoking heap below the Stockwell gradient. Other than the darting bull's-eyes of the Railway Police, the entire tunnel was a tube of utter blackness.

'I just don't believe it, Sholto,' John Thicke was saying. 'Another one right under my nose.'

'Don't reproach yourself, John. There are a lot of miles to cover.'

'I don't know.' Thicke hauled off his bonnet. 'Maybe it's time I hung up my chemise.'

'Now, don't say that,' Lestrade insisted. 'Good women like you are hard to come by. Let's have it again – from the top as I expect Squire Bancroft would say.'

'I was in a padded cell pulled by locomotive Number Eight. We'd just pulled in to Stockwell and I was about to change trains for the ride back when the lights went out.'

'All of them?'

'All the electric ones, yes. Even the gas gave a bit of a flutter. There was the most weird noise – I've never heard anything like it.'

'Can you describe it?'

'It was like . . . like a thousand nails scratching at once on a bucket. It was the sound of Fanny Chattox frying, dying on the line behind me.'

'But you must have been half a mile away.'

'I know. I grabbed the nearest guard and asked him what had happened. He said something or somebody must have fallen on the live rail.'

'You've examined the body?'

Thicke nodded. 'Seen my supper twice,' he said. 'Funnily enough, I don't remember eating any of it.'

'How do we know who she is?'

'Well, we don't. Not for sure. But one of the Railway boys found a handbag a few yards away. It's got her name and address in it. Duke Street.'

'Duke Street?' Lestrade's raised eyebrow was invisible in the darkness.

'That's what I thought,' agreed Thicke. 'A kept woman if ever there was one. The question is, who's keeping her?'

'Nobody now, I fancy. Have you ever seen an electrocution before, John?'

'Never,' said the Inspector. 'And I don't want to again, thanks. It's the smell, isn't it? That's the worst part. Sort of sickly sweet, like roast pig at the fair.'

'All right, have a cigar. Give me your bull's-eye.'

'Put that bloody light out!' a voice rang through the caverns measureless to man. 'We don't want anybody else going up in smoke.'

'Sorry!' Lestrade called and Thicke tucked the Havana into his garter for use on a later occasion.

The Yard man stumbled off down the line. The live rail was dead now, its current switched off. Still it shone deadly in his torch beam, a silver slash in the darkness rising a foot from the right-hand rail and mounted on curiously wrought glass insulators. The whole thing was about three inches wide where the locomotive's collector shoes nudged it in the course of a journey. And there was a three-inch gash across the face and breast of Fanny Chattox as she lay, done to a turn, staring at the blackness of the ceiling. She had been lovely once, Lestrade could tell, but her mystery paramour at Duke Street would not want to look at her now. Her skin was the colour of old mahogany and her hair like black wire. Her clothes lay in tatters around her and her boots lay down the line where the thump of the shock had blown them.

But it was the mouth that Lestrade would remember all his life – the lips peeled back from the bared teeth, the throat swollen as it had convulsed for the last scream that never came. Under the bodice and the once-voluptuous breasts the lungs had frozen and the heart had stopped.

He shook himself free of it, the nausea of death, and he walked back down the line, taking Thicke with him as he went.

'I want to see everybody,' he whispered, his words reverberating oddly in the dome of the tunnel. 'Everybody, do you understand, who works on this line. Day shift, night shift, it doesn't matter. Guards, engine drivers, platform porters, ticket collectors. And I want them here at Stockwell by midday tomorrow. He's not going to claim another victim if I can help it.'

He told them to be vigilant. The guards especially. But as one of the City and South London's more learned philosophers pointed out, 'Who guards the guards?'

It was thus that Lestrade had another look at the dusty old ledgers kept at Stockwell, among the peaked caps and gleaming ticket machines. On three of the Nights In Question, the murders of Fanny Chattox, Henrietta Fordingbridge and Verity True, the regular guards had gone sick with a curious malaise and A. N. Other had taken their place.

'Who are these replacements?' Lestrade had asked. And the supervisor had shrugged.

'Well, I thought I knew all the guards on this line,' he had said. 'The trouble is in the summer we're short-staffed. That Gladstone bloke's got a lot to answer for with the Annual Holiday Act. In my day . . .'

But Lestrade had had no time to reminisce. He questioned the three guards whose tours of duty had witnessed the three fatal rides up the line to death. Yes, they'd all come over peculiar the night before. Yes, they'd sent messages to the effect they wouldn't be in, but by the time the under-manager had gone to the locomotive locum register, somebody had already filled in a name. That was that. He assumed that the under-under-manager (an ambitious lad) had beaten him to it. And so Lestrade was left with three different names in the same spidery hand. Bearing in mind the patent nonsense spouted by the boffin at the Yard, there was clearly no point in showing the signatures to him. And anyway, they were obviously in disguise. Neither did the names mean anything to him – Hudson, Gooch and Hackworth. They sounded vaguely like a trio who might play with Dr Grace, but that was no help.

What of the other guards, Lestrade had asked – the partners of those who had gone sick? Had they noticed Messrs Hudson, Gooch and Hackworth? Well, not really. The other guard was three carriages away and it *was* always dark on the Underground. All they saw was a peaked cap and a whistle and a pair of flags. And these were available in the supervisor's office which was open day and night, and in any case there were replacements at every station to King William Street.

And so, tired and old before his time, Inspector Sholto Lestrade crawled back to the Yard, beaten, if only for now, by the appalling lack of observation of his fellow men. Tube travellers saw nothing, heard nothing, said nothing. And the staff were no better. Incompetence. Amateurism. Lackadaisicalism. What a way to run a railroad!

It was a grim-faced trio of bobbies who were lined up outside the office of Assistant Commissioner Nimrod Frost that afternoon. Constables Russell and Bromley in their brand-new detective serge. Walter Dew, an older hand altogether, his boater tucked into the crook of his arm.

'Mr Frost says you're to go in, sir,' Dew mumbled.

'Thank you, Walter,' Lestrade said, 'and cheer up. They haven't taken away your pension yet.'

'Guv'nor,' Dew blurted while Lestrade's fist was poised to knock the frosted glass.

'What is it, Walter? I'm a very busy man.'

The Constable thrust out a steadfast hand. 'I just wanted to say, sir, that these seven years have been . . . well, good isn't the word. You taught me all I know, guv, from petty larceny and safe breaking to the most indigenous forms of murder. I shan't forget that.'

'Good God, Walter, has His Nims got a scaffold waiting for me inside?'

'That goes for us too, sir,' Russell said. 'It's only been as many weeks as Mr Dew has had years, but it's been a joy to watch you working.'

'Pure delight, guv'nor,' Bromley said. 'There isn't a man in the Essex Force to match you.'

'Well, well, Bromley,' said Lestrade, 'high praise indeed. Now, I'm very grateful for the guard of honour and the kind words. I daresay His Nims will give me the clock. In the meantime, haven't you got any murders to solve?' And he knocked and entered.

It was not a gallows facing Lestrade, but it might as well have

159

been. The grey, pompous faces grouped around the room were infinitely more terrifying than Mr Berry the hangman or the Billingtons who had replaced him. There was even a vicar with his collar on back to front in lieu of the prison chaplain. Behind the great oak desk with its ormolu inkwells and blue lamp sat a stony-faced Assistant Commissioner and at his shoulder, like a self-satisfied parrot, the smug sidewhiskers of Chief Inspector Abberline.

'Gentlemen,' said Frost, 'this is Inspector Lestrade who until today was conducting inquiries into the Underground murders. Lestrade, these gentlemen are from the City and South London and Metropolitan and District Railway Companies. They are here to express their concern.'

'Good,' said Lestrade. 'Some two weeks ago I sent Detective Constable Dew to interview these gentlemen. They were, to a man, unaccountably busy and refused to see him.'

'How dare you!' a rubicund gentleman thundered, heaving himself to his feet. 'I see what you mean, Nimrod, about insubordination. Six women are dead, sir,' he rounded on Lestrade, 'and what are you doing about it?'

'You are, sir?' Lestrade asked.

'Bloody furious,' the man retorted, and in deference to the clergyman, 'begging your pardon, Bartholomew.'

'I fully understand, Basil. Our Lord surely had in mind the acquisition of a profit when he changed water into wine and fed the five thousand.'

'I mean,' said Lestrade, undeterred by puffing bullies like Basil, 'who are you?'

'Don't be impertinent, Lestrade,' Frost snapped.

'I believe I have a right to know my detractors,' Lestrade snapped back.

'Well,' growled Frost, 'we don't have all day.'

'I am Sir Basil Mott,' the rubicund gentleman said, turning such a shade of magenta that he threatened to cross the rubicund, 'resident engineer for the City and South London Railway. And to save you asking again, the clerical gentleman is the Reverend Bartholomew Dutts, principal shareholder and chaplain to the company.'

'Charmed,' lied Lestrade.

'This,' he indicated a foreign-looking gent with swarthy skin and a goatee, 'is Mr C. E. Spagnoletti, consulting electrician to the company.'

'Saluti.' The little Wop managed an icy grin.

'These are Messrs Hanbury, Hubbard, Robinson and Grenfell, directors of our company . . . and theirs.'

'We have elected Sir Basil as our spokesman,' Grenfell said, 'because although Sidney here,' he tapped Hubbard on the shoulder, 'is our elder chairman, he's not as compos as he was. Doesn't follow trains of thought. Do you Sidney?' he bellowed into the man's ear trumpet.

'A cup of tea would be lovely,' the old man agreed.

'Thank your lucky stars,' Grenfell told Lestrade, 'we left his dad at home this morning.'

'We haven't time for niceties, Charles,' Mott burbled. 'The point is that Bartholomew has hit the nail on the proverbial head. Profits. We are losing money to the tune of some . . . what is it, Bartholomew?'

'Three hundred pounds a day,' the vicar told him.

'Exactly.' Mott paced Frost's carpet in front of Lestrade. 'Nobody's riding the line any more. We used to carry fifteen thousand people a day. Now that deluge has slowed to a trickle – what is it, Bartholomew?'

'An estimated eight and a half thousand,' the Reverend intoned.

'Precisely.' Mott was in full flight.

'This fellow,' said Grenfell, 'this murderer chappie, seems to come and go like a will-o'-the-wisp. No one sees him. No one hears him. And the first we know of it is another grisly report in the morning papers. Sidney,' Grenfell flicked the elder chairman with his coat tail, 'don't do that.'

And the elder chairman desisted, at least for the time being.

'I am doing all that I can,' Lestrade explained, 'but you must appreciate the scale of the problem. With fifteen thousand people a day – even eight and a half thousand – to watch, my men are stretched pretty thin. I feel sure that Mr Frost has already pointed this out.'

'Frost carries the can,' Mott thundered. 'We're all senior executives here; we know the score. If something was amiss in my electrics, I'd expect to offer my head to the headsman. As would Bartholomew, if all was not well in his vestry. But . . .' and he closed to his man, 'at the same time I'd personally roast the underling who crossed the wrong wires – just as Bartholomew would excommunicate the curate who'd fouled the ecumenical nest; wouldn't you, Bartholomew?'

'It would certainly be a case of unction in the extreme,' the principal shareholder nodded.

'Well, there you are,' Mott subsided. 'Six women dead, profits vanishing. Any more of it, and I'll go to the Central London, as God is my witness – oh, saving your presence, Bartholomew.'

The clergyman nodded with a holier-than-anybody look on his face.

'That's enough!' Frost bellowed. He had been silent for a while and the explosion, when it came, moved mountains. The lamp shook and the pens jumped in their glass housings. Even Abberline moved away from the shock waves. 'We'll have no more talk of heads rolling,' he said. 'I may be a public servant, but by God,' and he made no apology to the clergyman, 'that's only a figure of speech. If I ran my detective force like you gentlemen run your railway, there'd be anarchy, gentlemen, chaos. This is still the safest city in the world thanks to men like Lestrade.' Frost was on his feet, easily out-Motting Sir Basil, thumping his blotting paper for extra effect. 'This man you see before you, gentlemen, is the very soul of integrity. A master of wit and repartee. Don't believe a word of the scurrilous nonsense written about him in the *Strand Magazine*. It's all patently untrue. And the fact that he has not taken out a writ of libel against Doctors Watson and Conan Doyle is testimony enough to the kind of man he is. He has faced knives, bullets, coshes, bricks in the line of duty. He has stared down some of the nastiest bastards known to man, solved the most ingenious of crimes, baffled the brains of the Underworld. The *Struwwelpeter* murders, the Brigade Case, the affair at Rhadegund Hall, the Pillow Case are the iceberg's tip of his triumphs, gentlemen. Now he has another job to do. And the best that the likes of you and I can do is to stand by and give him every assistance. Give him the tools and he'll do the job. Won't you, Sholto?'

Lestrade's mouth, like that of every other man in the room, was hanging open. He didn't realize that Frost even knew he had a first name, let alone that he might use it. 'Yes, sir,' was all he could find to say.

162

It was Mott who found himself first. 'Well, Nimrod,' he said, 'you and I go back a long way – when my father used to shop at your father's grocer's in Grantham. All I can say is, I hope you know what you're doing. You know I know the Commissioner, don't you?' And he raised a deadly eyebrow.

'Well, that makes two of us, Bazza, old boy. So bugger off!'

The clergyman dropped the top hat he was balancing on his knee.

'Come on, Sidney.' Grenfell helped the old codger to his feet. 'We've just witnessed the downfall of the Assistant Commissioner at Scotland Yard.'

'Oh,' said the elder chairman, 'I'll settle for coffee if you have no tea, I wouldn't want to be a nuisance.' And they helped him out.

The glass door slammed with a crash as the last of the railwaymen left.

'I'd just like to say, sir . . .' Lestrade began.

He was jabbed in the ribs by a stubby, exasperated finger. 'Don't, Lestrade. Don't say anything. Because if you do, I'm likely to commit detecticide. And with Abberline standing here, I probably wouldn't get away with it.' He looked at the Chief Inspector. 'Oh, I don't know, though. What I gave them is the same load of tosh I'd give Fleet Street. Confidence in my men, best man for the job, no stone unturned, etcetera, etcetera. In fact, Lestrade, this investigation of yours has been a bloody shambles from beginning to end. You've got constables and inspectors dressing up as women, pointless warnings to the passengers. You've been harassing librarians, fighting with ballet dancers . . . You tried to drown a writer the other day. And,' he lifted a wad of paper from his desk, 'I've got hospital bills coming out of my ears! Well, it's over, Lestrade. You may have missed my opening rejoinder when you arrived, so I'll say it again. You were, until this morning, in charge of the case. Now you're not. Abberline is.'

And the Chief Inspector couldn't resist a smirk at Lestrade's expense.

'Under my instructions, he will place uniformed men at every station and he will put a uniformed man on every train.'

'With respect, sir . . .' Lestrade began.

'Respect, Lestrade?' Frost roared. 'Respect? You don't know the meaning of the word.'

'That will only drive our murderer underground.'

'Oh, very droll, Lestrade,' Frost snarled. 'This isn't the Police Revue, man. This is murder. Worse, it's multiple murder. I'm talking about prevention. We owe it to the public to keep them safe.'

'Then shut the Tubes,' Lestrade said.

'Are you mad?' Abberline shouted.

'Shut up, Abberline.' Frost cut him dead. 'I'll question people's sanity around here. Are you mad, Lestrade?'

'That's the only way you'll stop him. Blanket policing can't do it. If you cover the City and South London, he'll just strike on the Metropolitan and District. Cover that and he'll hit the Central London. Cover that and he's back to the City and South London again. You don't have enough men to cover more than one line at a time. You know that and so does he.'

'Why do you think they built the Underground in the first place, Lestrade?' Frost was calmer. 'Because without it, you couldn't move on the streets. Man, you'd grow old crossing Whitehall. If we shut the Underground now, even for a day, it would stop the life of London. The metropolis would be dead inside a week, choking on its own stagnation. This is 1895, Lestrade. We are the Workshop of the World. The very existence of the Empire would be seriously threatened. Civilization as we know it would come to a squealing stop. The government would move to Birmingham.'

'So what do you suggest I do?' Lestrade asked.

An evil grin spread over the walrus features of the Assistant Commissioner. 'Ho, ho, for a moment there, Lestrade . . .' Then the grin vanished, and he held out his hand. 'What you will do is hand me your warrant card. I am suspending you without pay for the duration of this case.'

'Why? Because I haven't caught a murderer?'

'Don't presume to ask me for reasons, Lestrade.' Frost was almost inaudible in his fury. 'You don't have the rank for it. No, for the record, it is not because you have signally failed to catch the Underground murderer. It is because you allowed a female civilian, to wit one Agnes True to sleep . . . yes, *sleep*, Lestrade, under this very roof on no less than two occasions last week.'

'She did sleep alone, sir,' Lestrade pointed out, glaring knowingly at Abberline.

'I don't care if she slept with the entire Yard Glee Club and the Walthamstow Dog Handlers! The point is that Miss True is a) a civilian and b) a woman. We aren't a hotel, Lestrade. Neither are we a doss-house. What on earth were you thinking of, man?'

'She wanted to help, sir. Her sister was one of the Underground victims.'

'I know that, man,' Frost bellowed. 'Just because I am Assistant Commissioner doesn't mean I am a complete idiot. How could she possibly help by sleeping at the Yard?'

'Grief takes people in mysterious ways, sir,' the Inspector told him. 'I believe she needed to be kept busy. Her job at the library is very intermittent.'

'Yes, well, you'll be busy for a while too, Lestrade,' Frost snatched the warrant card from Lestrade's grasp, 'thinking up reasons why I shouldn't kick you back into uniform. Good afternoon.'

The Inspector spun on his heel. He'd been in this position before. It wouldn't break his stride.

'Oh and by the way,' Frost stopped him, 'that was a lie I told the railwaymen about not believing what Conan Doyle says about you. The only bit he's wrong about is that you're the best of a bad bunch!'

Lestrade threw his spare collars into his battered Gladstone, exchanged a few short words with Dew and Russell, brought himself to nod to Bromley and stepped out on to the Embankment. It was the afternoon of a glorious day in June. The sun danced and dazzled on the water and the happy shouts and laughter of the day trippers on the pleasure steamers drifted across the city. Knots of little girls with frothy dresses and wide-brimmed straw hats came running down the walkway as he wandered the water-wall.

'Inspector Lestrade.' A voice made him turn.

'Mr Lavender,' he said.

'This is a coincidence,' the museum man said, 'meeting you outside Scotland Yard and all. How is it going?'

'Badly, thanks,' Lestrade said. 'How are you on electrocution?'

'Er . . . rather vague, I'm afraid.'

'Look,' Lestrade had hit upon an idea, 'there's something I have to check. Do you mind accompanying me to the morgue?'

Lestrade had hoped that it was Igor's day off. Sadly, he was mistaken. The old mortuary attendant of Old Montague Street showed the gentlemen into the cold recesses of his lair. After the glare of the pavements above and the drone of the bluebottles around the horse manure, Igor's basement was a welcome relief.

'This won't be pleasant, Mr Lavender,' Lestrade warned the railway expert, not for the first time on this case. Igor, at a word from the Inspector, hauled back the linen shroud.

Lavender sucked in his breath and turned away. 'Good God,' he mumbled.

'Are those wounds constituent with hitting a live rail?' Lestrade asked him.

'I would think so.' Lavender declined the glass of water that Igor had thoughtfully provided. Like Lavender, it did look a little green.

'I am making the assumption,' Lestrade said, 'that she was pushed off the end carriage of the last but one down train near the Stockwell gradient last night. That would make sense, wouldn't it?'

'I suppose so. The conductor rail carries, I believe, a current of five hundred volts.'

'Enough to kill a woman?' Lestrade asked.

'Two hundred and fifty volts or less can do dat, Mr Lestrade.' Igor was polishing somebody's teeth. 'But of course it depends on de condition of de skin – moist or dry, de material vich de lady vas vearing, und zo on.'

'I had no idea you were such an expert, Igor.'

'All forms of death interest me,' the mortuary attendant sniffed. 'It goes viz ze job. It won't be long before ve are executing our criminals viz Old Sparky de vay de Americans do.'

'Do they?' Lavender had had to sit down.

'Oh, yah,' Igor told him. 'Dey pin a man into a chair, not unlike de one you are sitting in.' Lavender stood up immediately. 'Dey put his feet into a bowl of water und place wires on to his head. Dey say it takes eleven minutes to die. Und all de lights go out.'

'The smell must be awful,' Lestrade commented.

Igor sniffed, a martyr to mucus. 'I probably would not notice dat.' He joined Lestrade by the corpse of Fanny Chattox. 'Post-mortem's tomorrow,' he said. 'Vaste of time, really. Dere will be numerous subserous ecchymoses und capillary haemorrhages in de brain. De cytoplasm of de nerve cells vill hev undergone marked changes. De immediate cause of death will of course be cardiac fibrillation, I shouldn't be at all surprised.'

'No, Igor,' Lestrade slowly shook his head. 'There I must disagree with you. You see here, on the throat? Bruising. The immediate cause of death was a madman who leapt out at Miss Chattox. She struggled and she jumped, or was thrown, on to the line. We'll see ourselves out.'

'Come back sometime, already!' Igor called, waving the dentures at them.

Lavender at least was glad to feel the sun on his back in Old Montague Street. 'What now, Mr Lestrade?' he asked.

'Now every station, every train on the City and South London line will be guarded by uniformed police. Whether they'll leave my plainclothesmen incognito, I don't know.'

'They? But aren't you running the case?'

'As of this morning, apparently not,' Lestrade said. 'I've been suspended.'

'By what?' Lavender was shocked.

'The Assistant Commissioner,' Lestrade told him. 'Could have been worse. Could have been by the testicles.'

'What I can't understand is why the guard didn't see all this,' Lavender said.

'That's easy,' Lestrade answered. 'The man I'm looking for *is* a guard. Or at least, he's posing as one. I don't suppose the name Hudson means anything to you?'

'There was a clergyman of that name who perished on the Matterhorn a few years ago. And another after whom they named a strait.'

Lestrade shook his head. 'What about Gooch?'

It was Lavender's turn to shake his.

'Hackworth?'

'No, I'm sorry. I'm not being much help, am I, Inspector?'

'More than some, Mr Lavender,' Lestrade said. 'More than some.'

'What will you do now?' the railway expert asked. 'Grow geraniums like Superintendent Tomelty?'

'Probably,' Lestrade said. 'I've heard they sell some marvellous manure in Duke Street.'

The sun was still high when Lestrade found the number he wanted – thirty-five. It was typical of all the other terraced houses in the area, tucked away behind the bustle of Oxford Street, within hailing distance of the Row. This was not his first visit, nor probably would it be his last. And unlike the first time, when he was a green-as-grass rookie, he was on his guard. However placid the portico might appear, here was an avenue notorious throughout the metropolis. It ranked with the Ratcliffe Highway where policemen patrolled in fours, with Cleveland Street where, until recently, titled gentlemen whiled away whole afternoons with post office boys and the Nicol where London's gangland plied its grisly trade. He patted the brass knuckles in his pocket, just for good measure.

A black woman with the build of a goldfish bowl opened the door to him. She wore a tea towel around her head and her teeth shone like pearls. 'Yessir,' she bobbed.

'Is this the house of Miss Fanny Chattox?' he asked.

'Miss Fanny not at home today, sir,' and she began to close the door.

The Inspector was faster, however, and he winced as the oak pinned his foot to the frame. 'I know,' he said through swimming vision. 'I'll just wait if you don't mind.'

'Oh, no, sir. I can't let you in, sir. It's more than my job's worth, sir.'

'Now, now.' Lestrade wrestled with the woman for control of the door. If he hadn't brought his knee up sharply into the pit of where he guessed her stomach must be, she would probably have won. Holding her at arm's length was more difficult because she had the momentum of a rolling pumpkin.

'Let's calm down, shall we?' he shouted. 'I am a policeman. Inspector Lestrade from Scotland Yard.'

Her iron grip lessened and she stood hopping from foot to foot.

'Who are you?' he said calmly.

'I's Hecuba, massa,' she told him.

'Hecuba. You are Miss Fanny's maid?'

'Of all work, massa, yessir. Yessir.'

'Tell me, Hecuba,' he led her gingerly into a tastefully decorated drawing-room, 'whose house is this?'

'Is Miss Fanny's house, sir,' she told him.

'Yes, but who *owns* it, Hecuba? Miss Fanny just lives here, doesn't she? Who looks after her?'

'I do, sir. Hecuba look after Miss Fanny.'

He took her gently by her solid, gingham-wrapped shoulders. 'Not any more, Hecuba,' he said.

She looked at him, blinking uncomprehendingly.

'Can you read, Hecuba?' he asked.

'No, massa,' she said. 'Readin' is de work of de devil. No good person in Trinidad can read. 'Cept minister. An' he de biggest devil of dem all.'

'Yes, of course.' Lestrade had met ministers like that. 'Then you won't know,' he said. 'You won't have seen the papers. Come and sit down.'

'Oh no, sir,' and her huge eyes rolled in horror, 'I isn't to sit down in here, sir. Hecuba's chair is down de stairs. In de basement.'

'It's all right, Hecuba,' and he squeezed her ample buttocks into the Chesterfield, 'I'm sure Miss Fanny won't mind. I'm afraid I have some bad news for you. Miss Fanny isn't going to mind anything any more. I'm afraid she's dead.'

The black woman sat as though poleaxed, her eyes staring madly ahead, her arms crossing and uncrossing across her rolltop bust. She began burbling and muttering in a strange rhythmic hum. Lestrade flashed his hand in front of her face. Nothing. He clicked his fingers. No response. He stamped on her foot. To all intents and purposes, Hecuba was dead. He dashed to the kitchen in the basement, grabbed a jug of water and hurtled back upstairs with it. Hecuba was still humming like a Beyer and Peacock engine and he threw the contents of the jug full in her face. No response at all. The only difference was that instead of sitting there practising mumbo-jumbo she now sat there doing it wringing wet.

At that point, Lestrade, that most resourceful of detectives, knew when to give up on a lost cause and did a recce of the house. Miss Fanny's fol-de-rols, yards of silks and satins and lace, hung neatly folded by a Trinidadian hand. Other unmentionables still lay on her vast bed, but it was the bed itself that held Lestrade's attention, for carved into the gilt beading of the headboard was a family crest he thought he knew. Pausing only to check that the maid was still breathing, he saw himself out, and went down to the station and took him a train.

The Pelican Club was not so much a meeting of like minds; it was a meeting of no minds at all. And when Lestrade found them, it was on the evening of one of their annual – and clandestine – outings. He'd called in a favour from one of the minor aristocrats who owed him one and that minor aristocrat, loose of lip as well as of morals, had spilled beans in all directions. It had only taken a reminder from Lestrade that Henry Labouchere's Act, passed by both Houses of Parliament not eleven years ago, had been set up to deal with just the sort of acts that the minor aristocrat had practised. And the minor aristocrat had talked.

'For God's sake, Lestrade,' he had squawked, 'when you see him, don't tell him I sent you. And never, never, never tell him that I once knew Oscar Wilde.'

The trap left Lestrade at the entrance to the park, and the rest of the way, via the trout lakes and the stables, the suspended Inspector went on foot. As he passed the green gargoyles with their lichen and their verdigris, he heard the distant roars of a crowd, subdued, muted, as though buried beneath the earth. He slunk around corners, extricating privet from his person. The sun was nearly down, but his boater made too bright a target in its dying rays and he discarded it. Half hidden in the tangle of ivy was the iron-studded door that the minor aristocrat had told him about. Lestrade was grateful. Certainly he would never have found this for himself. He tapped on it with his fist.

An iron grille shot back and a heavy bloated face peered out. 'Yes?' it said.

'Queensberry rules OK.' Lestrade gave the password of the Pelican Club. There was a rattling and sliding of bolts and the heavy door swung open. The heavy bloated face belonged to a man with a heavy bloated body who pushed Lestrade against a whitewashed wall at the entrance to a tunnel and frisked him. Out came the usual – the string, the train ticket, the fluff and finally, with a raised, bloated eyebrow from the frisker, the brass knuckles with the murderous switchblade. But Lestrade was in no position to argue – he was after all the friskee; a guest and subject to the rules of the Pelican Club. He must play the game.

The heavy led him down a brick-built tunnel, like the sort they put over canals, and through another studded door just like the first. In the huge room beyond, top-hatted gents milled around on a straw-strewn floor. The whole place stank of sweat and liniment and blood, and in a sulphur-lit area in the centre two bare-knuckled boxers slogged it out, their hands raw, their faces masks of crimson. The grunts and thuds of their impact were drowned by the baying of the mob who roared for more in the raked seats around them, and Lestrade had never seen so much money cascading through the air in his life. A shirt-sleeved man rang a bell and the boxers collapsed into opposite corners of the ring to be fanned and doused with water.

A strange hush fell on the gathering and all eyes turned to Lestrade.

'Which of you is the Marquess of Queensberry?' he asked.

For a moment, no one moved. Then there was a stir in the crowd and a wizened little man with the stoop and sidewhiskers of an orang-utan shuffled forward. 'I'm Queensberry,' he rasped. 'Who the devil are you?'

'Lister,' lied Lestrade. '"Fighting Joe" Lister from Ballygowan.'

'You don't sound Irish to me.' Queensberry peered at him.

'You don't sound like a marquess to me,' Lestrade countered.

'How'd you get here?'

'Train, then pony and trap,' Lestrade said.

There were a few sniggers until Queensberry silenced them with a scowl. 'Oh, a wit yet,' he snarled. 'Fortinbras,' he summoned the heavy at Lestrade's elbow, 'did he give the password?'

'He did, my lord.'

'Well, where'd you learn that, buckaroo?' Queensberry pressed him.

Now, Lestrade knew the value of narks. The need to keep them safe. The vital necessity of not betraying them to anyone. He knew it and he approved it. However, 'Sir Roger Foulsham sent me,' he confessed. 'You know, the friend of Oscar Wilde.'

There was an inrush of breath. After that the only sound that could be heard was the dripping of blood from the boxers.

'That somdomite!' Queensberry snarled. 'So, you're another of those bloody Maryannes, are you?'

'No,' said Lestrade. 'In fact, I used to be happily married.'

'So did that somdomite Wilde. Threw me out of his house, he did. Cheeky little bugger.' Queensberry closed to Lestrade. 'Well, he's rotting now in Reading Gaol for his pains. They don't like Maryannes in prison. I'd be surprised if he survives. Either way, he's finished. Nobody'll watch that rubbish of his anymore – what's that one called – *The Importance of Being a Woofta*?'

'I came to play.' Lestrade flashed his wallet, careful not to let anyone see how empty it was.

'We'll get to that,' Queensberry said. 'But anyone joining the Pelican has to go through a little initiation first. Isn't that so, boys?'

There were shouts of assent all round.

'Yes, indeed.' Queensberry cleared the way. 'Any new bug has to go three rounds with the Masher.'

Roars of approval deafened Lestrade and he felt himself being lifted off his feet and up into the ring.

'Well, take your shirt off, Lister,' Queensberry shouted. 'Don't want to get blood over everything, do we?'

Lestrade slipped off the jacket, his regulation serge, then the waistcoat, carefully hooking up his half-hunter. While unbuttoning his cuffs, his opponent shambled into the ring. There were cheers and whistles, and the Masher raised his hands in the air in acknowledgement. He made the heavy on the door look positively dainty. His chest and back were a mass of matted hair and he had fists like sledgehammers.

'In the Red Corner,' a nattily titfered Master of Ceremonies suddenly announced, 'we have Maurice "The Masher" Melhuish, bare-knuckle champion of all Berkshire and a bit of Surrey. And in the Blue Corner . . . er . . . who?'

'"Fighting Jack" Lister,' shouted Lestrade, easily equal to the occasion (or so he kept telling himself as the butterflies prepared to leave his stomach in droves), 'the Ballygowan Bomber.'

There were howls of derision. Lestrade stood in his regulation trousers and his stockinged feet at a little under eleven stone. The Masher, with all the grace of a Clydesdale, must have been nearly twice that. The Master of Ceremonies called the contestants together in the centre and clapped a hand on each of their shoulders.

'Right, lads,' he said, 'I want a good clean fight. No gouging, no chewing, no kneeing in the bollocks. And when I say "break", I mean "break". All right?'

They pressed knuckles together and turned back to their respective corners, but as Lestrade turned, Masher didn't and brought a fierce fist crashing down on the Inspector's neck. Lestrade saw a mass of cheering, shouting faces, red with the heat and the excitement. Then he saw sawdust and felt a stockinged foot jab into his ribs. He rolled away from his opponent and managed to get to his knees before a hefty left foot pounded into his face and he went sprawling across the floor.

'Oh, dear, Lister,' he heard Queensberry bellow amid the cackling laughter, 'we said three *rounds*, m'boy, not three seconds.'

Lestrade shook the dust from his eyes and this time got to his feet. Masher was coming for him, swaying, his left arm held steady, his right pounding the air gently. If he could stay away from that right for long enough, he might just last the round. But his lungs felt like razors inside his chest and his vision was blurred. Two Mashers were more complicated – and four fists to watch out for. Lestrade stumbled backwards, Masher taunting him, dribbling saliva as he came. The crowd began to boo and catcall, clearly disappointed by the feeble show before them.

It was while Lestrade was watching Masher's right that the ground came up to hit him. That was because he had not been watching the left. Massive raw knuckles buried themselves in Lestrade's nose with a crunch and he bounced back, only to slump forward the next second as that deadly right caught him again. He was now in danger of forgetting what day it was and he kept telling himself over and over again as he fought to regain his feet that it was Thursday.

Four or five of the seven bells must have been knocked out of him already, but he couldn't hear the bell to end round one. That was because there was a permanent ringing in his ears. Masher came forward to deliver the *coup de grâce* as Lestrade swayed groggily, trying to keep his fists in front of his face. But the thug's swing was as wild as Oscar and it gave Lestrade an opening. He clasped both hands as though in prayer and smashed into Masher's paunch. The ox stood there stunned for a second, and Lestrade lashed the man's groin with his left foot. The moron was still on his feet, so Lestrade launched the other foot and Masher dropped to his knees, his eyes crossed, grunting like a castrated camel. The Inspector timed the next one carefully because he had a feeling it might be the last he was capable of, and with both fists he slammed the Champion of all Berkshire and a bit of Surrey into the middle of next week. The giant rolled sideways and lay motionless in the dust. Now, the cheering had stopped and the crowd was silent.

'Well done, Mr Lister,' said Queensbury. '"Fighting Joe" indeed. Come and have a drink with me. I think you've earned it,' and he nodded to men on his right and left as he led the battered brawler into an ante-room and poured them both brandies.

Lestrade's moustache was visible to both men as it stood so far out on Lestrade's swollen lip that he could see it easily. His nose was trickling blood and there was definitely a second Marquess of Queensbury, a little greyer and standing very close to the first.

'You've done that before,' the Marquess said. 'Now,' and he peered under the bloody gash across Lestrade's left eyebrow ridge, 'who are you really?'

'I told you,' Lestrade managed with his thick lip. The brandy stung like hell but it helped him focus.

He heard the door open behind him and an object hurtled through the air, narrowly missing his head. He recognized it immediately by its empty sound. His wallet.

'He's a bloody peeler, John,' a voice said. 'Scotland Yard, no less. Name of Lestrade.'

'Well, well, well.' Queensberry's face darkened. 'Come to infiltrate our little goings-on, have you? It's not going to work, Lestrade. You see, I'm the originator of the boxing rules the entire country goes by. Gloves, gumshields, fair play – that balderdash. Not for one moment would you get the world to believe that I run *this* side of the Pelican Club. A pity you didn't call tomorrow – I could have matched you against a bull terrier. I don't think you'd have come out of *that* one so lightly. Once those little beauties have their jaws around your vitals, that's it. Gangrene would set in before we could separate you.'

'What you . . . gentlemen . . . do in your spare time is of no concern to me,' Lestrade said. 'I am here about Fanny Chattox.'

The leer left the eighth Marquess's face and he snapped his fingers.

'Are you sure, John?' the voice said from behind Lestrade's head. The Inspector's neck muscles were too wrenched for him to turn round.

'Get out, all of you!' he screamed and waited until they'd gone. 'Well, what of her? What of Fanny?'

'She's dead,' Lestrade said.

The Marquess faltered for a moment then swigged the rest of his brandy. 'Dead?'

'Murdered. Electrocuted on the City and South London line late last night.'

'The devil you say.' Queensberry hit the bottle again, thinking. It was not the usual practice of the eighth Marquess. 'It's that mad Black who does for her,' he shouted. 'She's done for her.'

'She has?'

'Of course. Have you met her?'

'Hecuba? Yes, I have.'

'Well, there you are. Is she or is she not as insane as a snake?'

'Well, I . . .'

'Look, I'm an atheist. Refused to take the oath in the House of Lords. Load of Christian tomfoolery, that's what it is. But that mad nigger believes in witchcraft – hoodoo or voodoo or whatever they call it. Goes around like a bloody zombie half the time. She'll have put a spell on Fanny, you mark my words.'

'It is my belief,' said Lestrade, 'that Miss Chattox met her end at the hands of the Underground murderer.'

'Ah, another bloody Maryanne,' Queensberry snorted.

'Really?'

'Of course. It stands to reason. He doesn't like women, does he? That's why he kills them. Stands to reason.'

'Reason has little to do with murder, my lord,' Lestrade said, wiggling a wobbly incisor. 'The pederasts I've known have all been gentle men.'

'They're not gentlemen if they're Maryannes, Lestrade; look at that somdomite Wilde. Buggering young men on the couch in Tite Street. It doesn't bear thinking about. And that son of mine, the reptile. I stopped his allowance, I can tell you. He's a damned cur and a coward that somdomite and Bosie is no son of mine.'

'How long had you known Miss Chattox, my lord?' Lestrade slurred.

'Fanny? Must be three, no, four years.'

'And you ensconced her at Number Thirty-five Duke Street?'

'What of it? A man's got a right to his pleasures, Lestrade. If you'd met my family, you'd understand. They're all after my money, that's all. My eldest, Percy – do you know what that blighter did? He actually . . . God, I still can't believe it . . . he actually put up the bail money for that somdomite. There he was, buggering everything in sight . . .'

'Percy?'

'No, Wilde. Buggering everything in sight. They say even his canary wasn't safe from his bestial assaults.'

'Tsk, tsk.' Lestrade shook his head and instantly regretted it.

'And my eldest bloody son gives him his bail money. It's beyond belief, I tell you. When I saw him last he looked like a dug-up corpse. It's as true as I'm sitting here. Well, there y'are, y'see. Too much madness of kissing. I bumped into him at the corner of Bond Street and he demanded I stop sending obscene messages to that bloody awful wife of his. Know what I did?'

'No.'

'Hit him. Good and hard, too. If it hadn't been for the arrival of the peelers, I'd have belted him good and proper.'

'Have you any idea where Miss Chattox was going, on the Tube so late at night?'

'Not a clue,' admitted Queensberry, his usual predicament, 'But I'll tell you this. I'm getting that mad nigger out of there tomorrow. But I think I'll send Fortinbras round. Just in case, you know; in case she points a bone at me or something. Bloody somdomites.'

9

The man with the badly bruised face poured the contents of the watering can all over the geraniums. Craning as he did so by virtue of the rick in his neck, he could see over the sunlit roofs of the Walworth Road villas the great rococo façade of the Elephant and Castle Station, that bit of territory which had once, the historians said, belonged to Joanna of Navarre. It was now, to Lestrade at least, merely the site of a murder.

'Sholto!' He heard the voice behind him. 'I feel so dreadful about all this. It's my fault you're here at all.'

'Nonsense,' he slurred and saliva dribbled down his chin.

'It's true.' Miss True spun him round as gently as she could. 'You were suspended for allowing me to sleep on the couch at Scotland Yard. Didn't you explain you didn't want me to ride home on the Underground?'

'I don't think His Nims was in the mood to listen. He'd probably have suggested I get a constable to take you in a station wagon.'

'And then he'd have suspended you for improper use of a police vehicle. Either way, it's my fault.'

'No, no.' He blew as best he could through swollen lips to get rid of the aphids. They waved their tentacles at him in derision. 'This is just one of Abberline's little machicolations,' he told her. 'It's high time that bloke retired to Bournemouth.'

'Why doesn't he like you?'

'I've never really understood that,' he said. 'He was a rookie like me back in the seventies – in the old H Division based in Whitechapel. I suppose it was hate at first sight. But it's not exactly his fault. I must be difficult to work with.'

She took the watering can from him. 'And as a gardener,' she smiled, 'you make a damned good policeman.'

'I must admit,' he smiled, 'I'm happier with witness boxes than window boxes.'

'When you *do* retire,' she said, 'do you see yourself pruning all day long?'

'Retire? Me?' He laughed. 'Oh, no, I shall die in harness. Some dark alley, some winding stair. I'll be a bit slow with the knuckles one night and that'll be that. The last of the Lestrades. Killed in the line of duty.'

'What about little Emma?' She sat him down. 'She's a Lestrade.'

'Yes, she is,' he nodded. 'But that's precisely why I can't ever have her with me. She's happier in Somerset with the Bandicoots. It's for the best.'

'Well,' she patted his knee, 'you haven't told me about Queensberry.'

'How's the play coming along?' He tried to change the subject. 'Can Bancroft cope without a second gravedigger?'

'Without a second glance,' she said. 'If you'd read his atrocious little book *On and Off Stage with Mr and Mrs Bancroft* you'd understand it. The man's middle name is Ego.'

Squire Ego Bancroft Bancroft, Lestrade mused to himself. These theatrical types got sillier and sillier.

'Johnston is still very cut up about Henrietta, poor dear. I think he's become just slightly unhinged, you know. Handy, I suppose, playing Hamlet. Now, stop avoiding the issue and tell me about Queensberry.'

'Well, the man's an ape, there's no question of it. A total filistine.'

'I think he was horribly cruel to poor Mr Wilde, don't you?'

'Ah,' Lestrade shrugged, '"the British public in one of its periodical fits of morality".'

'Did Oscar Wilde say that?' She thought she had read both of his plays.

'No, but I bet he wishes he had. It was in a lecture I attended on Useful Quips for Policemen. Don't know why that one sticks in my mind particularly. Perhaps it sounds a shade brighter

178

than "Come along, now" and "Move along there".'

'What did Queensberry say about Fanny Chattox?'

'Not a lot. But I suspect he was fond of her, in his fashion. Fonder than of his family, anyway.'

'They say he's mad.'

'No question of it,' agreed Lestrade.

'Do you think he killed her?'

'No.' The suspended Inspector shook his head. 'No, he'd have got some lackey to do it. He had a whole army of toughs to call on. Any one of "the fancy" would slit his granny's throat for a quid. Or should I say guinea? Anyway, what would be the point? Why pay a fortune to equip a lady with fine gowns, an expensive town house and a maid, albeit black and mad, just to bump her off?'

She took his bruised hands in hers. 'You can't leave it alone, can you?' she said. 'Any more than I can? Me, because it's my sister. You, because . . . ? I don't know. Is it in the blood?'

'Perhaps it is,' he smiled.

'Well,' she said, 'two heads are better than one. What have we got?'

'Now, Trottie . . .'

She put a finger to his lips and he winced at the impact. 'Don't you "Now, Trottie" me, Sholto Lestrade. What have we got? What's the common denominator?'

He looked at her long and hard. If he could have screwed up his face to show disapproval without screaming, he would have done so. 'All right,' he sighed and rested his head against the high back of the Chesterfield. 'Six women dead in as many months and the pace is a-growing.'

'Which means?'

'I don't know. There's a lot we don't know about murderers yet. I always thought the phrenologists had the right idea, but it's old hat now, apparently.'

'Phrenologists?'

'Blokes who felt the bumps on your head. A certain pattern of bumps would indicate a criminal type. That way you can watch bumpy babies and prevent them from committing crime.'

'Sounds a bit too simple to me,' Trottie said.

'Most crime is. The trouble is that I keep running into the

clever ones. That doesn't do much for one's chances of promotion, one can tell you. Anyway, anybody feeling my bumps
this morning would have a field day. Perhaps our man feels
the compulsion to kill more strongly than before. Perhaps he
relishes a challenge.'

'A challenge?'

'Yes. If he's ridden the Underground in the past three days
he'll have seen coppers everywhere. Perhaps he sees it as a test
of his manhood.'

'There's nothing manly about killing defenceless women,'
Trottie reminded him.

'Ah, but that's not all of it. He's got to get past ticket barriers,
up and down staircases, in and out of hydraulic lifts. Then he's
got to get past platform officials, other passengers, guards and
drivers. He's got less than five minutes to find a victim, kill
her and get away. He probably thinks he's pretty slick.'

'What do you think, Inspector?' She gazed steadily at him,
her dark eyes burning into his own.

'I don't think he's a sexual maniac,' Lestrade said.

'Why not? He's killed six women. What about the Whitechapel
murders?'

'Totally different kettle of fish.' Lestrade shook his head
gingerly. 'A sexual maniac kills because he can only . . . er
. . . well . . . you know,' and he eased his collar a little.

'Come to fruition?' she suggested without a blush.

'Er . . . what? Oh, yes, quite. He can only fruit in the act of
or just having killed. *This* man doesn't have the chance to fruit
because of the time between stations. And he must know he
hasn't.'

'So he's impotent?'

'Possibly,' said Lestrade, 'but even impotent sexual mani-
acs kill when they'll have time to do the thing properly. I
remember Gerontius Hepplewhite, the Impotent Sex Murderer
of Mevagissey . . .'

'So what do you deduce, then?'

'This has to do with the Underground,' Lestrade said, 'not
with women. Whoever our fiend is, he wants us to *think* there's
another madman out there. Actually, he's as sane as you or I.'

'Did the women have anything in common?' Trottie asked.

'Apart from your sister and Miss Fordingbridge whose link

is actually fairly tortuous, I don't think so. At least we've found none and I've had Dew, Russell and Bromley wearing out shoe leather down that track. It leads to buffers.'

'Could it be a matter of copycat killing?' she posited.

'Perhaps,' said Lestrade. 'Perhaps George Culdrose *did* kill his wife back in February and someone else thought that was a damned simple way of killing someone.'

'But you said it wasn't.'

He blew outwardly with exhaustion. It felt as if there was a Beyer and Peacock Locomotive growling and rattling inside his head. 'Think about it,' he said. 'The first railway murder I know of was back in sixty-four. I was a mere stripling of ten, you weren't born and the Queen, God bless her, was still the Queen. A bloke called Franz Müller killed a bloke called Thomas Briggs in a railway carriage and just walked off the train. Too easy.'

'But they caught him?'

'Oh yes and hanged him. That's because friend Müller had the intelligence of a geranium, which is probably unkind to geraniums. There's no such thing as a perfect murder, Trottie, but you know what the nearest thing to perfection is?'

'No,' she said, waiting to be enlightened.

'Strangers on a train,' he said.

'What?'

'Take a tip from me. If you ever decide to murder someone, murder a complete stranger. Anyone known to you, and you run the risk of being questioned by us and something might slip. Choose a stranger and there's no chance of that. Select someone, anyone, sitting across the central aisle of a padded cell from you, choose your moment and walk away. Until they invent trains with corridors, you've got your victim – all to yourself – at least until the next station.'

'What about the alarm chain?'

'Ah, the lost cord. If the train has one, you've got, as a victim, I'd say, no better than a fifty-fifty chance of reaching it. Whether you'd have the strength to pull it in that situation is anybody's guess. Besides, not all trains have them, which is why, I suspect, our man haunts the City and South London line. That and the fact that you can't see into its carriages from the outside. No, Trottie, make no mistake about it. Our man is very, very clever, but he's rattled now. He's making mistakes.

Fanny Chattox fought back. I don't think he expected that. He got some scratches before. I hate to think what he looks like now. Damn!' And he caught his lip a nasty one on his coffee cup.

'Oh, Sholto,' she stroked his cheek, 'is it *very* painful?'

'Nothing that an old Stanwick like me can't put up with,' he said.

She leaned forward, her arms around his neck. 'You'll catch him, Sholto Lestrade,' she whispered. 'I know you will.'

Her face closed to his, her lips parted. Could he stand the pain? He was never to find out because the clanging of the door bell below drove the sleuths, amateur and professional, apart. Trottie looked out of the window. 'It's a station wagon,' she said. 'Walter Dew is at the door.'

'There's been another one!' Lestrade leapt to his feet and instantly regretted it.

'Gently, Sholto.' She eased him into his jacket.

He managed to stick his head out of the window. An odd combination of pink and purple, he clashed horribly with the geraniums. 'Where, Dew?' he shouted.

'Charing Cross, sir.'

'When?'

'Usual time last night.'

'Damn!' Lestrade hissed, fetching the back of his head a solid one on the sash. 'The Metropolitan and District line. I knew it. Frost and Abberline have got the City and South London sewn up with bobbies so he's bound to go elsewhere. But Charing Cross!'

'What about Charing Cross?' she shouted after him.

'It's probably the busiest station on the entire Underground. He's getting reckless.'

'I'm coming with you.' She ferreted for her hairpins.

'Not this time, Ophelia. You've got a part to learn.' And he slickly locked her door on the outside and left.

'All right, Dew.' Lestrade braced himself against the seat of the wagon. 'What have we got this time?'

'Blimey, guv'nor.' Dew had just noticed the contusions and the puffy cheeks. 'You look like you've gone a round with Maurice "The Masher" Melhuish.'

'Don't be silly, Walter. Morning, Russell.' He tried to smile at the lad. 'How are you enjoying the police force, sonny? Bromley,' he bellowed to the man perched with whip and reins on the box, 'imagine I'm a box of eggs and mind how you go. And no cracks – of the whip or of the wise – I'm feeling *particularly* fragile today.'

'Very good, sir,' and the wagon lurched forward.

'Tripe sandwich, sir?' Dew offered, ever-solicitous of his guv'nor's welfare.

'I'd love to, Walter, knowing, as I do, the love and care that Mrs Dew lavishes on them, but sadly . . .' he patted his face, 'the jaw . . . you understand?'

'Oh, righto, guv. Of course.'

'To cases then.'

'Well, this one's a bit different, sir.'

'Oh? In what way?'

'Well, for a start, sir, he's back to the Metropolitan and District.'

'Right. And?'

'Well, you'll never guess. It's the damnedest thing.'

'Dew,' Lestrade growled, 'I am forty-one years of age. I am under suspension. My head nearly left my shoulders for good two days ago and my entire career is hanging by a thread of intrigue. Now I don't have time for twenty questions, so I'll settle for one – what's different about this case?'

'Well, it's the victim, sir. He's a man.'

'A man?' Lestrade looked at Russell.

'True enough, sir,' the lad confirmed. 'Name of David Appleyard.'

'Well, I'll be buggered,' Lestrade said.

'Brilliant, guv,' Dew grinned, 'if I may be permitted to say so.'

'What?'

'That you knew Appleyard was a Maryanne.'

'What? Not as other commuters, you mean?'

'Well, other than Inspector Thicke and two rookies not a million miles from this 'ere wagon, I know of only one reason why a man puts on women's clothing.'

'Appleyard was in women's clothing?'

Dew nodded.

'A rather fetching little pink number with black ribbons,' Russell said.

'I'm afraid I can't take you to view the body, sir,' Dew apologized. 'Mr Abberline's strict orders. He's put Constables McIntyre and Burgess on the mortuary door.'

'So?' asked the green Russell.

'With the exception of Mr Dew and myself,' Lestrade explained, 'McIntyre and Burgess are the only two totally honest coppers at the Yard. I've got to hand it to Abberline; he can pick 'em. Do I take it from your attire, by the way, Russell, that you and Bromley are not buckling on your corsets on the Underground at the moment?'

'No sir. Mr Abberline's orders, sir. He's left Inspector Thicke going round in circles, still in a frock. Said he didn't want a man like that getting under his feet.'

'Quite. You've seen the body, Dew?'

'Yes, sir.'

'Fill me in, then.'

The detective consulted his notebook as the wagon jolted, despite Lestrade's express instructions to the contrary, round the bend by the Elephant and on in the direction of Vauxhall. Where the Pleasure Gardens used to be, Bromley applied the brake and parked illegally, willing a uniformed man to try to move him on. As always in these situations, there wasn't one to be seen.

'David Dunwoody Appleyard. Aged twenty-five. Address – "The Trossachs", Sussex Gardens. He's a printer's devil. Or he was.'

'I'm sure he was. Any printer in particular?'

'Anybody who'd ask, according to Mr Abberline,' Dew told him. 'You know how he feels about Maryannes.'

'Yes, well, be sympathetic, Walter. When you're married to a man in drag, as Mr Abberline undoubtedly is, it must be grating. Where did Appleyard hang out?'

'Well.' Dew's lips tightened. He was essentially a man of his times and thanks to Henry Labouchere's Criminal Law Amendment Act, the times ran against unnatural practices. So therefore did Walter Dew. 'If my experiences are anything to go by, a little below the waist.'

'No,' Lestrade smiled, 'I mean did he ply his trade in the Dilly? Underneath the arches?'

'We don't know yet.'

'Which way was he going?'

'On the westbound train,' Russell said.

'Last train?'

'Last but one.'

'No witnesses, I suppose?'

Dew shook his head.

'Who found him?'

'General labourer on the Metropolitan. He was going off shift,' said Dew.

'Cause of death?' Lestrade asked.

'Strangulation, same as usual.'

'Was he a big man, Walter, our Mr Appleyard?'

'No. Skinny. Couldn't have been more than five foot two.'

'An easy target, then?'

'Except that he was armed.'

'Armed?' Lestrade looked at his number two. 'With what?'

'A chiv.'

'You found it?'

'Lying next to the body. It had blood on the blade.'

'Where is it now?' Lestrade asked.

Dew smiled. 'I thought you'd never ask, guv,' he said, and produced the weapon from his back pocket. 'Ooh, that's better.'

'Tsk, tsk,' Lestrade chuckled, 'that's tampering with evidence, Walter. If Mr Abberline found out, you'd be back on the horse troughs.'

'Oh, I'm just borrowing it, sir,' Dew assured his guv'nor, wide-eyed, 'using a little initiative, you know.'

'Bless you, Walter,' said Lestrade. He cradled Appleyard's knife in his hand. It was an unusual type, with a tortoiseshell haft and a curved blade that slotted into it.

'Spanish, Mr Abberline says,' Dew commented.

'Well, who are we to doubt it?' Lestrade asked. 'How do we know this isn't the murderer's knife, Russell?'

'Not his modus operandi, sir,' the rookie said. 'Nor even his method of working. There were no cuts on the body of the deceased, were there, Mr Dew?'

'Nothing recent,' Dew said.

'So Mr Abberline thinks this is Spanish, does he?' He tossed the knife and caught it a few times.

'It says "Saragossa" on the blade, sir,' Russell pointed out.

'So it does,' Lestrade said, 'but isn't there a company with that name in the north somewhere? Walter, you remember it from the Cutlery Case?'

'Er . . . no, sir.'

'Yes, yes. Where was that? Sheffield? No. Rochdale?'

'Manchester, sir?' Russell piped up and as he did so, it was as though he felt the dead Maryanne's knife plunged into his own vitals. He'd said it. The one word in all the world that Constable Dew had told him to avoid. And he'd said it to the one man in all the world to whom it mattered.

'That's it.' Lestrade clicked his fingers. 'Well done, lad. Now, Walter, about this blood, the stuff on the blade.'

Dew had not forgiven the enormity of Russell's *faux pas*, even if Lestrade had feigned indifference. 'It was red, sir.' He scowled at the rookie.

'Yes, well,' Lestrade sighed, 'at least we know, then, that Appleyard was not of the aristocracy or it would have been blue. No one, I suppose, thought to have it tested?'

'Tested?' Dew and Russell chorused.

'I'm not surprised at you, Russell. Your knees aren't brown yet, but Dew, really! Time you attended a few lectures, my lad. They could at least have had a look under an Inspectorscope. Were you in at the kill, either of you? Did you visit the scene of the crime?'

'No, sir,' Dew said. 'Mr Abberline took his own lads along.'

'Right. So we don't know whether there was a trail of blood or which way it went or how much there was.'

'No, guv,' Dew admitted.

'You see, Russell, the thing about blood is that a little goes a long way. The head bleeds like buggery – especially, I suspect, in Mr Appleyard's case – though the wound itself may be slight. In other words, if the knife is Appleyard's and he fought back against his attacker, our man might be slightly, very or even fatally wounded. Nobody's reported a bloodstained man, I suppose?'

The constables old and new shook their heads.

'No, well, that was too much to hope for. All right.' Lestrade narrowed his eyes in thought. 'So our man made another mistake. Fanny Chattox tried to get away and if she hadn't fallen on to the live rail, could have survived and fingered him. David Appleyard is altogether the wrong kidney. Either it was blind panic or Appleyard was a damned convincing woman. I must have a word with John Thicke.'

Lestrade stuck his head out of the wagon window. 'Bromley, off your perch. Get in here.'

The old rookie duly obliged. 'Are you a married man, Constable?' Lestrade asked him.

'I am, sir.'

'What are your views on Maryannes?'

'Sir?'

'Homosexuals, Bromley. Those Who Are Not As Other Men. You must have them in Essex, surely? How do you feel about them?'

'I'd string 'em up, sir. Normally, I'm a live-and-let-live sort of policeman, but that's one thing I can't abide.'

'As I thought. Right, you and Dew sit this one out. It's a policeman's excuse me and Russell and I are partners. Walter, I want you to go home and borrow Mrs Dew's lipstick.'

'Mrs Dew doesn't wear lipstick, sir.' The Constable was outraged. 'She's a respectable woman.'

'Yes, of course.' Lestrade realized the social gaffe he had made. 'All right, Russell. Go to Lugley and Butterworth in the Strand. "Everything For Today's Thinking Woman". Buy a lipstick. Something like Love Lies Bleeding or Scarlett's Three Hundred should do the trick.'

'You know an awful lot about lipstick, sir.' Bromley's eyebrow was definitely raised.

'I know an awful lot about an awful lot of things, Constable,' Lestrade told him. 'That's why I'm an inspector and you're a constable.'

'May I ask what this is for, sir?' Russell said.

'Of course, dear boy.' Lestrade fumbled for a cigar. 'This evening, as the sun goes down, you and I will take a little walk down Villiers Street, past that shop that sells artificial limbs and other marital aids and we shall mill underneath the arches. We shall be wearing a particularly eye-catching shade of lipstick of the type you will have bought earlier. We will mingle with the Maryannes and keep our ears to the ground.'

'Won't that leave our backsides rather high in the air?' Russell asked. 'Besides, you haven't asked me my views of Maryannes yet.'

'You're too young to have views on anything yet, Russell. Besides, I need you. A half-dead old man like me wouldn't elicit much interest – you just might; among the silent community, I mean. One of them must know something about the late Appleyard.'

'Guv'nor,' Dew was deferential, as always, 'I don't want to pick flies, but bearing in mind what you look like already is it sensible to go . . . there . . . alone?'

'I was just telling a man the other day, Walter, how nice homosexuals are.'

'Oh, I'm sure they are, sir. But you remember Gervaise Hamilton, the Nasty Homosexual of High Wycombe . . .'

'Yes, as a matter of fact I do, Walter, and with good reason. But there are exceptions to every rule. Most coppers are half-way intelligent – but look at Abberline. And anyway, I won't be alone. Young Russell here will be with me.' And he winked at him. 'By the way,' the scarred face became grim, 'I want to thank you, *all* of you, for doing this. We all know that if the Yard found out, it would mean instant dismissal for you all. Just to be seen with me . . .'

'Oh, don't worry, guv,' Dew grinned. 'We don't intend to be seen.'

A helmeted face appeared at the window of the wagon and saluted. 'Mr Lestrade, Mr Dew, Russell, Bromley, good morning gentlemen. Do you mind tellin' me what you're doin' 'ere, parked in a no-waitin' area?'

The Press of course had a field day. All the late editions had it, blazoned across their frontages – 'Another Tube Slaying'. Some were quite discreet – 'Man In Compromising Costume' said the *Financial Times*; 'Colt Or Filly?' posed the *Horse and Hound*. Others were rather more forthright – 'Marjorie Gets Hers!' brayed the *Sun*. And it was surely a typographical error in *The Times* which had Chief Inspector Abberline quoted as saying that 'a maryanne was helping police with their inquiries'. But there was, in these frightened days, only one letter of complaint.

It was from a gentleman who preferred to remain anonymous but he gave his address as Reading Gaol.

Sunset over the City. A middle-aged man with what appeared to be eyeshadow and a superfluity of rouge walked down Villiers Streeet from Charing Cross Station. A younger man with him was more discreet on the make-up but drew attention to himself with the wiggle; to the extent that a trio of urchins ran behind with their hands down their trousers and their index fingers sticking out of their flies. It had been so for generations and no Act framed by that arch-hypocrite Henry Labouchere MP was going to make the slightest bit of difference.

The odd couple paused briefly outside the shop that sold artificial limbs and other marital aids, craning their necks in disbelief and then swept right, underneath the arches. The trains shook, rattled and rolled overhead as fashionable young men rubbed shoulders and other things against street urchins and mudlarks, and strange twilight creatures of an indeterminate sex undulated through the gathering darkness.

'You're sure you want to go through with this?' Lestrade hissed out of the only corner of his mouth still open.

'My only regret,' whispered Russell, 'is this bloody lipstick. I wish I'd bought Scarlett's Three Hundred now.'

The gas lamps flickered green and sent strange reflections around the glazed tiles of the caverns. In the gloomier corners, lovers entwined in semi-secrecy or stood whispering, their fingers locked, their eyes flaming.

'Welcome to the London nobody knows,' Lestrade said.

'Just as well,' a voice wheedled beside him, 'we haven't seen you here before, ducky.'

He turned to face a willowy young man with aesthetic blond hair that lingered for just a second on his velvet shoulders.

'No, we're new to the area,' Lestrade said, nudging Russell forward, 'Julie and I.'

'Oh,' the young man's face fell, 'my mistake, ducky. Three's a crowd.'

'Not at all.' Lestrade placed a hand on the man's chest. It was light enough to be friendly, but versatile enough to be turned into a police armlock if needs arose. 'I'm Fyllida.'

'Georgina,' the young man said. 'Well, what brings you to these parts? If you take my point?'

The look from Lestrade said it all and a jab from his elbow to Russell's ribs prompted him to look the same.

'Oh, I see,' Georgina trilled. 'Well, of course the place isn't the same these days. I don't know. The Naughty Nineties. It's about as naughty as saying "bother". Would you like to buy me a drink at the Gaiety? I'm parched.'

The Gaiety it was; opulent and gilded and candelabra'd. Lestrade was devastated. He'd forgotten his wallet. Luckily, young Julie had brought his and so all was well. He and his guv'nor stuck to halves, just to keep up appearances while Georgina had a crème de menthe with a dash of absinthe. When he bent low over the table, there was a real risk that all their eyelashes might have got entangled.

It wasn't the cosiest of tête-à-têtes. The management of course had long ago turned blind eyes to such unnatural goings-on. Indeed, Georgina spent most of the time blowing kisses to waiters. Lestrade on the other hand kept an eye out for any sign of Queensberry's toughs. It was well known that earlier in the year they had roamed the West End smashing cafés and restaurants frequented by the Wilde set. And they didn't come much wilder than the patrons of the Gaiety that night. Russell was on the look-out for any plainclothes presence except his own. Glad to help the guv'nor as he was, he knew he was sticking his neck out a long, long way and should there be a visit from the boys in blue or any other colour, he wanted to be sure he got to the door first.

At last Lestrade steered the conversation away from the price of mascara and what fun it had been at prep school and got on to the late departed.

'David Appleyard?' Georgina repeated. 'Oh, yes, we all had his number.'

'Shocking what happened, wasn't it?' Lestrade's lisp was all the easier to do with a thick lip.

'Awful. And of course it could be any one of us, couldn't it? Am I right, Julie, pet?'

'Oh,' Russell began in his usual timbre until a timely toe from Lestrade sent him an octave higher, 'oh you are, you are.'

'Look, Phyllida, love,' Georgina edged closer on the semi-circular seat, 'I don't want to pry, but . . . your face. Did you misread a situation? A certain sign? A flutter of the hand?'

'Well, I . . .'

'Oh, please.' He held up a hand with a glittering bracelet. 'You don't have to say a word, pet, not a word. I know.' He patted Lestrade's hand. 'I've been through it, you see, myself.' And he wiped a large, glistening tear from his eye. 'No one understands the hurt, do they? Oh, I'm not talking about your superficial wounds, your cuts, your bruises. It's only flesh and it'll heal . . . in time. No, it's the lacerations, the contusions to the soul; that's what hurts. Hurts and never heals. I know. I met this bargee once in Birmingham. Well, I know it sounds unlikely, but he had an ear-ring . . .'

'How well did you know David?' Lestrade asked.

'Not very,' Georgina said. 'Underneath the arches he was known as Davinia, of course.'

'Of course,' baritoned Russell, then higher, 'that's nice.'

'Well,' Georgina continued to edge nearer to Lestrade, 'I don't care a fig who knows it. I go for the older man. There, I've said it. I've come out of the water closet. I have to say, pets both, that Davinia wasn't exactly my type. I mean the full corsage, the corsets and so on – it's a bit tasteless in broad daylight, isn't it? I mean, in the privacy of one's own boudoir and then the colours should be hushed tones, all very well. But he was camp as a row of tents.'

'Even so,' Lestrade said, 'somebody had it in for him.'

'Oh yes, well, it's as I was saying – he asked the wrong question of the wrong person. You know what wouldn't surprise me?'

At that moment, Lestrade couldn't think of a single thing.

'That a policeman did it.'

'A policeman?' Russell and Lestrade outdid each other in terms of falsetto.

'Yes. Oh, they're rabid, you know. Trying to pretend they're oh-so-normal, whereas we know different. But if you're new here, loves, look out for them. The Metropolitans are the least understanding Force in the country.'

'In the world, I shouldn't wonder,' Russell added, frowning.

'One of them did for him, I'd stake my virginity on it,' Georgina said.

'Er . . . by "one of them", you mean . . .' Lestrade wanted to be clear.

'A peeler, pet. A policeman. You show me a nice policeman and I'll show you anything you like. My shriek, I believe. Clarence,' and he flicked his carmine finger-nails at a waiter, 'same again, lover, and a small one for yourself.'

'It's his family I feel sorry for,' said Lestrade.

'I don't believe he had any,' Georgina said. 'Some of us don't, do we? We even lose our nearest and dearest because of the way we are. Well, it's the way God made us. I wouldn't change a thing. Mind you, I'm lucky, I am. My dear old mum has always stood by me – Henry – never a cross word. She, poor old white-haired thing that she is – even makes my frocks – oh, only for indoors, of course.'

'Of course,' nodded Lestrade. 'Well, his friends, then.'

'Yes, I expect Aubrey's taking it hard.'

'Aubrey?' Lestrade squeaked, trying to look casual.

'Aubrey Beardsley. He's an insurance man or something, but what he can do with a pen and ink would make your garters quiver.'

'Comes here, does he, Audrey?'

'Aubrey, love, Aubrey,' Georgina corrected him. 'Bless you, no. But I can give you his address if you like.'

And he wrote it down on a napkin. It was at that moment that Clarence returned with a dimpled cheek and a tray of drinks, but Russell and Lestrade had gone, the Inspector's cigar still smouldering in the diamanté holder he had acquired years ago in the Case of the Diamanté Cigar Holder.

'Oh dear,' Georgina wailed, 'and I was going to take him home to meet mum.'

It was the next morning that Inspector Sholto Lestrade took advantage of his new-found freedom and hopped off the garden-seat omnibus and sauntered in the sun to Royal Arcade, off Old Bond Street. The door of No. 4 was opened by an extraordinary young man, no more than twenty-three, with a pudding basin haircut and a centre parting. His face was long and gaunt and his pallor deathly. The brightness of the sun at that hour of the morning seemed to dazzle him and he invited Lestrade in quickly.

'Aubrey Beardsley?' the Inspector asked.

'The same,' the young man bowed.

'Inspector Lestrade, Scotland Yard.'

'Ah, yes. Perfectly dreadful building,' Beardsley said. 'I was having breakfast. Would you like some coffee?'

'No thank you, sir. I had my breakfast two hours ago.'

'Yes, of course. I was up late working on some sketches.'

'I've heard great things of your artwork, Mr Beardsley.'

'How kind. *Salomé*, perhaps? *La Morte d'Arthur*? Not *Bons Mots*, surely?'

'No, sir.' Lestrade was at his iciest. 'It was a gentleman called Georgina who gave me your name and address.'

'Oh.' Beardsley's cadaverous grin faded. 'It's about poor David, isn't it?'

Lestrade sat in the chronically uncomfortable wicker chair Beardsley had offered him. 'Poor David. He once said I had remarkable hands.' He held them up for the Inspector's inspection. 'Do you think I have remarkable hands?'

'Unbelievable,' said Lestrade. 'What was your relationship, Mr Beardsley, with David Appleyard?'

'We were colleagues, Mr Lestrade,' the artist said, sitting with one skeletal knee crossed over the other and coughing quietly into an outsize coffee cup. 'He worked until the tragedy on the *Yellow Book*. God, it's extraordinary. I can't believe he's dead.'

'The . . . *Yellow Book*?'

'Yes, it's published by Messrs Dent and Company, publishers extraordinary. I am their art editor. David was a compositor.'

'A . . . ?'

'Compositor. He set up the type for the presses. Oh, a mechanical job, but a highly skilled one. One day I suppose it will all be done by electricity.'

'So your relationship was purely professional?'

'Of course. What did you expect?'

'I'm not sure,' Lestrade said.

'Look,' Beardsley squinted at him, 'do you mind?' And he sprang from his chair like a ruptured gazelle, framing Lestrade's face with his remarkable hands. 'Do you mind if I sketch you?'

'Well, I . . .'

'Oh, thanks. You have such strong features.'

'Well, I . . .'

'So . . . commanding. So powerful.'

'Er . . . my lip isn't normally out there.'

'No, I appreciate that. Bastards these critics, aren't they? So personally wounding.'

He ferreted in a drawer and perched on the table's edge, scattering the remnants of his toast. Then he crouched over a scribbling pad and made frenzied lines all over it. Lestrade tried to see, but was rebuked. 'Please, Mr Lestrade. All in good time. All in good time.'

'When did you see Mr Appleyard last?'

'May.'

'Not since then?'

'No, I've been at Dieppe, staying with friends; Arthur Symons and a group of other artists and writers. I only got back last week.'

'Did he have any enemies?'

'Which of us has not, Mr Lestrade?' Beardsley did not look up from his scribbling.

'Anyone specific?' Lestrade tried to narrow the field a little.

Beardsley looked up, coughing a little. 'He had what some might describe as a Bohemian lifestyle, Mr Lestrade. Such men court death as others court a lady. They are drawn like moths to a flame. And surely, his wings were burned.'

He put down his pad, his chest heaving convulsively, his hand trembling.

Lestrade had seen it before. His little sister, deathly pale under a thin coverlet in Pimlico, her golden hair matted to her head with the grip of the fever. 'A glass of water, Mr Beardsley?' he said softly.

The artist shook his head. 'Time enough for that, Mr Lestrade,' he said. 'I have work to do.'

And he handed Lestrade the half-finished sketch. The face was fine. The living spit of the Inspector, complete with boater and moustache. But the body was a long, elegant, black version of Beardsley's own, neither male nor female, like a human-turned-earthworm. 'Er . . . remarkable,' said Lestrade. 'Just like your hands, in fact Mr Beardsley. Tell me, do you ever take the Underground?'

'With these lungs?' the artist croaked. 'Ha, ha, Mr Lestrade.'

He fought for breath. 'The doctors say I have two good years left, maybe three. If I went below ground, they'd rediagnose that to as many days. I'm a creature of the shade, Mr Lestrade. Damned to all eternity. I cannot stand the sun but I surely cannot abide the total dark.'

'Thank you, Mr Beardsley.' The Inspector tipped his hat.

'Will you catch him?' the artist asked as he reached the door.

Lestrade turned to the young man who would never have time to become great. 'Oh yes,' he said, 'I'll catch him.'

Walter Dew had bought the lucky heather off the old crone who sold it at the corner of Old Bond Street and he lolled against the wall until Lestrade came out.

'What's that, guv'nor?' he asked.

'Nothing, Dew.' Lestrade stuffed the Beardsley sketch into his pocket. 'What brings you this far west?'

'You do, sir. I've got to hand it to Russell, pains me though it does to admit it. He'll make a good detective some day. Not that I'd let him hear me say it. They'd have to rip my tongue out first.'

'Let's pass over the cockney pleasantries, Walter. I've just met a young man who's put a cloud over the sun.'

'Ah, well, if it's good news you're after, I'm the bloke. Or rather Russell is.'

'Yes, Walter?' Lestrade stopped walking and turned to face his faithful lieutenant.

'A bloke came in this morning, sir, claiming to be the brother of Mr Appleyard.'

'And?'

'And he hasn't got a brother. At least, not according to our information.'

'So what happened?'

'Russell arrested him.'

'On what charge?'

'Impersonating a relative.'

'There's no such charge, Walter.'

'I know that, guv, and you know that. Unfortunately, Russell didn't know that.'

'Oh God!'

'But fortunately, the bloke didn't know it either. He's from South Africa.'

'South Africa? Did he say so?'

'Yes. Russell asked him why he hadn't come forward sooner. After all it's been in the papers for nearly twenty-four hours now. All the information anybody could want. He said he'd forgotten procedures. He'd left England years ago as a lad and hadn't long been back. Anyway, he talks funny.'

'Does he now?'

'And that's not all, sir.'

Lestrade hailed a hansom. 'Better and better, Walter. Go on.'

'Bromley recognized him.'

'No!'

'Yes. And that's not all.'

'Walter.' Lestrade swept into the cab. 'Scotland Yard, driver. Step on it. Walter, my cup runneth over.'

'I recognized him too.'

'Aha. Now, don't tell me. Let me guess.' The hansom jolted forward. 'He is none other than the father of Henrietta Fordingbridge and the husband of Emily Bellamy. Am I right?'

'No, guv'nor.'

Lestrade's face fell.

'But you're close.'

It rose again.

'I reckon they're brothers.'

'Brothers?' Lestrade frowned.

'You see, they're alike. But they're not alike.'

'Unless the others were in disguise.'

'It's possible,' Dew admitted.

'Does Abberline know about this other Appleyard?'

'Not yet. But it's only a matter of time.'

'Who's got him?'

'Corkindale.'

'Does he know about my suspension?'

'Come on, guv. Herminius doesn't know what day it is. No worries there.'

'All right, Walter. Good man. Driver,' Lestrade bashed the roof with his better hand, 'side door, under the planes. Savvy?'

196

It was a tricky operation certainly, but not beyond the wit of two intrepid policemen bent on nailing the bastard who had been terrorizing the Underground of a great city for the past six months. Dew kept a look-out, having paid the cab fare, in that Lestrade believed he must have inadvertently left his wallet at Beardsley's, and the Inspector slunk into the shadows to the west of the building. It was true that various MPs and civil servants saw him do it but assumed it was a routine Yard training exercise and thought no more about it. One of the more crime-conscious of them did pop into the darkened portico to inquire whether Lestrade was a member of the Irish Republican Brotherhood and on being told he wasn't, promptly went on his way.

On the inner staircase, Dew went ahead, checking corridor after corridor, ducking behind lockers where necessary until they got to the basement that led to Corkindale's domain.

'Oh, Christ!' the God-fearing Dew was heard to hiss. 'Mr Abberline!'

He was right. Cutting his customary swathe through coppers, the Chief Inspector of that name swept down the corridor towards them. Lestrade snatched up a saddle of the Mounted Branch that was in for repair work to the tree and raised it over his head.

'Morning, sir,' Dew called cheerfully as Abberline passed.

'It's afternoon, you nincompoop. Why wasn't I told about the man in Corkindale's cell?'

'Didn't Russell tell you, sir?' Dew asked, outraged. 'I'll have him back to the troughs, so help me.'

'*I'll* do the troughing around here, Dew, thank you.' Abberline had paused beyond the pair, trying to see under the dangling stirrup irons who the other one was. 'And no one is to speak to that man, do you understand? No one. Er . . .'

'Very good, sir. If we need you, sir?'

Abberline was already making for the stairs with a coterie of constables at his coat tails. 'Penge,' he snarled, 'I'll be in Penge. I'm getting pretty close to the flasher now.'

When he'd gone, the sigh of relief from both Dew and Lestrade was audible.

'Come on, Walter. So far, so good.'

'Afternoon, Herminius,' Dew said.

'Hello, Walter,' the ox grinned. Then he caught sight of Lestrade and saluted.

'Corkindale,' said Lestrade, 'open up, there's a good chap. I'd like to see the prisoner.'

'Oh, I'm sorry, Mr Lestrade, sir. I can't do that. Mr Abberline's orders.'

'No, no, Corkindale,' Lestrade laughed. 'That doesn't apply to me and Walter.'

'But you're under suspension, Mr Lestrade, sir. You shouldn't be here at all by right.'

'Ha, ha.' The grin froze on Lestrade's face. 'Excuse us,' he said and turned aside, placing an avuncular arm on Dew's shoulder. 'Doesn't know what day it is, eh, Dew? You do realize that Corkindale is that most feared of policemen, a powerful giant with the strength of ten and an honest streak a mile wide. If it now turns out that he has, against all probability, got a brain as well, we're sunk. Unless . . .'

'Unless, guv?'

Lestrade's index finger pierced the air. 'Plan B.'

Dew reached into his trousers for his truncheon with a heavy sigh.

'No, Dew,' Lestrade caught the movement, 'that's Plan C. I said Plan B. Er . . . Corkindale. You'll never guess who I met yesterday.'

'No, sir,' the Constable freely admitted, 'I probably won't.'

'Your old teacher. Mrs Minniver, isn't it?'

'Get away. Her from up at the school?'

'The self-same. She said to me, "How's old Horatius getting on?"'

'Herminius,' Dew hissed from out of the corner of his mouth.

'And then she asked after you, Herminius,' Lestrade continued, withering Dew with a single basilisk stare.

'How is she, sir?' And Lestrade fancied he saw a small tear glisten in the Constable's eye.

'White-haired now, of course,' Lestrade smiled fondly.

'Yes. She was then,' Corkindale remembered. 'How's her old trouble?'

'Oh, well, you know. As well as can be expected.'

'And her leg?'

'Er . . . which one?'

'The wooden one.' Corkindale was surprised that Lestrade had to ask.

'Oh, fine, Corkindale, fine. She made a special point of saying to me, however, that she hoped you were obeying your superiors, Corkindale, just like you used to. That whatever they asked you to do, you were to do it without question.'

'Oh, yes sir. You tell her, when you see her again, I always do.'

'I know you do, Corkindale.' Lestrade patted him on the shoulder. 'Now be a good fellow and open up the cell. I'd hate to tell Mrs Minniver that you hadn't been obeying your superiors.'

Mental anguish creased the Constable's brow. Dew's fingers strayed to his pocket again. He knew that Lestrade's Plan B was played out. If the big bugger didn't jump to it now, it would have to be Plan C and there would go, he'd wager, another broken truncheon.

'Well, all right, then,' Corkindale said slowly, hauling the keys out of his pocket at the end of a long chain. 'Just for that dear, white-haired old lady,' and he unlocked the door.

In the doorway, Lestrade gripped Dew's arm and flipped a coin, catching it expertly. 'Well, Walter?'

'Britannia,' said Dew.

Lestrade looked at the coin. 'Britannia it is.'

'Right.' Dew was across the room in one bound. Lestrade closed the door with a slam and let his Constable's nose scrape against that of the man sitting under the bare light. 'Now then, sunshine, I've had a lousy day so far. The canteen was shut and I can't find my favourite life-preserver, the one I usually use on blokes like you.' He sat on the table and hauled the man upright by his tie. 'So I don't want any nonsense, all right? Who the bloody hell are you really and why are you pretending to be somebody you aren't?'

The prisoner looked totally undeterred. 'I believe I have a right to a lawyer,' he said in the clipped dialect of Pietermaritzburg.

'Right? Right?' barked Dew. 'You're a bloody foreigner, son, you are. You sound like a bloody . . . what is it?'

'Kaffir,' said Lestrade quietly, standing behind the prisoner.

'Kaffir,' Dew shouted. 'That's what you sound like.'

'I am a British citizen,' the prisoner said, 'just like you.'

'Oh, no, son,' Dew screamed, 'not like me. Not at all like me. You see, I don't go around strangling women on the Underground.'

'Neither do I,' said the prisoner patiently. 'I told the other officer . . .'

'Never mind him. Chief Inspector Abberline is a vegetable. You're talking to me now.'

'I told the other officer that I have no knowledge of the circumstances surrounding the death of Mr Appleyard.'

'But you claimed earlier you were his brother when my other colleague asked you.'

'Well, we are all brothers, aren't we? One way or another?' Clearly the Afrikaner refused to be browbeaten.

'You may be, mate,' Dew snarled. 'Now, I want to know what your bloody angle is. And you're going to tell me if it takes all night. Got it?' Dew thrust his truncheon horizontally under the South African's neck. 'Why do you want to view the corpse of some bloke you know nothing about? Got a thing about corpses, have you? Eh? Eh?'

And he twisted the truncheon higher with each question.

'Walter, Walter,' Lestrade came forward and eased the oak from under the man's chin, 'we don't want any of that. I'm sure this gentleman meant no harm. Look, why don't you go and get us all a cup of tea while I have a chat with him. You'd like that, wouldn't you, Mr . . . er . . . ?'

A thump of the prisoner's epiglottis was answer enough. Dew broke away with some reluctance and marched to the door. 'Don't think I'm finished with you yet, son!' he roared and slammed the cell door behind him.

'Cigar?' Lestrade offered his second-best Havana.

'No thanks,' the South African said. 'About my lawyer . . .'

'Yes, of course. You are indeed entitled to one telegram. And afterwards, I'll post it myself. But first,' he pulled up a chair and sat facing the prisoner, 'you see, I really have to satisfy my superiors – and there are *some*, believe it or believe it not – that you're in the clear, Mr . . . er . . . ?'

'Of course.'

'Don't worry about Walter. He's just a little over-zealous, that's all. He can't help it. His mother was frightened by a suspect, I think, while she was carrying him.'

200

'Really?'

'Yes. He was three at the time. She dropped him on his head. He's never been quite the same since.'

The South African leaned forward so that the bulb from the bare gas light shone bright on his domed forehead and the auburn curls that crowned it. 'I am familiar, sir, with the nice policeman, nasty policeman routine. Unfortunately, I am from Natal. I thought that your man Walter was the nice policeman. Believe me, by comparison with the South African Constabulary, he is.'

'Oh,' was all Lestrade could think of to say. And then, by way of a probe, 'Mr . . . er . . . ?'

'No name. No rank. No serial number. Until I get my lawyer, you get nothing.'

And he folded his arms.

Lestrade scraped back the chair, 'Very well, Mr Appleyard, Mr Hudson, Mr Gooch, Mr Hackworth, Mr Fordingbridge, Mr Bellamy – I believe you have used all these names over the past months – I have no option but to accuse you of murder. My colleague will be back in a moment with the tea and he will formally charge you. I shall tell him you were not impressed before. Who knows, perhaps by now he will have found his life-preserver.'

And he saw himself out, carrying a saddle over his head.

10

So Goron had missed his man. By the time the magistrates at Clerkenwell had let him out and the French ambassador had threatened to insert his tricolour up Lord Rosebery's bottom in reprisal, Arizona John Burke had taken the skeleton crew of rough riders back to America with him, the Comte de la Warre among them. Now the Sûreté, it had to be said, was infinitely more generous with its expenses than Scotland Yard, where the old slate was minute, but even Goron balked at setting sail for the States. So he contented himself with a return trip to Soho where Chief Inspector Abberline took him on a tour of various nightspots. Then he caught another packet at Southampton and the next day sailed for home.

It was the day after that, a Thursday, that two rather familiar men turned up at Sergeant Dixon's desk, main vestibule, Scotland Yard. One had the unmistakable stoop of a man who had, at one time or another, seen service on the North-West Frontier and showed all the signs of having let the Khybers past. The other bore curious pale marks across his forehead that seemed to have been caused by dangling corks blotting out the fierce Antipodean sun. They had come, they said, in search of their brother, who had sent them a telegram the previous day. They wanted him charged or they wanted him released.

Sergeant Dixon was a copper of the old school. He knew which side his bread was buttered. 'Anything happens on the Appleyard front,' Abberline had said to him, 'you send for me straight away.' And an *in situ* Chief Inspector carried immeasurably more clout than a suspended Inspector. But somewhere Sergeant Dixon had a mind of his own. And he sent old Bromley round with a message to Mr Lestrade's.

'Forgive me,' the Inspector said, at a corner table in Gannet's Tea Rooms, 'for meeting you both here rather than at the Yard, but I have my reasons.'

'We've come for our brother,' said the Frontier man. 'You're holding him illegally.'

'On the contrary,' Lestrade said. 'We are holding him on suspicion of murder. The magistrate was kind enough to extend the writ. Tea?'

The waitress hovered, chewing her pencil stub.

'Thank you, no,' the Australian said. 'I lost the taste for it down under.'

Lestrade couldn't see what the man's sexual inclinations had to do with tea, but perhaps it wasn't his place to pry. 'One tea, please,' he said, 'and a Sally Lunn. Go easy on the sugar.'

The waitress bobbed.

'Scotland Yard's tab,' Lestrade called after her. 'Name of Abberline. You see, gentlemen,' the Inspector closed to the pair moving the table napkin into position down his collarfront, 'my first problem is that your brother refuses to give us his name. He calls himself Arthur Appleyard. And that just won't do.'

'He has his reasons,' said the Frontier man, 'as do we all.'

'I'm sure he does,' Lestrade said, 'and they probably involve the deaths of six women and one ... er ... man on the Underground since February last. Am I right?'

'We cannot comment on that,' the Australian said. 'We give you our word, however, that none of us is responsible.'

Lestrade sighed. He fished in his pocket and produced two crumpled sketches. He showed them to the pair. 'Look familiar?' he asked.

'Why should we?' the two chorused.

'No, I mean, do these drawings look familiar? They should. Constable Hockney is our police artist. He's coming on, isn't he? I remember when he used to draw horses with five legs. But that's quite a good likeness of you, isn't it, Mr Bellamy? And of you, Mr Fordingbridge?'

'What are you talking about?' snapped Bellamy.

'I know what you're thinking.' Lestrade's tea and cake arrived. 'Thank you, my dear. You're thinking that sketches like this are not admissible as evidence in court. Well, of course, you're quite right. There's a French bloke called Bertillon who's putting together hundreds of sorts of ears, noses, eyes and so on, like a jigsaw puzzle – a sort of kit to establish identity. All nonsense of course. It'll never work. But there's nothing like the real thing, is there?' Lestrade clicked his fingers and the waitress came loping over. 'No, dear, not you. Walter!'

The Detective Constable of that name appeared at his elbow from behind a frosted glass partition whose lettering read CREAM TEAS.

'Oh, yessir,' Dew beamed, 'this one's William Bellamy all right.'

'Thank you.' Lestrade clicked again. 'No, dear, I told you; not now. Bromley!'

The Detective Constable of *that* name followed Dew. 'Definitely,' he said. 'This man was calling himself John Fordingbridge not three weeks ago.'

'Thank you, gentlemen.' Lestrade sank his incisors into the gooey pastry. 'Your collar, I think, Walter. Read them their rights as you go. It's only a short walk to the Yard, Messrs Bellamy and Fordingbridge, and I believe you know the way. These officers will accompany you.'

'Are we under arrest?' Bellamy asked.

'I think you can assume that,' Lestrade said.

'On what charge?' Fordingbridge demanded.

'Lying to a police officer. Giving fictional names. Hampering the police in the course of their inquiries. That'll keep you for twenty-four hours anyway. I'll have thought of something else by then.'

'How dare you!' Fordingbridge snarled. 'This is outrageous. We've done nothing wrong.'

Lestrade clicked his fingers for a spoon. The waitress, tired of the policeman who cried wolf, ignored him.

'I've heard many a criminal say that,' Lestrade said, 'in a rather muffled way with a bag over his head and a rope round his neck. With my vast experience of the felonious classes, I believe that William and John *are* your real names. And your brother probably *is* Arthur. And there's no doubt about your familial relationship. All I need now is a surname. Do I have it? It makes the paperwork so much easier.'

No surname for the brothers grim was forthcoming. Dew and Bromley took them across the road to the Yard, under the shadow of Big Ben, and placed them in separate cells from their brother and each other with Corkindale minding all three.

And it was late that night that Lestrade found himself alone, padding slowly down the platform of Blackfriars Station, his hands locked behind his back, his bowler atilt on his head. The last train had gone. And the iron gears of the station clock chimed midnight. A passing pigeon, flapping homeward to its roost in the wrought-iron eaves, left its calling card on Lestrade's shoulder. He was about to deal with it as deftly as he could when a shadow flitted across the platform ahead. He broke his stride, half turned and flattened himself against the wall of the little covered waiting room.

There was no sound now, only the distant barges on the river wailing under the moon. The hiss of steam had gone; so had the clang of girders as they expanded and contracted in the summer's heat. He poked his head round the corner. Nothing. He edged one shoulder out, sticky with pigeon droppings, and he sidled into the moonlight. The waiting room, for all its glass sides, had dark corners, deep shadows. The Inspector felt the warm brass of the knuckles in his pocket and placed a foot gingerly on the brass step at the door. A faded poster urged him to take the Great Northern Railway to Doncaster, an invitation he found curiously easy to decline. Another, ripped and peeling, offered an exhilarating evening in the company of Martha Arthur And Her Amazing Chameleons. Sadly, Lestrade had missed it by nearly three years.

'Now, Ivan,' Lestrade said softly, 'we aren't going to have any tricks, are we? We're both too old for tricks.'

There was a chuckle in the darkest corner of the room. 'You always were a flatfoot, Sholto Lestrade. If I was a trasseno, you'd be dead by now.'

Lestrade swept off his hat and sat in the opposite corner. 'If you were a trasseno, Ivan, I wouldn't have come. How long has it been?'

A figure emerged into the light. A tall man with a curiously wrought walking stick and a stiff left leg. He extended a hand. Lestrade caught it.

'Too long,' the man said. 'How have you been, Sholto?'

'Better,' Lestrade confessed. 'But I'm a busy man, Ivan. And I'd dearly like to know why you asked me to meet you at midnight at Blackfriars Station.'

'"Under the moon at midnight",' Ivan corrected him.

Lestrade looked at his man. Older, certainly. Thinner of hair under the Homburg, he suspected. Gammier of leg than he remembered. But the same old Ivan. 'Don't tell me you're going to grow hair and start baying at it,' the Inspector said.

Ivan smiled. 'What do you know about me, Sholto?' he asked.

Lestrade looked at him in the moonlight. 'Ex-Inspector Ivan Corner, known to coppers and the Underworld alike as Ivan the Terrible and to the newspapers as Corner of the Yard. Joined the Metropolitan Police, M Division, in the Year of Our Lord 1840.'

'1839,' Corner corrected him. 'Lord Melbourne was Prime Minister and our great founder, bless his cotton underwear, had not yet taken the fall from his horse which was to prove his undoing.'

'Served two years as beat constable and became a member of that gallant band known as the Detective Branch.'

'In *old* Scotland Yard,' Corner remembered. 'That was a *real* police station in those days.'

'Worked with my old man on the murder at the village of Road – the Constance Kent Case.'

'I worked with Inspector Whicher,' Corner put him right. 'Your old man came along to polish our shoes.'

'Ah, we also serve who only stand and wait,' Lestrade said, in a rare moment of poesy. 'Rose to become Inspector. Feared by the bad, loved by the good. Retired with countless commendations on the occasion of Her Majesty's fortieth year on the throne. Like the Royal Canadian Mounted Police, to whom he gave copious advice on surveillance while wearing silly hats, always got his man. Ivan Corner, this is your life.'

'Not quite,' the old man said. 'That bit about always getting my man – sadly untrue.'

'Don't do yourself down, Ivan – allow me a little artistic licence, a few emblandishments.'

'No, no, Sholto. I'm not being modest. You see the one man I missed is back. Only now, he's killing people.'

Lestrade produced a cigar for them both. 'I'm sitting as comfortably as I can on a London and North-Eastern Railway seat at a little past midnight on a balmy night by the light of the moon. You may begin.'

'You haven't heard the legend of Blackfriars Dan, have you? It would be before your time.'

Lestrade shook his head.

'I'd been a detective for two years. Every copper south of the Humber had been drafted in to London for the Great Exhibition. You couldn't move for foreigners. And of course, one third of the visitors came by train.'

'Quite right.'

'Well, there weren't any trains when I was a lad, of course. All coaches and canals. I remember the first time I rode in a carriage. Shat myself because it was going so fast – but that's another story.'

Lestrade was glad of that.

'I remember it all started in the summer of fifty-one. A terrible, hot summer it was, like this one. We'd had reports of a maniac on the trains, interfering with young women.'

'Oh?' Lestrade was all ears.

'Whicher sent me out to investigate. It was like looking for a will-o'-the-wisp.'

Lestrade had been there before.

'He'd strike at night, in carriages, on lonely platforms. We couldn't find him.'

'What was his method?' Lestrade asked.

'He'd stand behind his prey on a platform and put his hand down the waistband of her skirts.'

'And in carriages?'

'Find one with a single female occupant and engage her in conversation. Then he'd try it on.'

'What?'

'An assault of a sexual nature.'

Lestrade clicked his tongue. 'Why Blackfriars Dan?' he asked.

'I plotted his attacks on a map. Dug out the area from the Map Room at the Yard and found that the centre of it all was here. Right here at Blackfriars. "Dan" because I knew who it was.'

'You did?'

Corner nodded, Lestrade's cigar clamped soggily in his teeth. 'Of course, looking back, it all seems a bit trivial now,' he said, 'but at the time the papers had a field day. Whicher's head was on the line; so was mine. That Jewish bastard Disraeli raised it in the House of bloody Commons. "The condition of England question," he said, "will never be answered while our policemen are of the calibre they are".'

'What did you do?'

'Drove out to Hughenden Manor, his country house, and shat through his letter box.'

'That did the trick?'

'Well, it was twenty years before he became Prime Minister. Obviously slowed him up a bit, you know; gave him food for thought.'

'So who was Blackfriars Dan, Ivan?'

'We narrowed it down to three possibles,' Corner said. 'One was a bloke named Felix Yusupov – of Russian extraction. I was able to rule him out because he was killed by a nervous bullock in Smithfield Market while the attacks were still going on. Pity, really; he was top of my list.'

'And number two?'

'Alexander Beardsmore, a defrocked clergyman from Devizes.'

'That sounds more promising.'

'That's what I thought. Until I realized that Beardsmore was terrified of trains.'

'He was?'

'Totally. Oh, he certainly molested young ladies, in hotels, shop doorways, on omnibuses, and we put him away for it. But trains, never. The fly bugger had buggered back to Devizes and when I tried to bring him back by train, he fainted on the platform. I thought he'd died. Both him and the engine, completely steamed up. I've never seen anything like it.'

'So Dan's your third man?'

'Ah, yes, the third man. One Daniel Sleigh, of private means. Married a rich woman to boot, so he had plenty of leisure. Time on his hands and money to burn – it's a fatal combination, Sholto.'

'So they tell me,' Lestrade said. 'Maybe I'll find out one day. What made you suspect him?'

'The description,' Corner replied. 'Three of the eight women saw him distinctly. Their accounts tallied in every particular – and they also fitted Sleigh.'

'And Yusupov and Beardsmore?'

'Yes,' shrugged the old man, 'but not half so well. Sleigh had no alibi for the nights in question and it was obvious when I spoke to his wife that he had . . . abnormal appetites.'

'What?' Lestrade frowned. 'You mean he ate a lot?'

'No, Sholto.' Age had made Ivan the Terrible short on patience. 'I mean matters of the flesh. Carnal relations.'

'The wife admitted this?'

'She didn't have to. I took the advantage of her afternoon nap to snoop around the house. There *was* a marriage bed, although she apparently napped downstairs of an afternoon and it had a bolster down the middle.'

'A lot of married couples employ that as a means of controlling births,' Lestrade said, although he and his Sarah had never found the need.

'Yes, but with iron spikes on the top? I tell you, Sholto, Daniel Sleigh was a fiend.'

'But you couldn't nail him?'

Corner shook his head. 'All these years it's bothered me. That's the sole reason I've never written my memoirs – that and the fact I can't write. Couldn't bear the duplicity you see, not to mention Blackfriars Dan. And couldn't bear the shame of mentioning him either.'

'What happened to him?'

'His wife had him put away.'

'Could she do that?'

'Well, let's put it this way. She did. Last I heard he was in a private sanatorium somewhere, chained to the wall.'

'What has this got to do with my case, Ivan?'

'Dan's back,' Corner said grimly.

Lestrade looked at him. 'No. How can that be? He'd be older than Methuselah by now.'

'Would he? When I talked to Daniel Sleigh he was my age – twenty-six at the time. That would make him, all things being equal, seventy now.'

'All right, then, Ivan, and I do beg your pardon, but are you seriously expecting me to believe that a seventy-year-old man could strangle six women and a man?'

'Simultaneously, no,' said Corner, 'but one at a time, why not?'

'Come on!' Lestrade was incredulous. Suddenly, he felt a thump to his temple. The cigar flew from his mouth and he found himself kneeling on the floor with Corner's left arm locked round his throat and his head twisted sharply to one side.

'And this is my bad arm,' the old copper grunted.

Lestrade slapped the man's forearm for all he was worth. The waiting room was beginning to swim in his vision and his chest threatened to burst. Corner released his grip, and Lestrade slumped forward. 'I thought we agreed,' he rasped, 'no tricks.'

'Sorry, Sholto,' Corner helped him up to the seat again, 'but I had to make a point.'

'Yes, yes, quite.' Lestrade tried to screw his head back on. All to no avail. It veered to the right for the rest of the night. 'All right. So a seventy-year-old man *could* strangle people, at least a seventy-year-old man with police training. How do you know Sleigh isn't dead? In my experience, people don't live long in those places.'

'He got out, Sholto, that's how I know. It was in *The Times*,

209

no less – a little piece just under the Hunjadi Janos Laxative advertisement. Back in February, this was.'

'February?' Lestrade made a valiant attempt to prick up his ears.

'Exactly,' Corner read the transparency that was Lestrade's mind, 'the month Mrs Culdrose died.'

'You've known about this all this time and you haven't come forward before?' Lestrade snapped. 'Why not?'

'At first, I wasn't sure. Remember that back in the 'fifties Sleigh didn't kill anybody. I reasoned after a while that that was because he didn't get the chance or because his mania hadn't fully developed. God knows what forty years of incarceration have done to his libidinous tendencies.'

'Not to mention his lusts after young women,' Lestrade added.

'I watched the papers. Mrs Hollander I wasn't sure about. She seemed to have so many men in her life, it could have been anybody. But by the time Miss Bellamy was found, I decided to act. I nipped into the Yard and got young George Dixon to look up Records.'

'And?'

'He found the name of the asylum where they put Sleigh.'

'Which was?'

'In Kent. Sandwich, to be precise.'

'Go on.'

'I went down there. They wouldn't tell me anything.'

'Nothing?'

'Asked me if I'd come to admit myself. I didn't like the look I was getting from some of the orderlies, so I left.'

'And that's it?'

'That's as far as I got. I had another of my turns a month ago – the old trouble. Been flat on my back since June. But he's out there, all right, Dan the lad, still up to his old nonsense. Only now he's hurting people. It's them I feel sorry for. His victims. Them and his family – those three little lads.'

'Little lads?' Lestrade asked.

'Yes. When I went to interview Sleigh's wife the first time, there were three babies, well, toddlers I suppose, scampering around with a bloody great Borzoi.'

Lestrade tutted. 'These damned foreigners are everywhere,' he said. 'So why come to me, Ivan?'

'It's your case, isn't it?'

'Not any more,' Lestrade told him. 'Not officially. I've been suspended. It could be serious.'

'Bollocks, Sholto!' Corner staggered to his feet. 'I was suspended more times than the Clifton Bridge. You can't claim to be a Yard man until you've been suspended at least three times. And even a suspended policeman can get into an asylum, as long as he doesn't tell them he's been suspended. An old one can't. Believe me; I've tried. Come on, we've got a long way to go.'

'We?' Lestrade stood with him.

'Well, I'm not passing it over now,' Corner assured him, grasping his stick firmly, 'old trouble or no old trouble. If I can nail this bastard, Sholto, I'll die a happy man. Oh, don't worry. You'll get the collar, of course.'

'But it's nearly one in the morning, Ivan,' Lestrade told him.

Corner led him onto the platform where the moon shone pale on the planking. 'Here,' he said, 'one night, one moonlit night like this one, I came as close to Blackfriars Dan as I am to you now.'

'What happened?'

'I told you,' Corner said, 'will-o'-the-wisp. He got away from me. One second he was there. The next, a gush of steam from the locomotive, and he was gone. To this day I don't know how he did it. But he did. Well, I'm a greedy bugger. I want that chance again. Come on, I've got a trap below.'

'I was afraid of that,' said Lestrade.

The sun came up over the Sandwich Flats as the policemen, ancient and modern, clattered through the barbican of the Cinque Port and on through its incomprehensible street plan. Perhaps incomprehensible was the wrong word, but then Lestrade was driving and was never at his best in control of a one-in-hand. Away to the north, the gallant little trains of the Dymchurch, Romney and Hythe Railway rattled through the morning, crossing many a fenny border, bringing the cheque and the postal order. They followed the North Stream of the River Stour, which struck Lestrade as odd because on the map it was very definitely to the south, and came to the rather imposing sweep that led to Mandalay, nestled behind a curtain wall of rhododendron bushes and guarded by sentinel elms where sentry rooks kept watch.

'You know,' Corner said as Lestrade reined in, 'before I met you at Blackfriars last night I had a nap. I dreamed I went to Mandalay again. And Daniel Sleigh took us on a guided tour of the rooms. Every man I've sent to the gallows was there, chained to the wall and heaping curses on my head. Do you ever have dreams like that, Sholto?'

Lestrade wavered for a moment, in mid-dismount. Then he smiled and tapped the older man's shoulder with his whip. 'You forget,' he said, 'we never sleep.'

'Daniel who?' Doctor McKechnie had had a bad night. 'Look,' he said, 'you'll have to forgive me. I've had rather a bad night.'

The policemen, past and present, exchanged glances.

'Take it from me,' he said, 'if you've never spent the night talking to Joan of Arc, you've never lived.'

'Sleigh,' Lestrade repeated, 'Daniel Sleigh. We have reason to believe that he was admitted to this asylum . . .'

'No,' McKechnie growled, then gentler, 'no, we no longer use that term here, Mr Lestrade. Asylum has connotations. People chained to walls, lashed into obedience, that sort of thing. Well, it may be all right for Bedlam, but it won't do here. We prefer the term "holiday camp". It has an altogether nicer atmosphere, don't you think? Here, our patients are guests, having an extended holiday. You're lucky, actually. Today's Friday – you can judge our Knobbly Knees Competition. Oh, don't worry. Absolutely no impropriety, I assure you. Chap guests only.'

'Well, that's kind of you, doctor,' Lestrade said, 'but I'm afraid my expertise doesn't run to knees. It's true I never forget a face, but below the waist is not my province.'

The doctor was clearly disappointed.

'But it's about impropriety and things below waists that we've come, in fact.'

'Oh?'

'Yes. Once again, the name of the luna . . . guest I'm looking for is Daniel Sleigh. S-L-E-I-G-H. Sleigh.'

'Thank you, Inspector, I can spell. Spelling is essential in a doctor of psychiatry – that word alone is a bitch – and a fluency in Latin gerundives is, of course, *de rigueur*.'

Damn, thought Lestrade, three of the very skills he lacked – spelling, Latin and Spanish. Had it not been for the way the Great Foreman in the Sky handed out jobs, he could have been wearing a white coat now, managing the loonies in the nuthouse.

'Ah, yes, of course. Dan. I do remember him actually. Let me see,' and he ran a medical finger down the lists in his ledger, 'yes, here we are. Admitted, 18 September 1851. He's not with us at the moment, of course.'

'He escaped?' Corner asked.

The doctor's face fell still further, but he screwed it into a determined smile. 'Again,' he said, struggling with his tombstone-sized teeth, 'not a term we use here. No, Mr Sleigh merely "went for a walk", as we say.'

Lestrade stayed frosty. 'Our fear, doctor,' he said, 'is that Mr Sleigh has been for several walks, always down the platforms of Underground stations and often committing murder on the way.'

'Impossible,' McKechnie said.

'That sounds a little definite,' Lestrade said. 'Is there something we don't know?'

'I know that Mr Sleigh is not the murderous type, Inspector. In fact, he's not a criminal at all in the conventional sense of the word. Oh, his tastes may be a little odd . . .'

'Why was he committed?' Corner asked.

'Oh, I couldn't possibly tell you that,' McKechnie said.

'Professional etiquette?' Lestrade asked.

'Lost records,' McKechnie confessed. 'No, I only have the bare essentials here. Lived in Portman Square and Cannes. Had a villa in Ventnor.'

'Who committed him, then?' Corner wouldn't leave it alone.

'It doesn't say,' McKechnie told him, 'but it's normally the next of kin – wife, husband, that sort of thing.'

'But you knew Sleigh,' Lestrade checked, 'before he esc . . . went for his walk?'

'Oh, yes.'

'What kind of man was he?'

The doctor perched the glasses on the end of his nose,

leaning back in the chair. 'Cultured. Intellectual. Not without a sense of humour. Suffers from obsessional neuroses of
course.'

'What?' Lestrade asked.

'He's mad as a snake,' McKechnie translated for the policemen's benefit.

'I assumed that,' said Lestrade, 'or he wouldn't be here . . .
would he?'

'Oh no,' McKechnie said. 'Some of our guests are as sane as
you or I,' but he squinted at Lestrade as he said it.

'They are?' Corner was surprised.

'I've got three crime writers in at the moment gleaning
research for their novels.'

'Isn't that a little unusual?' Lestrade asked.

'It's their funeral,' McKechnie shrugged. 'We've tightened up
on security since Sleigh "went for a walk". Walking is strictly
supervised now. They'll never get out.'

'Sleigh did,' Corner reminded him.

'We were perhaps a little under-zealous,' the doctor confessed.
'It won't happen again.'

'Do you know where he is now?' Lestrade asked.

The doctor consulted his hunter. 'Hephzibah's,' he said,
'taking breakfast.'

The policemen were astonished. 'I beg your pardon?' Lestrade
said.

'It's a little restaurant in the town,' McKechnie explained.
'They do a particularly choice scrambled egg.'

'Are you telling us that Sleigh is still in the area?'

'Oh, of course. The ways of the rationally disadvantaged are
strange, Mr Lestrade. Mr Sleigh was with us for over forty
years, before he "went for his walk". We are, effectively, his
home – the only one he can remember, anyway. It's typical
of the ambivalence of the neurotic. He can't live with us any
more, but neither can he live without us. We keep his room
free and his bed aired.'

'May we see the room?'

'I don't see why not.' McKechnie led the way through myriad
white-painted passages adorned with precepts pinched from
the workhouses – GOD IS LOVE and CHRIST IS KINDNESS. Under
these, various inmates, those presumably allowed relatively

214

sharp implements, had daubed FIND HIM IN ROOM 28. This had been crossed out several times and other numbers inserted.

'Free expression,' McKechnie explained as the policemen gazed about them in bewilderment. 'Many of our guests suffer from delusions of grandeur. Good morning, Your Majesty,' he bowed to an elderly gentleman in a little white lace cap. 'That one,' he whispered, 'believes he is Queen Victoria.'

'Isn't he a little on the male side?' Lestrade asked.

'Only slightly,' McKechnie said. 'These things take time. Some of our guests suffer from *folie à deux*. Good morning, sires,' and he bowed again to two men who walked stiffly down the corridor, as though in riding boots, their right hands tucked firmly into imaginary waistcoats. 'Napoleon and Lucien,' McKechnie whispered, 'the Corsican brothers. Ah, here we are.'

The room had no corners and only one small window. It reminded Lestrade at once of the stuffy padded cells of the City and South London line, except that it was a cold, almost painful white. Mechanically, he and Corner rummaged through the contents of a small wooden locker. Tucked away at the back, carefully, laid out in a line, were a number of tickets of the Underground railway, the Twopenny Tube.

'You'd better have a look at this, Sholto,' Corner said grimly.

He handed Lestrade a tatty manuscript with line after line and page after page in an untidy, backward-sloping scrawl. The younger policeman's eyes widened in disbelief. 'When he was four?' he asked aloud.

'It was the bit half-way up a church steeple that got me,' Corner said. 'Page thirty-eight.'

Lestrade flicked to it. 'Good God, yes. *And* it's Salisbury Cathedral which, if I remember my Church Architecture for Policemen lecture, is the tallest in England.'

'Ah,' McKechnie broke in, 'I see you've found Daniel's little opus. He intends it for publication. To be called "My Secret Life".'

'But it's obscene,' Corner said, 'or at least it was in my day.'

'It still is.' Lestrade was able to give his verdict from the viewpoint of current law. 'Makes Marie Corelli look a bit tame. I'm afraid we'll have to take this with us. And these.' He stuffed the tickets inside the book. 'I don't know about you,

Ivan, I could suddenly force down some particularly choice scrambled eggs.'

There was only one customer in Hephzibah's Tea Rooms at that hour of a Friday morning. Then suddenly there were three. This sudden upswing in her financial situation greatly pleased Hephzibah, but she was at a loss to know why the two newcomers insisted on sharing a table with the dear old gentleman who had recently become a regular. He *was* an old love, she realized, while beaming at him from the recesses of her kitchen. Perhaps a little fidgety of finger, a little likely to take liberties, and for that reason she never allowed one of her girls to serve him, always dutifully and altruistically braving his little lunges herself. It was, she explained to her girls, no more than her place as owner and manager of Hephzibah's Tea Rooms to bear his brunt and whatever else he ordered her to bare in the interests of customer relations. What those relations might be, no one was privileged to find out, because the dear old gentleman always paid his bill behind Hephzibah's beaded curtain, with a great deal of heavy breathing. Hephzibah assured them that the dear old gentleman was a martyr to asthma, tinged with tuberculosis, and the exertion of getting his wallet out was occasionally too much for him.

'Mr Sleigh?' Lestrade asked when he had ordered (Corner was paying).

'The same, sir. Who are you?'

'I am Inspector Lestrade of Scotland Yard. This is my colleague, Inspector Corner.'

'Good God,' Sleigh adjusted a smeary pair of pince-nez, 'so it is. It's been years, Mr Corner. I thought you were dead.'

'I thought you were,' Corner said, 'until recently.'

'Oh, I've been away,' Sleigh said, 'Morocco, Tangiers, south of France.'

'Blackfriars,' said Corner.

Sleigh looked a little uncomprehending.

'We recently visited the as . . . "holiday camp",' said Lestrade. 'Dr McKechnie was kind enough to show us your room.'

'Yes,' Sleigh was masticating his way around the last toast, 'pretty enough decor,' he said. 'Shame about the view.'

'In it,' the Inspector went on, 'we found a quantity of Underground railway tickets. Sadly of course, they don't carry dates.'

'Ah, I love the Underground,' Sleigh said. 'The darkness affords the most wonderful opportunities – not as many as in Morocco, of course. The Moroccans have this facility for yielding up their persons – and little boys are very cheap.'

'Yes,' said Lestrade. 'It's big girls I'm interested in.'

'Oh, so am I,' Sleigh enthused, catching his teeth just in time. 'Shall we compare notes?'

'Ah yes.' Lestrade waited until the naturally curious Hephzibah had served their breakfast trays and reluctantly retreated to her recess to prepare Mr Sleigh's elevenses. 'Your notes are something else we found in your room. It seems to be a catalogue of debauch since you were four years of age.'

'Do you know,' Sleigh reminisced as his pince-nez steamed up, 'I remember that serving girl as if it were yesterday. Enormous pair of . . .'

'Yes, I'm sure,' Lestrade interrupted. 'Tell me, Mr Sleigh, Mr Corner and I haven't had a chance to read your memoirs yet. I expect you've had some exciting encounters in the Underground, haven't you?'

'Not really,' Sleigh said, pouring himself another coffee. 'Oh, one or two frots on the platform, but I don't get up to town much these days. Too busy abroad, you see. I do remember two young lasses in a four-wheeler . . .'

'I remember you on Blackfriars Station,' Corner persisted. 'As do a number of ladies on whom you forced your unwelcome attentions.'

'Unwelcome? Unwelcome, Mr Corner? How dare you!' He shook with indignation. 'The only one to whom my attentions were unwelcome was my lady wife, Mrs Sleigh. And I believe she went to her Maker years ago. I've had duchesses, serving girls, errand boys, even a Yorkshire terrier, though it *was* a dark night. But to a man they've all given me their consent; all enjoyed a gentleman's little games. Even the Yorkshire terrier . . .'

'My God,' growled Corner, 'there's a law against that sort of thing. And if there isn't, there should be.'

'Yes,' Lestrade agreed. 'We'll pass these papers to the Royal Society for the Protection of Animals later. At the moment, I am concerned with six women and one man who have been murdered on the Underground.'

'Murdered?' Sleigh was aghast. 'Good heavens!'

'It can't have come as a surprise to you, Daniel,' Corner said, leaning forward, 'Don't you read the newspapers?'

'Only *Poules-de-luxe Volume III* – and to be honest, the standard of the drawings is going downhill. I honestly don't think the position shown in Number thirty-six is physically possible. Even when I was younger and fitter. Of course, they used to say about Catherine the Great . . .'

'Yes, I'm sure she was,' Lestrade interrupted. 'Tell me, Mr Sleigh, do you have children?'

'Oh, I expect so,' the old man beamed proudly. 'The length and breadth of the world, I should think.'

'No, I mean by Mrs Sleigh.'

'Oh, her.' He fished out a piece of toast where it had become sop in his coffee. 'Yes. Three boys.'

'Named William, John and Arthur?'

'Er . . . yes, I think so.'

'How old would they be now?'

'Ooh,' Sleigh sucked in his whiskers, 'getting on for eleven, I suppose. Look, I have to see my publisher today.' Sleigh folded his napkin. 'I'm not sure I want my name emblazoned all over the front of that.' He pointed to the pornography in Lestrade's hand. 'Not the sort of thing a gentleman does, show off. What about a *nom-de-plume*?'

'Not just now,' Lestrade said. 'The scrambled eggs were ample.'

'No, no, a pen name. Any ideas?'

Lestrade knew all about aliases. He looked at the ancient degenerate before him, his brain softened by years of excess. He thought of his own lieutenant, the strait-laced Constable Dew, who made Puritans like Cromwell look like libertines. 'What about Walter?' he suggested.

'"My Secret Life" by Walter.' Sleigh rolled the sound of it around his tongue. 'Yes. Yes. That's very good. Thank you, Mr Lestrade. Now, if that's all,' he reached under the flap of his waistcoat for his fly buttons, 'I must pay my bill. Not to mention a generous tip. It's a long way to Penge.'

'Penge?' repeated Lestrade.

'Where my publisher lives. I go there often.'

'By public transport?'

'Oh, yes. I do love the omnibus, don't you? Particularly watching young ladies walking upstairs.

'They don't often do that,' Lestrade observed.

'They do when I'm downstairs,' he beamed.

The policemen paid in cash and fled.

So Corner of the Yard had still not got his man. And the legend of Blackfriars Dan was destined to be buried in the dusty archives of Scotland Yard and the memory of an old copper. During their chat at Hephzibah's Tea Rooms, Lestrade had sized up the old reprobate. He'd also had a good, hard look at Daniel Sleigh. Wherever the old man had been, it was not Morocco or Tangiers. Neither, Lestrade suspected, was it the Underground. At least, not on the nights in question. He and Corner had made other inquiries around Sandwich and certainly, Sleigh had made a nuisance of himself from time to time. He had been caught leering outside the Sunday School on the day Sarah Culdrose had died. He had offered his services to help school children across the road when Jane Hollander was found. As Emily Bellamy had gasped her last, he was falling out of a tree overlooking a bedroom of the vicarage, and as Verity True expired he was noticed by the local constabulary adding to his collection (subsequently removed by the said constabulary) of ladies' underwear. In short, the bent old bastard had alibis for several of the nights in question and Blackfriars Dan had proved to be another red herring in a sea of red herrings. Whether Chief Inspector Abberline would overlook him on *his* suburban case was another matter.

On the journey home, Corner had a relapse of his old trouble and his protégé put him to bed, hanging up the old man's truncheon for the last time.

At least, though, Lestrade could eliminate three other people from his inquiries. Under cover of darkness that night, when the barges bobbed black on the river and the growlers ceased to growl under the stars; at a time when Chief Inspector Abberline was surveilling furiously at No Forty-eight Fitzloosely Street Road,

Penge, and Assistant Commissioner Frost was at home hardening his arteries, Lestrade crept into the Yard.

'Gentlemen,' he'd called all three into one cell with Dew and Corkindale at his back, 'John Sleigh, William Sleigh, Arthur Sleigh – I think it's time you all went home, don't you?'

The brothers looked at each other.

'There'll be a little delay,' the Inspector said. 'For reasons too procedural to go into, I am unable to sign your release papers tonight. Chief Inspector Abberline will do that, assuming he's mastered the joined-up writing by then. Goodnight, gentlemen.'

'Wait a minute.' Arthur stood up. 'What about our father?'

'Shut up, Arthur, you idiot!' John snapped.

'He knows, John,' Arthur said. 'If he knows our names, he also knows about Papa.'

'Do you, Lestrade?' William asked.

Lestrade looked at the brothers. 'More or less,' he said.

'You've found him?'

'Oh yes.'

'Thank God,' John said. 'Inspector, we have to know. Is it Papa? Is it he who has been carrying out these appalling attacks on the Underground?'

'No,' said Lestrade. 'I don't believe it is. By the way, he seems to think you three are nearly eleven.'

William shook his head. 'Poor papa,' he said. 'Mad as a hatter after all these years.'

'Would you care to tell me about it?' Lestrade lolled in the cell doorway.

'John?' Arthur said. 'You're the eldest.'

The eldest of the Sleighs stood up wearily. 'We are an honourable family, Mr Lestrade, I beg you to believe that. There was a Ranulf de Sley who came over with the Conqueror. And it was Aymer de Sley who handed King John his fountain pen to sign the Magna Carta. There was a regiment in the Civil War called Sley's Lobsters. We go back a long way.'

'I'd just like you to go back to 1851,' Lestrade said.

'In that year – we don't remember it, of course; I was three, William was two, Arthur one – in that year, our father, Daniel, was put away by our mother and her brothers. He was sadly deranged, responsible, she believed, for attacks on young ladies in railway carriages. The police were on his trail. It was either the asylum or the prison cell. She chose the former. But polite society shunned us. We toyed with changing the family name, but tradition dies hard. We'd all had our names down for Eton but they wrote to us saying there was no room. Trinity took us, however, in a fit of liberalism – but then, they took Lord Byron too, so that's no recommendation. When we were of age, we scattered to the corners of the globe. I enlisted in the Indian Army and became a Lieutenant in the Thirty-second Pioneers. William took to sheep-farming in the Dandenong and Arthur cattle-ranching at the Cape. Mama lived with my brothers by turns as soldiering was too impermanent a life for me to have her and she died some years ago.

'It was in the Chitral passes that I happened upon an old copy of *The Times*. It said a woman, one Sarah Culdrose, had been found strangled on the railway. I feared at once it might be Papa, up to his old tricks.'

'But he never attacked anyone on the Underground before,' Lestrade said.

'Only, I suspect, because there was no Underground in 1851,' Arthur said.

'Neither did he strangle anyone,' the Inspector reminded them.

'Perhaps no one had resisted him with enough vehemence before,' William said.

'Whatever,' said John, 'it was not a chance we could take. I sent a telegram to William and took ship from the Gulf of Cutch. Arthur and I reached London simultaneously. It took William longer, of course, from Australia.'

'What did you do then?' Lestrade asked.

'We knew that Papa had been incarcerated in the asylum at Sandwich. We learned that he had escaped, but had no idea where he had gone.'

'Down the road,' Lestrade told them. 'He seems to flit between the asylum and Hephzibah's Tea Rooms, with the possibility of the odd excursion to Penge.'

'Ah,' said William. 'This Hephzibah – big woman? Careless of dress? Morals not as rigid as they might be?'

'Hmm, possibly.' Lestrade wobbled his hand as a sign of

uncertainty. 'I didn't see her for long and her kitchen was a little dark.'

'That follows the pattern Mama told us about,' John remembered.

'Mama's words were actually "anything in a skirt", John,' Arthur corrected him.

'And then she was being kind,' William said. 'She might have added "or trousers".'

'Well, anyway,' John went on, 'the authorities at the asylum were singularly unhelpful and I smelt a cover-up. We feared the worst. Papa had absconded from the place in February, in time to attack Mrs Culdrose. In fact, by the time we'd all arrived, two other women had died.'

'Jane Hollander and Emily Bellamy.' Lestrade crossed their eyes and dotted their teas for them.

'So, we haunted the Underground,' John said. 'I never want to see an Underground train again. God, the sights we saw . . .'

'There was one chap who wore a frock,' Arthur remembered.

'David Appleyard,' Lestrade said.

'He looked as miserable as sin.'

'Ah, then that was Inspector John Thicke,' Lestrade told them, 'one of us.'

The Sleighs sincerely hoped not.

'But it was hopeless. Three of us trying to cover miles of the Underground. Thousands of passengers. We never even came close.'

'We hoped,' William took up the tale, 'that something in the method of murder, or the appearance of the victims or their clothes, that *something* would give us a clue.'

'So you pretended to be various relatives of the deceased?'

'We did,' John said. 'Like Daniel in the lions' den, but it had to be done.'

'We should have come to you in the first place,' Arthur said. 'We'd have saved a lot of time and worry. But the family name – it was too important.'

Lestrade nodded ruefully. 'What will you do now? Go for a bite at Hephzibah's Tea Rooms?'

'No,' John shook his head. 'We've never met our father, Mr Lestrade, and we've been brought up to despise him. We all have our lives elsewhere. If you're certain he's not the Underground murderer, we'll try to take up where we left off. I have to try to make my peace with the Colonel. I left him somewhere in the Chitral snows. Looked at one way it was desertion in the face of the enemy. I'll be lucky to escape a court martial.'

'I've got to round up a few thousand sheep,' William said, 'if the dingoes haven't got them.'

'Yes,' said Lestrade, 'we all have a touch of the dingoes from time to time. And you, Mr Sleigh?'

'I've got to go to the doctor back home,' said Arthur. 'See if I can't help change the course of Anglo-Boer relations and South African history.'

'Well, then, gentlemen,' Lestrade said, 'don't let me keep you from any of that.'

'And what of you, Mr Lestrade?' Arthur asked.

'Me?' Lestrade paused as he turned to go. 'I've got to catch me a murderer.'

11

'I thought you ought to see this, guv'nor,' Walter Dew said. He was unusually dishevelled for a smart young detective with a loving wife, but then he hadn't been home for three days and colleagues like Russell and Bromley were careful to keep upwind of him.

'What is it, Walter?' Lestrade hadn't slept either, but his dishevel wasn't so obvious.

'It's a letter, guv.' Dew was a *little* surprised at the Inspector's lack of perception.

'Thank you, Walter. Pull up a park bench.' He waved his hand at one where the starlings pecked at his breakfast.

Naked little boys splashed in the Serpentine some yards away, laughing and shouting.

'Shall I move them on, sir?' Dew asked.

'Certainly not, Walter.' Lestrade opened the envelope. 'They're doing no harm. Funny isn't it, we let our children do that and if

Daniel Sleigh so much as loosens his tie, we put him away for forty years.'

'They say they're the best years of your life,' Dew nodded, but Lestrade wasn't sure who he was referring to.

'Good God!'

'That's what I said,' Dew said. 'I said to Russell and Bromley, "Good God!" I said.'

'Well, well,' Lestrade folded the paper again, 'what do you make of it, Walter?'

'A hoax, of course.'

'Why?'

'Because I sent Russell round to Miss True's this morning, first thing.'

'And?'

'She wasn't there.'

'What?!' Lestrade was on his feet and the starlings, startled, flapped skyward.

'It's all right, guv. There was a note on the door saying she was at rehearsal at the Prince's.'

'And was she?'

'Er . . . ?'

'Didn't you check?'

'I sent Bromley.'

'Yes,' snarled Lestrade. 'That's like sending Edward Bayreuth to climb a rope. Last one to a cab is a blithering idiot.'

No, Squire Bancroft was adamant, he had not seen Trottie True that morning, only a tiresome succession of policemen. First, a detective constable who was clearly twenty years too old for the job. He had been spirited away by Mrs Bancroft who insisted on showing him her cuttings. Then had come Lestrade and some other buffoon, panting and worried. Why were they worried, Bancroft had demanded to know. *They* hadn't got to perform the Bard's most ambitious masterpiece in front of Sir Henry Irving in three days – and that without a second gravedigger. Yes, Trottie True *should* have been with them. She'd certainly promised to be the night before. But surely, Lestrade knew what women were? It *was* only half past ten – early yet. But if she'd responded to an emergency call from the library, he'd be furious.

Lestrade didn't wait to hear more. He dispatched Dew to the Camberwell Branch Library, extricated a sobbing Bromley from the clutches of the ghastly Mrs Bancroft and posted Russell on permanent duty outside Trottie's villa in the Walworth Road. None of which was bad for an inspector under suspension without actual power to break wind on his own.

In the growler back to Covent Garden, he read the letter again. No address of course. Even the envelope's postmark was smudged. Damn the General Post Office! A halfpenny to send a postcard was bad enough, but the gross incompetence of some anonymous sorter meant that Lestrade couldn't even pin down a postal district. At that moment, he would dearly have loved to have pinned down a postal sorter.

'If you want to see Agnes True again,' it read, 'you will come alone to Blackfriars Underground Station to catch the last train tonight. If you are not there and if you are not alone, they'll find what is left of Miss True scattered the length of the City and South London line. I am sure you follow my train of thought.'

And it was signed 'A. Commuter'.

Lestrade narrowed his eyes at the script – the same spidery hand he had read on the ledger of that company's duty roster, the hand that had forged the signatures of Hudson, Gooch and Hackworth. The dead man's hand. Male, certainly – look at the arcade letters. Was that an Edmonton slant? A Seven Dials scrawl? But it was broad daylight now – the Yard would be swarming with coppers of all shapes and sizes. He had about as much chance of getting to the boffin who understood these matters as flying to the moon.

He suddenly jabbed the roof of the lurching wagon with his fist and instantly regretted it. His knuckles were still raw from their close encounter with 'Masher' Melhuish.

'I'm putting you off here, Bromley. You catch another cab and get yourself over to George Culdrose's – I want his signature. If he's not there, get to Wandsworth and have a squint at his release papers. When you've done that, over to the Albany. I want to see William Bellamy's signature too. Got it?'

'Got it sir. What shall I do after lunch?'

'Don't be flippant with me, lad – I just saved your virtue from the She-Dragon of the Haymarket, did I not?'

'I owe you my life, guv,' Bromley said, still pale at the memory of it and jumped down from the cab.

'It's not your life that's on the line, Bromley, it's Miss True's.'

'Right enough, guv,' the ex-Essex man said. 'Where will you be?'

'Seeing if two ballet dancers can string two words together,' he said.

This time, Lestrade brooked no nonsense. He kept well away from the flying drop kicks of Cross and Holdsworth of the Ballet Rambo and demanded they write their names on a piece of paper. With much posturing and gesturing they did as they were told and he was able, through gritted teeth, to eliminate them from his inquiries. Camp they may have been, aesthetes to their tutus, and there was still an outside chance that one or both of them was a murderer; but they had not written the threatening letter – the one that threatened to snuff out the brief candle of Trottie True.

And when Lestrade and Bromley met up that afternoon, the signatures of Culdrose and Bellamy proved that they hadn't either. They went the pretty way, via the Walworth Road, which accounted for a pretty hefty cab fare that was put on Chief Inspector Abberline's tab. Russell was still there. Trottie was not. There had been no sign. A little further down the road Walter Dew had become involved in an extraordinary case involving a hysterical female librarian in Camberwell Branch Library who swore he had been looking up her index. Never was a man more delighted to see his colleagues, but he had to report there had been no sighting of Trottie True there either.

He checked, in the darkness of the stairway, where the down-draught caught the gasflame, that his switchblade still worked. The deadly four inches of steel flashed silver against the black. Then he walked on, his boots ringing on the metal treads. He fancied he saw movement below him, but it was only the light glancing off the ornate wrought iron.

What was she to him, he asked himself for the umpteenth time? What was he doing here, playing childish games with a practical joker? Walter Dew had told him not to; had told him flatly, then and there. There was no point. Either the madman had not got her and she was visiting a maiden aunt in Maidenhead or he had killed her already. And what if he had? What if his seizure of Trottie True meant that he had had all the time in the world to play his gentleman's games with her? No rush job in the four minutes between stations now. It didn't bear thinking about. Dew had been vehement; braver with his guv'nor than he'd ever been. Lestrade had silenced him with just seven words, 'What if it was Mrs Dew, Walter?' The detective had handed his guv'nor his boater.

The Inspector's instructions had been clear, whispered as they were as the four men fed the ducks in St James's Park. No one was to accompany him. No one was to follow. There would be a police presence anyway – Abberline's lads wasting their time. One glimpse of the genial faces of Dew, Russell or Bromley and the game would be up and they could all kiss goodbye to catching the Underground murderer and to Miss Trottie True.

So he was alone, pacing the dusty platform at Blackfriars. Above him, the great clock struck the half-hour. Half an hour to midnight. Above that again, up the crazy tangle of stairways that led to the surface station, no doubt the ghost of Blackfriars Dan stalked his victims, perhaps long dead.

No moon shone down here, only the green glimmer of the gas lamps. A half-whistled, half-hummed tune filled his ears. At the far end from him, where the tunnel loomed in blackness, a solitary cleaner, in the livery of the City and South London Company, was brushing his way towards him, his face a dark blur under the peak of his cap.

Lestrade turned to face him, hands in his pockets. As he neared, still whistling, the Inspector's left hand pulled free. The other cradled the knuckles.

'Oh, evenin' sir,' the man croaked, pausing to tug his peak. 'Last train'll be along in a minute.'

'Thanks,' said Lestrade.

'Good night, sir,' and he whistled on.

He was right. No sooner had Lestrade become engrossed

in reading Lady Fournier's remedy for sciatica blazoned over the concave station wall than he felt the wind rush along the line and whip the tails of his jacket. He held on to his hat and screwed up his eyes as No. 8 locomotive with its staring bright eyes and its yellow frontage hurtled out of the darkness, and slowed with a rush of steel and a whine of electricity. The lights in the padded cells dimmed and Lestrade checked the cars. No guards. No guards at all. He took the middle car and climbed aboard, letting his hand slide around the rail. Then he sat down on the empty, clanking train.

There was a tug on the electrics. The lights dimmed again and he was thrown sideways as the Mather and Platt's engines cranked into motion. He didn't see the puzzled look on the face of the platform sweeper. The old boy frowned up at the station clock. That was funny. The 11.38 was nearly seven minutes early.

So, he had followed instructions. Lestrade had caught the last train at Blackfriars. All he could do now was wait. No one got on at Blackfriars with him. And there was no guard to flag up the next station. The flash of light told him they were hurtling through a station, however, and he stood up to peer through the frosted windows above his seat. 'Elephant,' he said aloud.

He staggered to the end doors and rattled them. Nothing. They were locked. He ran now, colliding with the padded seats as he went, snatching the brass handles at the end he had entered by. Nothing. They wouldn't budge. Another flash of light. He couldn't see the station name, but that had to be Kennington. And what speed was that maniac doing? The madman at the controls. It was then that Lestrade realized it. The madman had been in control all along and now he had stolen a train. There must be signals forward? Guards and station masters on the platforms as they passed? One of them would telephone ahead, inform the police, kill the power at Stockwell. Then he'd have to stop. Without juice, he'd have no choice.

They took the curve by the Oval, Lestrade pressed flat into the cold leather, his boot heels dancing an insane jig on the slatted floor with the vibration of speed. A sign above him warned him not to smoke, but a quiet cigar now was the last thing on his mind. He could feel the engine racing, the car lift. The Stockwell gradient. The lights dimmed, then went out, and alone in the blackness, there was suddenly a scream of brakes. The dead man's hand slid home, and the whole train slewed to the left.

Lestrade was lying on the floor when he heard the front doors click open. He hauled himself up between the seats and whipped out the switchblade, ripping open the doors. There was no one there. He looked around him. If he'd cared to, he could have reached up and touched the blackened steel girders that ribbed the tunnel, like the skeleton of some great subterranean whale. He leapt over the metal tail gate and on to the next one. This time he was more cautious. He placed his left hand on the door handle, then wrenched. No one. Another empty padded cell, like the one he had just left. He walked steadily down it, lifting his boots as noiselessly as he could on the metal treads of the car.

Then he was there. The last doors. Beyond these, he knew, lay the Mather and Platt locomotive with its iron door. That meant a quarter of an inch of metal between him and a maniac. He swallowed hard, then hurled back the mahogany and stood, staring into darkness.

Someone had switched off the locomotive lights so that the cab's interior was dark. He could make out a silhouette in a peaked cap against the front window furthest from him, and the light from his own car fell on the uniform trousers of the City and South London line, encasing the legs of a murderer. He realized simultaneously that he was framed in light – a perfect target – and he knew that inches below him, just under his right foot, gleamed the live conductor rail.

'Well, well, Johnnie,' he said. 'No frock tonight?'

He saw the figure move a little, the shoulders quiver as though in a silent laugh.

'Where is she, Johnnie? Where is Miss True? You've already killed her sister. You don't want her as well. It's over, Inspector Thicke. Come on down.' And he made a step forward.

'This is all rather embarrassing, Inspector Lestrade,' he heard the killer say and he stepped forward a little too, just enough for Lestrade to see his face.

'Mr Lavender!' the Inspector rasped.

'I'm afraid so,' the railway expert smirked, 'hence the embarrassment. You see, I thought you were on to me. That's why I sent you that rather theatrical little note this morning. I thought it was time I shook you off, uncoupled you, so to speak. I knew your relationship with Miss True would bring you here as I asked, alone. And now it turns out you thought I was John Thicke all along. Well, well, there's no going back now, I'm afraid. No shunting aside.'

'You seem remarkably well informed,' said Lestrade.

'About Miss True, you mean? Oh, I'm not short of informants. Superintendent Tomelty of the Railway Police is as discreet as a loud hailer. Anything vouchsafed to him by your Mr Frost or Mr Abberline is instantly common knowledge. Then of course, there's railway gossip and the famous circumspection of Fleet Street, who will give a would-be murderer every detail about a killing he could wish to know. Helpful bunch, aren't they?'

'Melville Lavender,' began Lestrade, 'you are under arrest for . . .'

'Don't move, Lestrade!' The voice was harsher than he'd heard it, more malevolent.

'You are not armed, Mr Lavender,' the Inspector said, 'and I have reason to believe you are suffering from a knife wound inflicted by the late Mr Appleyard.'

'Ah, yes,' said Lavender, 'careless of me, that. It wasn't until my hands were round his throat that I realized my mistake. He made a damned good woman. It was only a scratch though.'

'Even so.' Lestrade stepped on to the locomotive platform, the switchblade upright.

'Even so!' Lavender screamed. 'You will stay where you are.'

He flicked a switch with his right hand and the front of the locomotive lit up. Lestrade stopped, his heart thumping, his eyes blinking in disbelief. In the locomotive's beams he could see the body of a woman tied as though to a crucifix, her arms outstretched, her body slumped. Her wrists were tied to the buffers at the end of a platform some ten feet away.

'Trottie,' he whispered.

'The same,' smiled Lavender.

'Is she . . . ?'

'No, Lestrade. She's not dead. If you're an observant copper, which sadly I know you are not, you will notice that my left hand has never left this throttle. That is my weapon, Lestrade.

You see, I am armed with a Number Eight Mather and Platt locomotive. It weighs three tons, Lestrade. I won't bore you with the velocity figure. But suffice it to say that even at ten feet, I can bring quite a bit of pressure to bear on Miss True – enough, at any rate, so that she will be unrecognizable when I reverse. Hydraulic death is not pretty – I know; I've seen it.'

'What is it you want?' Lestrade stepped back and dropped the switchblade to his side.

'You of course,' Lavender said. 'Oh, I don't think I'd get very far using my normal methods. So, if you'd be so good as to throw yourself on to the live rail . . . Now!'

His hand trembled on the cold steel of the controls. For a moment, time stood still. Lestrade could hear his heart thumping in his ears; felt his blood run cold.

'Why?' he asked. 'Why did you kill all those people?'

'Does it really matter?' Lavender asked wearily.

'Call it professional curiosity.' Lestrade played for time. He had to get that throttle away from Lavender – or Lavender away from it. Even without the locomotive as a ram, he knew that Trottie was unconscious and the strain on her heart and lungs from being hooked on those buffers would be fatal in minutes. God knows how long she had been there already.

'No,' said Lavender. 'You amuse me first. Let me be privy to your feeble attempts at deduction. Why did you think I was John Thicke?'

'It had to be someone with a knowledge of the Underground,' Lestrade told him, 'and who knew it better than a man who rode it every working day of his life?'

'A man who once owned a part of it,' Lavender answered. 'A man like me. Thicke wouldn't have known about this spur for example. It's only yards from the Stockwell Station, but you won't find it on any map.'

'I knew Thicke was tired of the work.' Lestrade kept talking, waiting, hoping, for his chance. 'I've known policemen go funny before. Overwork. Strain. Some of them crack. And who better to trust than another woman? It was perfect. Thicke had the perfect alibi – he was supposed to be here and we provided him with a disguise.'

'But he wasn't your only suspect, surely?' Lavender asked.

'No. For a long time, I suspected the men who turned out

to be the Sleigh brothers. They kept appearing at the Yard in various guises. But they cleared themselves – and their father – yesterday.'

'What of Bancroft? The papers were full of him.'

'It all adds up to more bums on seats for his show,' Lestrade shrugged. 'I was visited by an idiot named Galton the other week who had some half-baked theory about the little ridges at the ends of your fingers. Well that's patent nonsense; but Squire Bancroft has a hard, calloused ridge on his right thumb. That would have left an obvious impression on the dead women's necks – there wasn't one.'

'And Private Hitch?'

'He couldn't have done it himself for the same reason Edward Bayreuth couldn't – a useless right arm. Oh, he could just manage to drive a cab, but to strangle a woman – and one man – that would be impossible. Besides, you cleared him yourself when you wrote that note this morning. It wasn't the same hand as Hitch's – nor as Bellamy's, nor as Culdrose's. I suspect something about Hitch though.'

'And what's that?'

'That he didn't see his old comrade Corporal Schiess at all. I also suspect that you have a very strong facial resemblance to that gentleman. So when Hitch hailed you after you'd killed Verity True, you looked right through him.'

'Hmm,' nodded Lavender, 'I must go to a branch library somewhere – or perhaps the United Services Institute – and find a photograph of him tomorrow, when all this is over. What about the artist, Aubrey Beardsley?'

'The man's dying of tuberculosis. I know. I've seen it. His lungs couldn't stand a ride on the Tube, much less the exertion of killing anyone by strangulation. And you still haven't told me why,' Lestrade said, shifting his weight slightly to his left foot.

'And you haven't explained why you didn't arrest Queensberry.'

'I'd love to – and I might yet, one day, but your letter this morning clinched it. It was literate. He isn't. No man with his boorishness could possibly spell "commuter".'

'All right,' said Lavender, 'I suppose you have a right to know. It was the randomness that threw you, wasn't it? The fact that the victims had nothing in common. Oh, I know there was a connection between this lady's sister and the woman Fordingbridge, but that was a mere coincidence – coincidence, I'm happy to say that saw you Yard bobbies chasing your own tails. I didn't care who died. Anybody would do. But it had to be women. Women of all classes, not just the Unfortunates. Society had to believe that *no* woman was safe. And they never learn, do they? They still rode the Tubes after all the scaremongering from the Press and from Scotland Yard. I find the stupidity of Josephine Public quite incredible. It was terribly easy of course. I knew these trains and the stations like the back of my hand. At first I killed in my ordinary suit. Then *some* panic set in and ladies took to riding late at night with guards. So I became a guard.'

'Ah, yes,' said Lestrade, 'Messrs Hudson, Gooch and Hackworth. How did you manage that?'

'Simple. I was constantly nipping in and out of station masters' offices – they all know me here because of my railway museum. I was generous enough to buy the tea for the real guards and I slipped a certain substance into it – the same substance that has mercifully robbed Miss True of her consciousness at the moment. I simply slipped in early the following days and substituted myself on their shifts. I had the relevant uniform in my collection at home. The names were a bit silly, I realized afterwards – Hudson and Gooch, great railway magnates of the 'forties; Hackworth, the man who competed against the Rocket at the Rainhill Trials. Rather a give-away that, from a railway buff like me.' He eyed Lestrade carefully. 'I needn't have worried though, need I?' he asked. 'You were none the wiser until now.'

Lestrade shrugged. He'd die rather than admit it. And it looked as though, any moment, that could be arranged. 'You still haven't told me why,' he said.

'Revenge, if you like,' Lavender said. 'You see, when we first met, Lestrade, I told you a teensy untruth. I said that I had no head for business – that that side of the railways is a closed book to me.'

'Not so?' Lestrade asked.

Lavender shook his head slowly. 'I was the principal stockholder in the Charing Cross and Waterloo Railway. Ever heard of it?'

It was Lestrade's turn to shake his head.

'Sank without trace.' Lavender was shaking now, his fingers tightening on the controls. 'It was to have rivalled the Central. It would have been bigger than the Metropolitan and District, and would have knocked this tin-pot organization into a cocked hat. Then the government withdrew its support. The bill collapsed. And my personal fortune went along with it. Well, I plotted. Planned. Carefully, so carefully. Those bastards Mott, Dutts, Spagnoletti and the others – they're paying now just as I paid. Their profits have halved; no one's riding their lines anymore. Two, perhaps three more murders, and I'll have bankrupted them. Underground travel will be a thing of the past. And *my* personal reign of terror will have brought it all about. I even hinted at that after the third murder – that someone was out to discredit the company. I threw you the plausibility that someone in the City and South London was responsible. You fell for it superbly – "shitting on your own doorstep" you called it – very colourful.'

'Ingenious,' said Lestrade, 'but I fear you've forgotten one thing.'

'Indeed?' Lavender's eyes narrowed 'And what's that?'

Till his dying day, Sholto Lestrade didn't know how he made that shot, but make it he did. He hurled his switchblade at Lavender's left arm, the one rigid on the throttle. A miss at that moment and the madman would have jammed down the lever and Lestrade didn't even want to think about the result against the buffers. As it was, the blade bit deep into Lavender's forearm and the arm shot up in sudden agony. The Inspector threw himself forward, taking Lavender to the floor of the tiny cab with him. The blade and knuckles had rolled clear with the impact and they struggled together among the engine oil and the grime. Once, twice, Lestrade brought his fist smashing down into Lavender's face, but then he felt a bucket clang around his head and he rolled sideways.

In an instant Lavender was gone, bounding back through the cars, his arm useless and bleeding. Lestrade shook his head free of the metallic ringing and threw back the front door of the locomotive. He had to get Trottie. Before it was too late. He leapt down, landing perfectly on both feet. Then he froze. He daren't look. He daren't look. But he had to look.

His trouser leg was flapping a fraction of an inch from the live rail. One wobble now and the Inspector would be frying tonight. He lunged forward, hacking at Trottie's hands with the switchblade. Her right arm flopped downwards and he caught her, steadying her weight while he sawed frantically at the left. It gave way and he lifted her bodily on to the platform. For an instant her eyes flickered open, while he rubbed her wrists. She whispered, 'Sholto?' and her head fell back.

He patted her cheek, whipped off his jacket and threw it over her for warmth and turned back to the locomotive. As long as Trottie didn't roll off on to the live rail, all would be well; and Lavender was getting away. Lestrade ran down the spur to the Stockwell gradient. To his right, the lines curved downhill into the pitch darkness. It would have been easier for his man to run that way, but he had no torch and he was losing blood. To his left, the track rose steeply, but there was the pale light of Stockwell Station and a short ride to civilization and escape. He ran left.

Around him, the cavern of iron reverberated with his footsteps. The sweat ran down his face and he tasted salt on his lips. He had to keep his feet in a tight line or there would be an instant blue flash and a crackle and the lights would go out, probably all over Europe. Once, twice he stumbled, crying out in the darkness as he recovered, not daring to throw out his hands to save himself.

Then he was there, leaping up with a staggering gait on to the safety of the platform. No one. It was deserted. He looked back. It was a nightmare back there – a labyrinth of tunnels that interlocked with sewers and post office tubes and electrical subways. A man like Lavender probably knew them all. *That's* how he'd walked away from so many murders. He hadn't passed the guards at all. He knew a host of secret passageways, a myriad twisting ways where the sun never shone. It was hopeless. Lestrade had taken the wrong turning.

Then there was the click of a shoe on concrete and he saw Melville Lavender hurtle diagonally across the platform ahead. He saw what he was aiming at, too – the last lift was about to make its ascent.

'Come along there, please!' they heard the liftman say. Lavender had hung back for as long as he dared. He was in no shape for the stairs and he'd hoped that Lestrade would double back looking for him in the blackness. Now, he had no choice. The lift was already rising, the platform about half-way up the open entrance. The liftman saw Lavender too late and frantically tried to reverse his controls. The railway expert relied on split-second timing and his knowledge of Otis Elevators. But he was exhausted. His lungs felt like lead and he lunged too late.

The liftman was screaming at him not to jump but Lavender was already in the air and as his body hit the floor, his head hit the cross girder of the entrance and bounced back, rolling down the platform whence it came, like a cabbage kicked in the gutter, arcs of blood spraying where it came. The lift went on, dripping crimson to mark its path.

The station clock struck twelve.

By the time the photographs had been taken and depositions written and the Railway and Metropolitan Police had tramped all over the place, it was after dawn. As numbed, exhausted Inspector Lestrade took the stairs, rather than the lift, to the sunshine and as he passed the old crone selling heather, he saw a face he thought he knew. The face was familiar but there was something out of place.

'Mr Bayruth?' he asked.

'Bayreuth,' the Confessor beamed, 'and you'll *have* to arrest me now.'

'Really?' Lestrade pulled a cigar wearily out of his waistcoat pocket. 'Why?'

'Because I've got another arm,' and he waved it at Lestrade, 'what the doctors call a proscenium. Got it in that shop that sells marital aids in Villiers Street.'

'Good for you,' Lestrade grimaced, and took the offending limb in his hand, shaking it so hard that it fell off and landed with a clatter in Clapham High Street.

'You bastard!' Bayreuth roared. 'That's police brutality, that is!'

'Do you know,' said Lestrade, 'I think you're probably right.'

He turned on his heel. He had a lady to visit in Clapham General. Shock, the doctor had said, and the after-effects of a sleeping draught. She'd be perfectly up to dying on stage, indirectly at the hands of Mr Forbes-Robertson. Along, probably, with Effie Bancroft, who died whenever she appeared.

Lestrade watched them scurrying to the Underground entrance – the businessmen and the bricklayers, the telephonists and the typewriters – all bound for the Twopenny Tube, where all classes jostled together in the brave new world of technology and the Independent Labour Party.

He turned away, raised his arm, in fact, both of them, high in the air, just for the hell of it, and shouted, 'Cab!'

❑ Yes, please send my copies from the Lestrade Mystery Series as indicated below.

❑ Enclosed is my check or money order.

or

❑ Charge my ❑ VISA ❑ MasterCard ❑ 🔘 ❑ 🔲

Fax orders to 202-216-9183

Credit Card # _____Exp. date_____

Signature _____

Phone _____

Please indicate the address to which you would like your copies sent.

Name _____

Street _____

City _____State _____Zip _____

Mail this form to:

Gateway Mysteries c/o Regnery Publishing
P.O. Box 97199 • Washington, D.C. 20090-7199

CALL 1-888-219-4747

Qty.	Book	Code	Price	Total
	The Adventures of Inspector Lestrade	LST1	$9.95	
	Brigade: The Further Adventures of Lestrade	LST2	$9.95	
	Lestrade and the Hallowed House	LST3	$9.95	
	Lestrade and the Leviathan	LST4	$9.95	
	Lestrade and the Deadly Game	LST5	$15.95	
	Lestrade and the Ripper	LST6	$15.95	
	Lestrade and the Brother of Death	LST7	$15.95	
	Lestrade and the Guardian Angel	LST8	$15.95	
	Lestrade and the Gift of the Prince	LST9	$15.95	
	Lestrade and the Magpie	LST10	$15.95	
	Lestrade and the Dead Man's Hand	LST11	$15.95	
	Lestrade and the Sign of Nine	LST12	$15.95	
		Shipping and Handling		FREE!
RSP254			Total	